Letting Go of Gravity

Also by Meg Leder

The Museum of Heartbreak

LETTING GO OF GRAVITY

GO OF

GRAVITY

Meg Leder

Simon Pulse

New York   London   Toronto   Sydney   New Delhi

SIMON PULSE

An imprint of Simon & Schuster Children's Publishing Division

1230 Avenue of the Americas, New York, New York 10020

First Simon Pulse hardcover edition July 2018

Text copyright © 2018 by Margaret Leder

Front jacket design, hand-lettering, and illustration copyright © 2018 by Maggie Edkins

All rights reserved, including the right of reproduction in whole or in part in any form.

SIMON PULSE and colophon are registered trademarks of Simon & Schuster, Inc.

For information about special discounts for bulk purchases, please contact Simon & Schuster Special Sales at 1-866-506-1949 or business@simonandschuster.com.

The Simon & Schuster Speakers Bureau can bring authors to your live event.

For more information or to book an event contact the Simon & Schuster Speakers Bureau at 1-866-248-3049 or visit our website at www.simonspeakers.com.

Interior designed by Mike Rosamilia

The text of this book was set in Adobe Garamond Pro.

Manufactured in the United States of America

2 4 6 8 10 9 7 5 3 1

Library of Congress Cataloging-in-Publication Data

Names: Leder, Meg, 1974- author.

Title: Letting go of gravity / by Meg Leder.

Description: First Simon Pulse hardcover edition. | New York : Simon Pulse, 2018. | Summary: "Parker struggles to reconnect with her twin brother, Charlie, who's recovering from cancer, and to deal with her anxiety about her own future"— Provided by publisher.

Identifiers: LCCN 2017040121 (print) | LCCN 2017053296 (eBook) | ISBN 9781534403185 (eBook) | ISBN 9781534403161 (hardcover)

Subjects: | CYAC: Brothers and sisters—Fiction. | Twins—Fiction. | Family problems—Fiction. | Friendship—Fiction. | Graffiti—Fiction. | Anxiety—Fiction. | Panic attacks—Fiction.

Classification: LCC PZ7.1.L394 (eBook) | LCC PZ7.1.L394 Let 2018 (print) | DDC [Fic]—dc23

LC record available at https://lccn.loc.gov/2017040121

For my brother, SJL

Prologue

WHEN I WAS SIX, Grandma McCullough told me this story:

Once upon a time, there was a girl made of gravity.

Both of her feet were firmly planted on the ground.

Everywhere she went, she carried her heart around with her in a metal cage. It was comfortable there.

Her parents were made of gravity too, and they liked to keep her close, to keep her safe, everyone with their heart locked in their cage.

The little girl was mostly happy. She liked the garden behind her house with its red and yellow flowers, and having ice cream with her parents on special occasions. Sometimes she felt a little lonely, but then she'd take a walk in the woods and put her bare feet in the creek, or she'd lie on the grass and look at the clouds.

One night, in the middle of the night, the little girl heard a noise outside. When she looked out the window, she saw another little girl hovering in the air, one of her wings caught in the branches of the oak tree outside her window.

A helium person!

The gravity girl's parents had told her about the helium people. They came out at night and flew through the clouds and soared among the stars. They had wings made of moonlight, and their hearts lived outside of them.

("What does that mean, 'lived outside of them'?" I asked Grandma McCullough.

She clenched her hand in a fist and pounded her chest. "Their hearts are free on the outside! Not safe in a cage!" She stomped her Velcro sneakers against the foot guards in her wheelchair, her cancer-stale breath hot, her big eyes wild.)

"The helium people are reckless," the little girl's dad had said.

"Their hearts could fly away at any moment," her mom had said.

The little girl worried about the helium people, that they'd steal her from the ground, that she'd lose her heart.

But right then, the helium girl in the tree seemed more sad than scary.

"Will you please help me?" the helium girl cried. "I'm stuck here."

The gravity girl nodded and snuck outside. She climbed up the tree carefully, using all the gravity in her to make sure she stayed steady against the limbs.

She drew nearer to the helium girl.

She was close enough to see her eyelashes, as delicate as a spider's web.

She was close enough to see her eyes, all the colors of the sky.

"Hello," the helium girl whispered, fear making her voice shake.

"Hello," the gravity girl whispered back.

And then, with one arm clasped around the tree trunk for balance, the gravity girl gently shook the branch holding the helium girl's wing, setting a flutter of green leaves falling, the caught wing moving free.

The gravity girl climbed back down to the ground as the helium girl fluttered above her.

"I wish we could be friends," the helium girl said. "Would you like to visit the sky with me?"

"It's not safe," the gravity girl said, and held up her cage. "I don't want to lose my heart."

"But I'll make sure you're safe," the helium girl said. "Plus, the sky is the most beautiful thing you'll ever see! You can sleep on the clouds and touch the stars. We can be best friends!"

The gravity girl wondered what it would be like to take a nap on a cloud. She secretly wished she could keep a star in her pocket. She had always wanted a best friend.

So she nodded, and the helium girl took her hand.

"All you have to do is close your eyes, then jump up. You'll be able to fly too."

"But I don't have any helium in me."

"Everyone does. They just don't know it yet. Trust me."

So the gravity girl scrunched her eyes shut, but it was scary not being able to see the ground. When she tried to jump up, her legs simply wouldn't move. All she could think about was falling, not flying.

"I'm too scared," she whispered. "Something bad might happen."

"Something good might happen too!" the helium girl insisted. "You just have to trust me."

The gravity girl was too scared to change. It was much easier to believe there was no helium in her heart. It was much easier to believe she would fall.

But she didn't want to lose her new friend.

"You should stay here. With me. It's safer," she said. And she began to pull the helium girl toward her.

"I don't want to," the helium girl said.

The gravity girl tugged at her new friend even harder.

"Please let go," the helium girl cried as she began to resist, her heart straining, her wings aching to fly free.

The gravity girl could feel her hold on the helium girl beginning to slip, so she stretched out her other hand to grab tight, dropping her cage on the ground, her heart tumbling out onto the dirt.

She left it there, refusing to let go.

The helium girl's wings began to wilt, and her heart got smaller and smaller in its sadness.

But still the gravity girl didn't let go.

And so they stayed, heartsick and lost, both of them stuck in the in-between place for the rest of their days.

The end.

("What's the in-between place?" I asked, unable to stop myself.

"No place for anyone to live, that's for sure," Grandma McCullough said.

I wasn't so sure. Thanks to my copy of *The Big Book of Greek*

Myths, I knew what happened to kids who flew too close to the sun. The in-between place sounded a lot better.)

I remember telling Charlie this story later, how he wrinkled his nose, like I had just served up a plate of lima beans.

"Why didn't she just let go?"

"Because flying isn't safe!" I said, trying to convey the same amount of authority as Grandma McCullough.

But he seemed unmoved, which in retrospect isn't surprising.

Charlie's always been the one who wants to fly.

I'm the one who won't let go.

One

I CLEAR MY THROAT, one hand white-knuckling the edge of the podium, the other at my side, and remind myself I'm almost done. And it has gone perfectly—my voice clear, not too fast, not too slow, pauses just right.

I've practiced this end part so much, my body is on autopilot now. I hear the words come out of my mouth independently of me actually reading the typed pages: "And so, my fellow graduates, in conclusion, I leave you today with the immortal words of Lord Alfred Tennyson from his poem 'Ulysses.'"

And then, like habit, like breath, I look for Charlie, eyes darting to the row where he should be sitting.

I only see Christine Miller, intently focused on searching for split ends in her platinum-blond hair, legs crossed, impatiently tapping one stabby-looking high heel in front of her.

My eyes scan the crowd.

I meet Em's eyes, her wild blond hair a beacon amid blown-out highlighted waves, as she tugs at her necklace, smiling at me. Next to her, her cousin Matty gives me a reassuring thumbs-up.

No Charlie.

To the side, my parents. Dad—his grin so big, it looks like his whole body is in on the smile—and next to him, Mom, her love quieter, a low-level steady recurring pulse of warmth.

I still don't see my brother.

Principal Taylor clears her throat from behind me, and I realize my pause is too long.

"Lord Alfred Tennyson from his poem 'Ulysses,'" I repeat, trying to recapture my momentum.

But it's like someone's unplugged my speech, the words flickering to a black screen.

I can't believe Charlie's not here. I can't believe he didn't come at all.

I feel my grip sliding, my bottom right eyelid starting to twitch. I glance down at my one hand on the podium, and I'm not sure it's connected to me, that it's even mine anymore, and I miss it.

"Parker?" Principal Taylor says from behind me, touching my elbow, and I realize everyone's waiting for me, that anyone who wasn't paying attention before certainly is now.

"Sorry," I say, shaking my head and looking up, putting on a smile that isn't really mine.

"And so, my fellow graduates, in conclusion, I leave you today with the immortal words of Lord Alfred Tennyson from his poem 'Ulysses.'"

My finger shakes slightly as I trace the typed pages in front of me, and my bottom right eyelid is still twitching, but I force my voice to be steady, reminding myself I worked hard for this moment, that it's all mine.

"Though
We are not now that strength which in old days
Moved earth and heaven, that which we are, we are,
One equal temper of heroic hearts,
Made weak by time and fate, but strong in will
To strive, to seek, to find—"

And then, when I'm within four words of being done, a loud "Vroom vroom!" bursts into the air from the left side of the auditorium.

It stills everyone and everything, even me.

I see her: a dark-haired little girl, squatting in the aisle, gleefully running a toy car around on the floor.

The whole crowd shifts like they're waking up, adults smiling, people from my class laughing.

An older woman leans into the aisle, jerks the child's arm, and shushes her.

The little girl starts to cry, a wail echoing through the auditorium, and a man—probably her dad—scoops her up, heads toward the exit.

I stop, close my eyes, listen as the cry gets fainter.

In front of me, there are 233 fellow seniors in bright-red

polyester gowns, and I don't have anything real to say to them—not anything they care about, not anything that's mine.

I'm just quoting some words from a dead white guy.

I wish I had something of my own to say. Something totally new—words that no one in the entire history of the world has ever said before, a sentiment that is totally and perfectly and particularly mine.

But I wouldn't even know where to begin.

I open my eyes and finally see him, right under the exit sign.

Charlie.

My twin, my other half, cohabitant of our mom's womb, older by six and a half minutes, the person in the world whose DNA is the closest to mine.

Except my blood cells have always been orderly, behaved, healthy.

The light makes the brown fuzz of his newly grown-in hair look even softer.

He's leaning against the wall, arms crossed over his chest, legs forever too long for whatever space he's in, his face unreadable from where I'm standing, and I wonder when we lost each other.

"'—And not to yield'?" I finally say, making it a question.

There's an excruciating silence, everyone waiting because they're not sure it's the end of the speech—who ends an inspiring poem with a question? Tennyson didn't, that's for sure—but then Emerson starts clapping like she thinks I'm Oprah Winfrey and the Dalai Lama all in one, and then more people join in, and I step back, let out a long exhale, finishing up quite possibly the worst conclusion to a valedictorian speech in the history of vale-dictorian speeches.

Principal Taylor steps to the podium and thanks me, and I smile hard, because right now my teeth have a mind of their own and if I don't, I'm pretty sure they'll start chattering and never stop.

Sitting on a folding chair on the side of the stage, I tighten my hands in my lap, listening to Principal Taylor talking about this year's class of graduates—all the scholarships we've won, all the marvelous places we're going, the incredible adults we're becoming.

I pretend to listen, but really I'm promising myself that if I see Charlie again, everything—this summer, college, med school, my life—will be okay.

When I look back at the exit sign, he's gone.

Two

CHARLIE'S BEEN LEAVING ME behind since we were born.

He was the first out of the womb, a full six and a half minutes before me, a fact he never tires of pointing out.

According to our parents, he learned how to crawl a good month before me, while I remained stuck in tummy-time limbo, red-faced and furious, my fists clenching emptily in space trying to pull him back.

He was the first to learn how to walk, to utter "Da" and "Ma" and "cat," to lose a tooth (the front bottom one, earning him five dollars from the tooth fairy and plunging me into a frantic tooth-wiggling campaign of my own).

In fact, my earliest memory is of him leaving me. I don't know how old we were or where we were, other than old enough to walk and outside—a freshly mowed green lawn beneath my feet, the sun shining hard and yellow above us.

The memory is like a short home video.

First, an image of Charlie's back as he runs. He's wearing a red-and-blue striped shirt, gray sweatpants, and gym shoes, his thick, dark curls wild.

I can't keep up.

I know this because I can never keep up with him.

That doesn't stop me from trying.

I call out his name once and then again, my feet pushing on the ground, arms pumping faster, like I can catapult myself into supersonic flight, but instead Charlie gets farther and farther away, while I get a cramp in my side from running so hard.

And then I can't see him anymore. He's too far gone.

Right then, the sense of having lost something is so enormous and unbearable that I press my palms to my eyes, making sun spots dance in my vision, trying not to cry.

But here's the thing: Charlie comes back for me.

After a few seconds, I sense him rather than see him in front of me. I imagine him squatting down and resting on his calves, waiting for me to open my eyes.

"Parker," he says. "Why are you crying? I got you."

And without even needing to open my eyes, I know in the deepest parts of me that he does, because Charlie always comes back for me.

These days, I wonder if I made up the entire memory.

These days, I have moments when I see my brother and he's so impenetrable, so far away, that even his physical appearance has become unfamiliar, like I'm passing him on the street for the first time, noting his lanky frame, the way his ears stick out a little, how it's possible for brown eyes to burn.

He's become a stranger.

Mom insists it's just a phase, that our very natures are inseparable, that we'll always come back to each other.

For proof, she pulls out her old sonogram pictures, the ones that show Charlie and me curled around each other like a pair of opposing quotation marks in her stomach. "That's the thing about being twins: You'll *always* have each other. Always."

Dad says that before we learned to talk, we had our own language, speaking to each other in a strange mix of consonants and vowels no one else understood, that sometimes we were downright creepy: these two small people who came from them but clearly occupied a separate world.

When Charlie and I bicker now, Mom brings up the day in preschool I stayed home with the flu. I cried the whole morning—not because I felt sick, but because my brother wasn't there. Within the first hour, Mom got a call from the school saying Charlie was in hysterics too.

"You two were inseparable," she says again.

At times I've wondered if my parents invented these stories solely to demonstrate why Charlie and I shouldn't argue over who has the remote control or gets to use Mom's car on Friday night.

But then I remember those three words: *I got you.*

They're leftovers from a morning dream, the kind that as soon as you try to remember, you start to forget, making it easy to dismiss, to let go.

But there are traces glimmering on the edges of your memory, clues something more once existed.

I got you.

Here's the thing: Charlie and I don't hate each other now. At least I don't think we do.

We coexist at the same school and in the same home with a minimum of hostility and angst, like distant planets in the same solar system. Occasionally we hang out together when Matty and Em are involved.

But I can't imagine Charlie ever sitting down and confiding to me how he feels about not graduating with us.

I can't imagine confessing to him how lonely it is to be the one running ahead for the first time in our lives.

We don't have words in our vocabulary for that, let alone a secret language.

And these days, other than our mostly shared genetics, we could not be more different.

Charlie is confident and loud, popular and fearless.

I'm orderly, careful, introverted.

Charlie is tall and thin, his hair a lighter shade of brown now, a casual smattering of tasteful freckles scattered across his nose.

I'm far from tall, and thanks to some recessive German haus-frau genes from Dad's side, I have what I call extra weight and what Em insists are enviable curves. My dark-almost-black hair is so curly it verges on unmanageable, and my face looks like someone spilled a whole jar of freckles on it.

Charlie makes himself comfortable wherever he is—legs

stretched out, arms propped casually behind his head—while I wish I could curl into the smallest space possible needed to exist, like a pill bug.

Last spring, my brother pitched the school's baseball team to winning the national championship. He is loved by the band geeks and the jocks, the smart kids and the art kids, the loners and the stoners and the straight-edgers alike.

I have spent the past four years studying my ass off and padding my schedule with extracurriculars chosen solely to impress Harvard. The few acquaintance friends I have beyond Em, I've met through her.

And, of course, there's that one last glaring difference, the one I haven't mentioned yet, the one that even our shared DNA can't overcome:

Charlie got leukemia.

I didn't.

Three

THE LOBBY OUTSIDE THE auditorium is packed with seniors and parents, and in the middle of the crush, I see Mom and Dad.

No Charlie.

Mom waves, Dad beams, and when I reach them, they pull me into a group hug, nearly smashing the bouquet of yellow daisies Mom's holding against my chest in the process.

"Whoa," she calls out, holding them aside, but Dad scoops me in harder and Mom just laughs.

"We're so proud," Dad says when we finally part, and I realize he's tearing up a little bit.

"And your speech was phenomenal," Mom says.

"I loved that quote at the end," Dad says. "Brilliant. What was it again, 'Not to give up'?"

"'And not to yield.'"

"You must be so excited," he says. "This is it. Your whole life is in front of you." And he's right. I should be excited, but right then I wish I had given a totally different speech. I wish I were a totally different person.

"Have you seen your brother?" Mom asks.

"I was going to ask you the same thing," I say, scanning the crowd.

"Our reservation is at eight, so we should really leave soon," Dad says, checking his watch and frowning. "The traffic getting out of here is going to be a mess. And we might as well have parked on the moon for how close we are."

Mom sends me a quick eye roll at Dad's exaggeration, then pats him reassuringly on the arm. "Honey, why don't you and I go get the car while Parker finds Charlie? We'll pick them up on our way out."

"Okay, but if we're late . . ."

"Dad, don't worry. I'm on it," I say. "I'll text you guys when I find him."

I give them both another hug before they leave, then commence the search for my brother.

The lobby is packed. I duck out of the way as two guys from the football team tackle each other in what seems like a drunken hug.

"I'm going to miss you next year, bro," one bellows, while the other one gives him a dude clap on the back.

Across the way, I see Christine Miller of the split ends with her older sister, Molly, arms wrapped around each other as they pose for a picture for their parents, a row of lockers behind them.

I pass Jenna Lambert, our class salutatorian, embracing some guy with heavy-metal hair wearing leather pants, her hands hanging around his neck, his hands firmly clamped on her butt, clearly not caring who sees. She's a total badass.

There's Brian and Brad Vascek, the other set of twins in our grade, both in honors classes with me, both going to Miami University next year. Brad catches my eye and gives a wave, and I wave back, envying them their closeness.

Everyone around me seems completely at ease in their own skin. In obvious contrast, my eyelid keeps twitching impatiently, and I squeeze both eyes shut, trying to will it into stillness, my face scrunching with the effort.

When I open them, I realize I'm standing right in front of the picked-over Help Wanted bulletin board outside of the guidance counselor's office. Out of curiosity more than anything else, I scan the remaining listings: telemarketer ("Make $20,000 a month from home!"), dishwasher at a local diner, an assistant at a pottery studio, a full-time nanny position, a Kings Island hiring fair that happened last weekend.

Right then, arms circle me from behind in a hug.

"Park!" Em sings in my ear, and when I turn around, my face immediately moves into a real smile, one that mirrors hers.

"We did it," she says, then says it again, this time in a yell that makes several people turn around: "We did it! We graduated!"

She's practically bouncing in place, and I remember how my dad used to call her Tigger when we were little.

"Nice speech, lady," she adds.

I cringe. "I totally messed up at the end."

"I didn't notice. Besides, if you did? Who cares. You're the vale-dictorian, Parker McCullough. Not anyone else. You. That's a big freaking deal."

I shrug, embarrassed.

She leans closer, her voice lowering. "I know it must feel weird, Charlie not graduating tonight. But you can still be happy and proud of yourself, Park. I am."

I look away before she can see my expression, my eyes suddenly stinging. "Speaking of, have you seen him?"

"Not yet," Em says, standing on her tiptoes next to me. "Oh crap," she mutters, nudging my side and pointing across the room.

Em's ex-girlfriend, May Kim, is talking to Matty. Whether it's because May has chopped off her waist-length hair and is now sport-ing a chic pixie cut, or the fact that Em hasn't seen her ex-girlfriend since a teary breakup up last Thanksgiving, when May was home from Oberlin, Em sharply sucks in her breath.

"Of course she looks good," she murmurs.

"Why is she here?" I ask, immediately protective.

"Probably for Christine and Dolores and Jean and Clement. They were all on newspaper together last year."

Right then Matty sees us, his goofy grin growing, and he beck-ons Em over.

Em shoots me a confused look. "I should at least say hi, right?"

"It's up to you. But I've got your back no matter what."

She chews on her bottom lip. "Do I look okay?"

My best friend looks radiant—red flushing her cheeks, her

blond hair beachy and perfectly tousled even though it's only the beginning of summer and we're nowhere near the ocean.

I reach in my gown pocket and hand her my tub of sparkly lip balm. "It's got magic powers."

She dabs her finger in, gives her lips a quick swipe, then straightens.

"Perfect," I say.

She starts to leave, then turns back, pointing to the corner. "By the way, your brother's over there. But be forewarned: He's engaging in some major PDA with Erin right now."

I look in that direction and sigh.

Charlie and Erin are leaning against a wall of lockers, pressed together in a lip-locked embrace that's pushing the boundaries of PG-13. I make my way toward them, clearing my throat and tapping Charlie on the shoulder when I get there.

When he turns around, his cheeks are flushed, and the expression on his face falls a bit when he sees it's me.

"Hey," he says, pulling me into an obligatory hug, his arm angled awkwardly against me, like he's just fallen out of a tree and broken his arm, and the whole thing is super weird because I can't think of the last time we hugged, if ever. Not to mention he reeks of beer.

"Are you drunk?" I ask.

"Nice to see you too, Mom," he says, stepping back, shoving his hands in his pockets.

"Charlie," I say in warning.

"God, just trust me, okay?"

I look over at Erin for confirmation, but she's put on her special smile, the bright hard sunshiny one just like the one our mom uses when she wants to change the subject. "Parker! Happy graduation!"

"You too," I say.

"Congrats on your speech. It was really good," she says, looping her arm through Charlie's and looking up at him adoringly. "I wonder who'll be valedictorian next year for your class, babe? I bet half the people in this room will come back to see you graduate. You know I'll be there."

Right then, like they've practiced it, two of Charlie's baseball teammates, Steven Reiss and Jake Nolan, call out "McCullough!" in tandem.

A shadow flits across Charlie's face before he puts on a grin, clasping each of their hands and pulling them into one-armed guy hugs, complete with claps on the back.

They each hug Erin and me too, before turning back to Charlie.

"It's good to see you on your two feet, man," Jake says.

"Yeah, we've been worried," Steven adds, brow furrowing, voice serious. "How're you feeling?"

Charlie frowns at them before shooting Erin and me an exaggerated look of disbelief. "Jesus, you leave a baseball team for one season and everyone turns into total puss—"

Erin elbows him sharply.

Jake flinches at Charlie's tone, and Steven shifts uncomfortably.

"They're just being nice," Erin mutters under her breath.

Charlie shakes his head, dismissing her. "They know I'm just effing with them, right, guys?"

"Yeah," Steven says, nodding, like he's willing himself to agree. Jake offers a weak smile Erin's way.

"Congrats on Florida State, man," Charlie says to Steven. "And LSU?" he asks Jake.

"Yeah," Jake says. "Listen, we should probably . . . ," he starts, hiking his thumb over his shoulder toward the crowd.

"Maybe we'll see you at Chris's house later?" Erin says.

"Sure, yeah," Steven says. "Good to see you guys. And nice speech, Parker."

"Thanks," I say.

I watch them leave as Erin turns to Charlie. "Babe, you feeling okay?"

"Never been better," Charlie says, wincing out a smile, and even I can tell it's a stretch. But before she notices his expression, Erin's attention is caught by someone behind us, and she stands on her toes, waving enthusiastically, then grinning as Mr. Franklin, the school's baseball coach, lopes over, grabs my brother in a big bear hug, and lands two hearty claps on his back. "Charlie McCullough, it is really dang good to see you out in the world again."

Mr. Franklin has been Charlie's baseball coach since seventh grade, moving over to coach high school the same year we started as freshmen, and taking the team, with Charlie as the star pitcher, to first place in the state championship last year.

Last September, I'm pretty sure Charlie's cancer returning was as much of a blow to Mr. Franklin as to my parents. After Charlie went back in the hospital and the decision was made to hold him back a year, my parents went to tell Mr. Franklin in person. When they got home that night, I could tell they'd both been crying again.

"How are you feeling, son? Any word on whether we'll see you back on the team next year?"

"So far, so good," Charlie says, which isn't an answer, but Mr. Franklin visibly relaxes, patting Charlie on the back again.

"Good to hear. Good to hear. Looking forward to state championship number two with you on our team."

Erin flips her hair. "Coach Franklin, I was just telling Charlie and Parker that I bet most of these people will be back to see Charlie graduate next year."

"You bet," Mr. Franklin says.

So quickly I almost miss it, Charlie's mouth twists in a brief grimace before he projects a reassuring smile at Erin and his coach. "Thanks."

"Well, looking forward to talking more, Charlie," Mr. Franklin says. "Give me a call when you're ready to talk."

"Sure thing, sir."

As Mr. Franklin leaves, I turn back to my brother. "Dad's angsting about missing our dinner reservation because of parking lot traffic. You about ready?"

Charlie shakes his head, making that regretful clicking noise with his tongue on his teeth. "No can do. We're headed to a party at Chris Wilder's house."

"Wait, what?"

"I told you. We're going to a party."

"You're not going to dinner with us?" I ask, my words slower to catch up to the disappointment making its way through me.

"Nope."

"But I thought you were coming out with us."

"Jesus, Parker. No already!"

I stare at him. I know Charlie and I aren't exactly close, and I'm sure it wasn't easy to watch everyone graduate without him, but still, I never thought he wouldn't be part of this night.

I never imagined he wouldn't spend it with our family.

(I never imagined he wouldn't spend it with me.)

I straighten, try to push my heart back on the inside. "Did you tell Mom you're not coming?"

"No, but she didn't tell me about dinner, soooo . . ." He shrugs, looking to Erin for backup, but she shifts uncomfortably and focuses on rummaging through her purse.

"She probably just assumed you'd know we're having family dinner because it's graduation? A major night for us?" I search his face for some inkling he understands.

"You know what they say about assuming. Besides, it's not exactly a major night for me."

"Listen, Mom really wanted us to all be together. I think she's going to be bummed you're not coming. Will you please just come? You can go to the party after."

Charlie's face tightens, and I'm struck again by how much he looks like a stranger. "Parker, listen: I. Don't. Want. To. Go. To. Dinner. Okay?" He deliberately enunciates each word.

I cringe at the sharpness in his voice, blinking hard and trying not to cry, because I cry too much and I don't want Charlie to see me like that. But inside, the pressure is coming at me from everywhere, tightening my ribs, flattening my breath, squeezing my heart.

I can tell by the irritation that crosses Charlie's face that he knows I'm upset, but he doesn't care.

"Come on, Erin. Let's go."

Erin shoots me a regretful smile, but Charlie leaves without looking back.

I stand there, wishing I could tell him that it's not just Mom who will miss him tonight. That even though I see him every day, I've been missing my brother for years.

Four

THE MORNING AFTER GRADUATION, I wake up with a knot knitted behind my ribs like a clenched fist.

My clock says I still have another fifteen minutes to sleep, but my whole body is already awake, alert—my mind clear like a trumpet call: *Today is the day today is the day today is the day.*

I suck in my breath sharply, and for a second I wish I were sleeping in or going to babysit like I did last summer or getting ready to leave the country with Em.

But enough of that: I need to decide what to wear for my internship orientation.

Thirty minutes later, I'm headed downstairs, freshly showered and wearing navy capris, a crisp white short-sleeved shirt, and my navy-blue ballet flats, with a red striped cardigan slung over my arm. It feels like the right outfit—not too frivolous, not too flashy.

I'm ready.

When I reach the kitchen, Charlie's resting his forehead in his hands, a giant bowl of Cheerios sitting untouched in front of him.

I grab a bowl, a spoon, and the cereal box, which feels suspiciously light. My suspicions are confirmed when about eight Cheerios plink sadly into my bowl.

"Ugh."

Charlie raises his head, wincing.

"What?" I ask.

"You don't have to be so loud."

When I go to the pantry to find something else, all that's left is a box of HealthWheat, the disgusting health food cereal Mom wants Charlie to eat because she read about it in a cancer-free book.

"Charlie," I say, holding the box up and shaking it at him.

"I'm not eating that stuff today," he replies, slowly straightening, then jamming a spoonful of dry cereal in his mouth, talking as he does. "I've had it with garden-mulch cereal. No thanks."

I sigh, sitting down and shaking the HealthWheat into my bowl, the clumps landing with depressing thuds.

Charlie scans my outfit.

"What?" I ask, suddenly self-conscious.

He shakes his head, chewing.

"Charlie."

He swallows and slowly wipes the corner of his mouth. "You look like the American flag, that's all."

"Nice. Thanks for your support."

"You know I'm right." He shoves his barely touched bowl of cereal away and slouches back in his seat, closing his eyes.

"You're not even going to eat that?" I ask.

"Why do you care? You worried Mom's going to be disappointed again?" he asks, eyes still closed.

Dad strolls into the kitchen then, straightening his tie, and heads to the coffeemaker. "Good morning, guys. You ready for today, Dr. McCullough?" he asks.

Not for the first time, I wish I could tell him I miss the days when he called me by my first name. But ever since I got into Harvard, he's been downright giddy about my future plans, and I can tell he enjoys the nickname way more than I hate it.

"As ready as I can be," I reply.

"Do you think you'll see any patients today?" Dad asks.

"She's just doing an internship," Charlie answers.

"It's not just any internship. You know that, Charlie. And I bet you can still see patients in an internship," Dad starts, but Mom comes in before any of us can respond, giving Charlie and me cheek kisses before dropping her bag on the table and making a beeline for a mug and the pot of coffee.

She leans against the counter, sipping slowly. "Charlie, you're not eating your HealthWheat?"

"God, can't I eat what *I* want for once?" he snaps.

Mom flinches, a look of hurt crossing her face, and Charlie immediately slumps back in his chair.

"I'm sorry. I didn't mean it."

"No, you're right," Mom says carefully. "Besides, one little day without HealthWheat can't hurt, right?" She forces a smile and turns to me, and I can tell she really thinks one little day without HealthWheat could indeed hurt, but she's trying very hard to pretend otherwise. "I'm sorry we didn't get to see Em and Matty last night. When do they leave for Europe? I bet they're getting excited."

"Sunday," I say, realizing I only have a couple of days left with my best friend before she leaves for the summer.

"They're going to have such a good time," Mom says. "Phil, remember the first time we went to England?"

"Yeah, that was pretty amazing. But Europe is nothing compared to your summer, Dr. McCullough. This is pretty much the first day of the rest of your life."

"No pressure or anything," Charlie mutters.

"I guess—" I start before Charlie interrupts me.

"Don't forget my summer, Dad. Tutoring and support group every day. Now, *that's* amazing," Charlie says.

"Charlie, we all have responsibilities we don't want. You know I don't love my job. But I go," Dad begins.

I brace myself for the speech, the one about how he hates his job copywriting but does it for all of us.

"Fuck that," Charlie mutters.

I look up, shocked.

Dad stops midsentence, the confused look on his face evidence he didn't hear exactly what Charlie said. "What was that?"

"Nothing," Charlie replies.

Dad seems placated, but I shoot my brother a look, wondering why he's being extra unpleasant today.

"Hey, Mom," Charlie says. "Don't forget I need your keys."

She points toward her bag, holding her coffee mug close, like it's the only thing currently giving her life.

I straighten. "Wait, what? No. I need the car today, remember?"

Charlie digs through Mom's bag and pulls out the car keys. "Got 'em. Thanks," he says.

"But, Mom!"

"You are my beautiful, smart, grown children. I trust you can figure it out between yourselves," she says, heading toward the stairs again.

Dad follows her out of the room, pausing only to give me a corny Dad thumbs-up before he leaves.

"Charlie. I need the car."

"So do I."

"Since when? Your tutoring doesn't even start until next week."

"Mom said I can drop you off today."

"But that wasn't the plan."

He shrugs. "It is now."

"But, Charlie, I need the car. For *job* stuff," I add, trying to sound reasonable.

"But, Parker, I need it for *life* stuff," he says, shoveling in more cereal.

"Like what?" I ask.

"Got a comic book thing," he responds, but with the cereal he's just jammed in his mouth, it sounds more like "Cottacomma-boothig."

"I'll drop you off there, then."

He swallows. "No can do. It's in Louisville."

My hand falls on the table. "Louisville! That's, like, two hours from here! How are you going to get back in time to pick me up at two?"

"It's actually an hour and a half," he says. "Besides, you're done at five."

"No. I'm done at two."

He shrugs. "Mom told me five. That's when I'll be there."

"But it's orientation! I'm done at two. What am I supposed to do during those three hours, just sit around in the lobby? I was planning on hanging out with Em this afternoon."

"Can't you hang out with her tonight?"

"She has plans with her mom," I say, trying to stay patient.

"Maybe she can pick you up this afternoon instead?"

"No! Her mom's using the car today! That's why I need our car, so I can go to her house when I'm done today *at two*," I say, my voice breaking in frustration.

"Geez, Parker. Relax."

The knot behind my chest tightens more.

I try again.

"See, here's the thing. You know Em's leaving on Sunday? And I'm not going to see her for, like, ten weeks? And then I'm leaving for Harvard and she's leaving for John Carroll? So if you have the car, at least maybe you could try to get there earlier?"

"But here's the thing," Charlie says, mimicking me. "This is one of my last free days? Because on Tuesday I start weeks and weeks of tutoring? Because I missed school this year?"

LETTING GO OF GRAVITY

"Why are you being so nasty today?"

"Oh, I don't know. Maybe because I HAD CANCER?"

I flinch. "Fine. You take the car," I say.

Something flashes across his face, and I could swear he looks guilty, disappointed even. But then he breaks eye contact and nods. "Cool."

I focus on my bowl of HealthWheat, blinking hard, trying to push the disappointment of losing my afternoon with Em down deep inside.

Dad and Mom both come back in the kitchen then, and I wonder if they were eavesdropping, waiting to reemerge until we figured out the car situation.

"Everything settled?" Mom asks.

"Yeah. Charlie's going to drive me to my internship," I say.

"Good. Charlie, do what you can to pick your sister up as soon as you can today. Maybe you can get there a little earlier?" Mom leans down to kiss the soft new hair on Charlie's head, and like every other time she's done it since it started to grow back, I can see her marvel at its softness, its presence.

He ducks out from under her.

"Maybe I can get there by four thirty," he offers.

"That would be so thoughtful, thanks," she says.

Thirty minutes isn't nearly enough to salvage my afternoon with Em.

Dad hugs me so hard my shoulders wilt. "I can't wait to hear all about your first day. Remember, Dr. McCullough, you only get one chance to make a first impression," he says.

I force a smile.

He chucks Charlie's shoulder while Mom grabs her bag.

"Hon," Dad says, stopping her and leaning down to pick up a paper that's fallen onto the floor. Even from across the room, I can see her neat red handwriting all over some poor college student's essay.

"Thanks. Dinner at six tonight, guys," she calls over her shoulder as she shuts the door behind them.

Charlie stands abruptly, dumping his cereal in the garbage and placing the bowl in the sink. "Leave in ten minutes?" he calls over his shoulder before jogging upstairs.

I make myself eat more of the HealthWheat, despite the fact that it might be the worst thing I have ever tasted.

I tell myself that if I can make myself finish the whole bowl, Charlie will come back and selflessly offer me the car, or Mom and Dad will come back with a set of shiny keys for a new car of my own, or my previously MIA fairy godmother will suddenly appear and conjure up a whole new life for me.

But instead, Mustard the cat enters the kitchen and wraps himself around my legs. I can feel his throaty purr against my skin. He stops and licks my exposed ankle, and his tongue is all dry and scratchy, and then he stands on his hind legs, getting ready to jump into my lap, and I know he's going to shed all over my pants.

"Sorry, buddy," I say, pushing the chair back, giving up on the HealthWheat. He lets out a crabby meow. "We can't always get what we want."

I trudge upstairs to brush my teeth. If this is indeed the first day of the rest of my life, it's off to a sucky start.

Five

AS SOON AS WE hit I-71, it's clear Charlie's mood hasn't improved. He's going well above the speed limit, his crappy jam-band music filtering through the car. It doesn't help that Mom's ancient Tercel has black vinyl seats and no air-conditioning, that even with the windows down, I feel like I might melt.

"You're going too fast," I say, but Charlie doesn't slow down. If anything, he speeds up.

I lean over, turn down the music. "You're going to get a ticket."

He doesn't say anything, just turns the music back up.

I grip the side of my seat.

There's sweat trickling down my back. I mentally curse my decision to wear the white oxford and dark pants instead of a dress. I'm going to be thoroughly drenched by the time I get there.

Right then, Charlie slams the brakes, and the Tercel jerks to a halt behind a line of stopped cars in front of us, the seat belts yanking us back.

Charlie barks out a curse.

"God, Charlie! I told you to slow down!"

He mumbles something that sounds like "sorry," finally turning down the music, and I try to catch my breath.

We're stopped by the exit for the mall, and maybe it's the near-accident moment we just had, but I'm hit with a sudden wave of nostalgia for the Delaney kids, which is weird, because they were pretty much the bane of my existence last summer.

At first, the twenty dollars an hour Mrs. Delaney offered me to babysit her two sons seemed generous, extravagant even. But after my first hour with Todd and Ryan, I quickly came to the realization that two thousand dollars an hour wouldn't have been nearly enough.

They were, hands down, the worst kids I'd ever met.

Within the first week I watched them, Todd almost set the basement on fire (claiming he wanted to see if the fire extinguisher really worked), and Ryan intentionally locked himself in the bathroom for the better part of six hours. They both called me "Farter" instead of Parker, and the one time Emerson pinch-hit and watched them for me, she refused to talk to me for the next two days, accusing me of grossly misrepresenting what she was getting into.

Even with all that, I realize I would have done it again this summer. Once I learned their MOs—the way Todd would get real shifty and secretive when he was planning something, and how

Ryan started talking super loud when he was up to no good—I was a pretty good babysitter.

But I have my internship.

The internship I really, really wanted, the internship I beat out numerous other applicants for, the internship that's currently making me nostalgic for two near-homicidal children?

The line of traffic starts easing forward again, and for a while Charlie and I are both quiet.

I sneak a glance at him, wondering if he's thinking about Matty going to Europe—how Charlie was supposed to join him before he got sick again this past fall, how Em took his place instead, leaving us both without best friends for the summer looming ahead of us.

"Huh," Charlie says. "Look at that."

I lean forward to see what he's pointing at: bright-red capital letters spray-painted across the edge of the bridge: IS YR TIN CAN COMFORT PLUS.

"Wow. That's weird. What do you think it means?" I ask as we pass underneath.

"Not a clue."

"And how in the world could someone paint that up there without getting caught?"

"Maybe it was Spider-Man."

"Yeah, right," I say.

"Do you have a better theory? Seriously, painting that without falling into the traffic below? That takes some serious superhero mojo."

"And a total lack of concern for personal safety," I add. "Plus, would Spider-Man really do something illegal?"

"Maybe he got sick of fighting villains and rescuing people. Maybe, for once in his life, he just wanted to be someone else."

For a second I get it, but before I can agree, Charlie leans over and turns up the terrible jam-band music again, letting it fill up the space between us.

Six

AS CHARLIE PULLS UP to the Children's Hospital visitor
entrance, my breath sticks.

Other than driving by on the way to Em's favorite coffee shop, I
don't think I've been back to the main branch of Children's Hospital since Charlie was sick the first time, when we were nine. When
the cancer returned earlier this year, he went to Bethesda—it was
closer, and since he was almost eighteen, his doctors thought he
should transition to an adult cancer facility. And my internship
interview (which I nailed, talking about Charlie's history and how
it was why I wanted to be a pediatric oncologist) was at the Liberty
Campus in the suburbs.

Up until this moment, I didn't think it would be weird coming
back here. In fact, the thought never even crossed my mind.

But as Charlie slows the car by the front entrance, it's a

punch to the gut, my stomach literally turning at the sight of the blue-and-white logo of children holding hands, the pale tan color of the brick, even the shape of the font for the hospital's marquee.

And for the first time in years, I let myself think about that day in fourth grade when Charlie got the bloody nose.

Em and I were sitting cross-legged in a line of girls on the blacktop during recess, each person braiding the hair of the person in front of her. Except my hair was too short and too thick to do anything with, so I was at the end, sitting behind Em, trying to tame her soft blond curls into a neat French braid.

I don't know how long we'd been at it when we heard shouting and then saw our teacher, Ms. Dros, running across the blacktop toward a group of kids circled around something.

"I bet there's a fight!" Emerson said, turning to check it out and disrupting her braid in the process. I carefully angled her head back in front of me. I wanted to make the best French braid ever, if only to make up for my own hair.

But then I shot a quick glance over my shoulder, curiosity getting the better of me, and saw my brother bent over, his hands clenched around his face.

I dropped Em's braid, the strands unfurling like they were in slow motion.

By the time I got over to the group, Charlie was going inside with Ms. Dros and Matty, and the playground monitor made me stay outside with the rest of the class.

Caroline Bates, the class loudmouth, stood in the center of the lingering crowd, hands on her hips, telling everyone that Charlie's nose had started bleeding for no reason at all.

This I could imagine: bright-red life pouring out of his right nostril, down his Iron Man shirt, over his hands, just like last year when he tripped on the playground and fell on his face.

But Caroline also said Charlie started bawling.

This I didn't buy for one single second.

Charlie never cried.

So when she took it to the next level and called him a crybaby, I called her a shithead, a word I'd heard Dad use only when he was super mad about work.

Miraculously enough, I didn't get in trouble. With all the chaos of Charlie's bloody nose, no teachers heard it. And since everyone liked Charlie, no one tattled on me, not even Caroline, who seemed to know she was in the wrong.

I couldn't wait to tell Charlie.

For once, I felt brave. For once, I didn't cry.

That afternoon, Mom took Charlie to the doctor, so I stayed at school with Ms. Murray until Dad could pick me up. She asked me to feed our class guinea pig and to help put star stickers on the tests she graded. She even let me get M&M's from the vending machine in the teachers' lounge.

I remember sitting on the comfy couch there, legs propped up on the coffee table.

It was pretty much the best day of my nine years to date.

When Dad and I got home that afternoon, Charlie looked pale and worn-out. He didn't react when I whispered to him about calling Caroline that word, didn't laugh when I told him my new favorite knock-knock joke, didn't want our cat, Mustard, to sit with him.

He only wanted to curl up on the couch, his head in Mom's lap while she stroked his forehead.

Mom said the doctor thought it was probably sinus issues or allergies, but that they should keep an eye on Charlie just in case.

I didn't know what that "just in case" meant, but over the next few weeks, as I watched my brother, my heart started to worry, flitting nervously in my chest.

Charlie was constantly tired. He didn't want to play catch with Matty, said his hands hurt.

He turned down dessert, went to bed early.

He got another bloody nose, this time in the middle of Sunday breakfast, when Dad was making pancakes. Mom put both her hands on his neck under his ears, felt the space there tenderly, frowned, and made an appointment to take him to the doctor the next morning.

That night, when I made our secret knock on the wall, the one we gave each other every night before we fell asleep, Charlie didn't respond.

I got up, creeping carefully to his room. When I opened the door, he was sitting up in bed, the moonlight coming in from the window, sheets tangled around him. He was staring at his bare stomach, his Iron Man T-shirt wrinkled up in his grip, his hair pressed down on his forehead in sweaty curls.

"Charlie?" I whispered, my heart in my throat.

When he looked up, his eyes were wide and animal, and I could see the tracks of tears down his cheeks. I got closer and saw red mottled spots all over his chest and called out, my voice breaking with fear, *"MOM!"*

A week later, Charlie was diagnosed with cancer, specifically high-risk acute lymphocytic leukemia.

The doctors at Children's Hospital said it probably had been in Charlie for a while, but the bloody nose was the first visible symptom. They also said Charlie had an 85 percent survival rate, and Mom told me that was good.

But everything I saw wasn't good.

Charlie cried on a regular basis: when he had to go to the doctor, when Mom and Dad made the decision to take him out of school, when he had to get what I later learned was his first spinal tap.

Our cat, Mustard, began pooping in the middle of the dining room floor.

I started dreaming about helium people, variations of the same dream over and over: shadowy winged creatures with their hearts throbbing on the outside, trying to pull Charlie away from me, my bare feet curled against the dirt with the effort of trying to hold on. I couldn't tell if I wanted them to go away, or if I wanted to join them. But regardless of what I wanted, every time, the helium people won, Charlie's hand snapping out of mine, my eyes shooting open.

My parents tried to explain what was happening, that some of Charlie's cells were growing too fast, like the dandelions in the backyard, that Charlie was going to go to the hospital to get medicine to stop the weeds so they didn't take over all of him.

I pulled dandelions from the grass when no one was looking—from our backyard, on the edges of the playground, along the sidewalks in our neighborhood. I smashed them in my pockets, letting the yellow pulp stain my palms.

Mustard kept pooping on the floor.

A few weeks after Charlie's bloody nose, Grandma and Grandpa Rose picked me up from school.

"Your mom had to stay later with Charlie today and your dad's at work," Grandpa Rose explained. "But we thought we could get some ice cream."

That afternoon, we played Uno and I won, and then we watched *Snow White and the Seven Dwarfs*, my favorite movie. For dinner we went to Frisch's, and Grandma Rose let me bring home a slice of pumpkin pie in a plastic to-go container for Charlie, since it was his favorite.

But right before I went to bed, the phone rang. Grandpa's voice got quiet in the kitchen, and then Grandma Rose sat down and told me Charlie was going to stay in the hospital, that my parents were going to sleep over with him.

"Will they be home tomorrow?" I asked.

Grandma Rose shook her head. "Your parents will be, but Charlie's going to stay there for a while so he can get better. There are no germs there, and the doctors can take very good care of him."

I bit my lip. If Charlie wasn't in the bedroom next to mine, I couldn't give him our secret knock. He wouldn't know I was right there on the other side.

"But we get to stay here with you! And on weekends, your

mom arranged for you to stay with Em. Matty might sleep over too. Won't that be fun? It's going to be fine," Grandma Rose continued, her voice bright, but it was too bright, like she was trying to pretend it was sunny outside when it was really raining, and I knew it wasn't going to be fine.

"Not without Charlie," I said, and I started crying a little, and then more and more, until I was crying so hard, my breath flew away from me. It was terrifying, how I could feel my mouth gulping hard to find air, how my heart was on the outside, like the helium people.

Grandma Rose reached over and pulled me into her arms, holding me hard, shushing in my ear, rubbing my back steadily, until eventually my sobs slowed.

"It's okay to be sad with me and your grandpa," she whispered. "But right now your parents have a lot on their plate. I need you to be really brave for them, to be as good as you can. Can you do that for me? Can you be brave, Parker?"

I sniffed, nodding hard, my limbs suddenly heavy and tired.

"That's my girl," she said.

The next night, when Mom came home for dinner and asked me how my day was, I didn't tell her that I cried at lunch when Caroline Bates asked me if Charlie was going to die. Instead, I said that Caroline was praying for Charlie to get better. I watched Mom's smile come back from the faraway-Charlie-place, how when it rested on me, her shoulders relaxed just a little bit.

And later that week, when Dad gave Mustard a chin rub, telling me he was happy our cat had finally started using the litter box again, I didn't tell him about the messes I'd been cleaning up every day, the way I'd use a plastic bag to pick them up, hiding them in the bottom of the garbage can in the garage. Instead, I came over to pet Mustard too, letting his throaty purrs vibrate through my hand, calling him a good boy.

I worked hard on making the sadness small, making the fear invisible.

And it wasn't just with my parents. I made sure to thank Em's mom for having me spend the night. I did Charlie's chores without being asked. I gave Em all my winning Skee-Ball tickets when we went to Chuck E. Cheese's. After I saw Grandma Rose secretly crying in the kitchen one day when I told her I wished I could share my dessert with Charlie, I started lying to her and Grandpa, too, pretending to be the bravest girl in the world, making sure to hide under my covers when I cried at night.

And then, five months after Charlie's bloody nose, Dad came home from the hospital and taught me the word "remission." I was scared when his eyes got watery, but he told me it was because he was so happy. Charlie still had to get some more medicine to make sure the dandelions didn't grow back, but he was going to be okay.

I look over at Charlie now, nine years later—still skinny but much taller—and he's staring at the hospital entrance too.

I want to ask him what he's thinking.

I want to tell him looking at the hospital now makes my heart hurt.

But Charlie and I haven't talked like that for years, maybe not ever.

I fiddle with the door handle instead. "Well, have fun at the comic book thing."

"Yeah, good luck at orientation."

"Thanks," I say, but I still don't move, watching the automatic doors, the flow of families going in, a child in a wheelchair being wheeled out.

"Um, Parker?" Charlie asks, inclining his head toward the entrance.

I sigh, then grab my bag from the back and step outside.

As soon as I shut the door, Charlie's out of there.

Seven

OKAY, HERE IT GOES, *the first day of the rest of my life*, I think as the hospital doors slide open.

Stepping into the main lobby with its bright oranges and greens and yellows and blues is like going back in a time machine.

Focus, Parker. Focus.

I walk toward the front desk, and a friendly woman with short permed white hair and a name tag that says BETTY, VOLUNTEER cheerily says hello.

"I'm here for the internship program?"

"Another one of our interns! Welcome!" She hands me a temporary badge. "You'll get a photo ID later today," she says, motioning me to the elevator. "Second floor, head to the right. Room 221. Have a good day!"

My hands take the badge, and I smile automatically at Betty Volunteer.

The first elevator is too crowded. Even though a man in scrubs offers to make room for me, I shake my head, stepping back to wait for the next elevator.

As I'm standing there, my bottom right eyelid starts to twitch. I hope no one can see it.

Another elevator comes. There's plenty of room, but my legs won't move, and I shake my head politely when someone holds the door for me.

My teeth want to chatter, and I clench my jaw shut, feeling the energy building in the back of my throat.

A third elevator arrives, and even though the lobby is super air-conditioned, I'm sweaty all over and my head feels light.

I don't even look at the people in that elevator.

I remember standing in a waiting room, looking at my shiny red gym shoes, a nurse holding my hand as Dad walked down the hall, through doors at the end of the hallway, to find Mom and Charlie, and how right then, I knew with absolute certainty that it would be my fault if Charlie died.

I blink, trying to force the memory to leave, and everything around me gets extra loud and muffled at the same time. The volume in my ears is turned up to super sensitive, but I can't tell what anyone is saying, their words going in and out like trucks honking on the highway for no good reason.

The fourth elevator comes and goes.

I look at my watch. I have three minutes until the orientation starts. I know I should get in an elevator if I want to be on time, and I have to be on time. I can't be late for the first day of the rest of my life. It shouldn't be this hard; it's just getting in an elevator. But adrenaline is shooting through me, and I wipe my clammy palms on my pants.

When I look over my shoulder, Betty Volunteer is watching me, puzzled, and I think, *Parker McCullough, you are the valedictorian you are going to Harvard get your act together what is wrong with you there is nothing wrong with you you are healthy get in the elevator to strive to seek to find and not to yield. NOT to yield.*

I push the thudding heart coming out of my mouth back down in my chest where it belongs and squeeze into the crowded elevator.

"Can you press two, please?" I ask, my voice shaking.

When I enter the room, it's full, and everyone looks expectantly at me.

"Sorry I'm late," I say to the stern-looking gray-haired man at the front of the room. He glances at his watch and then points at the sign-in sheet. I sign the only blank space left while he speaks.

"As I started to say, I'm Dr. Gambier, the head of this internship program at Cincinnati Children's Hospital Medical Center. I'd like to take this opportunity to personally welcome each of you to our summer internship program. You've been accepted amid an elite group of students."

As he continues, I find the only empty seat, banging my thigh into the corner of the table when the girl next to me won't scoot in.

"Today is orientation. You're going to learn some of the basic procedures of working at Children's Hospital, in particular what you need to know about cleanliness. If you're in this room, you're already up-to-date on your vaccinations, which is great, but it's paramount that if you're sick, you call in. We want to minimize as much germ exposure as we can with our patients."

I look at the other people sitting around the table. Several of them are taking notes as Dr. Gambier speaks, so I grab a pen and pull the informational folder in front of me closer.

My mind wanders to the first time Charlie went through chemotherapy, how he got terrible sores in his mouth.

"Huh. So I guess we're partners," the girl next to me says, startling me out of my thoughts. Everyone around us is introducing themselves to one another.

I feel the same familiar terror I always feel when I have to talk to new people.

The girl is tall and thin, wearing diamond earrings that look like they cost more than our house. She smells like the entire perfume department at Macy's.

My nose tickles.

"I'm Laurel," she says, flicking back her long white-blond hair and not really looking at me. "I'm going to Harvard next year, focusing on pediatric endocrinology."

"Me too. I'm going to Harvard too, that is," I say, and Laurel gives me a closer look.

"Huh. Are you rushing anything?"

"No? I'm planning on finishing in four years?" I say, wondering if I should be finishing earlier. Would it improve my chances of getting into a good med school program if I completed undergrad in three years?

"I meant a sorority," she says.

"Oh, no, sorry. I'm not."

She looks disappointed. "Huh. Well, they're really great for connections and recommendations. You should think about it."

"Um, okay."

Laurel fiddles with a ballpoint pen, and I feel a desperate need to make this interaction work.

"So, why do you want to be a doctor?" I ask.

Laurel lights up so much, it's like she's a whole new person. "I love how bodies work. I've always thought it's kind of like we're a symphony, every part of us working together, contributing and playing its part, and when something's out of tune, it's a matter of finding that part, getting it back in tune, so the symphony's whole again. As soon as I was old enough to figure it out, I knew that's what I wanted to be. It's all I've ever wanted to be."

"Wow," I say.

"How about you?"

Around me, the other interns talk to one another. I try not to think about the day I found out Charlie's cancer had come back. Instead, I focus on getting my Harvard letter, Dad's joy, Mom's quiet pride.

"When we were in fourth grade, my twin got cancer, and I wanted to help other kids."

Across the table, two guys are intensely comparing notes on

Johns Hopkins's research program, talking about advances in gene research. I hear the guy to my right say that his dream is to join Doctors Without Borders and the girl he's chatting with say she wants to get into AIDS research.

I swallow hard. "I want to be a doctor so that kids like Charlie won't get sick again. . . ."

It's not enough.

The words fly into my mind, and even though I'm sitting, I feel like I'm going to fall over, my stomach turning and my body breaking into a cold sweat.

"Excuse me," I say, standing suddenly and pushing around Laurel, out of the room.

It takes me a second to find my bearings in the hallway, but when I do, I run to the restroom and into the first stall, kneel on the floor, and promptly throw up all the HealthWheat cereal I made myself eat this morning.

I wipe my mouth and stand up to leave, then lean over, vomiting again.

I try to tell myself I'm just nervous, that it's first-day jitters. Of course I can help kids with cancer. I've always wanted to be a doctor.

I owe Charlie this.

It's not enough.

I dry heave, then slide back down on the floor.

I hear clicks on the tile getting closer, two designer patent-leather flats ending up primly outside my stall.

For one desperate second I hope it's Betty Volunteer. I bet she'd find me a quiet dark room to sit in, would get me a soft drink and pat my forehead, would tell me it's all going to be okay.

"Dr. Gambier wants to know if you're okay," Laurel says.

I wish she were Em.

"I don't think so," I say.

"Huh," she says, and she and her designer flats click back out of the restroom.

I hug my knees against my chest and rest my head on them, not sure what to do next.

Eight

"I'M SO SORRY. I couldn't get ahold of my dad and my mom's teaching and Charlie's at some comic book thing in Kentucky," I say as I climb into Em's front seat.

"It's totally fine. I can't leave you sad and alone and barfing in the hospital lobby."

"But I know you're busy and your mom needed the car. Maybe I should have just waited until Charlie could pick me up." I can feel myself teeter dangerously near crying, but Em reaches out a hand and squeezes my shoulder.

"Park, it's okay. I promise. Mom was happy to hand over the keys so I could rescue you. Plus, this means I get to see you today after all."

I sigh, settling back into the seat as the beat-up old gray Fiesta pulls out of the hospital lot and toward the highway. Even though

Em's driving tends to make me a little carsick and she's playing her favorite terrible soft-rock station, I can feel the tension leaving my body by the second.

While Dr. Gambier couldn't have been more anxious to get my potentially contagious self out of there, Betty Volunteer was exactly as I imagined her to be—bringing me a ginger ale and periodically checking in to make sure I felt okay while I waited for Em.

"So, what happened in there?" Em asks.

I open my mouth to answer, but I feel dizzy again. I fix my gaze in front of me and grasp the door handle, white-knuckled. I need to get it together. Em's leaving. In two days.

"I think I ate some bad cereal," I finally say.

"Cereal can give you food poisoning?"

"I guess so."

She chews her lip, thinking carefully about what she wants to say next, while in the background some guy is singing about a horse with no name.

"Park, you'd tell me if something was wrong, right?"

"Nothing's wrong." I shake my head hard.

"You're lying."

I sniff tears back and think of the truest thing I know right now. "I'm just going to miss you so much. I'm sorry—that's selfish. I'm also totally excited for you."

She holds up a hand. "Listen, I know I'm great. You don't have to apologize for missing me."

I half cry, half laugh.

"But are you sure you don't want to come? We could still make it work—most of the places Matty and I are staying at are hostels, so it'd be easy for you to join us once you got to Europe."

I let myself imagine it for a minute—my entire life in a backpack, going to museums and pubs, wandering through beautiful cities and small towns.

Leaving Charlie behind.

"No. I have to do this internship, Em."

Em looks nervous and leans over to turn down the radio. "So, I don't want you to get mad. But there's something I've been wanting to ask you for a while."

"You don't want me to get mad? That sounds ominous," I say, letting out an unconvincing laugh.

"Do you really want to do this internship? Do you still want to be a doctor? Because ever since you got your Harvard acceptance, you've been kind of weird. I'm sure it'd be scary to change your mind now, but it's totally okay. You could . . ."

I zone out, thinking of the day I decided I wanted to be a doctor, how as soon as I said the words, Dad looked at me with so much love and Mom told me she was proud of me.

"Of course I do," I say, cutting off what she was still in the middle of saying.

"I mean, at the very least, maybe you could take the summer off to think about it. Because you're going to be spending the next God knows how many years studying your ass off."

A loud, weird laugh comes out of me. "I have wanted this since, like, fourth grade."

"I know."

"I mean, ever since Charlie got sick, I've known this is what I'm going to do."

"Park, I know, but . . . "

"This internship is so competitive and such an honor. Of course I want it! And anyway, can you imagine me telling my parents I don't want to do it? Ha! As if." I shake my head.

"Parker, you know they love you no matter what you do, right? I just think you might feel better if you talk with them. Or maybe you and Charlie could talk?"

"You're kidding, right?"

Em shakes her head.

"In what world would that *ever* happen?"

"He's going through things too, Park. And with all the Erin stuff and Matty being gone this summer . . ."

"What Erin stuff?"

"He didn't tell you?"

I shake my head.

"They broke up last night."

"What?"

"I don't know any of the details—Matty just told me they're over. But what I do know is that maybe he'll need a friend this summer. And I know this is totally corny, but maybe you need him too? It's just something to consider, okay?"

I don't reply.

She shoots me an anxious look. "Oh crap, are you mad?"

"No, I'm fine," I say, but it comes out sharper than I intended.

We're both quiet then, the noise of the highway competing

with both the car's muffler and the cheesy, heartfelt ballad coming from the speakers.

Em's coming from a good place, but she doesn't know what she's talking about with any of this: the internship, being a doctor, Charlie. Sure, she knows me better than pretty much anyone, but I want to be a doctor.

Then I remember Laurel's face when she talked about the human body being a symphony.

No.

I shake my head, clear my throat, make my voice light and breezy as Em pulls off the highway and onto Route 42. "So, do you have time for me to treat you to a root-beer float and a hot dog at the Float, as a thank-you for picking me up?"

Em looks doubtful. "Your stomach doesn't hurt anymore?"

"Weirdly enough, I'm actually kind of hungry," I say.

Em glances over, studying me, and whatever she sees must reassure her. She nods. "If we can get takeout, I'm in."

"Good, good," I say, looking out the window at the water tower we're passing. That's when I see it: another spray-painted message like the one on the I-71 overpass this morning, all in red capital letters, only this one spreads across the body of the metal tank: WHAT DO THE STARS LOOK LIKE YESTERDAY.

"Look," I say, pointing as we pass it.

Em laughs. "What do you think it means?"

"I have no clue. But whoever put it up there clearly isn't scared of heights. Charlie and I saw another one over I-71 this morning."

"Can you imagine being that fearless?" Em asks.

"No." What I can imagine is falling to my death onto the highway or crashing down onto the parking lot from the top of the water tower, but I don't say that. Instead, I sit back in the seat and try to pretend everything is just fine, which is a lot less terrifying than the alternative.

Nine

MAYBE BECAUSE IT'S HOT everyone thinks it's the perfect day for a root-beer float, or maybe the Friday lunch crowd is always this big, but there's a surprisingly long line at the Float, so Em drops me off while she runs to the bank to get some euros for her trip.

I stand in line, trying not to feel too bad for missing my first day of my internship and trying harder not to obsess over my conversation with Em. Instead, I study the sneakers of the girl in front of me, rearrange the letters in the first line of the menu to spell other words, try to recite all the words from the newest Taylor Swift song by heart, look at all the nearby buildings.

I realize there's a new storefront next to the Float where the Lucky Pup Day Spa used to be. The signage catches my attention. It's bright red and sky blue, painted like a graffiti tag, and it simply says CARLA'S CERAMICS. I always wished I could take ceramics or painting as electives in high school, but I packed my schedule with extra AP science classes instead. I wish I had time to do something like that this summer.

A perky voice interrupts my thoughts.

"Your order?"

The black girl at the counter has thick curls pulled up in a high ponytail, but even with that, I still have about two inches on her height-wise. She's wearing dark-framed glasses and has at least twenty dangly silver charm bracelets on her wrist. She stands patiently, smiling at me and waiting.

"Um, yeah," I start, but she's scrunching her nose and staring more closely at me. "Two root-beer floats, one with just half the ice cream."

Her face jolts with recognition, and deep dimples appear. "Wait! Aren't you this year's valedictorian?"

My face goes red, wondering if she heard me botch my speech at the end. "Yeah, that's me."

She leans forward on the counter. "Oh my God, you are, like, literally my total hero."

"I am?" I ask, letting out a surprised laugh.

"I pretty much want to be you when I grow up. Harvard, perfect SATs, scholarships from the National Merit Foundation *and* the Women in Medicine Foundation? It's awesome."

"Trust me, it's not all it's cracked up to be. My head's kind of a mess these days," I say, trying to make it sound lighthearted. However, I can tell by the way her expression stills that I wasn't successful. I immediately wish I could take it all back.

But then, surprisingly enough, the girl's face softens in sympathy. "I get it," she says, almost more to herself than to me. "My head is too."

Her honesty takes me off guard, and something vulnerable in me warms toward her.

The guy in line behind me interrupts the moment, saying loudly, "Any day now."

I cringe. "Oh God. I'm sorry. I'm holding up the line. I wanted to order two Jackie dogs. . . ."

She waves her hand. "He'll be fine. By the way, I'm Ruby Collie. I'll be a junior next year. You probably don't know me because I was just a sophomore, but I've seen you around. Maybe we could hang out sometime so I could ask you some questions about Harvard and your SAT strategy? I could really use your help." The words come out with a rush and halt to a stop, and she smiles hopefully, twisting her hands together.

And even though the last thing I want to do is to talk about Harvard, I think about what she said, about her head being a mess too. "Sure," I say. "I'm Parker, by the way."

"I know," she says, then cringes in embarrassment. "Not that I'm a stalker or anything."

A guy's voice calls from the grill. "Ruby, what's the order already?"

"Hold on to your butt, jerkface," she yells over her shoulder, and the sudden change in tone surprises me. She smiles awkwardly at me. "Sorry!" She grabs a pen and napkin, scribbles down her number and e-mail address, and slides it to me across the counter. "Call me, okay?"

"I will," I promise.

"Ruby, come on!" The guy from the kitchen emerges, wiping his hands on his apron, and my heart trips.

It's Finn Casper.

Even though I haven't seen him since first grade, I'd recognize him anywhere.

He's still pale with white-blond hair, but since I saw him last, his childhood scrawniness has become wiriness; he's all ropy sinews, and there's something that looks like a tattoo peeking out from under his T-shirt sleeve. His left eye is shadowed by a bruise—dark red and purple mottled spots.

His gaze moves over me as he takes in the crowd, clearly irritated. "Ruby! For chrissakes, there's a huge line!"

"Finally," the guy behind me mutters.

Without realizing it, my left hand has gone to my right wrist, circling it carefully. I drop my hand.

Ruby smiles at the line. "It's a beautiful day. I'm sure these fine people don't mind taking a few extra minutes to enjoy it. Am I right?"

More than a few people look surprised at being addressed but still nod in agreement.

Finn shoots an exasperated look at the flickering neon menu above him and rubs his hands over the back of his neck, under his short ponytail. His lips move, like he's counting to himself.

He lets out a long exhale and meets Ruby's eyes. "What's the order, Roo?"

"I told you not to call me that. God, you are such a crap bird, Finn," she says, giving him two middle fingers at the same time.

"Crap bird, that's a new one," Finn mutters. "Do you even know what the order is?"

Ruby looks back at me, putting on a sweet smile. "Two Jackie dogs and two floats, one with double the ice cream, right, Parker?"

I freeze when she says my name, but as Ruby looks triumphantly over her shoulder at Finn, I don't see any hint of recognition on his face.

I don't know if I'm relieved or disappointed.

"Half the ice cream. One with half. And extra sauerkraut on both dogs," I say tentatively, but Ruby's currently pretending to wind up her hand, just like a jack-in-the-box, as her middle finger slowly emerges in Finn's direction. She gives a triumphant "Ha!"

Finn rolls his eyes.

"You heard Parker's order. She is, in case you care, a total genius, the smartest person to ever live in this town, and she'll probably get a Nobel Prize in Life someday. Why are you keeping her and all these other fine customers waiting?" She gestures at the growing line.

Finn stalks back to kitchen.

"Extra sauerkraut, please," I call out.

"Parker, let's hang out soon, 'kay?" Ruby says as I hand her a twenty.

After I get my change, I move to the side, letting the impatient man behind me step up to order.

While I wait for the order, not entirely convinced the Jackie dogs will have any sauerkraut, let alone extra, Ruby shoots me an occasional conspiratorial grin, holding up her hand and mouthing, *Five more minutes!*

I realize why I instinctively like her so much: Her energy reminds me of Em's—immediately open and completely genuine.

Just then, Finn pokes his head out from the kitchen. "Order up," he says.

My mind flashes back to that day on the playground in first grade, the principal pulling Finn back by his arms as he kicked and screamed, how his hate echoed in my chest, and my hand returns to my wrist.

I feel a little sick again.

Ruby snatches the bag from him and hands it proudly to me. "For you!"

"Thanks, and nice to meet you, Ruby."

"You too, Parker!"

It isn't until I hand Em her order that I realize something: Even with Ruby busy teasing Finn and giving him the bird, he still must have listened to every word I said, because the order is perfect, right down to the extra sauerkraut.

Ten

CHARLIE AND I SPENT our first three years of school—two in preschool and one in kindergarten—in the same classes. But in first grade we were assigned to different teachers as well as different lunch hours.

Despite our parents explaining what this meant, I still wasn't prepared for the moment on the first day of school when Charlie was ushered through one door and I was ushered through another.

It was terrifying.

I slid into my desk and folded my hands tightly together. I blinked hard, hoping my eyes wouldn't tear up, and if they did, hoping no one would call me a crybaby. But then our teacher, Ms. O'Shaughnessy, came in and she gave us all a warm smile, and I felt myself relax just a little bit—not enough to talk to anyone during recess, but enough to get through the day.

There, I thought. *Done.*

I couldn't wait for the bus ride home, when I could catch up with Charlie again.

But when I climbed on, he was sitting with a boy I didn't recognize. "Parker, this is my new best friend, Matty Stephens!" I froze in the aisle, looking at the boy with wavy brown hair sitting in my spot, and then at all the other seats, filled with older kids I was too scared to sit with. Someone behind me jostled my backpack and I heard some girls laughing. My chest felt tight and my skin felt hot, and I didn't know what to do. But then Charlie flattened himself against the window. "Scoot over, Matty!" he said, and Matty grinned and squeezed himself against Charlie, and then I perched on the edge of the dark-green seat, hugging my backpack stiffly against my chest, trying not to topple into the aisle whenever the bus driver made a turn.

The next morning at breakfast, when I learned I had to go back to school again and that I still wouldn't be in Charlie's class, I cried so hard I couldn't get on the bus with Charlie, so Mom drove me to school.

When we pulled into the parking lot, she smoothed the bangs on my forehead, giving me a soft kiss. "Parker, I know it doesn't seem like it now, but it's good for you and Charlie to find your own paths. That's what growing up is about. You'll always have each other, but this gives you a chance to see who you are on your own."

That afternoon I wet my pants because I was too scared to ask Ms. O'Shaughnessy if I could go to the bathroom.

Over the next few weeks, things didn't get much better.

I missed being around Charlie with a loneliness so sharp it

made me get a weird fluttery feeling in my heart. Charlie was the friendly and brave parts of me—without him, I could barely talk to the other kids, words sticking in my throat like glue.

Charlie was the opposite. Even though he and Matty always made room for me on the bus, I was pretty sure Charlie didn't need me anymore. He and Matty joined Cub Scouts and started playing baseball after school, so they could be on the Reds team together when they grew up. Charlie talked about Matty all the time: how Matty insisted you could get gum out of your hair with Diet Coke, how Matty was having his next birthday party at Chuck E. Cheese's, how Matty got the highest score in the world in Super Mario Bros. When Matty came over after school, Charlie always invited me to join them, but it wasn't the same.

I didn't have a best friend anymore.

But then, one blue-skied October day, a kid from my class, Finn Casper, sat next to me on the playground.

"Do you want to hear something cool?" he asked.

I wasn't sure. Like me, Finn didn't have any friends. He frequently wore the same ratty Incredible Hulk T-shirt to school, and even though I'd never noticed it, I'd heard the other girls say he smelled and that he got his clothes from the lost-and-found box. He was loud and furious most of the time, the only kid in either first-grade class to routinely get time-outs, mostly for talking back to Ms. O'Shaughnessy, but once for shoving Eric Peterson over on the playground. While my unpopularity was silent, the type that at least allowed me to sit at the edge of the girls' table at lunch, Finn's was hard to miss.

I didn't know then about the rest of the Caspers: about how his brother, Johnny, a seventh grader, had been suspended for threatening to kill a teacher during the second week of school because she caught him smoking by the Dumpster; or Devin, his uncle, who was currently serving time for running a meth lab in a trailer in the woods behind his house. And then there was Mr. Casper, who ran Casper's Auto Body Shop, a store that never had any customers—clearly a front for something, but no one knew exactly what.

No, at that moment, I knew only that Finn was sitting right there, waiting, greasy white-blond bangs hanging in his eyes, and he wanted to talk to *me*.

"Okay," I whispered.

He pulled a duct-taped plastic box from his pocket, holding it out for my inspection. "It's called a Walkman and it plays music," he said, then continued to dig until he triumphantly held up a set of earbuds, grinning.

"Like an iPod?"

"Yep. But the music isn't on it—you have to put in old tapes." He showed me something he called a cassette, which had "David Bowie Greatest Hits" written in purple across the top, a heart dotting each of the *i*'s. "It was my mom's before she died."

I nodded, feeling sad he didn't have a mom, but he was too busy popping open the Walkman on the non-duct-taped side and placing the cassette inside to notice.

"You ready?" he asked, handing me an earbud.

I nodded. He started to press a chunky button, but stopped. "You have to close your eyes."

I closed them, hoping it wasn't all some mean joke.

But then I heard music start from far away and begin to march closer, getting louder by the second. A man began to sing, his voice deep and twisty like a wizard's, talking to someone named Major Tom, telling him to take pills and to put on his helmet.

In the background, another voice started counting down from ten to one, and my body leaned forward, wondering what would happen when he got to zero.

Then the guy said "Liftoff" and everything changed: the music twanging down to my toes before swelling back up, blasting through my chest and heart, up along my spine and through my ears, until it broke through the sky, flying.

It was the weirdest thing I'd ever heard, and I loved it.

I listened carefully to the words as Major Tom stepped outside the door into space. I wondered if that's where Grandma McCullough's helium people lived. I tried to imagine what being alone in all that dark sky would feel like. If it were me, maybe I'd try to steal a star, something prickly and hard and bright, something to keep close so I wouldn't be lonely, something that was mine.

My attention snapped back to the song when Major Tom said to tell his wife he loved her very much, which made me sad because I thought of Finn's dead mom and how much I loved my mom.

And then something went wrong, and the singer kept calling for Major Tom, but he said there was nothing he could do, and the music spiraled into mismatched blips and bleeps before it faded into silence.

I waited for Major Tom to come back.

Instead, I heard the click of the Walkman.

I kept my eyes closed for a second longer, and when I finally opened them, Finn was looking straight at me, and I could see the gap between his two front teeth, could see his eyes—the gray before a summer storm, occasional lightning at the edges, heavy with rain.

"My brother, Johnny, told me it's a true story," he said.

"Really?"

"Yeah. They still don't know what happened to Major Tom."

I thought about it for a second—about how his wife probably still missed him every day, how scared he must be lost in space. "That's really sad."

"Don't worry. I'm gonna find him someday," Finn assured me.

"You are?"

"Yeah. I'm learning to fly, and when I grow up, I'm going to fly into space to rescue him."

"You can fly?"

"I'm *working* on it," he clarified.

I thought about the helium people. The idea of flying made my stomach hurt. "That doesn't seem safe."

"It is. Trust me."

I looked doubtfully at the bruises on his arm, wondered if he got those from trying to fly. I felt a knot of worry start in my chest.

"This is all top secret," Finn said, his voice urgent. "You have to promise not to tell anyone about any of it."

"Can I tell my brother, Charlie?"

"Nope. Sorry. You can't tell anyone. You have to swear."

Even though I was still worried—about Finn's bruises, about

him breaking bones, about him falling from the sky—right then I felt a flush of warmth in my chest. This was what Mom was talking about: I finally had something that was mine, a secret, prickly and hard and bright like a star.

"Okay. I swear, cross my heart."

From that day on, first grade got a little easier.

I had a friend, someone who was just mine.

Finn frequently forgot his lunch money and never brought lunch, so I always split my PB&J sandwich with him, divvying up my carrot sticks and grapes. We made up knock-knock jokes, testing them out on each other. We ignored the girls who called him smelly.

On some days, Finn was extra quiet, moving his body stiffly, like he was a robot, and I knew then that he'd been practicing his flying. During those lunches, I gave him all my cookies. And I made sure we stayed extra still at recess, listening to the Major Tom song and then the other songs on the tape.

I especially liked the one about being heroes, and even though I never told him, I imagined him being king and me being queen, just like the song said.

All that time, I kept my promise, never telling anyone about his secret identity.

Not the day when I met his brother, Johnny, and Finn got suspended.

Not the day he stopped being my friend.

Not when he transferred out of our school.

Not a few months later when my dad gently informed me that the Major Tom song wasn't real.

Not in second grade when Em moved to town and became my best friend and we told each other all our secrets.

Not when I got older and realized Finn didn't forget his lunch money—he just didn't have any.

Not when Charlie got cancer.

Not when Charlie got better.

Not even years later, when I was learning to drive and heard that song "Space Oddity" for the first time again and remembered Finn, whose eyes were thunderstorms, who believed he could learn to fly.

Eleven

"DR. MCCULLOUGH! LISTEN TO THIS!"

I look up from the Harvard course catalog I was browsing.

Dad turns up the volume.

The music is not my favorite. It's edgy and off-key, reminding me of when my heart feels like it's going to jump out of my chest.

"Laurie Anderson. 'O Superman.' I didn't have this one yet," he says.

Dad is a music fanatic. A lot of the music he likes makes me nervous—it's experimental, loud and disorganized, wild on its edges. But I love watching him listen, how his whole self seems alert, intrigued, how you can literally see all the stress from his workday melt away.

I put down my Harvard course catalog, making sure to memorize the page number before I do. I'm not a fan of folding down page corners. "Where'd you get it?"

"I picked it up at Shake It Records on my lunch break."

"In Northside?"

"In Northside," he says proudly.

I smile, surprised, trying and failing to imagine my dad wandering the tattoo parlors and art galleries of that neighborhood. "How do you know about Shake It Records?"

"Your old dad had a life before you and your brother, you know." He settles back in the seat, pleased with himself.

"Time to eat," Mom calls from the kitchen. "And turn it down, Phil."

"It's stunning. That's the sound of someone doing what they love." Dad sighs wistfully before turning down the music.

I get up and follow him into the kitchen, my mind still caught up on whether or not I should take an extra class at Harvard first semester.

Yesterday, after Em dropped me off, I immediately went upstairs and fell asleep on top of my sheets, the air around me still, my room stuffy. When Mom woke me up for dinner a few hours later, at first I couldn't remember what day it was, or even where I was, but then, with a sinking feeling, the morning came back—the HealthWheat and Laurel and Dr. Gambier—and claiming continuing nausea, I went right back to sleep as soon as she shut my door.

Fifteen hours later, I woke up.

The heat had broken overnight, and the morning was the perfect amount of warm: no humidity, puffy white clouds, a light breeze making my curtains drift lazily back and forth from the windowsill.

My stomach didn't hurt.

I'm going to Harvard. I'm going to be a doctor.

Just thinking the words steadied me, and I slid out of bed and stood and stretched, ready to tackle my day. I reassured myself that getting sick the day before was just a hiccup—a product of first-day nerves and a gross old box of HealthWheat. On Tuesday I'd be ready to jump back into my internship.

The first thing I did was write Ruby.

Dear Ruby,

It was nice to meet you yesterday. Thanks for all the nice stuff you said about me. I'd be happy to meet up sometime.

Sincerely,
Parker McCullough

And then I spent the morning digging through my Harvard orientation packet and making lists of what I'd need to get for my dorm room. The afternoon was for starting Toni Morrison's *Song of Solomon*, the novel every freshman was reading as part of their First Year Experience, as well as reviewing the course catalog, debating how many classes I could squeeze in beyond the normal course load.

Five feels doable, but maybe I could do six, I think, entering the kitchen right as Dad, clearly still giddy from his new album, sneaks up on Mom and surprises her with a kiss.

She shrieks.

Charlie, already at the table, startles.

We all realize it at the same time: We caught Mom staring at Charlie from behind again.

My mom has always been a daydreamer, content to sit quietly amid their friends while Dad talks about the Reds or music or work. As a kid, I remember finding her more than once in front of the Christmas tree, her eyes lost in a content reverie.

But since Charlie's last bout of cancer, her daydreaming has turned to uneasy vigilance: carefully watching my brother from where he can't see her, every muscle in her trembling with the effort of staying still, like she wants to go hug him but she's worried if she moves she's going to lose him.

One time when Charlie caught her, he pretended to pick his nose, breaking her trance and earning him a playful swat on the arm. Tonight, though, he just looks back down at his plate.

Mom shakes her head and returns Dad's kiss.

I sit down next to Charlie, wondering if I should say anything about Erin, but I'm distracted by what we're having: meat loaf, Charlie's and my most hated food. When we were kids, every time Mom made meat loaf, he and I would chant, "Meat loaf, beet loaf, I hate meat loaf," our favorite line from the movie *A Christmas Story*. Even though we haven't done it for ages, I sneak a glance his way, wondering if he remembers it, but he's smashing a piece of American cheese on the mashed potatoes Mom's just dumped onto his plate.

She joins us, placing her napkin on her lap with a flourish. "So, Charlie, you want to tell them, or should I?"

Even though she doesn't seem upset, my chest reflexively tightens.

"What's going on?" Dad asks, his voice clipped.

Charlie won't meet anyone's eyes as he mumbles, "Dr. Travis called today."

"On Saturday?" I ask, my heart thumping.

"Don't worry—it's good news," Mom reassures us.

Charlie shrugs. "She just wanted to let me know my latest test came back good."

"Better than good," Mom chimes in. "His white blood cell count is back to a nearly normal level. Dr. Travis said this is one of the quickest recoveries she's ever seen."

Dad slams the table delightedly, making me jump, and leans over to pull Charlie into an enormous hug.

Charlie's limbs are slack, his face unreadable.

"So, does this mean you're cancer-free?" I ask.

"You saw how 'cancer-free' turned out last time. Seven years later and, surprise, it's back!"

"Now, Charlie," Mom starts. "You know there are all those studies connecting positive thinking and recovery."

"It could still come back. It came back once. It can come back again. No positive thinking's going to help with that," Charlie snaps.

Mom flinches, and Charlie immediately mumbles, "Sorry."

"It's okay. I know it's a lot to process. I'm really glad you're starting support group next week."

Charlie gives an unconvincing nod.

"Well, I think it's good news," Dad says, holding up his beer in a toast. "To one of the fastest recoveries Dr. Travis has ever seen."

"Hear, hear," Mom says, raising her iced tea.

Charlie and I join, raising our glasses of water, but I can tell by his expression, he's still in a mood.

"Have you called Coach Franklin to share the news yet?" Dad asks.

Charlie's face twists in annoyance, but Mom jumps in before he can say anything. "Well, Charlie just found out a few hours ago. But I thought I could give him a call on Tuesday, if that's okay with you, Charlie?"

"I guess," Charlie says.

"With a little bit of practice, I bet you could get back into fine pitching form for next season in no time at all," Dad says, his eyes lighting up. "You'll be ready for those college scouts this year!"

"Will that work for you, Parker? Not going to sabotage it this time?" Charlie asks under his breath.

I frown.

"Everything okay over there?" Mom asks.

"It's better than okay. It's fantastic," Charlie says, and I roll my eyes.

"Be nice," Mom admonishes him, but her tone is gentle.

For the rest of the meal, Dad's happily chatty, rambling on about the Reds' new pitcher and a records system they're testing at work.

Mom's talking about her summer sessions, but I see the exact moment when she registers all the food left on Charlie's plate, the way she bites her lip, choosing not to say anything.

As I poke at my meat loaf, I try not to obsess over Charlie's dig about last summer. But I'm feeling that weird mix of guilt and defensiveness and self-righteousness that always comes up when Charlie brings up last summer, so instead, I turn my attention back to my parents. Mom's done talking about her students, but Dad seems to be at the start of a long work story.

"So I told Stan, no, you're not going to win it if you approach it that way. And you know what he does?"

"Approaches it that way?" Mom asks.

"Exactly. And royally pisses off the client. Jeff's talking about giving him a promotion? I mean, come on! Guy can't find his own head in his ass."

Mom raises her eyebrow at him, but I can tell Dad's enjoying the rant.

"Well, it's true. He's going to lose this account, and we're supposed to toast him while he's doing it."

Charlie clears his throat and pushes his food around his plate. "Maybe he just wants to try it his own way for once. Maybe he's tired of everyone telling him what to do."

"Well, that's good and fine, except when his own way is the wrong way," Dad says. "Just last week, he presented a new campaign to Goldstar, against my advice, mind you, and it was so off base, we nearly lost the account completely."

"But sometimes the only way you can learn is by making your own mistakes, right? Didn't you tell me that?" Charlie makes eye contact with Dad.

Dad looks both confused and irritable, which usually means he's about ten seconds from exploding, so I jump in. "I'm thinking I might take an extra class at Harvard this fall," I say.

Mom turns to me. "That seems like a lot while you're getting settled, though, isn't it?"

"If anyone can handle it, I'm sure Dr. McCullough can," Dad adds.

But Charlie's not done with Dad.

"I'm surprised Stan hasn't quit with everyone up in his business," he says. "Life's too short for all that crap. And I'd know, wouldn't I?" He lets out a dry laugh.

Dad flinches, like he's been slapped.

I stare at Charlie. He literally got the best news he's had in at least a year today, and he's acting like a grade-A a-hole. "Is this about you and Erin?" I ask.

Charlie shoots me a sharp look. "That's none of your business."

"What's going on with Erin?" Dad asks.

"They broke up," I say.

"Jesus, Parker," Charlie says, slamming his fork down. "Is there anything in my life you don't report back to Mom and Dad?"

My face goes red and I look away.

"Charlie," Mom says, quick to intervene, her face concerned. "I'm so sorry to hear about Erin. Are you okay?"

"I'm fine. In fact, I'm better than fine," he says, his voice loud. He pushes his chair out, standing suddenly, and scratches furiously at the short hair on his head. "This effing itches, though. It's like I have bugs crawling over me every single second."

And on that note, he leaves. A few seconds later, his door slams upstairs.

I shoot a glance at my dad, and he looks so stricken, I have to turn away.

"Poor Charlie," Mom says, glancing at the hall, waiting for him to come back.

"But he just got good news. Incredible news!" Dad says in disbelief.

"It's a lot to deal with, Phil," Mom says to Dad. "Plus, if he and Erin . . ." Her voice trails off.

We sit quietly then.

I wish I could make it better for all of us.

I sigh, shaking my head, standing up. "I better get going."

"Tell Em and Matty bon voyage from us," Mom says, and I nod, not letting myself look back at them sitting alone at the table because I'm pretty sure I'd cancel my plans if I did.

Twelve

"SO YOU SAW MAY last night? I thought you had dinner with your mom?" I ask Em, following her on the barely there trail in the woods. The weeds we're brushing up against are practically up to my knees, and I scratch the two new bug bites on my arm.

Em shrugs. "I met May after. We had coffee, then wandered around Joseph-Beth for a little bit. And we might have made out," she adds.

I stop in my tracks. "Em!"

She sighs. "I knew you'd be upset. It's okay. I'm totally over her, I promise. Besides, you worry too much. I'm a grown-up. I know what I'm doing. This was the good-bye we should have had last November, you know?" she says. "Plus, I'm leaving tomorrow. I don't have time for her—I'm ready to fall head over heels in love with a French girl. No worrying, Park."

"Okay?" I say, her tone reminding me of the time she promised to quit smoking cigarettes and how I'm pretty sure she still sneaks one before school most mornings. But I can tell by the set of her shoulders the conversation is over and any attempt to the contrary will be futile.

"By the way, we're almost there. I promise." She turns around, walking backward, one hand crossing her heart, then faces forward, hopping stones over the rushing creek with ease.

"Are you sure you know where *there* is?"

"We're not lost!"

I approach the creek, tentatively placing one Converse on a stone and then stepping cautiously to the next. When I near the other side, I speed up, only to hit one super-wobbly rock. I try to catch my balance, but my foot slides into the creek, water filling my shoe.

"Argh!" I yell out in frustration, scrambling to the other side.

The bottom fourth of my leg is now wet. I remember that news story of the girl who got the flesh-eating virus from falling in a creek while zip-lining, and smack another mosquito—this one on my neck.

I'm just about ready to give up and go home when Em and I enter a clearing, the Little Miami River glowing under the setting sun. I see other people from our class gathered around a big bonfire, orange fire sparking, others lifting a keg from the back of a pickup truck. There's even a group wading in the river shallows. I hear a shriek as someone gets dunked, watch as she emerges, laughing.

"We're here!" Em calls out, grinning as Matty sees her. He

breaks away from the crowd by the keg and runs over, then lifts her off the ground in a big bear hug.

"EUROPE!" he bellows.

Em hugs him back, her curls smashing against his face before she bounces down. "You finally packed?"

He shrugs, and Em smacks him on the arm. "Matty, we're leaving in less than twenty-four hours. You're not going to be ready!"

"Um, Emerson, I'm a high school graduate now—"

"Just barely," she retorts.

"I got the diploma." He runs his hands through his hair, then rests them on his hips, looking nobly off in the distance. "Besides, can't you tell I'm an adult—full of knowledge and wisdom now? Of course I'll be ready."

She lightly punches his gut. "Full of beer is more like it."

"Harsh, cuz," he says, then lets out a huge belch and finally notices me. His grin gets bigger. "Parker! Our fearless valedictorian!"

"Thanks," I say, blushing. "Is Charlie here?"

"I saw him a few minutes ago," he says, looking over his shoulder and scanning the crowd.

"So, what happened with Erin?" I ask, but Matty's face has gone taut, his eyes on the river. "Crap, I told him that was a bad idea."

"What?" Em asks, but I'm following Matty's gaze.

There's a group of people gathering at the river's edge, and they're all looking at the opposite bank, the side with the steep cliff, trees at the top.

I glance at Matty for clarification, but right then, like Tarzan swinging through the jungle, a person soars out across the river, fifteen feet or more above the water, hands clenching a vine, a shape shadow-lit against the last of the sunset.

The crowd below starts cheering, and all it takes is one quick glance at Matty's blanched face to confirm my fear.

Em grabs my hand as I watch Charlie swing back to the tree and then out again, like he's flying, and then he whoops, no words, just a scream of pure joy and raw fury, a heart on the outside for everyone to see, right before the vine snaps and he drops like a rock, plummeting straight down into the dark water.

"Shit!" Matty says.

"Where'd he go?" someone behind me asks.

What if he hit his head what if he broke his neck what if he drowns?

Someone screams, and I realize it's me as I'm running toward the river, that I'm the one saying "CharlieCharlieCharlie" as I push through the people on the bank and splash into the cold water.

Em yells at me to be careful, and then Matty's by my side, his face looking as terrified as my insides feel, and we try to get to the spot where Charlie landed, but you can't run in water, can only push, stumble.

We're halfway there—the water up to my waist—when my brother surfaces, shirtless and skinny, alive and grinning, spitting water, pumping his fist, and yelling—no, roaring—with glee.

I stop, the relief washing over me so close to the fear I just felt, I can barely tell them apart.

Matty curses under his breath as Em arrives behind us, out of breath.

The crowd behind us begins chanting, "McCull-ough! McCull-ough!"

Charlie takes a few breaststrokes through the water until he can stand, at which point, my just-barely-cleared-of-cancer-for-the-second-time brother thrusts his arms up, like he's some avenging hero, like he's back from the dead.

I'm going to kill him.

"Little sister!" he yells at me, taking big clumsy steps forward, almost losing his balance more than once, words slurred.

He pulls me into a wet, sloppy hug, but my arms are flat against my sides, and despite all the river water around us, I can smell the liquor on his breath.

Face flushed, he turns proudly toward Matty. "Dude, did you see that?"

In reply, Matty steps forward and shoves Charlie right in the chest—not hard enough to knock him over, but enough to make my brother stumble a few steps back in the water.

"What the hell, Matty?" Charlie yelps.

"What the fuck were you thinking, Charlie?"

"Matty, he's pretty far gone," Em says.

"Which makes what he did just then even more dangerous!" he snaps at Em, turning back to my brother. "I have watched you do increasingly dangerous shit for the past year. I'm not doing it anymore. I'm done." Matty raises his hands and backs off, shaking his head.

Charlie sneers. "You were done a long time ago."

"What the fuck does that mean?"

"It means you don't seem so bummed to be going to Europe without me. I think you're relieved you don't have to be reminded of your own mortality by being around me."

"What the fuck are you even talking about?" Matty asks.

"Guys, guys," Em says, holding up her arms and moving between them.

I turn toward Matty, my hand on his elbow. "What are you talking about? What stuff did Charlie do last year?"

Charlie sways in the current, nearly falling over, and Matty winces. Em slings Charlie's arm around her shoulders, boosting him up.

Matty looks down at me. "I'm sorry, Parker. Now's not the time. I shouldn't have said anything."

Charlie's face twists in a snarl. "I'm not sick anymore. I don't need any fucking special treatment. Go ahead. Tell her. Parker loves ratting me out. You'll be in good company."

"Matty, please," I say.

Matty looks exhausted. He and Em are usually the ones who diffuse our fights. He's not used to picking sides. "Well, for starters, cheating on Erin. Smoking anything he can get his hands on. Last week, he was tripping on mushrooms when we were hiking at night at the gorge."

"*Mushrooms?* What were you thinking?" I ask.

Charlie lets out an aggrieved sigh, ignoring me. "God, Matty. You're making me sound like an addict. It's a little weed. And I tried mushrooms. Once."

My hand covers my mouth and I look at my brother, at the way his ribs are still showing because he's so skinny, how there's hardly any hair on his head to even be wet, the red raised scar from the chemotherapy port.

"You shouldn't be doing any of that stuff!" Matty hollers.

"He's right, Charlie," I add, trying to hide the tremor in my voice.

Charlie scowls, pushing Em off. "I can take care of myself. I don't need you guys." He makes a crooked path toward the riverbank.

He stops before he reaches dry land, joining a group of guys drinking in the shallows, high-fiving one of them and accepting a plastic cup of beer. He looks back at the three of us, then takes a long drink, finishing with a smirk, a deliberate taunt.

"Jesus," Matty says, and even though he's not religious, right then it's not a curse; it's a plea.

He doesn't deserve this from Charlie. None of us do.

My feet start moving, like I'm on autopilot.

"Parker, wait," Em says from behind me, but I wade toward my brother, unable to stop.

"I can't believe you," I say as I get closer.

He pretends not to hear me.

When I reach him, I push against his chest harder than Matty did. "I can't believe you."

"Whoa," he says as he spills his beer.

"Did you hear me? I can't believe you." I push again.

Words are building in me like a big wave, the one you watch for—with each second gaining momentum, power, the potential to destroy.

"Oh boy, here we go. Are you ready to go running back to Mom and Dad to tell them how horrible I am? That's your thing, right? Telling on me? Go for it. Be my guest."

I shake my head. "Do you know how hard it is to watch you be sick, Charlie? And this is how you take care of yourself?"

"Maybe instead of worrying about my life, you should get one of your own? How about that? Maybe you should try developing a spine." He laughs, and it's rusty and sharp, the type that draws blood.

I push forward anyway, pointing my finger at his chest.

"Do you know what Mom and Dad have given up for you? Do you know they're tens of thousands of dollars in debt and had to take out a second mortgage because of your hospital bills, that neither of them write anymore because they're too busy taking on extra hours at work?"

Charlie stares at me, his face impenetrable.

My voice wavers, and I realize I'm crying. "Do you know what Dad did when your cancer came back? Do you? He cried. The sound woke me up, and I came downstairs to find him sobbing in Mom's arms."

Charlie flinches, but I still don't stop.

"Do you know how hard it is to let ourselves love you, when we're terrified we're going to lose you any moment? You can't know! You can't! You wouldn't be doing stuff like that"—I point at the river—"if you did."

Charlie is stone-faced now, practically sober. "Go on. Say it, Parker."

"Say what?"

"It would have been easier if I had just died the first time, right? If you all didn't have to deal with this? Didn't have to pay my bills and change your plans and actually love me?"

"That's not at all what I mean."

"Sure, okay."

I look away, folding my arms against my chest.

Charlie leans close, gets right in front of my face, and his face is so hard, so gaunt, he doesn't even look human. His voice is low, casual. "It's okay to just admit it, you know. Sometimes I wish you were dead too."

As soon as he says it, he looks shocked at the words that came out of his mouth.

I can feel them hurtling forward, crashing into the soft spots of me, and I want to curl over, to crawl away on all fours.

"Go away," I whisper.

"Parker," he starts. "Come on, you know I didn't mean—"

But I shake my head, cutting him off, hugging myself tighter, my voice louder. "I don't want to look at you. Go away."

For a second I think he's going to argue with me, that he's going to try to make it better, but instead he sighs, muttering, "Whatever," and walks away, toward the group at the keg.

"What just happened?" Em asks, joining me. Matty's not far behind.

I shake my head. "I can't." My breath hitches, and I hold myself tighter.

I hear Charlie call out, "Anyone have any bourbon?"

Em wraps her arm around my shoulders, pulling me close.

"He's super drunk, Park. Whatever he said, he didn't mean it."

"He's being a dick, Em," Matty mutters, but she shushes him.

"That's not helping right now."

The three of us watch as someone lifts Charlie into a keg stand, and even from here I can see the outline of his ribs.

"I have to go. I can't be around this," I say, turning to leave.

"I'll go with you," Em offers.

"No. It's your night. You should stay. I'll be fine, okay?" I can't meet her eyes. This night was supposed to be our last really good night, and thanks to Charlie, it's ruined. "Matty, have a good trip, okay?"

He hugs me, and I can feel my sadness mirrored in him, even though he isn't my twin.

"I'll get him home tonight, okay?" he whispers.

And then Em pulls me into a hug, and it's hard, the way she hugs, fierce and furious strength against the smell of her strawberry shampoo, and for a second I let my shoulders fall.

"I'm going to miss you so much," I say against her hair.

"Will you promise to let me know if you need me? Like, seriously promise. Anytime, anywhere, okay?"

"I promise."

"Cross your heart?"

"Cross my heart," I say.

"I'll call you before I go tomorrow, okay?" she asks.

I nod and then I leave, finding my way to the path into the woods, back toward home, leaving everyone else behind.

Thirteen

THIS TIME, I SKIP over the creek with ease, which is ironic because both of my feet are already wet from trying to rescue my not-needing-to-be-rescued brother.

The moon is silvery from behind the trees, reminding me of nine-year-old Charlie staring at his stomach in the same light, the red spots all over his belly, and Charlie now, how he came up from the river like something from one of his zombie shows.

I don't know why tonight surprised me. When Charlie went through remission the first time, not only did he come back from the hospital skinny and bruised and bald, but he came back mean. He got irritated with our parents, didn't want to see Matty or Em, pushed away the hand-drawn cards from the kids in our class. Each time he found out he had to go back to the hospital for another stay, he cried hot furious tears and refused to talk to any of us.

He especially didn't want to hang out with me.

I brought him stickers and library books. Em and I choreographed an elaborate celebratory dance routine. I told him about all the stuff happening at school, making sure it didn't sound like too much fun without him. I explained how I was going to be a doctor when I grew up. I even let him watch whatever he wanted on TV.

Charlie responded by sulking. He picked fights. He told me he wished he didn't know me.

Mom told me to give it time, that it was probably hard for Charlie to see me healthy when he'd been so sick, that he still loved me no matter what. Dad told me that Charlie was lucky to have a sister who was going to cure cancer, that he'd realize that when he felt better again.

But I knew what had happened. Using his twin superpowers, Charlie had sussed out my secrets: that his bald head scared me, that I didn't like the way his medicine made him smell like chemicals, that I woke up every morning and felt a tiny kernel of ugly relief that my cells were okay.

So I tried harder.

I used all my allowance to buy Charlie a set of cool colored pencils and a big sketch pad. I made Mustard sleep in his room, not mine. I let Charlie pick the movie every Friday night. I asked Em and Matty to come over so we could replicate our game-night marathons but *with* Charlie this time.

After a few months, his hair began to grow back, a lighter brown like chocolate milk.

After a few more, he and Dad resumed throwing the baseball around in the backyard.

His weekly doctor checkups got changed to monthly ones, then every two months.

He caught up on all his missing schoolwork with his tutor, starting fifth grade with Em and Matty and me that fall.

He stopped scowling.

I stopped dreaming about the helium people.

Even now, looking back, I can't say if things over the next years got easier, or if we just got used to it all: the fact of Charlie being sick, of Charlie having been sick.

By the time we reached sixth grade, Charlie had finished all his maintenance treatments. Our parents took us to a Reds game to celebrate the fact that his body was finally, finally cancer-free.

But here's the thing: I don't think *we* were.

I don't mean any of us got cancer. No, it's more like this: Cancer moved through our family like a river wearing away its banks. You didn't notice it in the moment, but two years later, the essential shape of us was forever changed: rock worn away, movement altered, no going back to who we used to be.

I had become even more careful, a constant knot of worry in my chest.

Charlie, on the other hand, had become fearless.

He rode his bike with no hands, waving them carelessly in the air.

He skateboarded down the hill standing on one leg.

He tackled his opponents on the football field so savagely, he was routinely benched.

And then there was the day in sixth grade when he fell in the creek.

Thanks to a record foot and a half of snow overnight, we had a rare day off school. Charlie, Matty, Em, and I immediately bundled up and ventured outside, heading to the park, where we could sled down the big hill.

After an hour, our cheeks wind-burned, ice crystals frozen on all our eyelashes, I wanted to go home. But Charlie insisted we trek to the waterfall at the end of the creek, so Em and I trudged reluctantly behind him and Matty, already imagining the hot chocolate we'd have when we got home.

When we found the boys, they were investigating a freshly fallen tree. It spanned the width of the creek, a good six feet above the water below, a makeshift bridge.

"I dare you to cross it," Charlie said to Matty.

"No way," Matty said, and I felt relieved, because it wasn't safe. It was way too high and icy.

But then Charlie shrugged and stepped forward instead, carefully placing one foot in front of another on the log bridge, snow crunching under his bulky snow boots, his gloved hands balanced out like he was a tightrope walker, a confident grin on his face.

"Charlie, come back!" I yelled.

"Relax, Parker," he called.

"Charlie, maybe she's right," Matty said.

"I'm fine, halfway there!"

Em took my hand. "He'll be fine," she said.

I started to believe her. So much that I let myself turn away for just a few seconds. I was leaning down to grab a tissue from my pocket when I heard Matty yell and Em gasp and looked up to see Charlie's arms pedaling in the air, his eyes startled like a deer's, and then his body toppling backward, disappearing from my view.

The moment after Charlie fell, everything around me froze except for the snowflakes, still slow and lazy. An electric-blue current of fear started crackling around the edges of my vision.

I scrambled to the creek's edge, Matty and Em behind me, convinced Charlie had split his head open or broken his leg or worse, only to find him lying like a snow angel in the creek, one foot and his hat in the water, ice creaking underneath, a smile as big as the moon.

He started laughing.

In that moment, I wanted to push him off the bridge myself.

I watched Em and Matty ease themselves down the bank to pull Charlie up, and as soon as Matty had secured my brother's mittened hand, I turned and marched home, ignoring Em's calls to come back.

Watching him tonight at the river—fearless, reckless—reminds me of watching him that day.

Except worse.

Just then something behind me crashes through the bushes, and my heart jumps so far up in my throat, I nearly lose my balance.

When I look behind me, I don't see anything, but just in case, I pull out my key chain and open the scissors on my Swiss Army knife, the one my dad gave me for Christmas last year, holding the tiny blades extended at my side and feeling marginally more prepared to defend myself against whatever huge ravenous bear or murderous yeti is stalking me.

I walk for a few more minutes, just starting to feel okay again, but then a stick cracks over my right shoulder, and without thinking about poison ivy, I immediately run through the brush on my left, dodging branches and roots. It's a miracle I don't trip.

I run and run until I reach the road.

I bend over to catch my breath. It's longer this way, but at least I'll be on the road, where there are occasional cars and streetlights, and hopefully, no monsters.

I start the long walk home.

Fourteen

BY THE TIME I reach the covered pedestrian bridge that crosses Fosters Road, I've missed my curfew by almost an hour, a first for me. I must have run farther south than I thought.

I don't mind, though. I love the bridge. The way the arches curve and the spire reaches toward the sky . . .

I squint, wondering if I'm dreaming it or if there really are spray-painted words across the arch. THOMAS: CALL YOUR WIFE PLEAS.

It's just like the tin-can message, the one about the stars.

"Spider-Man," I say under my breath.

And then I hear it, a hiss coming from above me, over my right shoulder, a tense "Shhh."

I grip my tiny scissors tighter and look up.

A few feet into the bridge rafters—a boy: legs hooked around a beam, knuckle-clenching a spray paint can with one hand, his face hidden in the shadow of his sweatshirt hood and the eaves of the bridge.

He raises a finger sternly toward the direction of his lips, then points ominously toward my feet.

There, sniffing around and looking like it is in no hurry at all, is a big-ass skunk.

I suck in my breath and take a step back. The skunk jerks its head toward me, black beady eyes watching, tail twitching.

When I was in eighth grade, a skunk died under our front porch and it took three weeks for the smell to fade—you'd smell it when you opened drawers, turned on the AC, opened your backpack at school. Even our food tasted like skunk.

This is so not good.

"Don't move," Spider-Man whispers.

I look up, but he's pressed himself farther into the dark, making it even harder to see his face.

I slide my pocketknife back in my bag. Maybe if I back up slowly.

As soon as I move, the skunk hisses, a noise full of irrational hurt feelings and potential mouth-frothing rabies, and I jerk to the side, banging my knee on the edge of the bridge in the process and stifling a yelp.

"I told you not to move!" the boy says in a loud whisper.

Jerk.

"I hit my leg," I say as I ease back carefully against the bridge. My whole shin is throbbing, and when I look down, blood is welling up around the tender spot where I slammed it on the bridge.

I wonder how long it takes for tetanus to set in.

The skunk continues to nose along the base of the bridge path, but the boy and I are still, the only other noise an overly optimistic summer tree frog singing away.

Either ten minutes or two hours or eight hundred forty thousand years pass.

And then I feel it building in my left elbow, a right rib, both pinky toes: My body inexplicably wants to jangle and shake itself in a frenzy.

The longer I stand there, the more I need to move.

I press my nails into my palm.

I force myself to count backward from seventeen, then figure out multiples of twelve until I get to 372 and it gets too boring.

I weigh the merits of being able to disappear or run away at the speed of light.

I am just starting to wonder if my parents have sent out the police yet, if Charlie made it home already, when I hear a soft humming from above me, something familiar.

My mind tries to place it.

"Um, what are you humming?" I ask, my voice quiet.

The humming stops. "What?"

"You were humming something. It sounds like that new Taylor Swift song."

"No," he mutters.

"No, it isn't Taylor Swift, or no, you're not humming?"

"Crap," the boy says in a loud whisper. "Just let it go."

I frown. "Bully," I mutter under my breath.

The skunk, sensing the boy's sulkiness, settles itself down in the middle of the path, clearly not planning to go anywhere in the next five minutes, let alone five hours.

A few billion stars burn into existence and blink themselves out again.

"I'm not a bully," the boy finally says.

I feel a little bad that he heard me, but not enough to apologize.

I start to think about Charlie's words, but I can't go there.

Instead, I wonder what Taylor Swift is up to right now.

I contemplate the merits of tetanus.

Inside my head, I sing all the lyrics to the song the boy was humming.

I wonder what gymnastic maneuvering he had to utilize to get up on this bridge, if he knows how to rock climb.

I can't believe I thought he was Spider-Man.

If Spider-Man were real, he'd be way nicer.

I tell myself I'll count to one hundred and when I do the skunk will be gone.

I do, and it's not.

My mind goes back to Charlie—what it might have felt like swinging out over the river, what it might have felt like the moment the vine snapped.

My palms start to sweat.

What if he had landed in shallow water or hit his head on a rock?

What if he cut open his leg, and it gets infected?

Even though I'm standing up, there's a pressure pushing on my heart, like someone is sitting on me, like there's a family on top of me, a whole city, an entire world.

I wipe my forehead.

What if Charlie gets sick again?

What if Charlie and I are broken for good?

My legs start to go all pins and needles, and I grab the beam next to me.

The skunk stops moving, staring warily in my direction.

"Are you okay?" the boy asks.

"No," I say, bending over, my breath starting to hitch.

Charlie got sick and Charlie got better and Em and Matty are going to see Paris and in less than forty-eight hours I will be on my way back to my internship.

And then, in eleven weeks, I will leave for Harvard.

In four years, I will graduate from undergrad.

In eight years, I will graduate from med school.

In eleven years, I will finish a pediatric residency.

In fourteen years, I will finish a pediatric hematology or oncology fellowship.

In fourteen years, when I pass my board certifications, I will be a doctor.

I will be thirty-two.

I let out a strangled gasp.

The skunk stamps a foot, its tail poofing out.

"Parker, take it easy," the boy says from above, and a distant part of me wonders how he knows my name, but I push it aside, trying to breathe.

My body is sweating and pulsing, and my mind flashes to my first dissection in biology class freshman year, how the scalpel sliced through tissue-thin frog skin but not as easily as I'd thought, and how in med school you cut open people, and how the human body is so crowded inside it makes me claustrophobic—organs packed thick in muscles and tissue and fat.

"Oh my God," I say, conscious it's too loud, but I can't stop, my breath running itself in and out in sharp takes.

I hear the boy say "Hey, hey, now," note the quiet panic underneath the gruffness, but I'm thinking about how after our mom got her gallbladder removed, we'd catch her absentmindedly rubbing the incision site, like she was trying to reassure herself she was here, that not everything was gone.

I'm thinking about the poster on the wall of my dermatologist's office, the ABCDs of melanoma—asymmetry, border, color, diameter—the pictures of cells run wild.

I'm thinking about when Charlie barfed in the backseat after one of his first chemo treatments, how what came out of him was chartreuse and chemical-smelling, how I threw up next to him and our mom pulled over as quick as she could, all three of us crying then.

Sometimes I wish you were dead too.

"Just look at me. Look at me," not-Spider-Man says, but I can't.

All I can think of is cells and blood and bodies and cancer and how nothing is okay, not really, how nothing will ever be okay again, how it's never enough.

A loud moan escapes my lips, and at that second, the skunk puffs itself into a creature three sizes larger, its tail twitching.

I wonder fleetingly if it's pregnant, its belly is so low to the ground, and I see froth on its mouth and realize I am going to get sprayed and mauled by a pregnant skunk with rabies.

And then a spray paint can comes hurling down from the cosmos, thunking into my shin, and I yell "Oww!" right as not-Spider-Man yelps, falling from his perch on the bridge and onto the hard ground.

I scream.

The boy lies there, eyes closed, and I run around the skunk, fall to my knees, kneel beside him, then suck in my breath with a jolt of recognition.

Not-Spider-Man is Finn Casper.

This is who's leaving the messages?

His cheekbones look sharp enough to draw blood, everything about his face angles and hollows. Traces of the black eye remain, the skin around it mottled yellow and purple now, and there's a smear of red paint alongside his nose, like he accidentally scratched it.

I wonder if I should call 911.

But then Finn opens his eyes, and everything about him that's messy (his hair) or busted (the scabs on his knuckles) or crooked (his nose) or bruised (his left eye)—it all disappears in the dark gray looking back at me, still a storm growling heavy on the horizon, and I'm in first grade all over again.

The world tilts.

Finn slowly props himself up on an elbow, wincing, and I inadvertently scramble back.

He notices. "Did you get bit?"

"Bit?"

"The skunk?"

I scan the space behind me. No sign of the skunk.

"No. The can you dropped must have scared it off."

"I didn't drop it. I threw it."

"On purpose?"

"I was worried the skunk was going to bite you."

"Oh," I say, and then it comes back to me, the freak-out I was having right before Finn fell. "Oh," I repeat.

He studies me. "Help me up?"

"Yeah." He entwines his fingers with mine as I pull him to his feet.

He stifles a groan. "That is going to hurt tomorrow."

I look down at the discarded spray paint can, then the message written above us.

"So you're the one painting these all over town?" I'm too nervous to ask if he remembers me from first grade. "Aren't you worried about getting caught, you know, for defacing public property?"

He steps back, a dangerous flicker in his eyes before his expression hardens. "You won't report me, will you?"

"No, no." I shake my head hard. His gaze goes to my left hand, which is inadvertently circling my right wrist again. So quickly, I almost miss it, he winces.

I release my wrist. "Your secret is safe with me, Finn."

"You remember my name." He sounds surprised.

"I do. It's just, the other day at the Float, I didn't think you knew who I was. You didn't say anything."

He tightens his hands into fists. "You didn't either."

Now I'm flustered. "I'm sorry. I should have said hi."

He uncurls his hands, stretches his palms out flat, like he's steadying himself.

"You don't have to explain. I understand. After my brother . . ."

I shake my head, not wanting him to say anything more.

Crickets and tree frogs are making their night noise, and the creek is babbling below us, and my heart is knocking around in my chest. Finn bends down to grab his backpack, shoving the errant spray paint can inside. He stands, studies me. "Are you okay? Do you need me to call anyone?"

"I'm okay. The skunk didn't bite me or anything, thanks to you."

"I don't mean the skunk," he says.

My face goes hot. I can't believe he saw me like that. "Yeah, I'm totally fine. I'm really sorry for all the trouble. Seriously." I shift uncomfortably.

He looks doubtful but simply says, "Okay."

"Okay," I echo.

"Well, have a good night, then," he offers.

"Yeah, you too."

He slings his bag over a shoulder and starts to head to the bridge.

"Hey, Finn?" I call out.

He turns around.

"Thank you. For helping me." I swallow, the words hard to say. "I needed it."

He nods. "Anytime."

I watch him leave, wondering what just happened to me under that bridge.

Fifteen

I WAKE UP TO the smell of cut grass and the rumble of our neighbor's lawn mower, and squint at the clock.

8:04.

Mustard, wedged against the windowsill and the screen, stops licking his paw to study me, then stands, stretches, and pads his way over to my chest. He begins kneading it, happily drooling, a throaty purr.

I didn't sleep much last night.

When I got home, Charlie's door was half open, so I crept up, peeking in, making sure to angle myself to the side so he couldn't see me. But he was sound asleep, sprawled out on his bed, still in the shirt and shorts he was wearing at the river, snoring.

Even though he was on his side, I was worried about him throwing up, so I eased down against the wall outside, pulling my knees up against my chest and resting my head there, watching the slow rise and fall of his chest from the hallway.

I startled awake a little before five, but Charlie was still safely on his side, so I got up, massaging the crick in my neck, and made my way to my own bed, half awake, half asleep, wondering if I was dreaming the whole thing.

But the spot on my leg that I banged against the bridge is throbbing slightly, which means none of it was a dream: Charlie's behavior, Matty's revelations, Finn Casper and the skunk, whatever it is that happened to me when I was standing under that bridge.

What if I have some weird heart condition?

I remind myself I'd had to get caught up on all my vaccinations and pass a physical to be eligible for the internship program. There was nothing wrong with me then.

But there is now.

I'm all wrong.

I close my eyes, trying to still my body, but my mind doesn't quit, thoughts circling frantically like they're on a kids' race car track—no beginning, no end, just a frantic whizzing around and around.

Em's leaving today.

I have to go back to the internship on Tuesday.

Charlie's been smoking pot.

He tried mushrooms.

That second after the vine snapped, the water dark, my brother disappeared from the world.

(I don't let myself think about the words he said.)

I sit up, displacing Mustard, and lean over, resting my head in my hands, my breath coming in deep sharp gasps.

It is ridiculous, this panic. I don't even know what I'm panicked about.

But thinking that doesn't help.

Instead it makes it worse, my breath moving even faster, and I wonder if you can get heart attacks at eighteen.

I force myself to go through the yoga breathing cues Em taught me before I took the SATs, but my heart and brain are having none of it—they hate yoga as much as I do.

I'm going to die.

I stand up.

Em.

My whole body points itself to her.

I look at the clock. She hasn't left yet.

I could text her, but what would I say? "Em, I think I'm having a nervous breakdown. Text me back" doesn't feel right.

Besides, if I don't move my body soon, I feel like the panic may slip outside, swallow me whole.

I slide on a clean tee and my jean shorts and Converse from last night and slip downstairs. Luckily, Mom and Dad are reading the paper on the back deck and don't see me, so I don't have to explain to my poor parents that their daughter may be having a heart attack.

Outside, our neighbor Mr. Edwards waves at me from the lawn mower, but I can't deal with him right now, so I break into a jog for the five blocks to Em's house, even though I hate running as much as I hate yoga, and it's already too hot, and I forgot to put on deodorant. But after a few minutes, my feet start catching up with my heart—propelling me forward, outside of myself.

I round the corner to Em's and then stop, bending over and placing my hands on my knees, a knife in my gut, and try to slow down my heaving breaths, as big and deep as the time Charlie accidentally kicked a soccer ball into my stomach, knocking the air right out of me.

When I straighten, I see Em and Matty loading their backpacks into the car. He says something I can't hear, and she starts laughing, doubling over into one of her laugh-snorts—the only thing about Em that isn't obviously lovely—and Matty guffaws loudly in response.

I hear Charlie's words again: *Sometimes I wish you were dead too.*

At that second, I'm so envious of my best friend and her cousin, of how close they are, I'm pretty sure if a fairy-tale witch offered me the chance to steal all their happiness for me and Charlie, I would seize it without giving either of them a second thought.

What is wrong with me?

I back up slowly, then faster, then turn and start to run again until I'm sure they can't see me.

As my shoes slap the sidewalk, I try not to obsess about last night, what Matty said about Charlie.

About Charlie soaring across that river.

I massage the crick in my neck from watching him sleep, and the morning's sadness and anxiety start to morph into something else, something that makes me feel ugly on the inside, something that makes me run even faster.

What if Charlie hadn't come back up from the water last night?

What if he had thrown up last night and choked on it in his sleep?

I get angrier and angrier, and my shins burn.

Charlie's so close to getting everything back.

And he's messing it all up.

He's so selfish about his health, I want to shake him by the shoulders or kick him in the shins, something to get his attention, something to hurt him into taking care of himself.

He was awful to Matty and Em last night, and even though Erin and Charlie broke up, I'm sure Erin would be devastated if she found out he'd been cheating on her.

I shake my head, flex my fingers.

Not to mention Mom and Dad. If they lose him now, thanks to something reckless and preventable? They don't deserve that.

(And behind all of that, his words. *Sometimes I wish you were dead too.*)

I shake my head.

No.

When I get home, I find our parents at the kitchen table eating eggs and toast.

"Hey," I say, resting my hands on my hips, trying to catch my breath.

"You're out and about pretty early," Mom says. "Charlie's still sound asleep."

Of course he is.

"She's getting ready for those doctor hours," Dad says to Mom.

"I need to talk with you guys about something," I say.

Mom looks at me more carefully. "Everything okay?"

I shake my head. "Charlie was drinking last night."

"What?" Dad asks, putting his fork down.

"I'm sure he was just celebrating a little bit with everyone else, right?" Mom offers.

"More than that. He drank so much he could hardly stand. He was messing around at the river on this vine, and for a second we were all worried he drowned. And it's not just last night. Matty said he's been smoking pot and trying other stuff too. He's not taking care of himself."

Dad's palm slams down on the table. "For chrissakes. What's he thinking?"

Mom looks like someone's punched her in the gut, and I feel a twinge of guilt when I see her eyes glistening.

"I'm sorry, but I thought you should know," I say. "He needs help."

As the words leave my lips, I know I'm not wrong. Charlie's messed up in a way that goes deeper than the cancer in his blood. He needs help.

But the absolute certainty I felt in telling is short-lived when Dad stands up, hollering, "Charlie!" He goes to the bottom of the steps, yells louder. "Charlie!"

I hear a distant sleepy "What?"

"We need you downstairs. Now!"

"Just a minute."

Mom leans over, squeezing my shoulder gently, and I take that as my sign to leave.

When I get upstairs, Charlie's emerging from his room, rubbing his eyes. He smells sour, like beer and river, and I can tell from the expression on his face he's hungover.

"Jesus, what's up with Dad?" he asks in a half yawn.

I shrug, unable to look at him.

He immediately notices and steps forward, his face getting serious. "Parker, about last night. The stuff I said . . . you know I was just drunk, right?"

"Charlie!" Dad yells again from downstairs, and Charlie winces, looking over to me, confused.

"Why is he so mad . . . ?" He freezes, understanding dawning on his face. "You told them."

"It's for your own good," I insist.

"So you just went straight to Mom and Dad? You didn't even try to talk to me first?"

"Like you'd listen," I say, but my resolve fades further as his expression sharpens, turning dangerous.

"God, you are unbelievable. Remember this moment, little sister. Because someday you're going to mess up too, and let me tell you: I'm going to enjoy every single fucking second of it."

I try not to flinch, but his words are so horrible that I immediately have to head into my room and slam the door behind me before Charlie can see the way my hands are shaking.

The sound of Taylor Swift singing her heart out in my earphones is covering up most of the yelling currently happening downstairs.

In fact, I could almost pretend it's not happening, if it weren't for Mustard sitting next to me, perched at the edge of the bed, wary, his ears pushed back at attention.

I'm petting his soft orange head, trying to calm both of us down, when my phone buzzes.

Em.

On our way to airport but wanted to say hello. Missed you last night! How are things now?

I don't want Em to worry, so I weigh my words carefully before I reply.

C's hungover, but everything else is OK. Miss you already. oxo

Her response is immediate.

Serves him right.

Then she texts me our favorite emoji, the one of two girls with rabbit ears dancing together.

I respond with the cat with heart eyes, and then put my phone on the table and scoop my arm around my cat, humming along softly with the music.

I must fall asleep somewhere in the middle of that, because when I wake up, it's five fifteen, which means I've just slept for the past six-plus hours.

I could sleep for another six, another sixteen.

I take out my earbuds.

From the open window, I hear the sounds of Dad clanging around on the back deck, the smell of the grill wafting through the room.

I wonder what happened with Charlie and our parents but not enough to venture out of my room yet, that's for sure.

Mustard has relocated to the windowsill, watching me with interest. He meows, and I lean over and offer him a head rub, then press my palm against my sternum, breathe in deep, then stand, heading to my laptop.

When I log in, I have two new e-mails, both from "collier5."

Ruby.

I click on the first one, dated only a few hours after I sent my message to her.

> *Dear Parker,*
>
> *It was so good meeting you yesterday too! Thanks for writing me! If I didn't make it clear already, your kind of who I want to be when I "grow up" (haha). Did you apply to Harvard early acceptance? What were your SATs? (You don't have to tell me if you don't want!) Did you have good recommendation letters? When did you decide you wanted to be a doctor?*
>
> *I would write more now, but I'm on my phone at work and Finn Casper is being a total garbage monster and so I need to go.*
>
> *Thank you in advance for all your help!*
>
> *Your (hopefully) friend,*
> *Ruby*

For a second, I think about the logistics of trying to talk to her about Harvard, of pretending I'm as excited as I should be, about how things are so messed up right now, I don't know if I can be a role model, let alone a friend, to anyone.

And then I click to the next one, dated today.

Dear Parker,

Not to be all stalkery, but I wasn't sure if you got my last e-mail? If you did and are just too busy, I totally get it. I know I can be a lot sometimes! ☺ But if you didn't, maybe you're not getting this one either? Hmmm.

Also, I was rereading the note I sent you and realized I had a you're/your error in there. SORRY! If Finn hadn't been bugging the crap out of me when I wrote it, I would have caught it. So embarrassed. It's Finn's fault.

And again, sorry if I'm too much.

Sincerely yours,
Ruby Collie

My eyes hone in again on "a lot" and "too much," and something in my heart hurts.

I immediately feel awful that Ruby was waiting for a response from me, that she would think it has anything to do with her, that under all her bright light, she worries.

That part of Ruby doesn't remind me of Em.

It reminds me of me.

I start a response.

Ruby, hi!

I'm so sorry I didn't get back to you until now. My life has been kind of intense the past few days and my head isn't in the best place, so I haven't been on e-mail a ton. I'd still like to hang out sometime, though. I'll write you when things calm down, okay? And please don't worry—it's not you at all. I was really happy to meet you.

xox, Parker

I put aside my laptop and lie down. Mustard pads across the bed to my side, purring immediately and intensely.

He nestles his head against me and gives my hand small rough licks, like he's grooming me, and I let myself relax for a second.

But before he gets too settled, my e-mail chimes. He gives me a crabby nip as I pick up my laptop again.

It's a response from Ruby.

Hi, Parker.

*Thanks for your note! I'm sorry to hear
things are intense lately. I get it. Sometimes
being in my own head is a lot for me—
maybe that's what it's like for you too? I
know I don't know you that well, but if you
ever need a friend, I'm here. I look forward
to hearing from you soon.*

Your hopefully future friend Ruby

I lie back, in awe of her kindness. What would it be like to be
that open with people you didn't know?

Happy I'm paying attention to him again, Mustard gives my
hand another lick, then butts his head against my palm, reminding
me he's there, and for a brief, lovely second, I don't feel so alone.

And then I think about Charlie, about what he said to me at
the river, about how I told my parents, about the anger in his eyes
when he found out.

I scrunch my eyes shut and wait for the forgetfulness of sleep,
hoping when I wake up I won't be a mess anymore.

Sixteen

EVEN THOUGH I'M SITTING directly across from him as he drives down I-71, Charlie hasn't said more than five words to me since I passed him in the hallway on Sunday morning.

That evening, after my so-long-it-wasn't-right nap, I emerged from my room briefly for dinner. But Charlie didn't join us, and based on Dad's irritable mood and the circles under Mom's eyes, I didn't question his absence.

The next day, when we were getting ready to leave for the Schneider and Hall annual Memorial Day picnic, Charlie announced to our parents that he was going to skip it this year.

"No way," Dad said.

"Come on," Charlie said. "It's my last night without tutoring homework on my plate."

"You think you've earned my trust back after twenty-four

hours? At this point, I don't know if you want to stay home so you can try your hand at arson or do multiple lines of cocaine!"

"For God's sake," Charlie muttered.

"Phil," Mom started, but Dad held up his hand.

"I don't want to go to this picnic either, but we're all going if it's the last thing this family does!"

The picnic itself wasn't much better.

When Dad's colleagues weren't asking me about Harvard, they were talking about the humidity. And when they weren't talking about the humidity, they were talking about how great it was to hear Charlie was in remission.

"It's been a big relief for all of us," I said to Dad's boss when he asked. "I feel like we can all breathe again. Don't you agree, Charlie?" I asked, smiling, willing him to stop sitting at the edge of the picnic table, sullen, and to join me in the conversation.

He met my eyes evenly. "Actually, I don't," he said. "Not at all."

Six words.

I flinched, giving Dad's boss an embarrassed smile, while Charlie walked away, leaving me there.

We drive under Finn's message on I-71.

I shift uncomfortably, feeling a little guilty that Charlie's in so much trouble, but then I stop. This is all on Charlie, not me.

I turn to him as we pull off the highway onto the exit for the hospital and stop at the light.

"So, is this how it's going to go? You're never going to talk to me again?"

I wait, but he doesn't say anything. It's like I don't even exist.

The light turns green, and he guns forward. With the sudden movement, the textbooks stacked on the backseat slide onto the floor.

"Nice," I mutter, looking over at him, but his eyes are fixed on the road. I should let it go, but I can't help myself. "You know it was for your own good. That's why I told them, okay? It's because I care about you."

Charlie lets out a low whistle, shaking his head, like he can't believe what he's hearing, but he still doesn't say anything.

I look out the window right as we're passing the colorful mural on Calhoun. I must have missed it on Friday.

We passed that mural every time we went to Children's for his treatment the first time he was sick. It was the one thing I looked forward to: seeing the rainbow colors blur by from the backseat of the car.

Seeing it now doesn't help. I close my eyes, but I can't stop the bad feelings creeping into me again, my body bracing itself as we turn into the hospital drive. I've been so consumed by the drama with Charlie, I forgot I was actually going back to the hospital. And this time I can't blame it on HealthWheat.

Charlie jerks the car over to the curb so suddenly, my seat belt yanks me back. I open my eyes.

"Geez, Charlie! Watch it!"

He sits there, not moving, the car idling, waiting for me to get out.

"Okay, fine. Don't talk to me. I don't care. If that's what it takes to keep you alive, I'm fine with that." As I unbuckle the seat belt, I spill my purse, and lean down, trying to grab all the contents.

Charlie scoffs. "Yeah, okay, whatever lets you sleep at night."

I straighten, shoving my cell phone and sparkly lip balm back in my bag. "What do you mean?"

"What do you think I mean? You sold me out, Parker."

"You were putting yourself in danger! You'll thank me someday."

"Thank you for what? The fact that my crap-ass summer has now gotten five billion times worse? That I'm grounded from here until God knows when, or that if Mom and Dad catch the faintest amount of alcohol in my system, they'll take away my driving privileges and probably send me to rehab? Or maybe I should thank you for the fact that now, in addition to support group, I get to go see a therapist two times a week?"

"No. You should thank me for the fact that you'll be alive!" I yell.

He tightens his hands on the wheel, sucking in his breath, and when he turns to me, his eyes are so furious, I involuntarily shrink back against the seat.

"You know, the other night, the stuff I said . . ."

Sometimes I wish you were dead too.

"I figured it was probably just because I was drunk, you know? But it's times like this when I wonder if part of me really meant it."

As that sinks in, I push the car door open, but my legs aren't working. I lean over, like I'm going to be sick.

My vision is tunneling in, and I want to fold my body over and over until I'm so small, I don't exist anymore.

My heart's in my mouth.

It's happening again.

But even though my body is clumsy and confused like I

have extra limbs, I finally manage to stand, slamming the door behind me.

"Aw, come on, wait. You're blowing this all out of proportion," Charlie says. "I'm sorry, okay?"

I turn back to him, trying hard not to cry. "You really hate me that much?"

He sighs. I see it then—how bone-weary my brother looks. It's more than just circles under his eyes or that he hasn't gained back his pre-chemo weight yet. It's like something inside of him, the something that used to be bright and gleaming, the something that used to make everyone he met fall in love with him, is cracked in two, all jagged edges on the inside.

In those few seconds, his lack of a denial is all the answer I need.

"God, Charlie. What happened to us?" I ask.

His face breaks, and I see him there, the little boy who came back for me.

I want to say *I miss you.*

I want to say *Charlie, stay.*

But as if he's deciding something, he frowns, then guns the engine so hard, the tires squeal as the car peels out of the lot.

He doesn't come back.

I wipe my face on my arm and dig through my bag for a tissue, trying to calm what's happening inside me right as Laurel with the designer flats passes me.

"Hey, Laurel," I say, sniffling.

"Uh, hi?" she replies, and I realize she doesn't remember me as she breezes past, leaving a stench of perfume in her wake.

I can't do it.

I drop down on a bench outside—releasing my bag at my feet, resting my elbows against my knees, my head in my hands.

Behind me, the automatic doors slide open and closed, air-conditioning making its way weakly out between. I hear children and parents passing by and try to muster up the will to move because I can't screw this up. I already missed a day.

But I can't do it.

Charlie's words—I feel them in my lungs, how sharp they are.

My breath begins to hitch, and I push the heel of my clammy palm against my chest, pressing it hard against my ribs.

My thoughts become frantic and electric, banging around the insides of me, brittle and hard, and my heart is beating two words: *Not enough not enough not enough.*

"Are you okay, miss?" the woman in front of me asks. She's holding a little boy's hand, and he's hiding behind her leg because he's scared, because I'm scaring him.

I'm scaring a sick child.

I grab my purse and walk away from them and the hospital as quickly as I can.

My heart doesn't ease up.

I find a bus stop and crouch on the bench, leaning over and putting my head between my knees, trying to slow down my breathing.

I'm having a heart attack.

Everything in me is hot and frenzied and terrible, and I just need to get out of this place, out of my body, out of me.

But as I sit there on the bus stop bench, the sun beating down on me, I realize I don't have anyone to call.

Em's gone.

Matty's gone.

Mom and Dad are at work

And Charlie's not coming back.

I wish I had access to Mom's Uber account.

A cab. I'll call a cab.

I start digging through my bag for my wallet, but my hands shake more when I realize it's not there, that I must have left it on the floor of the car when I spilled my purse.

"Oh God, oh God," I mutter, resting my head in my sweaty hands.

I tell myself I can just wait, wait until Mom and Dad get off work, wait until someone can pick me up.

But even as I tell myself that, my breath speeds up even faster and my heart starts to move between my lips, and I choke, trying to keep it in.

I need help I need help I need help.

Ruby.

I hesitate for a second, but in her e-mail, she said being in her own head was a lot for her, too, and if I ever needed a friend, she was there. Maybe she could call me an Uber and I can pay her back later.

I grab my phone, fingers frantically searching for the number at the Float, hoping she'll pick up, but it's a guy on the other end.

"Float. How can I help you?"

"Is Ruby Collie there?"

"She's not in yet. We don't open until eleven."

Crap, I say inside my head. *Crapshitcrap*, my heart beats.

"Um, can you have her call me as soon as she can? 555-0165. This is Parker. Parker McCullough. Tell her . . ." My voice breaks. "Tell her I need help."

The voice on the other end makes a noise of recognition. "Parker? It's Finn Casper. What's going on?"

I feel my heart finally leave me then, floating up out of my mouth, away from me into the blue, light as helium, and I start crying, and even though the phone is still up against my ear and Finn is saying something, all I can hear are Charlie's words, the kind you can never take back.

Seventeen

"HEY, I HEARD SOMEONE needed a ride?"

I look up.

There's a beat-up old red pickup truck idling in front of the bus stop, and Finn's in the driver's seat, leaning over toward the passenger side, pushing the door open.

When I stand up, my legs are wobbly.

As I climb in, he takes my bag, puts it on the floor, and turns off the loud thrashy music coming from the speakers. "Sorry I'm late. I had to find someone to cover my afternoon shift."

"I'm so sorry," I whisper. "I didn't know who to call. I thought Ruby might be working."

He gives me a funny smile. "You know Ruby can't even drive yet."

I shake my head.

"It's okay. Fred owes me a shift. Hey, listen. Are you all right? You were pretty upset on the phone."

I shake my head—a brief no—but don't look at him. Instead, I focus on holding my hands together so I don't start crying again.

I wait for him to say something, but it is quiet and the quiet is terrible.

His hand lands lightly on my shoulder. "Where do you need to go?"

I can feel the tears gathering. "I don't know," I say, because I don't know anything anymore, and that is so terrifying, I'm pretty sure the fear is going to swallow up every single bit of me.

Finn looks like he's weighing options. "How about this: I'm hungry. Are you hungry?"

I sniff hard, my voice shaky. "I guess, yeah."

"Food it is."

He pulls away from the curb and into the lane of traffic, angling all the air vents toward me. But even then it's warm, the breeze from outside blowing almost hot against my face. Finn turns the radio back up, though not as loud. As he drives us through Clifton and onto I-75 South, I wipe my face with my arm, and then flustered, he leans over me to pop open the glove compartment and grabs a handful of White Castle napkins, shoving them my way.

"Thanks," I mutter, blowing my nose.

I'm still too mortified to look over at him, so instead, I lose myself in the rumbling of the muffler and the now-subdued background beat of the radio. There's sun on my face, and I can't even think too much about what is happening inside me right now, because if I do, I'm pretty sure something in me will break for good.

I wake to a nudge on my shoulder.

We're in a nearly empty gravelly parking lot, a blue neon sign saying THE ANCHOR GRILL flickering and spitting nervously overhead.

"We're here," Finn says.

I don't know what I'm doing, so I nod. Before I can make my way out of the truck, though, Finn's at the passenger side, extending a hand for me to hold as I hop down.

His palm is calloused.

For the first time since he's picked me up, I take him in. He's wearing old cargo shorts, a tattered heavy-metal T-shirt that says MEGADETH, his hair pulled off his face in a short ponytail. The black eye from the other day has morphed to a faint yellow-green.

He catches me studying him and looks away, inclining his head toward the entrance. "This way."

When we enter the Anchor Grill, we're greeted by the smell of grease and cigarette smoke. There's a counter in front of a kitchen, a lonely piece of not-so-fresh-looking cherry pie sitting under a glass dome on the corner.

Even though we're in a landlocked state, the decor is distinctly nautical—a ship's steering wheel on the wall, a sculpture of seashells behind some dusty glass.

"Um, what is this place?" I whisper.

"Covington's finest."

A grizzled heavyset guy wearing a trucker hat is sitting at the counter, talking to the waitress. She looks about eighty-five years old, her skin falling in heavy folds from her arms. There are brown penciled-in arcs where her eyebrows should be.

"Mabel," Finn says, tipping his head at her. She grunts in return.

I follow him into the next room, where the nautical theme continues. There's a life-size, crusty-looking old wooden sailor statue in yellow and blue lurking near the door, and paintings of lighthouses along the walls. The room is edged with red vinyl booths, and in the middle sits a table with a vase of dusty plastic flowers, a tarnished disco ball floating sadly overhead.

We're the only ones in this part of the restaurant.

Finn heads toward one of the booths, and I settle in across from him, avoiding the patch of split red vinyl that's duct-taped together farther in.

"So, do you come here a lot?"

Finn nods toward a faded red curtain halfway up the wall, about the size of a television screen.

"Just watch."

I squint. "What is it?"

He digs through his pocket, dumping five quarters out, and points to the corner of the table where a mini jukebox sits.

"Pick one," he says, sliding a quarter across the Formica. I start flipping through the jukebox tracks, but all the names are blurring together and I don't want to choose the wrong thing.

"I don't know what to pick," I say, and hand the quarter back to him.

He shrugs and clicks through the selections and drops the quarter in, pressing F17 and H2.

"Watch," he says, pointing at the curtain on the wall.

I hear things clicking from behind it, and then, with a rickety noise, the red curtain jerks open, revealing a glass panel with the words STRIKE UP THE BAND underneath. Behind the panel is a miniature six-piece band, the figurines dressed in tuxes. But something must have happened to one of them, because inserted in the mix is a Barbie wearing a gold minidress, her hair messily ratted up. She's strangely oversized compared to the rest of the band.

A light clicks onto the disco ball in the middle of the room. It starts a slow rotation, weird shimmers sparkling over the room, suddenly making everything kind of pretty, right as a warbly woman's voice begins haunting the room. "Craaazzzy . . . crazy for being so lonely . . ."

The dolls in the band begin to move in small robotic rhythms, playing along with the music, a hand strumming a guitar, another mechanically tapping a drum.

Only the Barbie is still.

"Whoa," I say, near speechless.

It's one of the most magnificent things I've ever seen.

I look across at Finn, who's watching me watch it, his expression unreadable, wary almost.

I can't believe I'm sitting across from him.

I can't believe I walked away from my internship and am sitting here right now.

I dig through my bag for my phone, see two missed calls from a 513 number and one message.

"Um, just a second," I say, clicking to my voice mail, then listen to the program assistant asking me if I'm still sick. I hit delete right as Mabel comes in and drops two sticky laminated menus on the table. She doesn't say anything, just holds a pad of paper and a pen, looking sourly down at me holding my phone.

"Sorry," I say, dropping my phone back in my bag and reaching for a menu, but Finn shakes his head at me.

"Two grilled cheeses with fries, two Cokes," he says instead to Mabel.

He gets a grunt in response, and she trudges out of the room.

"Sorry," I say to him, because evidently that's all I can say right now, but Finn shakes his head.

"Mabel hates everyone, cell phone or not."

"Ah, okay, cool," I say.

We sit there quietly.

I clear my throat. "So, what have you been up to lately?" I ask.

"Not much."

"Do you like working at the Float?"

He looks the other way. "It's okay."

"Cool."

The song ends and another clicks on, but this time I recognize the singer: Johnny Cash.

I fold the corner of a napkin. "Where are you going to college?"

Finn's breath pushes out in a gentle sigh.

"Did I do something wrong?" I ask, confused.

"You don't need to do that with me."

"Do what?"

"That small-talk stuff."

"I was just trying to make conversation. . . ." My voice trails off, my face hot.

Finn shifts awkwardly. "I'm sorry. I shouldn't have said anything." He looks frustrated with himself.

Mabel brings back our Cokes and two straws, and both of us are quiet, and I focus really hard on folding my napkin into an accordion, tiny pleats up and down.

Finn drops a few more quarters in the table jukebox, clicks a few selections.

So no small talk—only sitting here in silence?

And just when it's getting to the point where I don't think I can stand the silence one second longer and he's not helping the situation at all, I hear the words leave my mouth: "How'd you get the black eye?"

He lets out a sharp exhale—one that almost sounds appreciative.

I look him straight in the face, meet his gaze head-on. "You don't want small talk, so there. I'm making big talk."

"Big talk," he says, the corner of his mouth turning up. "Okay."

I try not to smile.

"I box."

"Oh," I say, and I see him register the surprise in my voice.

"Yeah, I started in second grade. I kept getting in fights in school, so boxing was suggested as a good way for me to manage all my 'anger issues,'" he says.

I nod, remembering that day on the playground in first grade when the principal pulled him away. "And the eye?"

Finn smiles fully for the first time then—big and real—and I see the sliver of space between his two front teeth I remember from when he was a kid. "Got my ass kicked in the ring last week. Moved too slow."

Silence settles in. Finn digs in his pocket for more change before flipping through the selections again.

I realize there's something about being here, with him, right now, that loosens the knot in my chest. For the first time in a while, I'm at ease.

It's like first grade all over again—this person sitting next to me on the playground when I was at my loneliest, this person sitting next to me now.

I look up. "My brother, Charlie—do you remember him?"

Finn nods carefully. "A little." He stops, recognition dawning on his face. "Wait. Charlie and Parker? Charlie Parker? Like the jazz guy?"

"You know him?"

"Just the name."

"My dad is super obsessed with all kinds of music. When he found out Mom was pregnant with twins, he came up with this mega list of possible names, all featuring his favorite musicians: Ella and Fitzgerald, Peter and Gabriel, Laurie and Anderson, Frank and Zappa, Bob and Dylan, you get the picture."

"Zappa?"

"Yeah, luckily Mom vetoed that one hard. But she really liked Charlie and Parker, so here we are."

"It's better than Finnegan," he says.

"I don't know. In grade school, this kid Felix in my class used to call me Parking Lot."

Finn snorts.

"I hated that so much."

His face goes red. "Sorry."

"You didn't call me that," I point out, but he doesn't say anything.

After a few seconds, he clears his throat. "What were you saying earlier, about Charlie?"

"We got in a huge fight this morning. And we had another one on Saturday night. It's bad, you know?"

Finn nods carefully.

"Charlie has cancer. Had it, I mean. Twice. In fourth grade and again this year. He's in remission now. And he's going to be fine. I know things aren't easy for him, so I try to give him the benefit of the doubt, but some of the stuff he said . . ."

I stop, realizing that even though he's my brother, maybe even *because* he's my brother, Charlie has the ability to hurt me more than anyone else I know.

"That must really suck," Finn says.

"It's been hard for him."

"I meant for you, too."

I give him a small smile. "Ever since I was little, I wanted to be a doctor so I could fix Charlie, you know? I was supposed to start an internship at Children's Hospital today. Friday actually. But I got sick on Friday, and when I tried to go in today, I just couldn't do it."

I look back down at my hands. I'm too embarrassed to look at his face when I'm telling him this, so I begin shredding my napkin into small bits.

"It's been happening more and more lately. It's like I psych myself out of doing what I want to do. My breathing gets all weird and I feel like I'm having a heart attack." I stop, Charlie's face flashing through my mind.

"I clearly just need to get over myself. I don't have anything to complain about. I'm healthy. I *wanted* this internship. I beat other people to get it. And I'm going to Harvard, and everything is good. It's really good. . . ." My voice trails off. I've missed the first two days. What if I can't go back? My heart speeds up, pumping blood faster and harder, like it needs to get as much life as it can to the very tips of me.

I've run out of napkin to rip, leaving only a small pile of sad confetti on the table.

"If the internship makes you feel like crap, don't do it," Finn says.

I look up at him then, feeling my stomach tighten. "It's not that easy."

"Do you need it for Harvard?"

"Well, I'm sure it helped with my application."

"But you can be a doctor without it?"

I nod.

"Screw the internship, then. If it makes you feel bad, don't do it."

My mind scrambles, panicking at the mere suggestion. "But I need the stipend—I need the money for the fall."

"There are tons of other summer jobs out there—my friend Carla's looking for an assistant at her pottery studio right now, in fact. I'm sure she'd hire you."

I try to imagine telling Mom and Dad I'm quitting the internship, the groan of disappointment from Dad, the look of concern on Mom's face.

No, no, no.

On cue, my eyelid twitches.

"I can't do that to my parents," I say, shaking my head.

"It's okay to tell them you don't want to do it."

"But I do want to do it. I want to do it because I want to be a doctor," I reply. "It's what I've always wanted to be, as long as I remember."

"Is it?"

"What else would I be?"

He looks at me. "Anything. Everything."

"Again, it's not that easy," I say. "Not at all. You don't know. I'm going back to the internship tomorrow. I'll figure something out—it'll be fine."

"All right," Finn says, holding up both hands in surrender. "Forget I said anything. It's none of my business anyway."

Right then, Mabel comes back in with our grilled cheese sandwiches and fries. She takes in the pile of ripped napkin bits in front of me and gives me a dirty look, dropping our plates on the table.

Finn immediately digs in.

I tell myself it isn't as easy as he says. He doesn't know the half of it. But that's not his fault.

I focus on my grilled cheese, take a bite, the orange-yellow cheese oozing out. I'm pretty sure I'm going to break out tomorrow, but I don't care. It tastes good.

"What's with all the messages you're leaving around town?" I finally ask.

"I just like street art, I guess. I like how it can surprise you."

"Oh," I say. "That's cool."

We're both quiet then, but weirdly enough, this time it's not awkward.

And as I watch the band of dolls move, I realize I don't want to leave.

Mabel comes in and drops a check on the table without asking us if we want more.

"Oh, crap, my wallet," I say, but Finn's hand darts out, grabbing the bill before I can.

"It's on me."

"But I wanted to treat you, for picking me up," I say.

"I got it," he says more insistently.

"At least let me pay you back later?"

His face goes red and he shakes his head, and I realize I just did something wrong even though I'm not sure what it was.

"Well, thanks. For everything," I say.

"You're welcome," he says, relaxing.

He nods, returns to eating his French fries. I study his sharp chin, the way blond hair is escaping from his short ponytail, how his wrists are thin but his arms look strong.

Anything.

Everything.

Inside me, something moves. Something made of feathers and thin bones, something made of sky.

Just recognizing it immediately makes it disappear.

But I can still feel the traces of it lingering, everything in my body reaching to get it back.

Eighteen

RIGHT BEFORE I DECIDED I wanted to be a doctor, I told my dad I wished Charlie was dead.

Of course, I didn't mean it, not really.

It was back when Grandma and Grandpa Rose were staying with us, but for some reason I no longer remember, that night they couldn't watch me. So Dad picked me up after school.

From the get-go, things weren't going so great.

Dad had just moved from his freelance writing gig to a full-time copywriting job, and from what I could discern, he hated it. "Another soul-killing day," he mumbled when I asked him how he was doing.

Meanwhile, my stomach was growling so much it hurt. I had skipped lunch because I hated the soggy fish sticks that were on the day's menu. Mom always packed my lunch on fish stick days, but Grandma Rose didn't know that.

Em split her banana and her oatmeal raisin cookie with me, and Matty let me eat some of his Doritos, but by the time Dad picked me up, I was convinced I was starving to death. I didn't want to be brave and good. I wanted to go through the McDonald's drive-through. Dad said we didn't have time if we wanted to beat rush-hour traffic.

But then we merged onto I-71, only to see an endless line of red brake lights in front of us. Dad cursed loudly, turning up the radio to get the traffic report.

By the time we passed the mangled cars and the sirens on the side of the highway, forty-five barely-inching-forward minutes had passed.

"I don't feel good," I said from the backseat as we got closer. I kicked his seat.

He didn't reply, turning right on Reading Road instead of going the way that took us by the mural on Calhoun.

"Wait!" I said. "You have to go that way! I want to see the painting on the wall!"

"This way works too," Dad said.

"But it's not the right way!" I kicked the back of the seat, my red gym shoes making a solid hit.

He didn't respond.

I watched boring buildings pass by and kicked the back of his seat again.

"I don't feel good."

Again, no response.

My red shoes took on a life of their own, kicking the seat, like they weren't even attached to me.

"I'm hungry," I said, louder this time, as he pulled into the parking garage, jerking the car to a stop. "Can we get something to eat?"

"Visiting hours are almost over," Dad said, getting out of the car and holding the door open for me. I climbed out of the backseat and started following him to the entrance. "We can get food on the way home."

"I don't want to wait that long. I'm hungry now," I said, my gym shoes kicking at a parking barrier, scuffing the rubber edges, and I almost tripped. I steadied myself and ran to catch up with him. "Dad, please," I said, tugging at the edge of his jacket.

"I said later, okay? We only have a half hour to see your brother."

He kept walking, and I stopped in my tracks, my eyes filling with hot tears.

"But I'm hungry!" I shouted.

Dad turned around. "Not now, Parker. I need you to work with me here. I had a really long day at work, and I'm hungry too, but I need you to be grown-up right now."

"I'm tired of being grown-up!" I yelled, and then I tried to think of the most horrible thing I could say. "I wish Charlie was dead!"

Dad didn't even pause for a second, his work shoes clicking hard against the concrete of the parking garage before he leaned down, grabbing my arm.

His face was so mad, so scary, that it stopped all my tears instantly.

"I don't *ever* want to hear you say that again. You are being self-ish. Do you hear me?" His hands hurt against my arm, and I knew it was serious because even though Dad got frustrated sometimes, he had never laid a hand on me or Charlie. I couldn't be sure, but it looked like Dad was crying then.

My heart tightened up inside me, like a tiny hard fist, and I nodded, and Dad let go of my arm.

"I'm sorry," I whispered.

"That's not enough! You can't say those things. Ever. Okay?"

I nodded again.

I looked down at those red gym shoes, watched them move step by step forward as I followed Dad into the hospital, watched them as I climbed into a seat in the waiting room, watched them as Dad asked the nurse at the reception desk to watch me while he visited with Charlie, watched them when the nurse asked me if I wanted a cookie or something to read.

"No," I said, my voice small.

I couldn't even look in the direction of Charlie's room, convinced Dad was telling Mom what I'd said, worried Charlie would overhear.

I closed my eyes tight, kicked my red shoes together three times, like in the movie with the flying monkeys, and wished I could trade places with Charlie, that I'd be the one who was sick instead. I wished so hard, my whole body scrunched up, like I could force the transformation into existence.

But when I opened my eyes, I was still in the waiting room.

When my parents came out later, I stood up, looked them both in the eye.

"I want to be a doctor to make Charlie better," I said.

"Oh, my girl," Mom said, rushing forward and pulling me into a hug. "I have missed you so much."

Over her shoulder I watched Dad, his face tired and tear-streaked, how he looked at me with so much love then, how I knew I'd finally said the right thing.

Nineteen

I SLIDE OPEN THE screen door to the back deck.

Dad's stretched out on a lawn chair, beer in hand, head tilted back, nodding slightly in time with whatever he's listening to on his iPod.

Mom looks up from the stack of student papers she's grading as I sit down next to her. "Hey, hon."

Dad takes off his headphones. "Dr. McCullough!"

"Hey, guys. Are we having dinner soon?"

"I'm thinking of ordering pizza in a bit. That okay with you? It's just the three of us, so we can get green peppers and pepperoni," Mom says, picking up the paper she's grading and fanning herself with it. Even though it's a little before six, it's still warm outside, the heat from the day sticking stubbornly to everyone's skin.

"What's Charlie doing?" I ask, trying to sound casual. Much to my relief, he wasn't home when Finn dropped me off. I'm not sure I'm ready to see him yet.

"Dinner with some of the people in his cancer support group," Mom says, blowing her bangs off her face.

Dad leans forward. "Soooo . . . ?" he starts, grinning.

I know exactly what's at the end of that question mark. I've been debating how to answer it ever since Finn dropped me off this afternoon. But now that the moment's here, seeing how happy he is, how relaxed Mom is, I can't believe I ever wondered what to say.

"So what?" I ask, purposefully acting nonchalant.

"Day two! How'd it go?"

"Pretty awesome," I lie, the words gliding easily through water, smooth and noiseless.

"I knew it!" Dad says. "How are the other people in the program?"

The sour face of the waitress at the Anchor Grill flashes through my mind. "There was one crabby nurse named Mabel, but everyone else was really nice. I think it's going to be really good working there. Not what I expected, but really good."

I don't tell them about my fight with Charlie.

I don't tell them about the e-mail that was waiting for me when I got home—the one from the head of the program asking me to call him immediately regarding my unexplained and unacceptable absence, reiterating how competitive the program was and how other students would welcome my spot.

I don't tell them any of this because I have to go back tomorrow. I'm going back tomorrow.

(My bottom right eyelid twitches.)

Dad takes a sip of beer and gets that look on his face, the surefire sign he's a little tipsy and about ten seconds away from getting sentimental. "Parker, when I saw you standing up there on graduation night, giving your valedictorian speech, it was pretty much the proudest moment of my life. If only your grandparents could have seen you. Your mom and me, we're so proud of you. You know that, right?"

"She knows," Mom says, patting Dad on the shoulder. "I'm going to order the pizza."

I watch her leave, resting my legs on the deck and flexing my bare toes.

"So, what's on the agenda for day three?" Dad asks.

"Why did you stop writing?" I ask instead of answering him, thinking of the concerts he used to attend when we were kids, the CDs he'd get in the mail to review, the prized *Rolling Stone* article he wrote about Pearl Jam, now framed in his office. "Why did you start at the brand agency?"

He looks surprised. "Things changed."

"But you loved writing."

"I did."

"And?"

"Your brother got sick. Schneider and Hall was looking for a copywriter. They offered a steady salary, better insurance than your Mom had at the university."

"Oh," I say, realizing even more keenly what he did to take care of us, everything taking on a new feel in light of the internship. "That must have been hard, giving up the music writing."

Dad leans forward, meeting my eyes. "If it meant helping your brother, I would do it again in a heartbeat. You know that, right?"

I nod. "But did you have to give up writing for good?"

Dad shrugs. "Your mom and I barely had time to sleep when Charlie was sick. And by the time he was better? I don't know, I guess you get so used to something, you don't realize it could be different." He squints, tilting his head back in the sun again. "Why do you ask?"

I fiddle with the hem of my T-shirt.

"I was just thinking about the day I decided to be a doctor. You had just started at Schneider and Hall. Do you remember that?"

"Of course. You were at the hospital with me and Mom."

"Because Grandma and Grandpa Rose were busy," I add.

"Yeah, that's right."

I brace myself for him to remember, my whole body tensing with shame over the memory of what I said in the parking garage.

Instead, he gets a nostalgic smile on his face. "You had to stay in the waiting room with a nurse. I felt bad leaving you, but when I came out, you were sitting there with your pigtails and a smile from ear to ear. You stood up and promised me and your mom you were going to be a doctor so you could make Charlie better."

"But—" I start, not sure what to say.

Dad doesn't even hear me. "It was the only good thing in the middle of all of that time. I was blown away by how smart you are and how big your heart is." He finishes his beer in one last gulp and stands, presumably to get another one, when he stops, looks down at me.

"Hey, you still didn't tell me what you're doing on day three."

"A tour of the oncology unit," I say. "It should be really amazing."

He leans down and gives me a kiss on the forehead before heading back inside.

I wonder if Charlie knows what Dad gave up for him.

For some reason, I kind of hope he doesn't.

Twenty

THAT NIGHT, I CAN'T sleep, my thoughts pinballing between imagining Dad's alternate career and the internship.

I'm going back tomorrow.

My skin itches and I want to crawl out of my body, crawl into someone else's life. I realize I'm picking at my lip and I drop my hand to my side.

I'm never going to fall asleep, so I get up and turn on my laptop, the screen light giving the room an eerie glow.

I click into my e-mail, and there at the top, like a gift from baby Jesus, like a sweet breath of relief, I see an exclamatory all-caps message from Em titled "HELLO FROM FOGGY LONDON TOWN!" My whole body eases for a second.

Park!

*Sorry I can't text—my cell plan is crap.
You're just going to have to deal with e-mail
or four-hundred-dollar phone calls—I'm
thinking e-mail, yes?*

*Do you remember how I told you about
that dream I had, where I got off the plane
in London and kept saying, "My feet are
on the ground in another country"? Well,
MY FEET ARE ON THE GROUND
IN ANOTHER COUNTRY! Matty and
I got to London early Monday morning,
and spent the day trying to catch up on
sleep in our hostel. This morning, though,
we wandered. Park, you would love it here.
Everyone sounds like Mr. Darcy. It's so
easy to get around on the tube (what they
call the subway), and today we got to see
a cat mummy in the British Museum. I'm
officially in love with this city—the voices
and color and pace.*

*Tomorrow we're taking a street-art
tour, which makes me think of that weird
message on the water tower. Who knew
Cincinnati was on the cutting edge of
street art (ha!).*

Hope you and Charlie are talking again.
How was your dad's Memorial Day picnic?
How is the internship?

Miss you, oxo, E

God, I miss her.

I wish she were here. I wish I could tell her about the internship. I wish she could tell me what to do.

My bottom right eyelid is twitching again.

I gaze at my bulletin board: my Harvard acceptance; a picture of Charlie and me when we were little—him with a toothy grin, me with a fierce scowl; the blue first-place ribbon I won in my fourth-grade science fair; formal pictures from junior-year prom—one of me and Em making faces and wearing terrible bridesmaids dresses we found at the Salvation Army. Another of us with Charlie and Matty—Em and Matty squeezed together in the middle, Charlie and me bookending them.

Maybe this summer is what happens when Em and Matty aren't there to stand between us anymore.

Maybe this summer is what happens when Charlie and I aren't even in the same picture anymore.

Like a whisper, I hear Finn's words: *Anything. Everything.*

I try to steady my breathing, and on an impulse, I Google Image "street art."

Color explodes on the screen.

There are tiled mosaics of old Pac-Man ghosts and small space invaders. Each one is totally different, and they're placed on buildings all over the world—Paris, New York, Hong Kong—by an artist who keeps his identity secret, just like a superhero.

There are bright murals of yellow men and women in colorful clothes, dreamy and weird, like they walked out of a fairy tale, painted by Brazilian twins.

There are images of work from a guy named ESPO, sayings in bright letters: LETS ADORE AND ENDURE EACH OTHER. EUPHORIA IS FOR YOU AND ME. IF YOU WERE HERE ID BE HOME NOW. They remind me of Finn's messages.

I go further down the rabbit hole, discovering even more artists: Ben Wilson, who paints tiny works of art on chewing gum stuck to the sidewalk in London. ROA, who creates detailed black-and-white illustrations of rats and squirrels. Olek, who does something called yarn bombing, where she crochets around trees and bikes.

It's not the stuff of my high school art history lessons, works I had to memorize, movements I had to put into historical context.

This is on the edges, messy and uneven and rough. It makes me feel a weird sort of jangly, but not in a bad way.

Mustard wanders into the room and jumps up on my lap, and I absentmindedly pet him, clicking through more and more links.

Small figures casting shadows on curbs. A rendering of that famous wartime photo of the kiss in NYC, only with a rainbow behind it. A guy called Hanksy who paints Tom Hanks puns.

This is art that rises from hidden tunnels, that floats off walls and over bridges.

All this art where it shouldn't be.

All this art not to make money, but just because.

My hand hovers over the mouse, frozen.

What would it be like to do something not because you had to, but just because you wanted to?

But I have the internship.

And right then, it's not Dad's words, or Charlie's, or even Finn's, that come to mind.

Instead it's mine—one simple gorgeous word: *No.*

The sureness of it moves through my body, my bones settling into their joints, my thoughts slowing down.

What if I don't go back to the internship?

I wait for something to happen, for my dad to rush into my room and tell me I'm out of my mind, for my mom to come in and talk me out of it, for Charlie to get an insta-bloody nose.

But nothing happens.

So carefully, one more small thought at a time, I begin to imagine what it would be like to quit.

I'd have to do it in a way that didn't necessitate the program calling Mom and Dad, who, to put it mildly, would not be keen about my decision. And I'd have to make sure it wouldn't jeopardize my Harvard acceptance in any way. I'm already in, but despite what I told Finn earlier, what if the director called Harvard, told them I was a big, selfish disappointment? I can't risk that.

I scratch my arm.

Mono. I can tell the program director I have mono. It's contagious. I can't be around sick kids.

What else?

I'll need to find a compelling reason Charlie doesn't need to drive me to the internship I'm apparently still participating in. I'll have to find a job to make up for losing the internship stipend, which I needed to buy textbooks for next year. And at some point, I'll have to tell my parents.

This lie is going to need constant maintenance and nurturing, not just today but throughout the rest of the summer.

I don't know how I'm going to manage any of this.

But when I think about not going back to the internship?

The breath in me changes.

This time, it's not being snagged on thorns. It's not scary.

Instead, it's like earlier, at the Anchor Grill with Finn: breath arriving, the whisper of wings.

Behind it all, steady heartbeat: *Anything. Everything.*

Twenty-One

WHEN I WAKE UP the next morning, I'm lighter than I've been for ages.

I'm not going back to that internship.

By the time I'm dressed and eating cereal—a new box of Cheerios Charlie hasn't plowed through yet—I'm mentally reviewing the plan that I came up with last night. And it's weird to admit it, but it feels good. I haven't felt this on top of things since I was preparing my early-decision application for Harvard. Back then, I had to make sure every piece of the application machine was ready to do its part: SATs, recommendations, extracurriculars. Now it's making sure all my lies are in place.

From behind me, Dad is whistling at the coffeemaker, and I can hear the sounds of Mom getting ready upstairs.

My "no" is a life raft—I'm not letting go.

Charlie eases into the seat across from me, pouring yet again an obscene amount of Cheerios into an oversized bowl.

I steal a glance at him, wondering if he's feeling even a little bad about our fight yesterday, but he looks disinterested, half asleep.

For a second I wish it were different, but then I remember Charlie has always been able to tell when I'm lying, so maybe us not talking right now is actually a good thing.

"Can one of you guys put the potatoes on the stove when you get home tonight?" Mom asks as she enters the kitchen.

"Sure," I say.

She kisses me on the forehead, runs her hand over Charlie's head, and grabs the cup of coffee Dad's holding out before rushing out the door.

Dad dutifully grabs the stack of papers she's accidentally left on the counter, then turns to us.

"Have fun changing the world today, Dr. McCullough!"

I feel a pang of guilt and shovel more cereal in my mouth.

"And, Charlie. Enjoy tutoring. Remember: 'Any fool can know. The point is to understand,'" he says, clearly quoting something.

Charlie gives an exaggerated grimace. "Are you calling me a fool?"

He automatically looks to me for confirmation that Dad is being corny, but then looks away quickly, like he just remembered he hates me.

Dad gives a goofy wave and leaves.

I poke at my cereal, not feeling very hungry. This is the first time I've been alone with Charlie since our fight at the hospital yesterday.

I wait for him to apologize for what he said, because there's no way I'm going to make the first move.

But the longer we sit there, I realize Charlie's not going to either.

I feel my bottom right eyelid start to twitch, and I squeeze it hard, willing it to stop, and focus instead on carefully chewing my cereal.

After a few more minutes of nothing but the sound of cereal being consumed and Mustard chirruping at birds in the backyard, Charlie stands and brings his bowl to the sink. He turns to me, expressionless.

"Thanks to you, I have therapy today after tutoring, so I can't pick you up until at least six."

I try to ignore the knot in my chest. "I don't need you to drive me anymore. A girl from the program can pick me up and drop me off for the rest of the summer. So feel free to take your time at therapy. I figure you need it."

Charlie flinches. *Good. I can hurt him, too*, I think, and for a brief moment I feel satisfied.

And then the guilt starts to seep into my edges.

He grabs the car keys without looking back, mumbles, "Later," and is out the door.

I wait until I hear the garage shut behind him before I let my breath out.

I did it.

I pulled off the first step in freeing myself of the internship.

I wait to feel giddy or relieved, but I can't shake the memory of the wounded look on Charlie's face when I made the therapy crack.

I stand, dump my leftover cereal milk in the sink, and then jog upstairs. I change out of my black pants and navy shirt into my favorite light-blue-and-white spaghetti-strap sundress—something I never could have worn to intern at the hospital.

Mustard pads into the room, surprised to see me there, and makes little cat chirps as he winds himself around my legs, his purring audible.

"I'm happy to be here too, buddy," I say, bending down and giving him a vigorous chin rub. A blue jay outside my window catches his attention, so he leaves me, springing up onto the windowsill.

I take in my breath, shake off the bad feelings. I'm not going to let Charlie ruin my day.

First things first.

I pull up my laptop and start an e-mail to the program director of the internship.

The words come out without a second thought, no pausing, no second-guessing:

Dear Dr. Gambier,

After speaking with my doctor yesterday, I regret to inform you I have to withdraw from the Children's Hospital internship. What I thought was a twenty-four-hour virus has just been diagnosed as mononucleosis. Since I'm contagious for the foreseeable future, I can't in good conscience

continue to participate in the program.
I'm so sorry for any inconvenience this may
cause, and I truly regret I won't be able to
benefit from such an amazing program.

Sincerely,
Parker McCullough

I hit send and slump back against my chair, light-headed with relief.

I did it.

With one e-mail, I wiped out my summer plans, and instead of being completely terrified, I feel kind of awesome.

This is the feeling I was waiting for.

Mustard has fallen asleep in a ray of sunlight on the windowsill, his tail waving lazily, content.

Next up: replying to Em's e-mail.

Em!

London sounds awesome. I'm so happy for you.
Have you met any charming British girls?
Even if you do, you have to come back to the
States, remember? You promised. Did you go to
the Tower of London? Did you ride the Eye?

I pause.

*Nothing much here, except AND YOU
CAN'T TELL ANYONE THIS . . . I quit
my internship. You were right: I just think
I need a break this summer before the fall.
But I haven't told my parents or Charlie—
they'd freak—so if you randomly run into
any members of the McCullough family in
Europe (haha), not a word, 'kay?*

xox, Park

At the window, Mustard's paws and whiskers twitch, like he's having a dream about chasing birds.

I hit send.

Another rush of relief moves through me, taking with it the last of the lingering Charlie feelings.

This is Brand-New Me.

No internship.

A big beautiful summer ahead of me.

Anything and everything.

Now, to find my new summer job.

Twenty-Two

NEW ME IS FLOUNDERING.

I've spent the past two hours canvassing any business within walking distance that my family won't frequent during the day and that might be hiring. So far, I've been shot down by the vegan restaurant, a stamp and scrapbooking store, a children's play zone, the library, and the ice cream store Serendipity.

Turns out, as at least three different people tell me, the last day of May is way too late to line up a summer job—have I tried Kings Island Amusement Park yet?

I sit on the bench outside Serendipity, trying to enjoy my scoop of chocolate peanut butter ice cream, wishing I'd had my internship epiphany before I turned down babysitting the Delaney boys, and pretending my eyelid isn't twitching again.

I've clearly made a hideous mistake. I debate writing Dr.

Gambier back, telling him the doctor misdiagnosed me and I'm actually not contagious, it's a miracle, and can I come back?

But just thinking about walking through those doors again?

No.

I toss the last of my ice cream in the garbage and start walking home.

I slow as I pass the Float. There's a small line forming for the lunch crowd, and I'm wondering if Finn is working when my eyes rest on the small white building next door, the one with the spray-painted sign out front that says CARLA'S CERAMICS, and in the front window, scrawled in big red letters, HELP WANTED.

I remember Finn's comment about his friend Carla needing a studio assistant and realize now that if anyone put two and two together, the store signage looks a lot like all of those messages showing up on bridges around town.

This must be the place.

I know nothing about ceramics. But at this point, what do I have to lose?

When I enter the studio, a loud bell jangles above me. Three older ladies turn to look at me. They're all sitting on stools around the tables and seem to be in the middle of painting mugs.

"Hi?" I say tentatively, looking for someone in charge. "I'm here about the sign?" I cringe internally at the unwelcome return of the question mark.

"Carla!" yells a stout white woman with wild, uncombed gray hair. She is wearing a garish flowered muumuu. "Someone here for you!"

A voice yells, "Just a minute!"

"Harriet, you don't need to be that loud," says a tall, thin white woman elegantly decked out in pearls and lavender with matching lavender hair. Her sleeves are neatly rolled back, and her posture makes me feel exhausted just looking at it.

To my surprise, the loud muumuu woman—Harriet—gives Lavender the finger, and Lavender frowns, like she's just smelled spoiled milk.

The black woman sitting next to Lavender is wearing a yellow shirt, red pants, a bright-orange scarf, and a huge sun-shaped brooch. She's looking anxiously between Harriet and Lavender, and I get the feeling this isn't the first time they've fought.

I step farther into the shop, taking in the surroundings. The space is bright, large windows letting in the morning sun, a tangle of hanging plants growing wild under the skylight. There are shelves of white unpainted ceramics lining the front: mugs and plates and plaques, but also statues—frogs and cats and puppies.

That's when I notice the fourth woman. She's sitting at a table by herself in the back, her hands folded neatly in her lap, a blank mug and a paintbrush on the table in front of her. She's slight, short silver hair clipped close, pale white skin, and she's staring out the window at the creek behind the studio, a dreamy lost look on her face. Her expression reminds me of Grandma Rose in the months before she died, how she got quieter and quieter, not always completely with us.

"Does it still smell like wet dog? You can tell me the truth."

When I turn around, a ruddy-faced, middle-aged woman is

standing behind me. Her thick brown hair is pulled back in a plaid bandana, freckles dotting her sunburned cheeks, and she's wiping what looks like mud from her hands across a mud-stained apron.

"I have tried and tried to get the smell out. I figure once I get the kiln going, it'll either kill it completely, or make it smell like my side business is cooking Fido. But I needed a larger studio space, and the landlord offered me a great deal."

I try to look like I know what she's talking about.

"Turns out this space is the perfect atmosphere for clay. Not too humid, not too dry, though every time I go outside, some blue jay won't stop scolding me."

She stops herself, realizing I haven't said anything, and I wish I had, because now there's a weird silence between us. My eyelid twitches once, and then again, and I hope she doesn't notice.

"Um, do you need help?" I ask.

"With the bird?"

"No." I point at the sign. "You're hiring, right? I saw the sign, and I know Finn. He said you were looking for an assistant."

"You know Finn?" she echoes, clearly surprised.

"Kind of. We were friends a while ago and just reconnected."

"What's your name?"

"Parker McCullough."

Her eyes go to my hands.

"You ever work with clay?"

I debate lying but figure I could fake my way through that for only so long.

"Not since Play-Doh."

She snorts. "Good. I can show you the right way to use it. No bad habits to undo. You good with difficult people?"

I'm guessing that even though they're kids, Ryan and Todd Delaney count as difficult people. "I hold my ground okay."

"You okay with thirty hours a week, ten bucks an hour?"

I nod, hardly believing this is actually happening, that I might have just landed myself not only a job, but a job that pays more than minimum wage.

"Got any bad habits I should know about? Drugs, cigarettes, that stuff?"

I shake my head vigorously. "No, not at all. I can provide references, too."

"That'd be good, but to be honest, you're the first person who's come in, and I have to believe it's meant to be. Can you be here every weekday from ten to four?"

"Absolutely." Yes, yes, yes.

"Can you start tomorrow?"

I realize I've been nodding too hard, so I try to slow down and smile like I'm quietly excited and professional, not a bobbleheaded version of myself. "Yes."

She reaches out to shake my hand. "I'm Carla. You're hired. See you tomorrow. I'll have you fill out a W-4 then. Bring your references, too."

"Cool, yes!"

"Ladies, I finally have an assistant," Carla announces to the four women, before she waves and heads to the door in the back. "See you tomorrow, Parker."

169

Lavender nods, and the sunshine woman smiles, but Harriet just rolls her eyes and mutters, "About time."

I look at the quiet woman, to see if she's changed position, but she's still staring out the window.

"Oh, Alice doesn't talk anymore, dear," Lavender says to me.

"Her Alzheimer's is pretty bad," the sunshine woman chimes in. "Sometimes she just likes to sit by herself and watch the creek."

"With the current company, I don't blame her," Harriet grumbles.

"Well, see you later," I say, and as I leave, I hear Lavender murmur, "Such a lovely girl."

It's not until I'm halfway home that I realize two things: I'm not sure what my new job entails, and I'm strangely okay with that.

Twenty-Three

THAT EVENING, I STAND on my tiptoes, trying to see who's working at the Float. I smile when I locate Ruby at the counter—she's half of the reason I'm here.

The other half—Finn—hasn't made an appearance yet.

I fidget with my phone, trying to calm the jitters in my stomach.

It's no big deal. I'm just stopping by to see if Ruby wants to hang out sometime and to thank Finn for the ride and the job lead.

But I still feel a mix of weird and excited to see them both again, the same giddiness that was tripping around me this morning. I want to tell someone on this continent that I quit the internship and found another job, that it feels like everything's coming together, that maybe things could be *good*.

I want them to be my friends.

Speaking of . . . I open my e-mail to start a note to Em about Carla's, but there's already a response from her in my in-box.

> *Park,*
>
> *So, I got your note about the internship, and I tried to call you, but my cell service is crappy, so e-mail it is. . . .*
>
> *First, I'm really proud of you for figuring out the internship isn't for you. That's a big thing, and it couldn't have been easy to make that decision, and you're smart and brave and awesome.*

I feel a flush of pride and keep reading.

> *That being said, and I hope you're not mad at me for saying this, but I really think you should tell your parents. It feels like maybe you're not dealing with everything, the reasons you quit in the first place, etc.? Plus, are you just going to lie about it all summer? I don't mean that in a judgy way, just that it sounds really lonely to carry that lie all by yourself, Park. I really think you should talk to your parents.*

> *I'm sorry, but I had to be honest. I love*
> *you to pieces.*
>
> *oxo, Em*

And just like that, my good feelings go down the drain.

Frowning, I inch forward in the line and reread the e-mail. Why can't she just be happy for me? She knows how my parents are, especially my dad. Does she honestly think I could tell him the truth? He would be so disappointed, I doubt he'd be able to look at me. I can already see him marching me right back to that internship the next day.

Plus, what is it she told me when I worried about her hooking up with May again?

My thumbs fly across the keyboard:

> *Em, thanks for your note. But I'm a*
> *grown-up, and I got it. You don't need*
> *to worry. Park*

I hit send.

I feel triumphant, righteous even, for about ten seconds.

And then I start second-guessing the e-mail and myself.

What if she's right to worry? What if I can't carry this lie the whole summer?

"Can I help you? Oh, Parker, hey!"

I look up to see Ruby pushing her glasses up the bridge of her nose and smiling.

"Ruby, hey!"

"How are things going?"

"They're a little better," I say, thinking of my new summer job. "Actually, I was going to see if you wanted to grab lunch soon?"

Her face opens up. "Really? Oh my God, yes. That would be awesome."

"I'll e-mail you," I say.

"I'll bring all my Harvard and SAT questions for you!"

The guy behind me in line clears his throat significantly, and Ruby rolls her eyes, but I jump in.

"In the meantime, one root-beer float. Small."

"One large float!" she calls out.

"Small," I say, but she winks.

"Upsizing you and giving you the employee discount," she whispers. "One dollar."

"You don't have to—"

"I know I don't *have* to, but I *want* to."

As I hand her the money, I try to angle my gaze toward the kitchen, but I can't tell who's back there. I drop two singles in the tip jar and move to the side to wait. The guy behind me starts to order, but then I can't help it, and I lean around him.

"Ruby?"

The guy at the counter gives a weary sigh.

"Yeah?"

"Is Finn working tonight?" I ask.

Ruby wrinkles her nose. "Finn?"

"Yeah," I say, deciding not to explain any further.

"He's on his break, probably out back," she says.

"Great, thanks," I say, taking my float. "Talk soon! I promise." She gives me a cheery wave.

I take a sip of my float, and it's the perfect mix of creamy vanilla and sharp root beer. I smooth my sundress and take a deep breath, heading toward the back of the Float.

It's quieter here, not meant for customers. There are no picnic tables, only a Dumpster and a flickering overhead light casting the whole place with a weird industrial glow.

"Hello?"

Right then, a guy comes from the side of the Dumpster, leaning over so he can light something as he walks. At first I think it's Finn, because the guy has the same blond hair, the same razor-sharp build, but when he stands, inhaling, and sees me, my breath catches.

Even though Finn's brother, Johnny, must be in his midtwenties by now, he looks like he's about forty. He's literally skin and bones, a shadow version of Finn. I register the line of scabs on his arm.

The corner of Johnny's mouth creeps up right before he exhales a cloud of smoke, skunky and dank. His eyes narrow, like he's trying to figure out who I am.

"Can I help you?" he asks.

"Um . . ." I step back. "I was just looking for someone, but he's not here, so, um, yeah, have a good night?"

He gives me such an obvious once-over, eyes lingering at my

chest, leering, that I immediately want to take a shower.

"You sure you're not looking for me? I've got stuff you might want." He holds up what he's smoking and licks his lips slowly, then stares at me harder. "I'd even be open to trading, figuring out a special arrangement between you and me."

All the blood in me freezes, and for a second I can't move, I hate him so much.

He narrows his brow. "Wait a minute. Do I know you?"

I shake my head. "No, and no thank you. Have a good night," I say, walking as fast as I can back to the front of the restaurant, tossing my float in the nearest garbage can.

I cringe at my ever-present manners, the fact that I just politely declined some creepy sexual harassment. Johnny didn't deserve that. What he deserved was a solid kick in the shins, or elsewhere. I can't believe I told him to have a good night.

I'm moving so quickly, second-guessing myself, that I nearly run right into Finn.

"Whoa," he says, hands resting on my shoulders for a second to slow me down, his face lighting up when he sees it's me. His hair is pulled back in a messy ponytail, an apron folded down across his waist. I can see more of his tattoo: a skull and crossbones.

His smile is easy. "Ruby said you were looking for me."

I take a step back, force a smile of my own, but I can't meet his eyes. I wonder if he knows what his brother is doing out back. I wonder if he's going to join him.

"Hey, so I've still got ten minutes on my break. Want to hang out for a bit?"

"No." My voice is shorter than I intended, but I want to get as far away from Johnny as possible.

Finn looks confused, and I fumble through my bag and grab the gift card, holding it out, my hands still trembling slightly from my encounter with his brother. The navy polka-dot ribbon I tied around it earlier looks pathetic now.

He looks at it in my hands but doesn't move to take it. "Parker, are you okay? Did something happen?"

"This is for you," I say. "For the art store on Route 42—Vinchesi's? I thought you could use it to get some more paint. For your messages."

He's still standing there, so I move a step closer, but he doesn't take it.

Everything around me feels hot and dizzy, my vision too sharp.

"I wanted to thank you for the ride and for the job lead. I quit my internship after all, and I'm working at Carla's now." My words are rushed, and I just want him to take the gift card already. "So I picked this up for you, to pay you back."

"Parker, you didn't have to get me anything."

"I know I didn't. But I figured you could use it. And now we're even."

His face hardens and he steps back, changing in front of me. "I don't need your charity."

"That's not what I meant."

"Sure it isn't."

I look at him, trying to find the boy who helped me at the bridge, who helped me at the hospital, but the person in front of me is furious. I don't know what just happened. I try to review my words, but I'm so flustered from my encounter with his brother that everything around me feels too electric and nervous to make sense. And then, like I conjured him Bloody Mary–style at a slumber party, Johnny comes around the corner.

"Finny. There you are. I was looking for you." He chuckles when he sees me. "Girlfriend trouble?"

"No. Parker's not my friend," Finn says, his voice far away. "She's just paying back a debt."

"Will you please take it?" I ask, shoving the gift card against his chest, trying not to look surprised at the strength there, how he doesn't waver even with my push. His gaze is like ice.

I let go of the card and it drops to the ground. I sling my purse over my shoulder, leaving Finn Casper and his brother behind me.

I keep my gaze forward, my walk purposeful, speeding up as I get closer, until I can shut myself in Mom's car, my hands still shaking as I lock the doors.

They don't stop until I'm halfway home.

Twenty-Four

WHEN I WAS IN first grade, Finn's brother, Johnny, broke my wrist.

It was a chilly January day, and Finn had entrusted me with his Walkman while he ran back inside to get his hat. I was listening to the heroes song when an older kid, one with dirty-blond hair, came over and stood in front of me. I had seen him once or twice—I was pretty sure he was a seventh grader.

I tried to focus on the music, hoping if I didn't look up, he'd just go away.

"Hey," he said.

Then again even louder. *"Hey."*

I hit stop and took out the earbuds.

He pointed at the Walkman. "Where'd you get that?"

"It's my friend's," I said. My shoulders were scrunched up by my ears, my body trying to shrink into itself.

"Is your friend Finn Casper?"

I didn't know whether to nod or not, but the boy sneered.

"I *knew* he stole it. Give it to me. Now."

I didn't like this person. I didn't like what he'd said about Finn and how he was trying to scare me. I shook my head, my voice small. "Finn said not to give it to anyone."

The boy laughed then, and it made me want to hide.

But I held on to Finn's Walkman, my fingers pressing harder against the plastic.

"Tell Finn he's going to be sorry," the boy said, turning to leave. I started to slump back in relief, my fingers loosening, right as the boy spun around and triumphantly snatched the Walkman out of my hands.

"No!" I cried. "It's not yours!"

He started walking away. "Whatever. Tell Finn to come get it from me if he wants it back."

I looked at my empty hands. I couldn't believe he took it. I didn't know what I'd tell Finn. I was pretty sure that Walkman was what he loved most in the world. So I stood up and started running toward the boy's back.

"Hey!" I yelled. "Come back!"

Johnny turned and started laughing at me.

"Give it to me!" I yelled, catching up with him. He dangled the Walkman right above my grasp, and I jumped, trying to snatch it back.

Johnny kept laughing. "Guys, look at the puppy!" he said, turning to some of his friends.

The moment of distraction was the window I needed, and finally, my fingers touched the Walkman. Unfortunately, my grip wasn't secure, and instead of taking it back, I pulled it out of Johnny's hands and it fell out of mine, onto the blacktop, cracking.

I will never forget the look on Johnny's face then, how for a second he looked soft and sad. And then he turned toward me, his whole body twisting into a snarl, and he shoved me so hard, I fell backward, my hands flailing out uselessly behind me.

I heard the crack as my body slammed against the pavement, my right wrist folding under me.

The pain was like my scream—white-hot and sharp—and I curled to the side, around my arm, sobbing.

Kids started gathering around, trying to figure out what had happened, and someone called for a playground monitor, but I was having a hard time focusing. Johnny had picked up the Walkman and was wiping his eyes with his arm, trying to press different buttons.

In the distance, I saw Finn coming out of the school, tugging his hat on. My vision honed in on him, the only clear thing amid the stinging of my knees and elbows, the dizzying pain coming from my arm. He registered me on the ground and started walking faster, then slowed as he took in his brother at the edge of the crowd. Finn's eyes went back to mine, and the storm in them broke, the sky opening.

I can only describe what happened next as the type of transformation I'd seen in Charlie's superhero movies, when Wolverine slid out his claws or that guy turned into the Hulk.

Finn's whole face hardened and he started running for Johnny. He hunched forward as he ran and aimed straight for the back of his brother's knees, screaming as he made contact, knocking his brother off his feet so hard that both Johnny and the Walkman smacked against the blacktop at the same time, the Walkman shattering into multiple pieces this time.

"You can't hurt her. I *hate* you!" Finn howled, his fists pummeling Johnny's back. His brother struggled to turn over, to push Finn off him. But Finn didn't stop, landing a blow in his brother's stomach and then right on his nose, continuing to yell. "You can't hurt her, too!"

At this point, the third-grade teacher, Ms. Felleman, was helping me up, leading me gently by the arm that wasn't hurt, while the fifth-grade teacher, Mr. Dufault, and Principal Fitzgerald were pulling Finn off Johnny.

Finn was furious, his face red, his arms struggling against the men lifting him, his legs still spinning in the air, while he yelled over and over at Johnny, "I hate you. I hate you. *I hate you!*"

Johnny, meanwhile, pulled a hand away from his face, dazed, seemingly surprised by the bright red blood there.

"*I hate you!*" Finn continued to scream, and right then, even though he was my friend, all that hate scared me so much, my teeth started chattering.

I turned to Ms. Felleman. "I need to find my brother," I said. "I need Charlie."

She led me away, and I left Finn behind, his screams echoing inside me for hours after.

That night, when I came back from the doctor's office, Charlie decorated my cast for me, filling every inch of white space with color and words—pictures of superheroes and cats and knock-knock jokes—making sure to leave space for my parents to sign their names. Matty added to it the next day after school. In fact, the cast was so full that by the time I went back to class two days later, my classmates were disappointed there wasn't more room for their autographs.

I was surprised they cared.

Turns out, everyone wanted to see my cast. The boys asked if it was true that I had heard my wrist crack when I fell (yes) and if my bone had poked out through my skin (no). The girls, the same ones who had called Finn smelly and said all those mean things about the lost-and-found box, invited me to join them at lunch, offering to carry my tray for me and splitting their favorite desserts. I never had to sit by myself during gym class either—a few kids routinely took turns joining me on the bleachers, while everyone else ran around wild, played basketball, or ran relay races.

A week later, when Finn finally came back after his suspension, he sat by himself at lunch, scowling. I waved from my new spot with the girls, but he ignored me. After lunch, I approached him carefully.

"Finn?"

He looked up, squinting, furious.

"I missed you," I said.

His face broke into a sneer just like his brother's. "Why?"

I stepped back, my hand half circling my cast. I didn't recognize him, and it felt like my heart was on the outside.

Finn's eyes took it all in, how I backed up, my hand on my wrist, how I was scared of him. "You're not my friend," he said.

It was like breaking my wrist all over again, only worse. This time the insides of me were breaking.

My parents had talked with me the night before, telling me Finn needed a lot of help, gently suggesting maybe I should find some other friends. I didn't want to listen to them.

But right then, all I could see in front of me was Johnny's brother, not my superhero friend.

"Go away," he said, his voice a growl.

I took another step back, trying not to cry.

"I said *go away*!"

I flinched and ran, not looking back.

Finn and Johnny transferred out of our school a few weeks later.

I never got to ask Finn if he was mad at me for not protecting his Walkman and his cassette tape.

I never got to ask him if he found Major Tom.

I never got to ask him if he ever learned to fly.

Twenty-Five

THAT NIGHT WHEN I get home from the Float, I hear Dad upstairs in the home office, his voice raised and irritable, which means he's on a work call.

There are quieter voices out back, so I follow them to the deck, only to find Mom and Charlie in the dusky light.

I falter for a second. I don't know if it's seeing Johnny tonight, or thinking about Johnny and Finn back then, but right now, even though things with Charlie suck, I need my family.

I slide open the screen door and poke out my head. "Do you guys want me to turn on the light?"

"No. We're looking for lightning bugs," says Mom.

"And we don't want more of those guys," says Charlie, pointing up to the moths batting themselves to death against the screen of Dad's office window.

Mom points at an empty seat. "Come join us."

I slide the door shut behind me, pretty sure I just let in a moth or two. "Dad sounds pretty crabby."

"He's on the phone for work," Mom says. "There's some problem with a client presentation."

"Avoid him at all costs," Charlie mutters, and I feel my shoulders ease. A muttered warning is better than silence.

"So how was your internship today?" Mom asks.

"Good." I pause. "I met my supervisor. Carla. I mean Dr. . . ." I scramble for a second. "Dr. Smith." Em's words replay in my mind, but there's no way I can tell my parents the truth. "I think she's pretty cool. She's going to be a good boss for the summer."

"That's wonderful, Parker," Mom says, but she's stopped by the sound of Dad's raised voice coming from upstairs.

"But it happens every single damn time!" he yells.

I feel rather than see Charlie tense, hear his exasperated sigh.

"You know, I was thinking maybe for Dad's birthday this fall, we could do something that would encourage him to get back into writing about music again," I say.

"That's a really cool idea, Parker," Mom says, sounding surprised. "What made you think of that?"

"I don't know. I guess I was just remembering how much he loved doing that when we were kids. Do you remember that, Charlie?"

He doesn't respond.

"What did you have in mind?" Mom asks.

"Maybe we can find him a writing retreat weekend or something?

There's that new Writer's Space place in Hyde Park. Or we could set up a blog for him? I don't know. I'll have to keep thinking on it."

"It's a good idea. I'll think on it too," Mom says, right as Dad yells, "Are you kidding me? That's a terrible idea!"

She sighs and stretches. "I'd better go see if your dad's okay."

"Good luck with that," Charlie says.

She leaves, and I remember the day Johnny broke my wrist, how Charlie got to the nurse's office before Mom arrived. I couldn't stop crying, but he waited with me, his arm sure around my shoulder, his low voice whispering, "I got you, Parker. I got you."

I turn to him now. "How was tutoring?"

"Fine."

"And therapy?"

"We're really going to do this?" he asks.

I sigh, worrying the fabric of my sundress between my fingers, and try again. "Have you talked with Matty since he left?"

I'm obviously a glutton for punishment.

"No."

This conversation clearly isn't going anywhere, and I'm just about ready to leave when Charlie says, "But I texted him an apology for some of the stuff I said on Saturday."

"You did?" I don't know if I'm more surprised that he apologized or that he's telling me about it.

"Yeah. I don't know if he got the text, though."

I choose my words carefully. "What were you apologizing for?"

"Because I gave him shit for going to Europe without me."

I let out a small surprised breath. As far as I'm concerned, he has a lot to apologize for regarding that night, but this would never have crossed my mind.

"I should never have done that. I'm glad he went to Europe without me. He's the only one doing what he wants even though I had cancer."

"What do you mean?"

He turns to me, and I can see his face in the light filtering out from inside. "Do you know Erin turned down a full scholarship to USC so she could go to school at Xavier? Ever since I've known her, Erin wanted to move to California. But I get sick again, and all of a sudden, she couldn't be more excited to stay in boring old Ohio."

He rubs his scalp.

"Why'd she do that?"

"I don't know. I think so she could be close by, since I was sick," he says.

"Oh," I say, remembering a similar conversation with Dad last December, how I was prepared to defer Harvard a year if Charlie's last round of chemo didn't work. "That's really thoughtful," I add.

Charlie lets out an exasperated sigh. "This past year, I wasn't her boyfriend," he says. "I was her boyfriend *with cancer*. She dropped out of cheerleading because she was missing so many games. She skipped Homecoming and the Winter Formal because I was in the hospital, even though I would have been cool if she went with someone else. I even told her to go with Matty."

"You were better by prom, though. Didn't she want to go?"

"I didn't want to go, so I didn't bring it up. She didn't ask. Instead we watched *Die Hard*. She doesn't even *like* action movies."

"So you're mad at her for being nice and not pushing you to go to prom and watching a movie you wanted to watch instead?" I ask.

"I didn't ask her to do any of that stuff, but she did," Charlie says, his voice breaking in frustration. "It's effing exhausting."

I can't believe the words coming out of his mouth. "Charlie, she loves you. That's why she did all that stuff."

"I didn't ask to be the person everyone sacrifices crap for. It's too much. I owe everyone too much already."

"You don't owe anyone anything—it's not an exchange. That's just what people do for the people they love."

Right then a door slams hard upstairs.

Charlie laughs. "I never asked for any of this, Parker. Erin giving up her dream school, Dad taking a shit job, you becoming a doctor."

"But I want to be a doctor."

He snorts. "Sure you do. Matty's the only one I can stand being around right now, to be honest."

"That's a really mean thing to say, Charlie."

Charlie scoffs, but his voice isn't angry. It's sad. "God, it must be nice to live in your perfect world."

"What does that mean?" I ask.

"Valedictorian? Full scholarship to Harvard? An internship you beat out . . . how many other candidates for?"

I don't answer.

"What is it Dad would say, 'The world's your oyster'? It is, Parker. But it's not mine."

He stands, stretches, heads inside.

I want to call him back.

I want to tell him the truth about everything, how for the first time in my life, I dread things: the internship, our parents finding out the truth. How I'm pretty sure there's something wrong with me, the terrible way my heart jumps too hard and fast. How my world is far from perfect.

And then I think about him being held back senior year.

About the cost of me telling our parents about his cancer coming back last summer.

About cancer, twice.

The knot of guilt tangles itself further in my chest, so instead I just sit there in the dark by myself, holding all the words in, letting them fade with the last of the light.

Twenty-Six

LAST JUNE, EM DECIDED to throw a surprise birthday party for Matty at Erin's house so we could use the pool. "He's always punking me—it's my turn to catch him off guard."

"Wow. That's a pretty sinister revenge plot," Charlie said to Em. "A secret pool party with his best friends? You'll show him."

"Shut up," Em said, swatting him on the arm. "You're not helping."

The day of the party, everything was going as planned: Erin's parents were out of town, and Em, May, Charlie, and I had gotten there early to help her set up. Charlie had the grill going, the guys from the baseball team had miraculously arrived on time (Em had significantly padded the arrival time solely for their benefit), and even though it was totally a mistake, we couldn't stop laughing at the birthday message on Matty's cake: HAPPY BIRTHDAY PATTY!

"Shhh!" Em said when the doorbell rang, holding up her phone to record Matty's reaction.

When he slid open the patio door, calling for Charlie, and we all jumped out screaming "Surprise!" Matty let out such a high-pitched yelp, Em did a victory fist pump. "Totally posting this on YouTube right now," she said, looking at her phone as she automatically held a hand up for a high five.

Everything was perfect that day, even the imperfect cake.

And then I saw Charlie.

I was by the pool, drying off in the sun, a warm towel wrapped around my shoulders, half listening to May talk about the political science classes she was taking at Oberlin in the fall, when Charlie passed in front of me, pulling off his Cincinnati Reds T-shirt and, with a wild whoop, cannonballing into the water right next to Erin.

I froze, watching him.

Erin shrieked as Charlie surfaced, scooping her up, threatening to dunk her.

"Charlie, I just got my hair blown out!" she said, but she was beaming at him, her arms around his shoulders.

I stood up.

"Park?" Em said.

"Just a minute," I said, walking over to the pool, as close as I could get to Charlie without actually getting in. By this point, he and Matty had started their "synchronized swimming" routine, the one that involved them holding their noses and jumping up and down in tandem.

I rubbed my eyes, just in case I was seeing sun spots, but no, as Charlie bobbed in the water, I could see them all over his back: tiny broken blood vessels, just like the ones on his chest when he first got cancer. With all the chaos and sunlight and splashing, I guessed no one else had seen them yet.

I rocked back on my heels right as Charlie looked at me, swimming over and splashing me from the pool.

He squinted up at me when I didn't move, his ears sticking out from his wet hair. They looked like they were getting burned, and I realized he probably didn't put any sunscreen on his ears, and he really should, because of skin cancer, because of cancer, and I swallowed hard.

"Parker, you okay? You look like you're going to throw up Happy Birthday Patty cake all over the place."

The sun was too warm on my face and I could smell chlorine in my hair, and I hated what I was going to do.

"There are spots on your back," I said, keeping my voice quiet.

"What? Bug bites?"

"No."

"It's probably heat rash or something."

"Charlie, they're like before."

He craned his neck back, twisting his whole body, so he could see. I watched his face fall amid all the life around him: Matty jumping into the pool, Erin laughing at his belly flop, Em and May sneaking a kiss.

"I'm sorry," I said.

"No. Fuck. No." He pulled himself up out of the pool and

193

grabbed a towel, wrapping it around his shoulders and yanking his T-shirt off a table before stalking into the house.

"Charlie?" Erin called from the pool.

"He'll be back," I said, following the trail of pool water until I found him standing in front of the bathroom mirror, angling his body to see his back.

The red spots looked like a map of constellations on his skin.

His eyes met mine in the mirror.

"My last blood test was good. I'm fine," he said.

"Yeah," I said, trying to sound like I believed it, like I wasn't terrified. "You're right. And I bet Mom and Dad can get you in to see Dr. Travis tomorrow and she'll rule it out, and it'll all be good."

He pulled his T-shirt on, shaking his head.

"I can't tomorrow."

"What? Why not?"

"I've got the baseball recruitment camp in two weeks. I'll go to the doctor after that."

"Charlie, you can't wait. If the cancer's back, it could be spreading. You know every day matters."

"I'm not missing the camp. All the good coaches will be there. Coach Franklin thinks it'll up my chances of getting recruited for Duke or Vanderbilt's team next year."

"But couldn't you go to the doctor and still go to the camp after that?"

"Not if I'm sick again."

"But if the cancer's back, the camp won't make any difference!"

Charlie flinched.

"I'm sorry, I just mean, if it's back, you probably couldn't play next year anyway, right?"

"You don't know that. If I get accepted, I could defer for a year."

"God, Charlie," I said, my voice cracking in frustration.

"Just give me these two weeks, okay? I promise, as soon as the camp is over, I'll tell Mom and Dad and I'll make an appointment with Dr. Travis. But, Parker, you have to let me do this on my own terms."

Charlie's voice was desperate, and I had to look away.

I took a step back, hugging myself, shaking my head. "No."

"Come on."

"No."

"Parker, if you ruin this for me, I will never forgive you," he said, his voice choked up, a mix of fury and heartbreak.

"I'm sorry," I said. "Tell Matty I said happy birthday. I'll see you at home tonight."

"Parker!" Charlie yelled as I left, but I didn't turn back, just started walking toward home.

As soon as I got there, I told my parents.

Before Charlie even got home that night, they had booked him into a nine a.m. appointment with Dr. Travis the next day and blood tests later in the afternoon.

I don't know how he took the news, if he was as furious with our parents as he was with me. I was too busy hiding upstairs in my room, afraid to face him, unable to shake the feeling that even though I'd done the right thing, I'd still done something really wrong, the type of wrong you could never come back from.

Four days later, Em and I were at the mall, hanging out on her break from the yogurt stand, when Mom called from the hospital to tell me it was official: Charlie had relapsed acute lymphocytic leukemia.

After I hung up, I was trying so hard to be matter-of-fact, but as soon as I told Em, her face screwed up and her eyes welled up, and then I couldn't look at her, because I knew if I did, I'd lose the little bit of myself that was still holding the rest of me together.

Our parents withdrew Charlie from the baseball camp, told Coach Franklin the news.

I did everything I could to avoid Charlie, while he did everything he could to indicate how much he hated me.

Our communication was limited to the basics of simple human interaction: *Good morning. Can you pass me the milk? Good night.* When I did meet his eyes, his gaze was so leveling, so devastating, I couldn't shake the feeling that this was all my fault: him missing the camp, the cancer coming back.

That September, Charlie started chemo again for his reinduction therapy. Mom began leaving metal pots around the house again—by the couch, at the foot of Charlie's bed—for when his treatments made him throw up. Dad took on as much overtime as he could get to help with the bills. I mailed off my Harvard early-action application packet.

In November, Mom and Dad told me that Charlie was taking off at least the first half of the year so he could focus on his treatments, meaning he wouldn't graduate with me and Matty and Em. That night, I heard him crying quietly on the other side of the wall.

I raised my hand, wanting to send him our old knock, but my knuckles froze inches from the wall, unable to bear the possibility that he might not knock back.

The day my Harvard acceptance packet arrived was our first snow of the year. Nothing heavy, just delicate December flakes, the type that make you forget the piles of gray snow that will come later in the winter.

As soon as I opened the letter, I felt my future solidify in front of me, edges sharp, colors bright: green rolling lawns, redbrick buildings, a stethoscope, scrubs, Dr. McCullough.

"I got into Harvard," I heard myself say to my parents.

"Holy cow!" my dad yelled, doing an enthusiastic fist pump. He pulled me into a hug that crushed my ribs against each other, letting go only so Mom could hug me too.

I gulped hard, trying to swallow, and at that second, I thought of the Wicked Witch of the East, the one who gets crushed by a house right at the beginning of the movie.

Dad put his hands on my shoulders. "Heck, let's go out to celebrate! Skyline Chili?"

I wanted to say, *A house has landed on top of me. There's something wrong with me. Something bad is happening.* But my head bobbed automatically, my mouth moved into a smile automatically, instinct taking over, and I nodded.

"If we go now, it won't be crowded," he said.

"I'll see if your brother feels well enough to join," Mom said before following Dad upstairs, calling Charlie.

I sucked in my breath and it got caught on a tangle inside me, and I held my head down on my lap, trying to find oxygen in the dark tent of my arms.

Harvard.

Premed.

Dr. McCullough.

It was what I'd always wanted.

But my heart felt sweaty, and my legs felt jumbly, and I couldn't get out from under that house.

"Parker?"

My head jerked up. Charlie was standing in front of me.

It was the first time he had looked at me in months when his gaze didn't make me shrink, didn't make me hate what I'd done.

"I got into Harvard," I said.

"Is this what you want?"

I stared at him. He looked gaunt, and I saw the new patches where his hair had come out in clumps. "Yes."

He didn't react, just turned and left without another word, not joining us for dinner that night.

At the time, I had hoped the being-crushed-by-a-house feeling was just nerves, being excited.

But afterward, I started dreaming about the helium people again.

I dreamed about them flying near my window at night, tapping on the glass pane.

I dreamed about them following me when I walked outside, pulling on my hair as I curled my toes against the earth.

I worried about their insides being exposed, convinced it

couldn't be good to show your heart out in the world like that.

Each time, late in the dream, I realized (or maybe just remembered) that Charlie was standing next to me too, right as one of the helium people took his hand, lifting him off the ground.

He always looked so happy, yelling, "Happy Birthday to us, Parker!"

And each time, I grabbed his foot, circled my hand around his bony ankle, tried to keep him tethered to me.

But I couldn't keep him close—the helium people were too strong—and with a cry, I watched Charlie break free, leaving me behind, my gravity feet on the ground.

I always woke up with loss aching through me, a sense of missing something so essential, it took me a while to remember where I was, even who I was, to remember I hadn't done enough to save my brother.

It was never enough.

Twenty-Seven

WHEN I ARRIVE FOR my first shift at Carla's, the four older ladies from the previous day are already there, this time painting what appear to be small shallow dishes.

All of them except for Alice, that is. This time she's actually sitting at the same table as the other three, but she still isn't painting. Instead, she's staring at her hands in her lap, neatly folded. The crabby one from yesterday, Harriet, just grunts, but the other two murmur hellos.

Right then, the front door opens behind me, and both Carla and Finn come in, boxes stacked in their arms.

Finn stops in his tracks when he sees me.

My heart does a weird optimistic surge, hoping maybe what happened the other night between us wasn't as bad as I remember, but he only nods, walking past me.

"Parker! Good to see you," Carla calls out, following him toward the back staircase. "Just give me a few minutes. We have to bring some clay downstairs."

"I told you I got 'em, C," Finn says. "Just put your boxes there and I'll make another trip."

"Such a well-mannered young man," says the woman who was decked out like the sun last time. Today she's in blacks and silvers, with a marvelous shooting-star pin on a sparkly sweater.

"Yes, but he could use a haircut," the lavender-haired woman says too loudly, and Finn's already red face goes redder.

Carla drops her three boxes on the back counter and shakes out her arms afterward, rolling her shoulders. "Morning workout!"

She tries to ruffle Finn's hair as he passes, but he ducks. "Thanks, Finnegan."

"Anytime," he says as he troops downstairs.

"Parker!" Carla says, motioning me over.

I hand Carla my W-4 and references, but she only glances at my paperwork before shoving it in a drawer and leaning conspiratorially forward.

"So these four are from Wild Meadows Retirement Community. They're here as part of an art outreach program."

"Oh, that's nice—" I start, but Carla flaps her hand, motions me closer, and drops her voice to a whisper.

"They fight. All the time. Harriet over there, the one in the green muumuu? She's usually the instigator, but I can assure you Miss Peggy—the one with the purple hair?—she isn't blameless. It's like a grade-school playground. All I need you to do for the morning is to babysit and make sure they don't destroy anything valuable or each other."

A babysitter for old ladies? My face must be betraying my surprise, as Carla pats my hand reassuringly.

"Trust me. I need you up here. The real pottery stuff will come later."

Right then, Finn comes back upstairs and grabs the remaining boxes. I can see the muscles in his arms, and I blush, looking away, meeting Harriet's eyes.

She winks at me.

"Just yell downstairs if there are any customers or if you need me—I'm going to go help Finn." She turns toward the table. "Ladies, I'm leaving Parker in your good hands. Be nice." She looks relieved to leave.

I listen to her follow Finn down the stairs, and I realize I have no clue what to do next.

"Hi?" I say to the ladies.

Harriet snorts, stabbing her paintbrush in black paint. Her bowl's design seems to consist solely of sharp, jagged lines.

"Parker, it's so nice to meet you," says the lavender-haired woman. "I'm Miss Peggy."

The woman with the star pin pats the empty stool beside her. "I'm Lorna. This is Alice," she says, nodding toward the quiet woman.

"And *that's* Harriet," Miss Peggy says.

"Nice to meet you all," I say.

Harriet glares in our direction from across the table.

"What is it you do, Parker?" Miss Peggy asks.

I nearly mention the internship, but I catch myself. "I just graduated. I'm going to Harvard next year. I'm going to be a doctor." As the words leave my mouth, they feel hollow. But what's on the other side feels too empty to begin to contemplate.

"That's very impressive," Miss Peggy says, and Harriet sniffs loudly. Lorna shoots an anxious glance in Miss Peggy's direction, but she seems to have missed it.

"My husband, Leonard, was a dentist," Miss Peggy says. "The hours were hard, but it was worth it, knowing he was making people's lives better."

Out of the corner of my eye, I see Harriet grimace.

Miss Peggy begins listing all the sacrifices she made as a dentist's wife, while Lorna nods sympathetically in response and Harriet ignores all of it.

Alice is in her own world.

While they talk, I study the space around me. There are a few painted objects on the shelves, and I can hear the creek babbling softly through the open window, a hearty laugh from Carla downstairs.

When I got up this morning, Charlie had already left for tutoring. My parents were in the kitchen, Dad in a much better mood than the previous night, both of them discussing the morning's news. I tried to ignore the pangs of guilt in my stomach when they both wished me a good day at my internship.

Miss Peggy's voice brings me back to earth. "In other news, I also heard we're getting a new resident on the second floor."

"Interesting!" Lorna says. "How'd you find that out?"

"I have my sources. And guess what?" She waits, clearly savoring having the knowledge. Even Harriet seems to be leaning slightly closer.

"It's a man. A *widowed* man," she adds.

"Well, that's something!" Lorna says, immediately patting her hair, trying to push the curls into shape.

Harriet shakes her head and points at Miss Peggy. "No one likes a know-it-all."

Miss Peggy rolls her eyes.

"I think Miss Peggy is just sharing some information," I say, somewhat surprised by the unprovoked aggression, but Harriet only shrugs, while Miss Peggy whispers something in Lorna's ear.

Whether it's due to hearing aids, passive-aggressiveness, or a healthy degree of both, it's definitely more of a declaration than a whisper, and I suspect even Carla may hear it: "They clearly cut back on Harriet's meds."

Lorna cringes.

Harriet glares murderously at Miss Peggy, then bellows, "I can *hear* you, asshole!"

My mouth drops open.

"Takes one to know one," Miss Peggy retorts.

At this point, Harriet wags her head at her and slowly draws a finger menacingly across her throat.

Lorna gasps, looking to me for reassurance.

I can't believe these are grown-ups.

"All right," I say. "Enough!"

Everyone looks surprised at my tone, and I feel a little guilty about the ensuing sulky silence, but then I remember this is what I was hired to do—to make sure these ladies don't kill one another.

I turn my attention toward the tiny woman sitting next to me. "How are you doing, Alice?" I ask.

Everything about her is fragile and thin, like a bird. She doesn't respond, just hums softly to herself, smiling at her hands, still folded neatly in her lap.

I pick up a paintbrush, watching to see if she responds, and then reach over and grab the sky-blue paint.

"This color reminds me of your sweater," I say softly to her, holding it up against her vintage cardigan, decorated with tiny pearly seed beads. "And this one"—I pick up a mossy green—"is the same color as your eyes."

I dab the brush in a little bit of the blue. "Is it okay if I paint for you?"

She keeps humming, so I lean over, lightly feathering the rim of the bowl with the brush and the blue paint. "Maybe you can keep this bowl on your dresser for earrings. I like the ones you have on— they remind me of dragonfly wings. Have you seen a dragonfly before? They always seem like characters from a fairy tale, I think."

I continue painting the bowl, careful, slow, light strokes, talking to Alice the entire time, until the edges of it are as bright as a cloudless sky.

"This looks nice, doesn't it?"

I rinse the brush in water and then move to the moss green, creating a solid border around the base. "This color reminds me of the ponds my brother, Charlie, and I used to explore when our family was on vacation in Ludington, Michigan. We'd take the trail with our parents and we'd run ahead, and when we rounded the corner, we'd find these green ponds, filled with lily pads with bright-yellow flowers in the middle. Usually there were turtles sunning themselves on the rocks. Did you ever wander when you were a kid? The world just felt a little more magical back then."

I lean back to assess the colors together, and that's when I register the stillness in the room. None of the other ladies are talking, but next to me Alice is silent as well, no longer humming. Miss Peggy's and Lorna's gazes are directed curiously toward Alice, and even Harriet's expression has softened.

Alice is looking directly at the bowl in my hands, her fingers fluttering excitedly in the air, like bird wings.

I hand her the bowl, and she holds it carefully from the bottom, an expression of deep contentment on her face as she lets the paint dry.

Twenty-Eight

"SO, DID YOU TAKE your PSATs in sophomore year?" Ruby asks as she dumps half a bottle of ketchup on top of her already mustard-and-mayo-drenched fries, then sips her Cherry Coke.

"Yeah, and then again in junior year."

"That's what I'm going to do. I hope I can get a National Merit scholarship like you."

I nod as Ruby begins to outline her SAT strategy as well, and bite into my hot dog.

I have approximately twenty-four minutes left on my lunch break. Much to my relief, there's no sign of Finn yet, the grill at the Float being helmed today by an extremely crabby old man who told Ruby she had to pay for my hot dog. When I offered to pay her back, she flapped her hand at me. "Fred'll get over it. He's all bark and no bite."

It's been almost a week since I started working at Carla's, and this is the first day I've actually had time to eat a real lunch, instead of slapping together a peanut butter sandwich from Carla's mini kitchen in the back room. Lucky for me, when I texted her, Ruby was able to meet last-minute for lunch.

The job has been surprisingly busy. Along with watching over Harriet, Miss Peggy, Lorna, and Alice every other day, I've also gotten to help out with a few mommy/kid painting parties, as well as a raucous group of middle-aged women who were fooling no one when they insisted their plastic bottles were filled with pink lemonade, not rosé.

So far, no one in my family seems to have caught on. But ever since my night on the deck with Charlie, I've been paying more attention to how we talk to one another: Charlie gives one-word answers about tutoring and support group while Mom watches him and chews on her nails until she catches herself. Meanwhile, Dad complains about work, unless he's asking about my internship or drilling Charlie on what he's thinking about baseball next year.

I'm not sure any of us are being our real selves right now.

But when I'm at Carla's, I can breathe. It seems simple, but I like how it feels to help people. I love encouraging the Wild Meadows ladies to paint new things, to go outside of their comfort zones. I love watching how excited the little kids are when they come back to pick up their freshly glazed creations, how they hold their new pieces reverently.

The only not-great part of the new job has been the Casper brothers.

Each afternoon I leave Carla's, I see Johnny leaning against a beat-up old blue Datsun at the edge of the lot, smoking a cigarette or furtively shaking hands with different people, clearly passing things back and forth. He's taken to giving me a two-finger salute when he sees me, nodding his head and grinning.

Two days ago, though, I saw Finn standing across from him. Finn had his apron on, his hair knotted up, and I could see him pointing at Johnny, who was slouched back against the car. It didn't seem like a friendly conversation.

But Finn doesn't seem to be into those much at all. He's been doing his best to avoid me, and when I do see him, he ignores me so hard, so fiercely, it's obvious to everyone within a five-mile radius. Yesterday I overheard Carla, after witnessing one of our exchanges, say to Finn, "I thought you guys were friends?"

I left before I could hear the answer.

Ruby leans forward, interrupting my thoughts.

"So, how long have you wanted to be a doctor?" she asks.

"Since fourth grade," I say, choosing not to explain that the revelation came about after wishing out loud that my sick brother would die. A trickle of sweat makes its way down my back, my legs sticky against the picnic table. "How about you?"

She sits up, her whole face getting smilier—a reality I didn't think was possible. "So, last summer, my church group went down South to volunteer to help the communities hardest hit by the hurricane, and it was totally life-changing. The fact that I could actually help people? I knew then that I wanted to be a doctor more than anything else in the world. I mean, I always knew I was interested in being a doctor, but that solidified it. I never felt so sure about anything in my life."

She's so excited and so passionate, the sun so bright behind her, that it's hard to look at her. I pick at a splinter on the table.

"And then I read this whole profile about the people who started Doctors Without Borders, and it just blew my mind," Ruby continues. "That's what I ultimately want to do. And I feel like if I can get into the best programs, I can make the most difference, you know?"

I give a halfhearted nod.

"Like, don't you get excited thinking about it? How you can work with people and save their lives? It's like being a real-life superhero, but you don't need powers, and . . ."

As she continues to talk about all the amazing things we'll get to do as doctors, for the first time since I wrote that e-mail to Dr. Gambier, I realize that even though I got out of the internship, there's still Harvard, and after that, med school, and after that, the rest of my life.

This summer is only a reprieve.

"I was thinking about trying for a summer internship at one of the hospitals. Didn't I hear you were doing something like that?" Ruby leans forward eagerly.

I look at her open smile and think about Em and how she was right; keeping this secret is lonely. I don't want to lie to Ruby.

I shake my head. "I had one, but it didn't work out. I'm working at a pottery studio instead. But that's a secret."

Ruby looks surprised, and I immediately wonder if I should have told her the truth, because the more people that know, the more chance there is of my secret being blown. But what do I think will happen at the end of the summer? Do I really think I can get away with this for the rest of my life?

"Is this part of . . . ?" She stops, then starts again. "Is that why things were hard at the beginning of the summer, when we met?"

I nod, picking more intently at the picnic table.

"Your parents don't know?"

I shake my head.

"Are you going to tell them?" she asks. She sounds like Em, and I feel myself bristle at the reminder.

"I will. Soon." My voice is sharp. It's a lie, but it's easier than the truth.

"I'm sorry. I shouldn't have pried," she says, clearly embarrassed.

"No, it's not you. I just . . . It's really not a big deal, I promise." I wave my hand, like I can brush the whole thing off.

But I can tell by her uneasy "Okay" that Ruby isn't at all convinced.

"So, tell me more about what you want to focus on in med school," I say, hoping to change the subject.

"Um, I was thinking of focusing on emergency medicine, but then I wonder if I might do more good in something more research based."

She grows more confident when she talks about being a doctor, but as she continues, I feel that familiar hitch in my heart—a feeling I haven't had in the days since I quit that internship, a feeling I was pretty sure I was done with.

This isn't good.

In my head, I start singing a Taylor Swift song, hoping that will calm me down. My hands are hard at work at the splinter on the table as Ruby continues to muse over all the different types of medicine she likes.

"Oh crap, I've done it, haven't I?"

I look up at Ruby, surprised. The expression on her face is stricken.

"Wha—"

She drops her head to her hands, digging her hands in her curls, and lets out a strangled moan. "This is exactly what my mom told me not to do."

"Ruby—"

She lifts her glasses, rubs the bridge of her nose. "I just get so excited about all this stuff and then I talk too much, and I know it's weird and I'm too intense, and my mom keeps reminding me that I need to listen, too."

"No, it's fine—"

"I'm just not good at talking to people sometimes? I totally think it's because I'm the youngest in my class, and even though my parents thought it was fine, I feel like I missed out on something important, like there was some how-to-make-friends phase I skipped over."

She frowns, shaking the ketchup bottle furiously on top of her fries again.

"But—"

"I tried to be friends with this group of girls in my honors classes, but they never invite me to anything. One time I invited them to a study group at my house and I even made cupcakes. But no one came, and then I saw all these Instagram pictures of them hanging out together at the mall. Can you believe it?"

I shake my head, trying to get a word in, but she's on a tear, not paying any attention to the huge glops of ketchup now soaking her paper plate.

"It's not like I wanted to go to the mall anyway. I mean, I don't think I'd want to go to the mall, but it would have been nice to be invited, you know? And this summer I invited Annalise and Mallory to go swimming, but they never even replied, and—"

"Ruby—"

"Maybe there's something wrong with me, like maybe I'll never have friends. Maybe—"

"*Ruby!* Hey!" I gently grab her. "It's okay."

She freezes, her golden-brown eyes meeting mine across the picnic table. "Oh, crap on a Ritz cracker," she whispers.

And then I can't help it—maybe it's the frayed nerves from my own impending freak-out, or that Ruby's finally rendered herself speechless, or maybe it's because it's so hot my float is now just a soupy mix of root beer and congealed ice cream, or maybe it's just the simple reality that this girl across from me cusses more creatively than anyone I've ever met before—I feel a laugh building in me.

I cover my mouth.

Ruby's eyes are wide, and I shake my head. It's like the time Charlie farted in the middle of our great-aunt's funeral and he and I got totally inappropriate giggles—the laughter is a force of its own, rising up, unstoppable and enormous and invincible.

"Crap on a Ritz cracker?" I ask, giggling.

She nods.

"That is amazing," I manage to eke out.

"Really?" Ruby asks, her grin starting to grow.

"I liked it," I say, gasping for breath, "when you called Finn a crap bird too.'"

She giggles. "It's pretty good, right?"

Tears stream out of my eyes, and I clutch my chest.

"I've also called him a turd burglar," she says, half shy, half proud.

This elicits a whole new round of laughter from me, and then Ruby joins in.

"And a fartmeister," she says, giggling.

"Stop," I say. "I can't."

"And His Royal Pain in the Ass, High Prince of Finn-land."

"Oh my God," I gasp. "That doesn't even make any sense!" I drop my head on the table, burying my head in my hands, my shoulders shaking. I haven't laughed so hard since Em left, maybe even longer, and I didn't realize how much I'd missed it until right this second.

When I finally lift my head, Ruby's wiping tears off her face too, and I'm pretty sure they're happy.

Before I can think twice about it, I reach my hand across the table and give hers a quick squeeze. "Those girls are garbage people."

"You think?" she asks, and her face is so vulnerable that I make a decision right then and there.

"Listen, my friend Emerson told me once that she wished I could like myself as much as she likes me."

Ruby sighs. "She sounds like a good friend."

"She is," I say, thinking again of how much I miss her and trying to ignore the twinge of guilt that comes from the fact that I haven't written her back since the day she told me to tell my parents about the internship, that I haven't really wanted to. "That's what friends do—they remind you of who you are underneath all the stuff people believe about you, all that stuff you believe about yourself."

"I need friends like that," Ruby half whispers, and then she flinches. "Oh gosh, I didn't mean to say that out loud."

I remember when I first met Em. It was the summer before second grade, and even though Finn had been gone for months and I had some friends, I still missed him. But then in July, Matty's aunt Marly and his cousin Emerson moved to town, so Matty started bringing Em when he came to hang out with Charlie. Em was mouthy and wild and had a laugh that made me nervous, but she also wanted to see my dollhouse. She made me a beaded friendship bracelet with my name misspelled (Parer) because she couldn't find a *K*. She invited me to a real sleepover. And on the first day of school, she sat with me at lunch. There wasn't even a question—Em had picked me.

I realize now that Ruby needs what I needed back then.

She needs someone to pick her back.

"I'm glad we met," I say.

"Really?"

"Yes. Cross my heart."

She straightens, using a napkin to dry her face, and then stretches her drink out to me. "To being friends!"

"We're toasting?"

"I don't know if you know, but ancient legend has it that a toast on a Cherry Coke and a root-beer float means your friendship will weather every storm."

I laugh. "Really?"

"Yes. And also, Cherry Coke makes everything better."

I don't think I've ever toasted with a root-beer float before, but then again, I don't think I've ever been friends with someone as openhearted as Ruby before. And I'm starting to realize I need her as much as she needs me.

"Friends," I say.

Her big eyes dart to something over my shoulder, and she scowls.

"Ugh. He's back."

I look over my shoulder to see Johnny's rusty blue Datsun pulling into a spot at the far edge of the parking lot. My stomach tightens. Ruby looks over her shoulder and nods to Fred, who's also glaring at Johnny's car from behind the counter.

"You going to call?" she hollers.

He nods, shuffles back into the kitchen.

"Call?" I ask.

"The cops. We don't want Johnny dealing in our lot. Fred's niece is on the force, and anytime we see Johnny here and Finn isn't working, Fred calls his niece, who's always happy to stop by for a free root-beer float."

I must look confused.

"Finn made us swear not to call the cops on his brother, but

Fred and I figure offering his niece food isn't exactly calling the cops on his brother. It just gets them here, and Johnny always leaves as soon as he sees the police car."

I'm afraid of the answer, but I ask anyway. "Why doesn't Finn want you to call the cops on his brother? Is he involved in all that drug stuff too?"

Ruby's quick to shake her head. "Oh God, no. Finn hates it. But Johnny's gotten two strikes already, and a third strike means major jail time. Finn doesn't want that for him. I guess at the end of the day, they're still brothers."

Right then, a police car pulls into the lot.

"Wow, that was fast."

"The station's right around the corner. They could walk, but Fred and I think the car looks more intimidating."

At this point, Johnny's already pulling out of his spot, but as he drives by Ruby and me, he slows his car and leans out the window.

"Hey there, Parker," he says, smacking his lips and making a kissing noise. "Here to see your boyfriend Finn? Can't get enough of the Casper brothers, huh?"

I shudder, but Ruby doesn't hesitate, immediately flipping up both her middle fingers.

Johnny laughs as he drives away.

Ruby turns to me. "What was that all about?"

"It's no big deal," I lie, trying to ignore the way my heart is scrambling for safety inside me.

"Parker, that wasn't nothing. It was super creepy."

"I knew him when we were kids. It's really nothing. I'm sure if

I ignore him, he'll just go away." I realize as I say it that I'm trying to convince myself as much as I am her.

Ruby looks unsatisfied with my answer, but I lean forward. "Can we have lunch again, maybe tomorrow?"

"Yes," she says, grinning, and the smile I return feels like my first genuine one in ages.

Twenty-Nine

MAYBE IT'S THE FACT that the meager air-conditioning at Carla's is no match for the day's humidity, especially with the kiln blazing in the basement. Or maybe it's an effect of their ride over with the new bus driver, who all the ladies think drives too fast. Whatever the reason, when the Wild Meadows crew arrives the next afternoon, Carla lasts about thirty seconds before shooting me a sympathetic look and fleeing back downstairs.

The ladies are in a mood.

I can see the warning signs immediately, like prickly little flashes of heat lightning: Miss Peggy's extra-straight posture, Lorna's anxious hair patting, Harriet's misapplied makeup, Alice's inability to make eye contact with anyone or anything other than the floor.

"Hey, everyone!" I say.

"These paintbrushes are dirty," Miss Peggy says as she sits down, holding up a handful.

"We had a kids' birthday party in here this morning," I say, taking them from her and heading to the sink. "I probably didn't clean this bunch yet."

"You could have cleaned them yourself, Pegs," Harriet points out, and I smile since I couldn't say it myself. But my appreciation for Harriet is short-lived. "Ugh, are we just painting boring old mugs again? I don't need any more mugs. I have mugs coming out of my ears and mouth and—"

I interrupt before she can name any other body parts. "There are also bowls and plates," I offer. "And some cat and dog figurines?"

"We've painted all those already," Lorna says. Today she's decked out in purples—lilacs, lavenders, grapes—with a small delicate violet brooch. "Before you got here. But that's okay. There're always new ways to paint old dogs!" She chuckles appreciatively at her joke and grabs one of the dog figurines. "Get it? New ways? Old dogs?"

I smile weakly, but Harriet rolls her eyes and even Miss Peggy seems offended by how bad the joke is. Lorna immediately deflates.

"Boring," Harriet mumbles, tapping her fingers on the table, and I wonder if she's always been this rude, or if she's just letting it all out now that she's older and no one's stopping her. "Dying of boredom here."

"We should only be so lucky," Miss Peggy declares, snatching the newly cleaned brushes out of my hands.

God, these two are being awful. I suck in my breath, choosing to ignore them, and sit next to Alice instead.

"How about we work on this one?" I ask her, holding up a smiling ceramic flower and grabbing some bright-yellow paint. She looks harder at the floor, but I pick up the brush and start painting the petals anyway.

After ten minutes, the atmosphere in the room has gotten worse. Sure, Lorna is painting, carefully biting her lip as she coats her dog statue in an electric-blue color, but Alice seems to be getting smaller and more withdrawn by the second, actively shrinking from me each time I show her the smiling flower. Harriet has fallen asleep and is loudly snoring. Miss Peggy still hasn't settled on a paintbrush, drying each one by hand and then holding it up to the light, insisting, "It's very hard to work with substandard equipment."

It pretty much stinks.

I scowl at the smiling yellow flower I'm painting and set it down on the table.

Right then, Harriet bolts awake and belts out, loudly and off-key, the opening lyrics to "Piano Man" by Billy Joel.

The interruption startles all of us.

Lorna's hand jerks in surprise, and blue paint accidentally spatters across the dog's face. She mutters "Drats!" right as Miss Peggy drops a handful of paintbrushes on the table. Even Alice jumps in place, the outburst is so unexpected.

". . . play us your songs right now . . ."

"Oh, Harriet, honestly," Lorna says, looking sadly at her ruined dog.

Miss Peggy shakes her head. "Her voice is going to give me a migraine."

"Harriet, can you please sing more quietly?" I ask.

She ignores all of us, crooning, "We're all in the blue for your memories . . ."

"Those aren't even the right words!" Miss Peggy cries.

". . . and you left us wanting you all night!" Harriet bellows, sweeping her hand dramatically across the table, knocking my smiling yellow flower onto the floor, where it breaks in half.

"Oh no," Lorna says, sounding so dismayed as I pick up the pieces, I'm worried she might actually start crying.

Miss Peggy looks smugly at me, like, *See? I told you she was trouble.*

Harriet seems slightly chagrined. "I can glue it back together—"

"Argh, enough!" I stand, grabbing my phone, and walk hastily over to the stereo. I find a USB cord on the side and plug in my phone.

I can practically feel the ladies watching me through my back, waiting to see what I'm going to do next, but I don't turn around, instead scrolling through iTunes until I find the playlist I put together for Dad's birthday last year. It's big-band music, but as I'm guessing no one in this room is a Taylor Swift fan, it's the closest thing I have to anything they might like.

I hit play.

"Sing Sing Sing" by Benny Goodman starts playing, punchy and lively. I don't always love Dad's eclectic tastes, but this song makes me want to move, to tap and shake my hands and dance.

I turn around. "Paint this."

"What?" Harriet wrinkles her face.

"You're bored? Paint this. Paint this music. Go on. Let the music dictate your choices."

Lorna looks helplessly at her dog. "You can keep painting that, Lorna, if you want. But the two of you?" I point to Harriet and Miss Peggy. "My grandma used to say only boring people get bored."

As soon as the words leave my mouth, I worry I've gone too far. Even though they're not acting like it, these are grown ladies, not the Delaney boys, and I can't imagine Carla would take kindly to the rest home withdrawing their business because I'm being a disrespectful jerk.

But then, much to my surprise, Miss Peggy sits up straighter and pushes her sleeves back, like she's rising to the challenge. She picks out a thin brush and a magenta paint and then begins to sweep lively loops all over a plate.

Lorna returns to painting her dog, contentedly humming as she works the misplaced splash across the face into the design.

Alice has closed her eyes, but there's a small smile on her face as the music dances through the room.

And then I look over at Harriet, who's nodding appreciatively at me, tapping her hand on the table with the beat. "Not bad work at all, girl," she says, before picking up a paintbrush and an empty mug.

I fall back in the chair, exhausted with the close call, but feeling strangely proud of Harriet's compliment. Not bad work at all.

Thirty

"I'LL TAKE TWO CHEESE Coneys, mustard, but no onions, and water," Ruby tells the waitress.

"A Three-Way, dry, and a Diet Pepsi," I add.

Last night, when my parents mentioned that they were attending an outdoor concert of Broadway's Greatest Hits in Sharon Woods tonight and wouldn't be home for dinner, I texted Ruby to see if she was free to grab Skyline Chili with me. She texted back with an immediate My parents are going to the same concert and this gives me the perfect reason not to go with them, which is good because Broadway show tunes are so earnest, they make me embarrassed, so YES YES YES!!!

The waitress drops off a bowl of oyster crackers for each of us, and Ruby turns back to me. "Harriet and Miss Peggy *both* liked the big-band music?"

"Yeah. Turns out I might have accidentally discovered the one thing in the world they agree on. I don't know if Lorna is as big a fan, but she seemed happy no one was fighting."

"That's a really cool idea. How did the lady with Alzheimer's do? Alice, right?"

"That's the most amazing part. She actually picked up a paintbrush for the first time since I started! Her hand was shaky, but I helped her steady it, and she made all these tiny dots across a plate."

"Parker, that's really cool," Ruby says, popping an oyster cracker in her mouth.

I try not to grin too hard, but she's right—it's the coolest thing I've been part of in ages. After the ladies left today, Carla told me, "You have a real knack for working with them, Parker."

I wish I could tattoo her words on my arm, a reminder for when I'm not sure what I'm doing. Even now, two and a half hours later, my limbs still feel buoyant.

"How was the Float today?" I ask.

"It was okay. Finn's been in a super-crappy mood lately, so that's not fun. But he's been asking about—" She stops as she looks up behind me. "Um, hi?"

I turn around to find my brother standing there.

"Oh, hey," I say.

He nods awkwardly, and the two of us don't say anything further, until Ruby extends her hand. "I'm Ruby," she says.

"Charlie McCullough," Charlie says, shaking her hand back. "Parker's brother."

I wait for Ruby's face to register who he is, the subsequent face-fall of sympathy, but she brightly smiles, squeezing his hand instead.

"If you're half as cool as your sister, I like you already."

Charlie blushes.

That I did not expect.

"Well, I'll see you at home," I start to say to him, but Ruby's a step ahead of me.

"Are you eating by yourself?"

"Getting takeout," Charlie says.

"Why don't you join us? That's okay with you, right, Parker?" She turns to me, her smile as big as it was the night I met her.

I frown. I don't want to disappoint Ruby, but considering Charlie's and my exchanges of late have been downright nuclear, the last thing I want to do right now is hang out with him.

But Charlie's got this look on his face that I haven't seen in a while—he actually seems nervous I'll say no.

He *wants* to join us.

"Yeah, okay," I say, and it takes approximately two seconds for him to slide into the booth next to me.

Charlie smells sweaty and he's taking up too much space, and I immediately regret my decision. He leans over and grabs a huge handful of the oyster crackers from my bowl.

The waitress comes by again. "Something for you, too, hon?"

"A Five-Way, please," Charlie says to her.

She nods and heads back to the kitchen area.

Charlie starts his ritual of intricately dripping hot sauce into a partially cracked oyster cracker and then eating it.

"Do you go to our high school?" Ruby asks him.

Charlie swallows. "I'm going to be a senior next year. You?"

"Junior. But I'm 'young for my class,'" she says, making ironic finger quotes. "I'm taking my driver's license test at the end of the summer."

"Well, when the time comes, I hope you're a better driver than Parker," Charlie says.

"Why? What happened?" Ruby asks, looking between us.

Oh, for God's sake. "Our parents are terrible teachers. And learning on a stick is impossible," I say, indignation making my voice louder than I want.

"She's not good at not being good at something," Charlie whispers to Ruby, who giggles.

I scowl.

"After she applied the clutch too hard one too many times, our dad took the keys and left her in the car because Parker was making him carsick. And our mom, who's a teacher, mind you, said she never met anyone who was worse at learning something," Charlie says.

"Dad was being a jerk and Mom kept yelling at me. That's not a productive learning environment."

"It sounds hard for everyone," Ruby says diplomatically.

"Meanwhile, I learned in about five minutes and passed the test a full month and a half before her," Charlie says. "I'm clearly a natural."

"Wait a minute. Why did you take yours at the same time?" Ruby asks.

"Twins," I say, making room on the table as the waitress brings us our food.

"No way," Ruby says, looking rapidly from me to Charlie and back again.

"She got the brains. I got the looks," Charlie says, and Ruby giggles.

I realize with a shock that Charlie is flirting. I've never seen him flirt before. It's totally irritating and gross.

But the chili smells delicious, so I twirl a big mess of spaghetti and cheese and meat sauce around my fork, trying to ignore Charlie.

All three of us are happily eating, when Ruby stops, Cheese Coney in hand. "Wait. If you're twins, how come you're a senior but Parker graduated?"

I swallow quickly, not wanting Charlie to have to explain, but he gets to it first. "I got sick last fall and I missed a lot of school, so they held me back. It was going to be just a half year, but it took longer than we thought for the treatment to work."

"Sick?" Ruby asks.

My whole body tenses, and Charlie gives a terse nod.

"Leukemia," he says.

"Whoa. That stinks," Ruby says.

"I'm better now, though," Charlie adds quickly.

Ruby's sprinkling oyster crackers on top of her Cheese Coney, and I can see Charlie stiffen, waiting for her response. Finally, she looks up. "It'd be cool to be friends with a senior next year. If you see me in the halls, you won't pretend you don't know me, will you?"

Charlie's smile is genuine. "I don't think I could forget you," he says.

"Well, that's good news," she replies matter-of-factly, but underneath all her cool, she's beaming as hard as Charlie.

Even though I'm totally irritated with everything Charlie-related right now, I have to stop myself from hugging Ruby Collie right then and there. I haven't seen him like this in ages.

"So, do you want to be a doctor like Parker?" she asks Charlie.

"God, no!" he says. I'm surprised by how vehement he is. "I've had enough of hospitals to last me the rest of my life. I don't know how she can stand that internship."

Ruby shoots an uncertain look at me, and I subtly shake my head. She recovers quickly. "What do you want to do, then?"

Charlie opens his mouth, but nothing comes out.

"Baseball," I say. "Charlie's a phenomenal pitcher."

"Not anymore. I'm too out of practice for the recruitment camps this summer."

"That doesn't mean you couldn't still get on a team next year—" I start, but Charlie interrupts me.

"I don't know if I want to do that anymore."

"What?" I ask. "But it's what you've always wanted to do!"

"Where was all this support last summer, Parker? I didn't really have an option in my future then, did I?" Charlie asks, and I look away, my face flushing.

"Well, maybe it's time to make it an option again," Ruby says.

My stomach does a little somersault.

Charlie scoffs. "It's not that simple."

"It totally is," she replies.

I give her a warning glance, but she's not watching me. Instead, she's using the last bit of her bun to soak up the chili grease on her plate.

Charlie shakes his head, but Ruby jumps in before he gets a chance to say anything more.

"Did you know that in Spanish, the future tense also works to express possibility in the now?"

I slowly shake my head, and Charlie looks confused.

"It works like our future tense, like *Trabajaré este sábado*—'I will work this Saturday.' But you can also use it to wonder now—*¿Quién será el?* 'I wonder who he could be.'

"I like thinking of time that way—that it's a little more fluid in Spanish. Like maybe to start thinking about the future, you need to think about the possibility in the right now, you know?" Ruby looks first to Charlie for a reaction, then to me, but Charlie's face is skeptical, and I'm sure I look equally flummoxed.

Ruby immediately deflates, her whole body cringing. "Oh God, sorry. I'm doing that thing I do."

"What's that?" Charlie asks.

"Nothing," she mumbles. "Forget I brought up the Spanish stuff. I'm sorry."

"Ruby," I say.

Her eyes meet mine. "I know I'm too much for people sometimes. Even my mom says so." She tries to smile, like it's not a totally terrible thing for a mom to say to her kid, then sucks in her breath and straightens. "Anyway, subject change, like I was saying earlier, Finn's been asking all about—"

"Hey—" Charlie starts to say, but the look on Ruby's face is desperate. She wants to change the subject.

I bite. "What was he asking about?"

She lets out a grateful little sigh. "You."

"Who's Finn?" Charlie asks.

"No one," I say too quickly.

Charlie perks up, smirking, and I mentally curse myself. "Doesn't sound like no one," he says.

"He works in the kitchen at the Float," Ruby says. "You probably know him. Finn Casper?"

I hold my breath, hoping he doesn't remember.

"Finn *Casper*?" Charlie says, shooting me a disbelieving look. "The one who broke your wrist?"

Rats.

"Hold on, what?" Ruby asks.

"He didn't break my wrist," I say. "His brother, Johnny, did."

"But didn't he get expelled for attacking a teacher?" Charlie asks.

"Again: his brother."

Charlie lets out his breath in a scoff. "Come on. Finn's still a Casper. Wasn't their dad in jail for running a meth lab?"

"I don't know," I say, purposefully focusing on my bowl of chili.

Ruby gives me a doubtful look before turning back to Charlie. "When he's not being an asshat, Finn's actually a really good person. It sucks he has the family he does, but he's more than just them."

Charlie ignores her, focused on me. He lets out a smug chuckle. "This is amazing. My perfect little sister's associating with the Caspers."

I fix him with a furious glare. "I'm not perfect. And I'm not associating with Finn Casper!"

Ruby looks surprised. "You and Finn aren't friends?"

"We are," I start.

But Charlie snickers, muttering to himself. "'Not perfect'? As if."

"What does that mean?"

"Four point oh? Weekends spent cramming for the SATs? Harvard? Scholarships? Future doctor? Never once disappointing Mom and Dad? Your noble, noble life?"

If he only knew about the internship, about the e-mail Em sent me telling me to tell my parents, about the way my eyelid twitches and my heart races.

"That's not true," I say, but he ignores me, turning to Ruby.

"Sometimes I wonder if I'm the real kid and Parker's the cyborg version, the one our parents ordered from a factory, customized with 'good grades and a friendly disposition'!"

Ruby smiles awkwardly, and Charlie takes it as encouragement, getting even more animated, adopting an infomercial voice.

"Our Parker four-point-oh model does her chores, has excellent manners, and never ever talks back. Plus, she has a four-point-oh average, hence the name!" He winks.

"Shut up," I say.

"Parker four-point-oh model is the perfect child to make all your parenting dreams come true!"

"Stop it."

"And don't worry, kids. Parker four-point-oh will always do the right thing, no matter whose future it screws up."

"Well, have you ever thought I'm this way because you got cancer?" I snap, then stop, surprised at the words that just came out of my mouth.

Charlie lets out a slow whistle between his teeth, shaking his head, satisfied. "Finally, there it is. After all these years, a glitch in the system. Honesty."

"You're being an asshole."

"At least I'm being an honest one. You should try it sometime."

Ruby glances between us, tapping her fingers uneasily on the table, her bracelets chiming, and then she must make a decision, because she leans toward Charlie, holding out the bottle of hot sauce.

"Tell me, what do you do with this again?"

Charlie looks like he's not done with me, but Ruby shakes the bottle so insistently at him, it's clear he doesn't have a choice. He sighs and begins an elaborate demonstration of how you find the ideal oyster cracker and add the perfect amount of sauce. Ruby tries the concoction, her nose wrinkling up.

"Why in the world would you *want* to do that?" she asks, after gulping down half her glass of water.

"You're kidding me, right?" Charlie asks.

I only half listen to Charlie enumerating all the reasons eating oyster crackers with hot sauce is awesome and then Ruby sharing all her counter-reasons for why it violates the "sacred integrity of the oyster cracker."

I'm not hungry anymore.

Instead, I'm too busy thinking about the words I just said, the unbidden truth in them.

It's like when you surprise a flock of birds, how they swoop out of rafters and eaves in a wave of flustered feathers, half squawks, how they leave you standing there, heart startled and terrified, as they take flight.

Thirty-One

THE NEXT DAY, MY shift at Carla's is quiet. The ladies from Wild Meadows Retirement Community have a field trip to see the butterfly exhibit at Krohn Conservatory, and the kids' birthday party I was supposed to supervise canceled late yesterday. I offered to stay home in case Carla didn't need me, but much to my happiness, she insisted I come in anyway.

Each day, I love being at Carla's more and more. And it's not just the fact that no one there calls me Dr. McCullough or that my eyelid never twitches when I'm around the Wild Meadows ladies. It's more that Carla's feels like home, a place where my shoulders aren't tight, where I laugh without thinking about it, where I can simply breathe.

After I finish dusting and straightening the front room, I sit at the counter for a second, watching the dust motes in the sun coming through the room, then reread the e-mail I got from Em last night.

Park, so I haven't written you back since you told me you were a grown-up and I shouldn't worry about you, as I figured I pissed you off and you needed some space. But I miss you too much to give you any more space, so here I am! Seriously, I'm sorry if my advice rubbed you the wrong way. I still think you should tell your parents (sorry not sorry), but I will try not to push you on it. That being said, I cannot promise I will stop worrying, because you are my best friend and I want good things for you and that's just how I'm wired. But please know that whatever you decide, I'm here for you no matter what, okay?

Things here are good. We've been hiking in the Lake District. I know! I'm all naturey now! Do you remember when we read that Wordsworth poem in Mr. Fontana's English class about the lake and the sublime? At the time, I thought, "Ugh, another white guy poet," and I *still* maintain that our syllabus that semester was crap, but being here, I kind of get part of it now. It's otherworldly. This morning I got up and sat *by the lake and just sketched. There was mist coming off the lake and I honestly expected a sword to rise out of the water, like it was Excalibur. It was totally badass.*

Also, maybe, just maybe, I met a very nice Scottish girl named Tamsin who is also backpacking through Europe this summer and is going to school at Indiana University next year and perhaps we might have made out a little bit before promising to stay in touch when she moves to the States this fall.

Maybe.

(Actually, totally. She is gorgeous. And smart. And kind. I think you'd like her.)

Please write back and let me know you're okay, that we're okay.

Miss you bunches,
E.

PS: Matty says hi to you and Charlie. Evidently, Charlie e-mailed him and the two of them are getting along again? Who knows. Boys are weird.

PPS: Your parents will love you no matter what.

I don't know how to respond.

I wish she'd stop pushing me to talk with Mom and Dad.

If she really trusted me, like she says, she'd drop it.

I let out a frustrated sigh, deleting her e-mail, and then decide to see what Carla's up to.

I make sure the register is locked before I call out her name down the steps.

"Come on down, Parker," she calls.

I walk carefully down the narrow basement steps.

The studio downstairs is a completely different world from the one upstairs. While the main room is bright and cluttery, crowded with shelves of white to-be-painted ceramics, this room is shady and cool and organized, eight pottery wheels accompanied by stools arranged in a half circle in the space, the door in the back opening directly to a patch of grass in front of the creek. I see a picnic table out there covered with lumps of clay drying in the sun.

Carla's currently hunched over one of the wheels, a lump of wet red clay smacking against her hands as the wheel spins.

Her arms push strong against the clay—I can see her muscles working as she shapes the mess. She lifts her hands, sprinkles water over the clay, and then drills a finger down the middle, opening it up.

She sees me, nudges her head toward an empty stool.

I can't take my eyes away from the wheel spinning.

"How long have you been doing this?" I ask.

"Since freshman year of high school. Art elective. But I loved it so much, I took it all four years and fit it in through college, too."

"Did you start the studio after college?"

"Oh no. I majored in business, got a job as an account manager at Proctor and Gamble after graduation, and rented a wheel through a space downtown. But about seven years ago, my dad passed away and left me some money. Finn and his brother had just moved out, and I was feeling out of sorts, so after talking with my husband, I decided to try opening a studio of my own. I quit P and G, got a business loan, covered the rest with all of my savings. It did better than I hoped, and this spring I decided to find a bigger space. And here I am."

Carla's fingers are so light against the clay right now, they're barely touching it.

"I didn't know Finn lived with you," I say.

"He didn't tell you how we met?"

I shake my head.

She straightens, turning the wheel off. It slows to a stop, leaving a large bowl, its graceful walls rising like arms welcoming the sun. Her eyes meet mine. "My husband and I fostered Finn and his brother for two and a half years, while their dad was serving time. Finn was six when he moved in, Johnny was eleven. For two and a half years, those boys were ours." She smiles wistfully. "Johnny hated every single day, but I still would have adopted him if I could. And Finn? Letting him move back in with his dad was the hardest thing I've ever done." She sighs. "So, I put all that love into my own pottery place. Speaking of, you ready to try?"

I want to ask her more, but it doesn't feel like it's my place.

"Try what?" I ask.

"Throwing some clay."

"But don't you need me to do some work? Like cleaning or . . . ?" My eyes sweep the room.

Carla rolls her eyes good-naturedly. "Parker, this is still work, you know. Besides, it's good for you to know how to do this, in case I need you to watch a studio class for me someday. Come on. Grab an apron, and let me show you how to wedge the clay."

I follow her to a smooth counter in the back, where we each scoop out handfuls of red clay from a bucket. She shows me how to knead the lump over and over, folding it in on itself. The clay is cool against my hands, leaving a brownish-red tint on my palms.

"You have to work any potential air bubbles out of the clay. They can threaten the stability of what you're throwing," she says.

When both piles of clay meet her approval, she digs through a jar of tools, handing me a few, as well as a sponge and a bucket. "You can borrow these, though someday you can get your own set."

She points me to a wheel, and I sit down as she hands me a removable round plate called a bat to put on top of my wheel. She grabs the stool next to me, takes her huge lump of clay, and throws it down hard right in the center of her own bat, the clay making a thick thwacking sound. She pinches the edges onto the surface.

"Try it," Carla says.

I move my clay from hand to hand and then let it fall.

"Harder. You're giving it its foundation. You want it to be a good, stable one."

I throw it with force this time, pleased with the satisfying smack it makes.

"Good!"

Carla wets her clay with water from the bucket. "You ready?" She starts the wheel spinning slowly and leans over and puts her hands in a V around the clay. "It comes from your shoulders, not your hands."

She begins walking me through what she calls centering—getting the clay evenly weighted on the wheel through pushing and shaping—and then beginning to turn the lump into a bowl.

I try to follow her directions.

"Slow down your wheel," she says. "And when you pull up the walls, don't let your wrists touch. Push hard with the left hand, use the bend of your index finger on the right."

My hands are covered in muddy wet clay, my arms, too.

I'm pretty sure I'm doing it all wrong.

It's weird, the feeling of my hands against the clay, how my fingers seep into the messiness. I've always hated for my hands to be dirty—I hate syrup on pancakes because it makes my fingers sticky; I hate manicures because it feels like there's dirt I can't see underneath the bright colors.

Charlie's the exact opposite—or at least he used to be. When he was a kid, he loved playing in dirt. He went through an entire stage where he thought if he dug hard enough, long enough, he could reach China. Then he gave up and began digging for buried treasure. Dad wasn't pleased when he found the holes all over the backyard.

I always watched from the porch, because the few times I did help out, I couldn't shake the feeling of mess on my clothes and skin, the disorder in the previously smooth green yard.

This is a similar feeling, but surprisingly, I don't totally hate it.

Sure, my hands are covered in glop, and I'm grateful I can periodically wipe them on the apron. But I'm so focused on the wheel, the constant calming hum of the spin, my arms strong in front of me, that when I finally do pause, I realize I haven't thought once about the internship or worried about Charlie.

The quiet in my mind feels like a certified miracle.

I look over and admire Carla's creation. Her bowl is sturdy and graceful at the same time—something of dirt and earth made light and lovely.

But before I can even compliment hers, one of the sides on my bowl completely flops over, the walls collapsing inward on themselves.

"Crud," I mutter, turning the wheel off, my eyelid giving a warning twitch. I don't want to seem ungrateful that she taught me in the first place, so I shrug and smile. "Clearly, a career as a potter isn't in my future."

"Parker McCullough, are you seriously giving up after the first try? I think it took me about one hundred tries before I ever threw something worth firing. And then I picked an ugly glaze and didn't apply it well."

She points to a small crooked bowl sitting in a spot of honor amid other beautifully glazed vases and dishes.

It looks like the sad runt of that litter.

"High school art class, 1992. The first bowl I ever successfully threw. No matter what stuff I throw today, that one will always be my favorite. Go on. Go look at it."

I walk over and pick it up, careful not to knock into either the green-hued bowl that's the color of April leaves or the luminous fluted blue vase on either side of it.

Carla's old bowl is glazed brownish red, and the bottom is super heavy. One side is thicker than the other, and the glaze on the inside isn't consistent, spots where it didn't stick showing speckled stoneware underneath. There's a chunk missing from the corner and several big cracks running around the base, like it was glued back together at some point.

"This is your favorite?" I ask, unable to help myself.

Carla nods. "We all have to start somewhere. That little pot was the beginning of my love affair. Besides, it's got character, don't you think? If it came to life in a Disney movie, some cantankerous old-man actor would definitely voice it."

"But it'd still have a heart of gold?" I ask, smiling.

"Indeed."

I let my finger run over the rough edges of the bowl, wondering what it'd be like to make a mistake and let myself love it.

Thirty-Two

AS SOON AS THEY open the gates at Kings Island Amusement Park, Ruby breaks into a half walk/half run, dodging around some families with small kids and jogging backward to make sure Charlie and I are following her.

"If we hurry, we might be able to be first in line for the first ride of the day on the Beast!" she says. "Come on, this way. We can totally beat the crowd!"

Right then Ruby reminds me of Em and how sometimes she gets so excited it's like her body can't even begin to contain all the possibility in the world around her.

For Ruby, evidently, that possibility is roller coasters.

I look over at Charlie, irritated all over again that he's crashing my hangout time with Ruby.

This morning, when I was waiting outside on the porch for

Ruby's mom to pick me up, Charlie came out, swinging Mom's keys.

"You ready?"

"Ready for what?"

"To go pick up Ruby?"

"Her mom's picking me up. And since when do you care?"

"Since I'm driving you to pick her up, and we're all going to Kings Island together. She invited me to join."

I fixed him with a disgusted look. "You're kidding me, right?"

"Nope. I'm serious as death right now. Which, you know, I know all about, because—"

I held up my hand, cutting him off, and walked to the car.

When we got to Ruby's, I gladly relinquished shotgun, using any chance I could to glare at Charlie from the backseat while Ruby outlined her roller coaster plan: spending the day trying to ride the first seat in all of the park's roller coasters.

So here we are now, weaving around families, following Ruby through the crowd, and I'm convinced the whole day is a loss.

But then, in our haste to keep up with her, Charlie nearly runs smack into a group of preteen girls, and they giggle when he bows in apology. He turns and shoots me a smile before jogging to catch up with Ruby.

It stops me in my tracks.

Charlie just smiled at me.

There was no irritation there, no hidden agenda. Just my brother smiling at me without thinking twice. It's such a small thing, but it's also big as the universe.

And the thing that's even weirder is I'm pretty sure I smiled back.

Maybe it's not so terrible that he's here today after all.

Sure, it's not great. It's not what I wanted.

But maybe it's not terrible.

I feel good until we reach the nonexistent line for the Beast. Ruby is downright gleeful as she tears through the winding path toward the front of the coaster, scooting into the line for the first seat behind two men holding hands, and beckoning me to join her.

Crap. I didn't think this through.

I haven't been on a roller coaster since the summer before third grade. I was so scared, I started shrieking before the ride even pulled out of the station. Em tried to calm me down, but I wasn't having it, and the teenagers working the booth had to stop the ride and let me get out before the train left the station.

I thought I'd be fine by now, but looking at the tracks in front of me, I realize I seriously overestimated my ability to get over it. I have no desire to ride this roller coaster.

I look up at Ruby to confess, but she's bouncing on her toes.

"I'm so excited to do this with you guys. I have wanted to ride the first seat on every coaster for ages." She motions us into a huddle. "I have no clue how these people beat us here," she says in a too-loud whisper, pointing to the couple in front of us in the turnstile. "I really thought we'd be the first seat on the first ride of the day."

I shoot an anxious smile at the couple, but if they've heard, they don't seem to care, the taller man leaning down to kiss his partner. "You'll be fine," he says.

His partner looks like he might throw up before even getting on the ride.

I want to take that guy's hand and pull him right out of the line, so the two of us can make a break for it.

A rickety old car pulls into the station, the turnstiles open, and the guys in front of us file in. An employee starts checking to make sure everyone's safety bars are secure.

"You should take off your glasses," the worker says to the nervous guy. "Don't want to lose them along the way. Want us to hold them?"

As the guy hands them over, I turn to Ruby.

"So, I think maybe I'll wait for you guys—" I start, right as the employee raises his hand in an all clear and the train takes off.

Ruby doesn't hear me over the noise of the train. "Did you guys know the Beast is the longest wooden roller coaster in the United States? There are other smoother rides, but this one is a classic."

Smoother?

"I've actually never been on it," Charlie replies.

"*What?* I'm so excited for you!" Ruby yells, leaning over and squeezing Charlie's arm, then dropping it almost as quickly. "When was the last time you rode a coaster?"

"When we were kids. Before I got sick, right, Parker? It was the kids' one. I think it was called the Fairly Odd Coaster." Charlie looks to me. "Wasn't that the time you started to get on but you were crying?"

I frown, shaking my head.

"That coaster's still here," Ruby says, right as an empty set of cars pulls in front of us. "I think they call it Woodstock Express now. Or maybe that was the name last year? Whatever it's called, we'll hit it later."

"But isn't it for kids?" Charlie asks.

"Oh, we're doing them *all*," she assures us.

I look for the guy with the glasses, but the car in front of us is empty, and maybe every single person flew out of their seats and isn't coming back, but then I feel a slight nudge on my shoulder, Charlie bending down close to my ear so Ruby doesn't hear.

"They run two trains at a time," he says. "The first group is still in the middle of their ride."

"Oh, yeah, of course. I knew that," I say quickly, even though I didn't.

Ruby climbs into the front seat and carefully puts her glasses into a case and then into her purse, then shoves her purse on the floor of the car. Charlie hops into the seat behind her, riding by himself. I look down at both of them, my feet frozen on the wood platform.

I don't know why I can't just tell them I don't want to ride the coaster.

But the words are stuck in my throat.

The employee is checking all the bars and moving toward the front of the ride, and I still don't move.

"Parker?" Ruby asks.

"I don't. I can't."

The employee stops at our cars. "Are you getting on?"

"I just think, maybe, I don't . . . ," I stammer.

"Here," Charlie says, half standing, patting the seat next to him. "It'll be okay. Sit here."

I hesitate for a second, but Charlie meets my eyes. "You got this."

Shaky, I climb in next to him, my legs already sticky with nervous sweat against the vinyl seat, watching as he lowers the padded safety bar against our legs.

Charlie leans forward to Ruby. "You okay by yourself?"

She nods happily. "Oh yeah. I'm ready."

I grip the safety bar in front of me as the train starts to move onto the old wooden track, everything clunking and knocking like it has arthritis.

My hands are knuckle-locked around the bar, like they were during my valedictorian speech. I try to breathe as the train begins to ascend the first hill.

"Don't throw up on me," Charlie says, and I'm tempted to snap, *Vomiting is the least of my worries*, but then I see his face and realize he's trying to calm me down, so I force out a strained smile.

"I'll try to angle it over the side."

We move up the big hill slowly and steadily, and I look enviously at the emergency steps running parallel with the track, wondering if there's anything I could do to stop the train at this point and then make my way down.

I venture a look below. Everything is getting smaller by each second—trees, houses, buildings, lives.

Ruby pokes her head between the seats. "How are things back there?"

"What do you say, Parker?" Charlie asks. "You doing okay?"

I know he's asking about riding the roller coaster, but the question could apply to so much more.

I want to tell him I'm terrified of becoming a doctor.

I want to tell him that I'm even more terrified of not becoming one.

I want to tell him that everything is a mess, that I hate the in-between space, that my feet ache for the ground, that a very small, very scared part of me wants to touch the sky, and that that is maybe the worst thing of all.

The train starts to slow as it gets near the top of the hill.

"I don't know," I finally say, which is the truth.

Charlie puts his hand on top of mine, holding it tight, anchoring me. "It's okay. I got you now, okay? I got you," he says.

I look over. It's the first time he's had my back in ages, the first time he's tried, the first time I've let him. I nod. "Okay," I say.

For one agonizing second, it feels like we actually stop at the peak, the train poised between the past and the future, and then the first seat starts to tilt over, and both of Ruby's hands shoot straight up, and then our car is at the top, and I gulp hard, looking at my hands, and it's still there, Charlie's left hand clasped on top of my right, keeping me from flying away.

I squeeze my eyes shut, and we fly down, down, down, so fast, and I open my eyes, and the world is a blur around us, the seats shaking on the wooden track, the wind blowing fast and strong, and my mouth pulls back in a smile, because Charlie's not going to let me go, and it all feels familiar then, my brother's hand on mine and the soaring feeling—a feeling I thought I never had—the memory of wings.

Thirty-Three

WHILE WE'RE WAITING FOR Charlie to bring our LaRosa's pizza, Ruby and I watch the Diamondback coaster glide down the hill, all power and momentum, slicing through the surface of the lake below it, water splashing everywhere.

"I want to do that one next," she says.

"White Water Canyon," I remind her.

Since riding the Beast this morning, we've tackled the Banshee, the Racer, and the Vortex roller coasters. While the lines for each have gotten longer as the day's gone on, the rides have also been a little less scary each time. Turns out, roller coasters make me laugh, which isn't the worst thing. That being said, the upside-down loops on the Vortex left me feeling both queasy and hungry, and as the day is getting progressively warmer, rather than going straight to another coaster, I insisted we stop for food and then a nice hill-free water ride.

"All right, all right. I guess we have time for something else," she says with an enormous dramatic sigh. She looks over her shoulder for Charlie, then leans closer. "So what's the deal with you and Finn?"

"Nothing. There's no deal," I say.

"You came looking for him that night at the Float, and then next thing I know, you're not 'associating' with him," she says, doing finger quotes.

"It's more like he's not associating with me," I say. "He doesn't want anything to do with me."

Ruby rolls her eyes. "Oh my God, you guys are both such dork-wads."

"Hey! What does that mean?"

"He said the same thing when I asked him about you. He said you blew him off."

"That's totally not true!"

"He said the last time you talked, you couldn't get away from him fast enough."

I try to remember our encounter at the Float and shake my head. "Not him. Johnny."

Ruby straightens. "Did something happen?"

I shrug.

"Was it more of that crap he pulled the other day with you in the parking lot?"

I don't answer.

"Parker, you should tell Finn."

"No, it's fine. Besides, it was more than that. Finn also got super weird when I gave him a gift certificate, going on about charity."

I stop.

Kids in our class used to say Finn got his clothes from the lost-and-found box, that he never had any money for lunch.

Charity is the last thing he wants from me.

"Crap," I say, burying my head in my hands.

"What?" Ruby asks, but I just shake my head.

"Listen," she continues. "Maybe give the friendship thing another chance. I know I complain about him. But he's like my brother. He can be really thoughtful when you need a friend."

Her words remind me of how quickly he came to my rescue the day he picked me up from the hospital, how he adjusted the air vents in his truck so all the cool air would blow my way.

"One day when I just started working at the Float, all those girls from my honors class came in, the ones I was trying to be friends with?" Ruby nervously moves one of the twenty silver bracelets she's wearing back and forth on her wrist. "They had just come from prom and were with their dates, and it took them, like, five minutes to even realize they knew me. But I'm pretty sure Finn took extra-long with their orders because he could tell I was upset."

Of course he did.

"Finn Casper is actually a really good person, though if you ever tell him I said that, I will deny it to my dying day. Besides, he keeps asking if you're doing okay, and I'm tired of answering for you."

"Why wouldn't I be doing okay?" I ask, even though I know exactly what he's referring to.

She takes a steadying breath and then looks me straight in the face, and in the sunlight, I can see the specks of amber glinting gold in her eyes. "Truth time? Maybe it's because you haven't told any-one in your family that you quit your internship yet?"

My stomach tightens. I wondered if Ruby was going to bring that up. She clearly caught my lie at Skyline. I've been avoiding Em for this very reason, and the last thing I want to do is fight with Ruby about it.

"It's not that easy," I say, and as the words leave my mouth, I feel myself get hotter, sweat pooling behind my knees, my palms getting clammy.

"I'm not saying it is. I just think maybe you should talk about it with someone." She looks away, fidgeting even more with her silver bracelets, the charms as jangly as she is, and then the realization dawns on me with all the subtlety of one of those cartoon anvils dropping on someone from overhead.

"Oh crap. Ruby, I'm so sorry. I didn't mean to put you in an awkward position."

She looks up, confused.

"It's not fair of me to ask you to keep my secret in front of Charlie. I'm sorry!"

Ruby lets out a relieved half laugh. "No, that's not it at all. It's just, well . . ." She looks over at the Diamondback roller coaster, like she's nervous about what she's going to say next. "I just thought *I* could be the someone when you want to talk. No pressure or anything."

"Oh," I say. "I mean, thank you."

She nods, and the two of us are quiet. I can see Ruby's eyes tracing the path of the cars as they sleekly move along the tracks.

"You really love roller coasters, don't you?" I ask after a few seconds.

She nods easily. "Totally. If I didn't want to be a doctor, I'd design roller coasters."

"You'd be awesome at that."

"What would you be?"

"What?"

"If you weren't going to be a doctor, what would you be?"

"I . . . I don't . . . I'm not . . ."

Ruby waits, squinting in the sunlight, her attention fully on me.

The range of possible answers feels as dark and endless and lonely as outer space, but I remind myself this person in front of me wants to be my friend.

"I have no clue," I finally admit.

"Was there something you wanted to be when you were a kid, before you knew you wanted to be a doctor? I thought I wanted to be an artist who painted roses." She laughs at herself.

I pause for a second. "Actually, I wanted to be my dad," I say, surprised at the memory.

"You wanted to be a copywriter?"

I shake my head. "No, I just wanted to be happy like him. And this was before he worked at the copywriting firm. Back then I didn't know what he did exactly, but I knew that's what I wanted— to come home and be as happy as he was."

Before I can focus too much on it, Charlie returns. "One large pepperoni pizza," he says, sliding the box onto our metal table with a flourish.

Ruby looks like she wants to say more about the internship, about our dad, but I'm ready to change the subject.

"Why does the pizza always smell so much better here than it does at the actual restaurants?" I open the box and grab a slice, cheese pulling apart at the edges.

Ruby hands Charlie a ten, but he shakes his head. "I got it, Roo."

I expect her to reprimand him for the shortening of her name like she did with Finn, but instead she smiles shyly.

I bite into the cheesy goodness and try not to think too hard about my conversation with Ruby.

I try not to care.

But after a few minutes of pretending to listen to her and Charlie rate the roller coasters we've ridden this morning, I realize I can't stop thinking about it.

I used to look forward to growing up.

And now that it's in front of me, I'm terrified.

I don't know if I want to be a doctor.

And I don't know who I am without that.

I look over at Charlie, to reassure myself that he's there, and that's when I see the purple blooms on his upper arms—twin bruises, round and large, in near parallel positions.

"Charlie!" I grab the closest arm, pulling it toward me.

"Geez," he snaps, yanking his arm back before seeing what I see. His eyes widen, but then he shakes his head slowly, calmly. "The doctor said this could happen for a while. It's not a big deal."

"It kind of looks like a big deal," I say, panic coursing through me.

"Relax. My last test came back fine."

I shake my head. "Maybe we should just call it quits. What

time is it? Two? I can call Mom, and I bet she can get you a doctor appointment this evening."

"Parker, you're not listening to me."

"It's probably from one of the rides," Ruby adds, but I'm already cleaning our table, tossing napkins in the nearby garbage can, folding the pizza box top closed.

"I mean, I know it's the weekend," I say. "But Dr. Travis knows you. She'll make an exception." I grab our pizza box and stand, but Ruby and Charlie haven't moved from their seats. Charlie looks irritated, but Ruby just looks nervous, glancing between the both of us.

"We're not leaving. I'm fine," Charlie says.

"You can't be too safe," I say.

"You can when it's ruining our day."

"So you're not going to leave? You're just going to let this go?" I ask, my voice getting louder.

"Hey," Ruby says quietly, but I ignore her.

"Yeah, I'm going to let it go," Charlie says. "Because *it's nothing.*"

"How do you know it's nothing? You don't know that."

"Um, Parker?" Ruby says more insistently, and maybe it's all the built-up adrenaline from the coasters or the too-bright sun or the fact that I don't know who I am, but the one thing I do know is that I'm not letting this go.

"For chrissakes," Charlie says. "So you want to go straight to our parents again? I can't believe how fucking predictable you are. You can't leave me alone for more than two hours, can you? I don't want you up in my business, Parker. I don't know how many times I have to tell you."

The words sting, but I don't care. If he's still sick, it doesn't matter what he thinks.

Ruby stands up. *"Parker."* She points to my upper arms, the same area where Charlie's bruises have formed. There are two round reddish spots, smaller blooms than Charlie's, but most likely the start of bruises too.

I push the spots gently, feel the tender skin.

"I bet they're from the shoulder braces on the Vortex. If you hold them like this . . ." Ruby demonstrates an arm hold just like the one I used. "You probably held on so hard you bruised yourself. You both did."

Charlie folds his arms. "See?" he says, his voice still sharp, furious.

"Just sit down," Ruby says. "We'll eat and then we'll do White Water Canyon and take it from there, okay?"

Chagrined, I put the pizza box back on the table, but the joy of the morning is clearly gone. Charlie and I are quiet, and Ruby talks in double time to try to make up for our sullen silence.

After a totally unpleasant hour-long wait for White Water Canyon, followed by an equally tense ride, I tell Charlie and Ruby I'm going to watch a musical show in the Festhaus and that I'll meet up with them later. I wait for Charlie to point out that I hate musicals, but he can't get away from me quickly enough.

I don't watch a show. Instead, I spend the next two hours sitting by the long line of fountains by the entrance, watching families pose happily with costumed characters, unable to escape the feeling that I can't blame Charlie. I'm not sure I want to be around me right now either.

Thirty-Four

"ARE YOU SURE I can't tempt you to stay and practice more? It's air-conditioned in here," Carla calls out as I scoop up another mess of a failed bowl and try not to dump it too forcefully into the scraps pail.

It splashes unpleasantly, a thick gloppy *thunk*, and I shake my head.

"No thanks. I have plans." I hope I don't sound too eager to leave, because Carla is only being nice. But I am 100 percent willing to risk the 100-plus-degree weather if it means not spending another second feeling miserable and failing miserably on the wheel.

Since Carla first showed me how to work the wheel two weeks ago, I've spent a few hours every shift trying to throw something worth keeping. Carla has been nothing but encouraging, going so far as to put up the closed sign during our lunch break so she can give me individual instruction.

"You're helping me practice my teaching skills for when I start classes up in the fall," she insisted the first day.

I suspect I'm helping her practice patience more, because, to put it bluntly, I'm really, really terrible at pottery. Anytime my hands get near the wheel, it's like they're drunk.

They're always in the wrong place.

They're always pushing too hard.

Or not hard enough.

Yesterday, I tried to get out of it. I had such a good morning with the Wild Meadows ladies that I didn't want to ruin it with feeling bad about myself.

"I don't think pottery is for me," I said.

But Carla wouldn't have it. "Can't go over it, can't go under it, gotta go through it," she said cryptically.

When I told Ruby about it at Graeter's over ice cream sundaes last night, she suggested that maybe Charlie was right: that what I'm not good at is not being good at something. Immediately cringing as the words left her mouth, she then apologized for accidentally saying what she was thinking out loud and continued to do so for the next five minutes.

But she never said she was sorry for being wrong.

I say good-bye to Carla and head outside, groaning as soon as the wave of heat hits me.

After five minutes of walking, everything around me is melting—the soles of my Converse, the blacktop, my mood. There's no shade, no breeze, just shimmering heat rising from the street and several beads of sweat making their way down my back. When I check my weather app, it says the heat index is 107 degrees.

I should have stayed at work.

Ever since the bruise incident at Kings Island, Charlie and I are back to ignoring each other, and despite how much I try to forget it, I feel terrible anytime I think about Finn and the gift certificate.

I'm flat on the inside—like I've been reduced to just two dimensions. The only bright parts of my life are getting to know Ruby better, and my time working at Carla's. But if I'm not with my new friend or at the studio, I'm stretched on my bed, trying to sleep in the heat, wishing Mom would just turn on the air conditioner already.

I'm sleeping close to twelve hours a day.

A small part of me, something bright and small and brave, knows this much sleeping isn't normal, but the rest of me doesn't care.

By the time I'm halfway home, I'm pretty sure I might be close to a literal sunstroke, but I push myself forward, intent, eyes practically squinted shut, not paying much attention to the world around me.

And then someone calls out my name, and I almost trip on the sidewalk.

I look up.

Finn Casper's in his red truck, driving slowly behind me. He pulls up next to me, leans over from the driver's side.

"Parker, hey." His face is open, tentative, and I stop, wondering if it's a mirage. "Can we talk?"

Based on how badly I messed up our last conversation, I don't think Finn and I are on the same friendship wavelength. "I should probably head home."

"Please," he says, and it's the note of pleading in his voice that gets to me.

"Okay," I say.

He pulls the truck against the curb and leans over again, turning the ignition off. The truck shudders to a stop like it's exhausted too.

"I wanted to . . . you know . . ." He shrugs, like I should know what he means.

"I don't know."

"To say I'm sorry."

"For stalking me on my walk home like a creeper?"

The corner of his mouth curls. "No." But then he takes in a deep breath, his face getting more serious. "I'm sorry for jumping to conclusions that night at the Float. Ruby told me why you wanted to get out of there. I'm sorry for Johnny, too."

I shake my head. "That's not your fault."

"He won't bother you anymore, okay? And I wanted to thank you for the gift card. I put it to good use."

"It wasn't charity," I say. "You saved me, Finn. Twice. Once from a skunk, once from a hospital parking lot. I'm really grateful for that," I say, having a hard time looking at him as I say it.

We're both quiet for a second, until he clears his throat. "You want to see something cool?"

I look up. Maybe it's the meltiness of the heat, but it's like I'm looking at six-year-old Finn that first day on the playground again, his gray eyes serious, asking if I wanted to hear something cool.

I nod.

In response, he leans over and pushes open the passenger door, and I climb in.

In the heat, even with the windows down all the way, the inside of Finn's truck smells earthy, a mix of sweat and paint and guy. There's a pile of newspapers between us, and the one on top has individual words and entire phrases circled in black ballpoint pen.

Finn's tapping a thumb nervously against the steering wheel, but when he catches me studying him, he stops.

"So, pretty hot today, yeah?" he asks.

"No way," I scoff.

"What?"

"Finn Casper's making small talk? It's a miracle."

His face goes red. "I deserve that."

I shift my gaze to the floor—an old spray paint can rolls around by my feet—and then to the cup holder near the gearshift. It's filled with pennies and a small, dirt-covered pink plastic ballerina—the kind you get on cupcakes from grocery stores. I pick up the ballerina and start scraping dirt off her tutu.

"Do you like working at the pottery studio?"

"That's better," I say, and he rolls his eyes with a grin. "I do like working there. Carla's really great."

"Yeah, she's not so bad," he says.

"Some of the customers are a handful, but it keeps everything interesting. And there's this one older lady, Alice, who has

Alzheimer's, and some days, even though she doesn't talk, she really gets into the painting. Alice is most responsive when I play certain types of music, so I've been experimenting. She really likes Billie Holiday and Vivaldi. Soft rock, not so much."

"I don't blame her. Have you told your parents about it yet?"

I shake my head, trying to ignore how my heart is speeding up, and fiddle with the ballerina. She's just about free of dirt, but I keep working my fingernail in the groove of her tutu, digging in hard, taking a break only to point left toward my street. "My mom would worry so much if she knew I quit the internship. And my dad? No."

"Parker, the internship wasn't making you happy."

"But—" I start, my eyelid twitching.

"I know. 'It's not that easy,'" he says, echoing my earlier words. "But I bet it sucks, not telling them. It seems really hard and lonely to hold on to all of that by yourself."

I don't respond, keeping the eye that's twitching angled away from Finn. I try not to think too much of how similar his words are to Em's and Ruby's.

I close my hand hard around the ballerina, feeling her tutu impress into my hand, not letting her go.

Thirty-Five

WE'VE BEEN DRIVING ON quiet roads, passing through shady patches of woods and by sleepy-looking farms for at least twenty minutes. Finally, Finn pulls the truck over to the side of the road.

"Here? I really hope you're not taking me to some survivalist cult compound," I say, only half joking, as I get out.

"Trust me," he says, grabbing an old canvas rucksack from the back of the truck. I can hear the clatter of spray paint cans as he motions me to follow him.

We start making our way through a tangle of ragweed and Queen Anne's lace, which eventually eases into woods. Maybe it's the shade from the enormous trees tunneling over us—the only sunlight coming through in small dappled spots—but it immediately feels cooler.

I stop at the top of a terrifyingly steep hill as Finn starts to make his way down, using trees for balance. He turns around to check on me.

"I don't know if I'm up for this," I call out. "I don't want to break my leg. I read some terrible story last year about a guy who fell down a hill—"

Without saying another word, Finn scrambles back up and holds out a hand.

I suck in my breath, but then I take it. He wraps his fingers around mine as we start down the hill. Finn leads, offering me his arm for support as I take small angled steps behind him.

When we get to the bottom, I see rusty train tracks leading into a tunnel, forest growth sprouting up between all the rails. Finn lets go, walking ahead only to stop at the mouth of the tunnel, pulling a flashlight out of his bag.

"Come on."

I follow him in, then stop, speechless, as I take in the tunnel walls.

What's around me is worth risking the scariest cult compound in the world, worth suffering a hundred broken bones.

Between the beam of Finn's light and the drowsy sunlight coming in from the other end of the tunnel, every inch of the tunnel is exploding with bursts of color, fireworks in apple reds and sky blues, bright oranges and deep violets, neon yellows and piercing pinks. It's luminous and alive, life where you'd least expect it.

"Finn," I breathe, unable to say more.

It's a secret cathedral, the moment of the big bang, the electric of dreams.

I venture in farther, tracing my fingers along the cool stone wall. Amid the dim, I see color around me, above me. The deeper I go, the more it all comes to life, swirling and blooming, blue vines creeping up the walls, small bursts of silver stars on the ceiling, moons shattering into pieces, white clouds morphing into storm clouds.

Woven between it all, messages from Finn:

FLOATING FALLING.

CAN YOU HEAR ME?

YOUR WIFE LOVES YOU SO VERY MUCH.

THEY'RE THE SAME STARS.

"Oh my God, your messages. They're all about Major Tom, aren't they?" I ask, looking back at him.

"Just in case he's listening," Finn says.

I do a double take. "You know that's not real."

"Yeah, I know it's not real." He laughs.

The art stops two thirds of the way through, after turquoise and emerald waves, purple bubbles rising from them, octopus tentacles creeping around the edges.

"I'm not done yet," Finn says from behind me.

I turn back to him, shaking my head in disbelief. "Finn, I don't. I can't." I stop. "I don't have the right words. It's phenomenal, Finn."

He smiles, and I can tell he's more than a little bit embarrassed, but there's pride there too. He opens his bag and grabs a can. "Want to try?"

"I couldn't."

He tosses the can toward me, and I barely catch it in time.

"Come on." He motions toward an empty patch.

"I don't want to mess up what you did."

"You won't mess it up. Plus, that's the good thing about walls. I can just paint over what you did if I hate it."

"Hey!"

"Kidding. Here, let me show you." He hands me a surgical face mask from his bag, pulls one over his mouth too, then shakes the can for a good long while.

And then, holding it out six inches from the wall, he starts creating streaks of sea green, shaking the can in between every few strokes, building up layers of stripes, like a mint bumblebee. He points at my can.

"Your turn." His voice is muffled.

I take off the lid and face the nozzle toward the wall, then start shaking the can, the rattle strangely satisfying. And then I press the nozzle, and a scattered spritz of sky blue comes out.

"Shake it more," Finn says. "Then press harder."

I do, and this time a solid line of blue paint comes out, so I fill in the blank spaces between Finn's green stripes, and the color is running behind Charlie on a summer day, the ice cream truck singing in the distance. It's lying on my back in the grass, watching clouds with Em.

It surprises me, the joy I feel in making this mark on the world.

And then a big drip of blue paint goes rogue, streaming down over one of Finn's streaks.

"Argh, I'm sorry," I say, dropping my arm to my side.

Finn shakes his head, then digs through his bag, finding a new can. After a vigorous shake, he creates similarly sized drips of indigo paint, layering them until they start trailing down over his green and my blue.

I laugh, then add some more sky-blue drips, until between the both of us, we've created something that looks like a striped jellyfish. We stand back, studying it. For the first time in weeks, months even, I feel myself tilting toward possibility, that moment at the top of the roller coaster.

This time I'm not scared.

"Why?" I ask, turning to him, lowering my mask.

His brow furrows and he lowers his. "Why what?"

"Why did you start? Why here? Why the bridges? Why do you keep it secret? Why aren't you in art school? Why aren't you sharing this with everyone?"

"Parker," he says, his voice reluctant.

"Please. I want to understand."

He's quiet for a second, shifts awkwardly, kicks the edge of the track. "When my dad went to jail for dealing meth, Johnny and I were put into foster care. That's how I met Carla and her husband, Noel. She was my foster mom."

I nod carefully, not wanting him to stop.

"When I was little, I was pissed. All the time. And after we moved in with her, it got worse. It was like all this fury was building inside me waiting to explode; it made me want to rip off my skin. But then Carla signed me up for boxing. That helped. It was the first time someone saw that anger in me and didn't think it was bad—just that it hadn't found the best way to express itself yet.

"Johnny was never happy at her place. But, for a while, I was."

He sucks in his breath, clenches his hands and releases them slowly.

"One day, Carla told us Dad was out of jail. He had secured a job at an old competitor's—Tom's Auto Body—and he had the house back and was getting it ready for us to move home. Carla said he was coming to see us the next day, and he'd keep coming to see us until we could move back in with him. Johnny was pumped. I knew I should be. But inside?"

Finn shakes his head, his expression dark.

"That night, after everyone went to bed, I found every piece of pottery Carla had in the house and smashed it on the driveway."

The cracks in Carla's first crooked bowl, the one she glued back together—it all makes sense now.

"Noel found me first, and he started yelling, and then Johnny and Carla came downstairs. And the look on Carla's face?"

Finn can't meet my eyes then.

"Johnny couldn't stop laughing, and Noel was calling me ungrateful, but for the first time in a long time, I was totally empty inside, and it was a relief."

He blinks hard.

"The next morning I could tell Carla had been crying, but she told me she wasn't mad, just disappointed. She said I wasn't being very creative with all my anger. She handed me a paintbrush, opened up a few cans of paint, and told me to go to town on the back patio. So I did. For the next six months, after every one of my dad's visits, I'd go out on the back porch and paint every bad word

I could think of. I drew bloody daggers and guns and monsters. I wrote mean things. I painted that seven-by-seven rectangle every single day until I felt empty. Carla never censored me. She'd only look at what I was doing, nod, and go back in the house.

"When we moved home for a trial basis, Carla sent me with a whole box of paintbrushes and notebooks and paint. And after my dad got custody again, she kept dropping stuff off. My dad wasn't crazy about her stopping by, so she never stayed for long, but Carla was the one who got me started. It all grew from there. Now it's like a habit, and not just when I'm mad. I like it." He shrugs.

"Carla's really great at encouraging people to try things," I say, thinking of her gentle nudging with me not to give up on the pottery wheel.

"Yeah, she is." Finn nods solemnly.

"And all this?" I point to the walls. "You're really talented, Finn. You should think about art school. UC has a good program—I bet Carla could help with that, too."

He lets out a dry laugh. "You sound just like her."

"Is that a bad thing?"

"Parker, I'm not the college type."

"That's not true."

"I didn't even graduate from high school. I dropped out last year."

"Oh," I say. "But that doesn't mean you couldn't still—"

"With what money?"

"Scholarships and loans," I start.

He shakes his head. "My dad, Johnny, and I are saving to buy back the old auto body shop so we can have a family business again. Dad hates working at Tom's, and it's been the plan for forever, ever since he got out of jail. It's what we all want. So please, let it go."

Staying here, with Johnny? But Finn's shoulders are braced, and I bite back what I want to say next.

He grabs a new can of paint, tosses it at me. "Want to make another go of it?"

I nod, shaking the can, appreciating the way the color paints over all the uncertainty inside me, around me, in front of us, between us.

Thirty-Six

WHEN I GET TO Carla's the next day, there's a weird under-current in the room. I don't see Alice, but Miss Peggy and Lorna are whispering and sneaking glances at Harriet.

"Hi, Carla," I call down the steps, which earns me a "G'morning, Parker" shout in return.

Harriet, much to my surprise, is holding up a tiny hand mirror and applying bright-coral lipstick in an uneven line across her top lip, then her bottom. She smacks them together loudly.

"Where's Alice?" I ask.

"Sick," Miss Peggy says.

"Is she okay?" I ask right as the toilet flushes, and all our heads swivel expectantly to the bathroom door. I'm hoping it's Finn, but instead, an older Asian man with silvery black hair, a tweed cap, and a bright smile emerges.

"Good morning!" he says to me.

"Henry, this is our Parker. And, Parker, this, *this*, is Henry Chee." Miss Peggy's voice is practically a coo as she gestures toward him. "He just moved into Wild Meadows last week, and I told him he had to come with us today."

"Nice to make your acquaintance," Henry says, giving me a firm handshake.

"Likewise."

Harriet looks like she wants to burn down the whole building when Henry chooses to sit on the empty stool next to Miss Peggy.

"I thought we could do something a little different today, if it's okay with you guys?" I ask the group.

"Sure!" Lorna chirps.

"If it's okay with Henry," Miss Peggy says, patting her hand gently on his.

"Why wouldn't it be?" Harriet barks. "It's all new to him!"

Henry shoots me an anxious glance, and I immediately feel deeply sorry for him stuck between Harriet and Miss Peggy. I shake my head subtly, sending him psychic messages not to engage. "We're going to do a group activity."

"Oh Lord," Harriet groans.

Last night, I couldn't fall asleep, but for once it wasn't because of dread circling around me. Instead, my mind kept racing with possibility—the hyper colors of Finn's secret cathedral like sun spots when I closed my eyes. I ended up getting up in the middle of the night and Googling more about street art, which led me to a page about Stik, a formerly homeless artist who invited a bunch of local schoolkids to paint murals with him in London.

It sparked today's plan. I wish Alice were here, as I was hoping the activity would pull her out of her shell a little more, but figure it's worth trying now anyway.

I grab five blank mugs and paintbrushes and pass them around. I pull out my phone, then sit down next to Harriet.

"Nice lipstick," I murmur. She harrumphs in response, but I could swear she straightens up and puts her shoulders back too, like a bird preening.

"So today we're going to paint together. You'll start on a mug, and after three minutes, you'll pass it to the person next to you. We'll go around in a circle until we finish all the mugs."

"But what if we don't like what other people do on our mugs?" Miss Peggy asks.

I feel Harriet suck her breath in right as Henry says, "We won't know until we try. I like to think everyone has something to offer."

Miss Peggy grimaces, while Harriet looks as pleased as a cat who not only ate the canary but scarfed down every other bird in the pet store.

"Okay." I set the timer on my phone. "Go!"

Everyone starts to paint.

"Henry, what did you do in your earlier days?" Miss Peggy asks.

"I was a doctor," he says, reaching for the red paint at the same time as Lorna. She demurs, pushing it his way. Today, she has on a pale-green shirt, lime-green pants, a bright-green parrot pin.

"Parker here is going to be a doctor too!" Miss Peggy smiles generously at me.

Henry arches an eyebrow as he paints his mug handle red. "Is that so?"

Miss Peggy replies for me. "She's going to Harvard in the fall. Full scholarship. She's super smart, this one."

"Time!" I say, preferring to pretend my future doesn't exist right now.

Lorna looks fretfully at the outline of the blue flower she's started on her mug. "Pass them on," I say. She reluctantly hands it to Harriet, who passes me a mug with her furious black slashes around the edge.

"Henry, this is lovely. Such vision," Miss Peggy says, holding up the mug he started.

"But it's just a red handle," Henry says uncertainly, and Harriet chuckles.

"I like red," Lorna offers. "Maybe I will wear my red outfit tomorrow."

"And next round . . . three, two, one, go!" I say.

"Parker will make a wonderful doctor, just like you," Miss Peggy says, batting her eyelashes at Henry.

"That looks great, Harriet." I point at the small black polka dots she's painting inside Lorna's blue petals. They're not slashes, but they're still very Harriet.

"Oh!" Lorna says when she sees what Harriet's doing, clearly surprised but not unpleasantly so. Harriet tries to hide a smile.

Miss Peggy clears her throat. "My son Frank said we'll need more doctors in the next fifty years than ever before. We're both widowed," she says to Henry, pointing at herself and Lorna. "God rest our dear husbands' souls."

Henry looks uncomfortable with the turn in the conversation and focuses on painting yet another mug with a red handle. "Well, Harvard is a great place to be. It has one of the best premed programs in the country," he says.

I smile weakly at him, leaning over to grab yellow so I can outline Harriet's jagged black edges.

Miss Peggy puts her brush down and rests her arm on Henry's. "Perhaps you could mentor her. I'm sure she'd love to hear more about your days in medicine."

"Oh, for chrissakes," Harriet grumbles. "Just let it be."

Surprised, I glance over at my ally. Harriet winks at me.

Miss Peggy looks wounded, and Henry is focusing intensely on adding another coat of red to the handle of his mug.

"Time's up. Pass the mugs again. Now go!"

I get the mug with the blue flower petals filled with black polka dots and pick up green paint, starting to draw elaborate vines and leaves around the flower.

Lorna looks slightly confused with the mug she's received. It's one of the red-handled ones Henry started. Miss Peggy simply painted more red around the rim. Lorna hesitantly picks up orange paint, looking up for approval, and before I get a chance to nod, Henry leans over to her. "That orange looks really nice with my red."

Lorna smiles.

For the next few minutes, everyone seems to be focused on their painting, but then Miss Peggy clears her throat. "I was just proud of Parker. I didn't realize it was a problem to be happy for someone here."

"It'd be fine if you were doing it for reasons other than your vagina," Harriet said.

"Harriet!" Miss Peggy and Lorna and I all exclaim at once.

At first Henry looks startled, but then he chuckles, giving Harriet an admiring look.

"Vulgar," Miss Peggy grumbles.

"Listen, I appreciate *everyone's* support," I say. "But let's not talk about me anymore."

"So what kind of doctor were you, Henry?" Lorna asks.

"A cardiologist," he says, pressing his hand to his chest, wiggling his eyebrows. "I was an expert in matters of the heart."

For a second I debate asking him if it's possible for an eighteen-year-old to have a heart attack. I'm pretty sure it's all in my head, but what if there's something really wrong with me, like there was with Charlie?

But then Harriet cackles out loud. "Aren't you something?"

My eyes meet Lorna's across the table, and she looks just as shocked as I feel: Harriet's flirting. Meanwhile, Miss Peggy sulkily pushes away the red paint she was using and grabs a dark brown instead, painting brown blobs over Henry's red handle.

After the last round, it's clear Miss Peggy's feelings are still hurt, as she won't respond with anything other than monosyllabic grunts and has refused to paint anything other than brown spots on the red handles Henry has added to every single mug.

Henry, Harriet, Lorna, and I, however, are having a good time.

Lorna tells us all about her days as a court stenographer in downtown Cincinnati and how she always wished she could be a lawyer. Her eyes are dreamy, wistful, and more than once I see Henry sneaking glances at her.

Meanwhile, Harriet regales us with tales of her time as a showgirl at a Coney Island dance revue and how she had so many lovers, she lost count.

I blush at Harriet's stories, focusing on my painting, but Henry laughs throughout, and even Lorna looks impressed.

When Carla comes up an hour later, she lets out a pleased chuckle, and for the first time, I take a closer look at our work. Surprisingly enough, the mugs look kind of good. Lorna's blue flowers have just the right amount of edge with Harriet's black accents, and I think the touches of yellow and green I've added complement Miss Peggy's and Henry's polka-dot handles.

"Nice job, everyone," she says delightedly.

Miss Peggy mutters something under her breath, but Carla smiles at me across the room.

Good work, she mouths to me, and I feel something warm in my chest, a sun rising.

Thirty-Seven

"HOW IS THE CANCER support group going these days, Charlie?" Mom asks.

"Shockingly not terrible," he replies, and I look up from my plate, surprised. Dad's fork freezes midair.

Up until now, anytime any of us have asked about Charlie's group, we've gotten noncommittal grunts in response.

Dad and I gave up a while ago, but Mom keeps trying. Even though she's nicer about it, underneath she's just as stubborn as Charlie sometimes.

"There's a new counselor named Peg," Charlie continues. "She's a breast cancer survivor and she's pretty badass. She was talking about how when she finally went into remission, things weren't as easy as she expected, but she kept focusing on hope. . . ." He stops when he notices the looks on our faces. "What?"

"Nothing. It's just good to hear you talking about it, that's all," Mom says.

Charlie shrugs. "By the way, can I use your car tonight?"

Mom gives me an inquiring look, and I shake my head. "I don't have any plans."

"You heading to the batting cages?" Dad asks.

"No," he says, not meeting anyone's eyes. "I'm going out with my friend Ruby."

"*Your* friend Ruby?" I ask.

"Is this a date?" Mom asks.

I expect Charlie to explode, but instead he just blushes.

Dad looks confused.

"You're going on a date with Ruby?" I ask. "My Ruby?"

"She's not *your* Ruby," Charlie says.

"Who's Ruby?" Dad says.

"I'm happy to hear you're making new friends," Mom adds.

"I don't know if that's a good idea," I start, thinking of what Matty said about Charlie cheating on Erin.

"Will someone please tell me who Ruby is?" Dad asks.

"Does Ruby want to come over for dinner sometime?" Mom offers.

Charlie groans. "This is why I never tell any of you anything."

"We're sorry," Mom says.

Dad still looks confused. "What are we sorry about?"

"I'm not sorry," I say. "You should have told me."

Charlie grabs a dinner roll, stuffing half of it in his mouth while talking. "I'm telling you now. Besides, why do I have to tell you anything? She's my friend too."

I fix my gaze evenly on him. "Charlie, if you mess with Ruby's heart, I will murder you."

He rolls his eyes.

"I'm not kidding. I know about you and Erin."

"What happened with Erin?" Dad asks.

"Nothing, all right?" Charlie snaps at him before turning back to me. "You don't know the first thing about me and Erin."

"I know what Matty told me that night at the river."

His face blanches. "God, I can't catch a break with you, can I?" he asks, voice cracking in frustration.

Mom clears her throat, giving Dad and me warning looks before turning back to my brother. "Charlie, I'm sorry we're not respecting your privacy," she says. "We all look forward to you sharing when and if you want to share."

"But—" I start, but Mom cuts me off, her face making it clear we are changing the subject. Right. Now. "Parker, how was your internship today? You haven't talked much about it lately," she asks.

Crud.

I slink back in my seat. "It's good," I offer, which isn't exactly a lie. After class today, I overheard Henry telling Carla he was so glad he came. "It's really good, actually. There was a new patient in the pediatric ward today named Henry, and I think he was feeling really overwhelmed about being there, but I helped him fit in."

"That must be so hard for his family," Mom says, and for a second I feel guilty about my lie.

Dad jumps in. "Are you making some good contacts? You

know, any contact you make now is only going to help you in the long run. These are the people who might hire you someday."

"Mmm-hmm." I nod, purposefully shoving a forkful of salad in my mouth.

Dad looks pleased, but when I look over at Charlie, he has this knowing expression on his face, like he can tell I'm lying.

I shift uneasily and remind myself he doesn't know anything about the internship.

"Oh, that reminds me," Mom says. "I ran into Mrs. Delaney at the grocery store the other day. . . ."

This change of subject 100 percent works.

"She was asking all about you. She says the boys miss you a lot. Evidently, they locked their new babysitter out of the house. Helen had to come home from work to let her in."

"That sounds about right," I say. "Remember that afternoon I had to call poison control to determine if eating toy slime was dangerous?"

"It's a miracle those kids are still alive," Dad says.

"Helen also said she thought she saw you the other afternoon, at the Float in the middle of the day. . . ."

Uh-oh.

"But I told her you must have another twin out in the world."

I smile weakly, but Charlie leans forward eagerly. "That's weird. A Parker look-alike at the Float when the real Parker's at her internship? Huh. What *are* the odds? Do you know, little sister? It's not like you could be in two different places at the same time." He gives me a taunting smile, and my mouth flaps open, then closes again, the rest of me freezing in sheer panic.

Charlie knows.

I don't know how he found out, but he knows.

I abruptly stand. "I'm going to start the dishes," I say, taking my half-full plate of chicken and rice and walking into the kitchen.

Underneath the sound of my heart, I hear my parents in the dining room.

"Hon, we need to talk about our strategy for winning euchre tonight. I'm tired of the Dickersons winning."

"I'm all ears."

As they discuss the benefits of "leading trump on defense," I scrape my leftover food into the garbage and rinse the dishes before I put them in the dishwasher.

I'm trying to stay calm, but what I really want to do is throw the dishes on the floor and run out of the house and keep running and never stop.

Charlie saunters into the kitchen with his dishes, Mustard following him in a quest for table scraps, and I take Charlie's plate, wishing he'd just leave already.

Instead he leans against the counter, arms folded, legs crossed, expression smug, like he's watching a tennis match and his guy is winning.

I cut to the chase. "How'd you find out?"

"I stopped by the Float at lunch earlier this week and saw you going into that pottery place. And when I went back the next day, you were there again. Your nails finally made sense."

"My nails?" I look down.

"Yeah. There's been a lot of dirt under your fingernails. You wouldn't last more than two minutes at Children's with those germ-infested fingers." He shrugs, but then he looks at me, and this time his expression is more careful, arms at his sides. "Is everything okay—" he starts.

"Are you going to tell Mom and Dad?" I interrupt.

He rolls his eyes and looks away, folding his arms again. "That depends."

"On what?"

"Are you going to warn Ruby off of me?"

I frown. "Is this blackmail?"

He sighs in frustration. "I was kind of hoping it was more me asking you to give me a chance with her, but yeah, if you want to put it like that, be my guest."

"Ruby's my friend, and she has a really big heart, so you have to be careful with her. I'm not kidding, Charlie."

"I'm not either!" he snaps. And then he takes a breath, refusing to look at me. "I like her, all right?"

His confession sits there still and heavy between us while the world goes on around us, the sound of Mr. Edwards mowing the lawn outside the screen window, Mom and Dad still strategizing in the dining room, Mustard chirruping at my feet, twining himself between my legs.

I wish I could let it go, but I don't trust him not to hurt her.

"I just don't think you and Ruby are a good idea," I say.

"God, I'm so sick of this," he mutters.

"Sick of what?"

"Sick of how you treat me. Sick of how you won't ever give

me a chance. Sick of how you constantly think you know what's best."

I flinch.

"You want blackmail? Okay, here it is. You do anything to ruin me and Ruby, the jig is up on your internship, okay? How's that for a 'good idea'?"

My heart is pounding so hard, it might fly out of my mouth. "I don't even know who you are anymore."

"Well, that makes two of us."

I turn my back on him, focusing on washing the food off the plate so he doesn't see my hands shaking. "If you even remotely think of breaking her heart, all bets are off," I say.

I wait for him to agree, but when I look over my shoulder, he's long gone.

Thirty-Eight

AN HOUR LATER, I'M sitting on our porch swing with my laptop, one foot tucked under me, replaying Charlie's words, debating whether or not I just made the wrong decision regarding him and Ruby.

I feel gross and sad and anxious and complicit and then sad again.

I try to shake it all off, looking up from my laptop.

Even though it's getting pretty dusky, next door, Mrs. Edwards is working on her garden, planting marigolds in neat lines, Mr. Edwards puttering behind her on the lawn mower, still. I honestly don't know how there's any grass left to mow at this point.

From the other side of our screen door, Mustard lets out a mournful meow.

"You know you can't come outside right now," I say to him. "It's getting too dark." He blinks slowly at me, his tail swatting impatiently, and then he sees a moth batting against the porch light and he makes a weird little *yip* noise.

I go back to reading Em's latest e-mail.

Park, either you still don't want to talk to me, or the entire city of Cincinnati, Ohio, has fallen into some weird alternative dimension where e-mails can't be sent or received. I'm going to assume it's the latter because you know I love you and I'm so sorry if I made you mad and I just want good things for you, okay? Okay.

So yesterday Matty and I decided we'd had enough of lovely ol' England. We had brunch with Tamsin, and then she and I said good-bye at the train station (so romantic). After that, Matty and I hopped on a train to Wales and then got on a boat. Guess where we are now? IRELAND! We're in Dublin tonight—tomorrow we're taking a bus across the country—we're going to some place called the Dingle Peninsula. (Every time I say it, Matty snickers under his breath.) Evidently, they have a dolphin living there that everyone calls Fungie (terrible name, no?). And cliffs and hiking

and old ruins. And the hostel we're going to
stay at is haunted!

It's been cool traveling with Matty—it's
nice not having to share rooms at hostels
with strangers—though he never wants to
go shopping with me. I miss you pretty much
all the time, but that's one of the times when
I miss you the most.

How are things going with everything?
Have you told your family about the
internship? I'm thinking of you.

Miss you, xoxo, Em

She's right. I don't want to talk to her. It's unfair and unreasonable, but it's so much easier to ignore the pangs of guilt about the lies when someone isn't pointing them out to me.

At least it was until tonight. Now that Charlie knows, things are going to get even harder.

The pool of dread in my stomach stirs right as a horn honks.

Finn's truck is idling in front of our house. He's leaning across the passenger seat, looking at me through the open window.

Despite my mood, I smile. "Hello, Finnegan!" I yell, and I see him frown at the name.

Mustard meows behind the screen.

Mrs. Edwards sits back on her feet, squinting in Finn's direction, trying to make out who it is in the twilight.

I wait for him to say something.

"Um, yeah, so do you want to hang out?" he finally says.

I look at the blinking cursor of my screen and then back up at the only person besides Ruby who knows my secrets right now.

Correction, the only person besides Ruby and my brother.

I slam my laptop shut. "Give me a second."

I see Mrs. Edwards purse her lips and shake her head, standing up and going inside.

When I push the door open, Mustard tries to wrap himself around me, but I shoo him to the side, earning a bite on my leg.

"Little jerk," I say to him as he stalks out of the room.

I leave my laptop on the coffee table and grab only my purse and keys, locking the door behind me.

Finn's truck rolls to a stop on the side of the road.

When I hop out, I'm greeted with evening. It's cooled off now that the sun's set, and the world around us is musty with goldenrod and Queen Anne's lace, itchy with nettles and weeds. Finn heads toward the left, parts the brush in front of us, holds it to the side for me.

I pause. "What if there are snakes?"

Finn shakes his head. "No snakes."

I nod and step forward.

We're in front of a large fence, one that stretches to the right and left of us, as far as I can see. On the other side is a runway lined with blue lights. There's a tower at the end of it, more flashing lights behind it.

"The airport?"

He nods.

"But isn't this trespassing?" I ask.

"Not on this side of the fence."

"Are you sure?"

"I'm sure. Not trespassing. No snakes. You're not going to break your leg. It's not a survivalist cult compound. Trust me."

I flush red.

He settles down on the grass facing the runway and then lies down all the way, cradling his head in his hands. I hear him humming softly—Taylor Swift again—and I give in, lying down next to him, my hands fretting at the corner of my T-shirt.

"I'm sorry I worry so much," I finally say. "I don't mean to. But it's like my brain can't stop."

He waits for me to say more.

"I used to think it started with Charlie being sick. But even when I was little, I worried about stuff. I worried about getting bit by a spider or Charlie leaving me behind. I worried about there being ghosts in the basement. I worried about getting kidnapped by the helium people."

"The helium people?" Finn asks.

"Yeah. When I was little, Grandma McCullough told me this story about gravity people and helium people that totally freaked me out. Being a helium person sounded like the worst fate ever."

"Why? What's a helium person?"

So I tell him the story of the little girl who was made of gravity, who spent all her time on the ground being safe. And how she met another little girl of helium, who spent all her time flying in the sky.

"I realize the point is that the gravity girl's fear gets the best of her, that she's missing out on the world around her, that she's holding her new friend back. But when I was little, I was convinced she was doing the right thing by not letting go."

"Huh," Finn says, his voice doubtful. "That's a pretty shitty story."

I laugh, surprised. "Don't hold back."

"Come on. The gravity girl was terrified. I don't blame her for holding on to the helium girl. Sure, it might not have been the best thing, but she was just a scared kid."

A jolt of surprise runs along my arms like static electricity.

"No offense to your grandma or anything," he adds quickly, propping himself up, anxious he's overstepped.

"None taken. Really, it's okay."

He flops back down, clearing his throat after a minute. "When I was a kid, I was scared of the dark."

This time I wait.

"Johnny used to tell me he saw our mom outside the windows at night when it was raining, and she was all bloody and broken from the car accident, and her teeth were sharp and pointed like a vampire's."

I make everything in me go still, the words I want to say, the way my hand wants to reach out to his.

"At first, anytime it rained at night, I'd try to man up and stay awake, because I wanted to see her, you know? But then I'd lie there, thinking more about it, and the thought of those teeth? Scared the crap out of me. I'd close my eyes and my whole body would freeze up, and I was too much of a baby to even go to the bathroom. I wondered how I'd ever see my mom again if I was scared of the dark. But I still couldn't open my eyes."

His words remind me of the first time Charlie was in the hospital for an extended stay. I'd wake up, convinced I heard him on the other side of the wall, and then I'd remember he wasn't there, and then I'd stare at the ceiling, unable to move, wondering what was in his room instead.

Fear is so lonely making.

"Every time, I somehow managed to fall asleep anyway. And then I'd wake up in the morning needing to pee like no one's business, and outside, everything looked normal, like the night before was never real, like my mom had always been gone."

"Did you ever see her?" I ask.

"Johnny was just screwing with me."

"I know, but maybe she was still watching over you, without the scary teeth, you know?"

Finn shakes his head. "No. The moment her car hit that telephone pole, she was gone."

"I'm sorry," I say.

"I don't really remember her. Johnny insists there was nothing to miss, that she was just as much of an asshole as the rest of us."

I suck in my breath. The grass is itchy against the backs of my legs, and I can hear Finn breathing next to me, see the rise and fall of his chest.

"But you're not an asshole," I say, my voice soft. I nudge him gently on the shoulder with my hand and he nudges right back. He stretches his arms farther behind his head, and the corner of his T-shirt hitches up. Even though the light is dim, I can still make out his skin underneath, the way it's entirely covered with faded yellow bruises.

"Finn," I say under my breath, half sitting up, and his smile fades as he jerks the T-shirt back down.

"It's fine." I hear the note of exasperation in his voice.

"I know I don't know much about boxing, but are you supposed to get that hurt?"

"It's not a big deal."

"But what if your organs are hurt?"

"Parker, my organs are fine, okay?" he snaps. "Stop worrying about everything."

I flinch, wishing my brain were different.

But what if he's really hurt?

After a few seconds, Finn clears his throat. "I'm sorry. That wasn't the right thing to say."

I turn my head to look at him, but his eyes are closed, and I can see the kid in him, face scrunched tight against the dark, against a ghost of a mom with teeth.

"Okay," I say. "But will you just be careful when you box? Please? Now that I found you, I don't want to lose you again."

As soon as I've said it, I wonder if I've said too much, but Finn nods, inclining his head slightly, so it's angled against my shoulder.

"Okay," he says.

From the distance, I hear an engine and realize it's coming from the runway, and it's getting closer, and then I see lights heading our way, getting bigger and brighter.

"Here we go," Finn says, and there's something in his voice I haven't heard before, something bright and untarnished, something new and vulnerable.

I watch as the lights get closer, see the airplane taking shape against the black of the sky behind it, see the enormity of it like it's going to run us over, like it's going to run our hearts into the ground.

Right then, Finn carefully twines his fingers in mine, giving my hand a gentle squeeze, and I realize maybe what we have isn't exactly just friends anymore, but then the engine is roaring, the wind force pushing our hair off our faces, and the plane lifts off right in front of us, its nose rising into the night above us, and then the rest of it, leaving the earth, and for a second it's so close, I could put my free hand up and touch it, all of gravity holding me close as tons of steel take flight, light as helium.

Thirty-Nine

MY ELBOWS ARE BENT, resting on my knees, and I'm pushing everything I have into the mound of red-brown clay in front of me. One side is uneven, the heel of my palm bumping into it every time it passes under my left hand, leaving a brief phantom space right after. But I wedge my right hand hard against it, pushing gently with the left, until it's smooth and centered on the wheel.

Maybe it was the little bit of creative confidence I got from painting with Finn in the tunnel last week. Or maybe it's just all the extra practice I've had on the wheel. But the past few times I've tried, I've managed to center the clay. And each time it happens, I feel this rush of satisfaction, that I've wrangled the heaviness into something grounded and steady.

I start to form the lump into a bowl.

Carla is bustling around behind me, taking pots out of the kiln, making small sighs of appreciation as she notices the way her new batch of glazes is settling.

But it's all background noise, because to my astonishment, for the first time since I started this, the clay in front of me is doing what it's supposed to do.

I feel a knot of tension in my shoulders, but the rest of me is assured, my fingers lifting up and out, the curve of clay following my lead, walls rising.

"Not bad at all," Carla says, and I look up at her, startled. She points at the clay in front of me, clicks off my wheel.

Sometime in the past half hour, I have managed to shape something shapeless into a bowl, high and small and not nearly big enough for salad but maybe okay for some ice cream.

"Huh," I say, looking at it, still dazed. "It's kind of crooked around the top. And the bottom is heavy."

"That's what trimming is for," Carla says.

"I don't love this bulge in the middle. I guess I didn't wedge it enough."

"Parker, you threw a bowl."

I wipe my clay-covered hands on my apron. "But it's not—"

"Stop," Carla says. "You did this. It's yours. Not to get all hokey, but you gave it life—you found its shape."

I look up at her, a smile tugging at the corner of my mouth.

"That is kind of hokey," I say.

Carla rolls her eyes, shaking her head. "That bowl doesn't suck," she says.

"It doesn't suck," I admit, looking at the weird crooked thing I made sitting on the wheel.

"And it's yours."

"It's mine," I say.

And it is. It's something I made with my two hands, something that didn't exist in the world before me, something that wouldn't exist without me.

And for those ten to twenty minutes I was shaping it, my mind was quiet. My hands were steady, strong, my feet solid against the ground.

It's a terrible bowl. I know that.

And there's still trimming to get through, which means that I might cut a hole through it or not trim enough. Or glazing: I could pick an ugly color. I might put on too much, and it will run, the pot sticking to the kiln. I might not put on enough, leaving bald spots. The pot might crack under the heat.

I know these things too.

But I think about the day I got my Harvard acceptance, how it felt like a house landed on my chest.

I think about the first day of my internship, how I was too terrified to even get on an elevator.

And I think about now, how I feel like I belong at Carla's, how I made something that has nothing to do with my parents or Charlie or cancer or Harvard.

I made this.

It's a terrible bowl, and I feel prouder of it than I did of my SAT scores and Harvard scholarship combined.

I take a wire and slide it under my creation, then use the silver spatula to wiggle the bowl off the bat and onto a piece of particle-board, taking care to tuck plastic around it, keeping it safe until the clay is dry enough to trim.

Carla helps me find a good spot for it on the shelf.

"By the way, I meant to tell you, I finally talked with the volunteer coordinator at Wild Meadows," she says. "Alice isn't coming back for a while."

"Is she okay?"

"They think she had a stroke last week."

"Oh," I say, feeling a little crack in my heart, thinking of Alice's hands fluttering over the paintbrush. "I hope she's okay. I'd been researching some things to try with her."

Carla nods. "That's a good idea, Parker. You know, I took some art therapy classes back in college. I still have a few of the books, if you want to borrow them."

"Yeah, actually that'd be pretty cool."

Carla nods toward the clay, and I go over and grab another chunk and start wedging it on the block. As my hands move through it, kneading it, working the bubbles out of it, I wonder if I should tell Carla about Finn's bruises. But then I remind myself of how I overreacted with Charlie at Kings Island, how I worry too much.

"Do you think it'd be okay for me to visit Alice? Maybe tomorrow afternoon?" I say instead, turning around to look at her.

"Sure, yeah. I bet Alice would welcome a visitor. I can make a call to Nancy, the volunteer coordinator, to see if it's okay. I've got that conference in Dayton tomorrow, but it's fine with me if you close up for the day. I can text you."

"Thanks," I say, nodding. "I'd like that."

Forty

THE NEXT MORNING, I brace myself and press the doorbell, then step back, my Converse kicking the concrete like a nervous habit.

It's overcast and muggy, the sky expectant with rain, like it would take one wrong word for it to just let loose.

Carla texted me last night, giving me the go-ahead to visit Alice, but I realized I didn't want to go by myself. Plus, I needed a car.

I hope it's okay that I'm here. What if Johnny answers the door? What if Finn's too busy? What if he's tired of bailing me out whenever I need a car?

But then the door opens and he's there, wearing an Alice in Chains T-shirt and his usual cargo shorts, feet bare, hair tousled, like he just woke up.

He gives me a small smile.

It's natural and easy, a smile that shows the gap between his two front teeth, and right then it moves over me like the sudden introduction of light into a dark room, everything making itself known in the new brightness.

Being with Finn is about more than needing a car.

When I'm with Finn, I can be myself.

It's like talking with Ruby or being at Carla's. No one's expecting the valedictorian, the healthy sister, the responsible daughter, the future doctor.

They're just expecting me.

The simple realization makes me want to cry with relief.

"Parker?" He steps outside, shutting the door behind him, shoving his fists in his pockets. "How'd you know where I live?"

"Internet. Hey, can you drive me somewhere right now?"

He waits a second, to see if I'm going to say more, then nods. "Just a minute." The door shuts behind him.

I hug myself and look around. The lawn is overgrown. Finn's truck is in the driveway, along with Johnny's Datsun, its hood open, insides exposed to the elements. The woods behind their house are encroaching onto the edges of the backyard, as if in another five years, the trees and roots might just swallow the whole house. From the corner of my eye, I see a hand nudge aside bent window blinds, then drop them back just as quickly.

There's no way I want to run into Johnny.

I go over to Finn's truck and open the passenger side, climb in, jiggling my leg, the change in the cup holder rattling with the movement, and watch a squirrel dart across a phone line and leap onto a tree.

I leave the ballerina where she is.

Finn slides in a few minutes later, smelling like soap and minty toothpaste. "Where to?" he asks.

I don't say much on the way to Wild Meadows, and Finn doesn't either, which I appreciate. I haven't been to Wild Meadows since Grandma McCullough died when I was in second grade, and I can't say I'm looking forward to it.

"Here," I finally say, motioning him to the visitors parking.

As soon as I take in my surroundings in the lobby, I feel like I've jumped into a time machine and gone back to when Grandma McCullough was sick. The faux-homey decor is exactly the same: a maroon and pine-green flowered print, innocuous art, a grandfather clock, even a glass aviary with small finches hopping around.

Charlie and I used to wheel Grandma to the aviary while Mom and Dad talked with the doctors. We'd sit with her there, watching the birds, while she told us stories about the cowboy music society and helium people and George Bush offering her a cream puff.

It was a few years before I realized her chemo made her confused, that she hadn't really met George Bush.

"Parker?" Finn asks, his hand light on my elbow, and I shake my head.

"Sorry." At the desk, a perky blond-haired woman with a name tag that says PAM looks brightly up at me. "I'm here to see Alice Roell," I say.

"Oh, are you her niece?" the woman asks. "I'm so excited you finally made it!"

"No. I work at the place where Alice comes for her ceramics classes."

Pam smiles and shakes her head. "I'm sorry, of course."

"Alice has a niece?" I ask, signing my name and Finn's in the visitor log.

"Yep. Her name's Lily," Pam says. "Come on. I'll show you to Alice's room."

As we follow Pam down the hall, she keeps mindlessly chatting, clearly glad for the company.

"I help Alice FaceTime with Lily and her son, Jack, every week. He is just the cutest thing! I'm not sure how much of it Alice actually takes in, but she's always calmer after hearing Lily's voice."

"FaceTime?" I ask. "Why doesn't Lily visit?"

"She lives in Texas. She's a single mom, and I don't know that she can afford a ticket up. But she makes sure to call every Tuesday and Thursday at six thirty p.m., right after Alice has dinner."

I nod as Pam points us down a hall. "Room 116," she says. "I'll buzz you through. Have a good visit!"

When we enter Alice's section, my breath catches.

This section doesn't remind me of my grandma.

It reminds me of Charlie.

Of hospitals.

Of sickness and generic cleaning supplies and vanilla pudding cups.

The hallway is spotted with residents sitting in wheelchairs. Some of them are sleeping. One older man has his mouth open and is breathing heavily, and another older man is muttering under his breath about bacon.

Without thinking, I reach my hand out toward Finn, and he takes it, holds tight.

"Alice?" I say as I knock on the open door of 116.

She's lying in the bed, awake, but her eyes are glazed over, and I'm not sure she sees us or even knows we're there. She looks so small and flat against the sheets.

I motion Finn to the chair near the window and pull another up next to her.

"It's Parker, from Carla's Ceramics. I'm here with my friend Finn."

She doesn't respond or move, but I continue talking.

"We've missed seeing you. I'm sure you know already, but there's a new guy, Henry? And Miss Peggy and Harriet both have a bit of a crush on him. Oh, and we made something for you."

I dig through my bag until I find the brightly colored vase we all painted for her, round-robin style. There's a plastic pitcher filled with daisies on the bedside table next to her, and without asking, Finn takes the vase from me and grabs the pitcher of daisies, heading to the bathroom. I hear him pouring out the water from the pitcher, filling the vase.

I take in the picture next to Alice's bed—one of a couple on their wedding day, the woman tiny and birdlike, the man dapper, with a sparkle in his eye, a man and woman standing at each of their sides, the best man and maid of honor.

I realize the bride must be Alice.

"Your husband was so handsome, Alice! And look at how beautiful you are," I say, leaning over and taking the picture, studying it more closely. "This bridesmaid has to be related to you, yes?"

I take in the two women, each with meticulously curled hair, the same button noses, careful posture, high cheekbones. The bridesmaid is breaking the pose and squeezing Alice's elbow, just as excited as Alice is.

Even though I don't know for certain, I feel like she has to be Alice's sister, Lily's mom.

I look back at Alice, her eyes gazing vacantly at a spot on the wall, and I wish her sister were still alive now, holding her hand, or that Lily and Jack could be here.

A fierce wave of missing Charlie comes over me then, and I remember running after him and losing him, how he came back for me.

I'm not sure he would do that for me anymore.

Finn returns with the flowers in our vase, placing it where Alice can see it. He grabs his chair and scoots it closer to mine, and I pick up Alice's hand, her skin tissue-paper thin.

"Alice, did you know my friend Finn is an artist? He paints amazing messages to people all over the city. You'd like them. They make you think outside of what's around you. They take you to other places. And he has a secret tunnel, too. It's like a superhero hideout but with art. It's the most magical place I've ever been, but I'm not supposed to tell anyone about it, I don't think."

I sneak a glance at Finn. He's leaning forward, head in hands, looking at the floor, and blushing something fierce.

I gently turn over Alice's hand, holding the palm open.

"What's your message to the world today?" I ask Finn.

"You are here," he replies.

His words remind me of raising my hand in class during attendance, saying "Here," of the map near the information desk at the mall, marking your location in the middle of all the neon lights and window displays, of the poem I nearly used for my valedictorian speech, one from Walt Whitman I had to memorize for English class: "That you are here—that life exists and identity / That the powerful play goes on, and you may contribute a verse."

Finn is here, next to me, waiting.

With my index finger, I slowly trace a *Y* on Alice's palm and then an *O*. She closes her eyes as I do, her breathing steady and even, and I keep tracing, talking to her in a low, steady voice.

"You're here," I say, as much to myself and Finn as to her. "You are here."

Forty-One

"PARK THERE," I SAY to Finn, pointing to the empty meter we've just passed. He jerks the truck to a stop, earning a deserved honk from the driver of the BMW behind us, who then screeches around us, giving us the finger.

Finn laughs under his breath, putting his arm on the back of my seat and craning his head around, parallel parking in the spot.

Just as he turns off the ignition, the sky opens up in sheets of rain.

"Come on," I say. "We can run."

The two of us wait in the truck cabin for a break in traffic on Delta Avenue, and as soon as I see one, I yell, "Go!"

We tear out of the truck, doors slamming behind us, and run across the street in the downpour. I hunch into myself the whole way, trying to make myself smaller and not get so wet.

We burst into Zip's like an entire army is after us, earning a shocked look from the waitress.

We're drenched.

Finn wipes his wet sneakers in the entryway, his T-shirt clinging to his chest.

I wring out my hair. "Sorry," I say as the water runs off us in rivulets.

"It's fine. Y'all are brave to venture out today," the waitress says, hands on her hips, watching us both. "Two drowned rats, I swear. Just a minute."

My wet skin and hair feel chilly in the air-conditioning, and Finn doesn't look much warmer. But the waitress comes back with two pink sweatshirts, a Zip's logo emblazoned across the fronts.

"Left over from when we sponsored the Flying Pig Marathon," she says, handing them to us. "Sorry about the color."

Finn shrugs, pulling his on, and I giggle when I see him.

"What?"

"It's a far cry from Alice in Chains," I say, pulling mine on too. It smells musty, like it's been shoved in a box in the back of an attic, but it's dry and warm. "Thanks," I say to the waitress.

"Sit anywhere you want," she replies, heading back to the kitchen. Since it's only a little after eleven thirty, there are tables to be found, and I grab a booth on the side.

"I've never been here," Finn says to me, taking in the surroundings.

I try to see Zip's through his eyes, like I haven't been going here once a month for as long as I can remember. It's cozy and dark in the rain, the Reds away game playing on the TV in the corner, the toy train that circles the top of the main room chugging merrily along its track.

"My favorite part when I was a kid," I say, seeing Finn notice it.

"Nice," he says.

As soon as we sit in the booth, Finn grimaces. "Do you like baseball?"

"Eh, it's okay," I say. "Why?"

"Big talk?"

I nod.

"If I sit in this seat, the television is over your shoulder and I'm going to watch it the whole time, no matter how much I want to watch you. Switch?"

I'm grateful it's dark enough that Finn doesn't see me blush, so we stand, shuffle awkwardly around each other, and settle on the opposite sides of the booth.

The waitress comes over, hands us menus.

"What's good here?" Finn asks, scanning the laminated menus.

"Burgers. You have to get a burger. That's what they're known for. That's what I'll have," I say, turning to the waitress. "A Zip's Burger and fries and a Diet Coke."

"Same thing," Finn adds. "But a regular Coke."

My eyes dart to the game on the television screen behind him. The Reds are currently winning.

When I look back, Finn's watching me—I see his eyes moving from my hair to my cheekbones, to my lips, to my eyes.

"Do I have something on my face?" I ask, reflexively wiping my lips.

"No, not at all," he says. I blush. Again.

"What's the deal with this place?" he asks.

"It's been here since the 1920s. My great-grandpa first met my great-grandma here. It was before he left for overseas service, and he said this whole family of beautiful girls came in from church, all dressed up in hats. My great-grandmother was the youngest of five sisters. My great-grandpa originally had a crush on her older sister Irene, but when he came back from his time overseas, my great-grandma was all grown up, and he realized she was the sister for him. My mom loves telling that story about her grandparents."

Finn nods, fiddling with the napkin in front of him, suddenly quiet.

"But it's no Anchor Grill, you know?" I tease.

He doesn't respond, and we sit there quietly, and I'm about to ask him what just happened, why he got so quiet, when he mutters something.

"What?" I say.

"Alice is lucky to have you," he says, slightly louder.

"Oh," I say.

The waitress comes with our food, and the burger bun is glistening with butter on the top, the fries golden, and my stomach gives a loud embarrassing growl.

We eat in silence, until I get the courage to say what I've been mulling over since the night at the airport.

"I've been thinking about your bruises, and I wonder if maybe you should take a break from boxing. Have a doctor check them out, you know?"

"Parker."

"I just think getting hurt like that over and over can't be good for your body. Maybe your coach should take it easier when you're practicing."

"It's not even all from boxing," he snaps, then immediately looks like he wants to take it back.

"What do you mean it's not all from boxing?"

Finn lets out a loud sigh. "Johnny and I got in a fight last week."

"What?" The question comes out as a strangled little shriek.

"It's fine."

"Your brother did that? That's not fine!"

"Seriously, it was just a fight, okay? Brothers fight."

"God, why do you put up with him, Finn?" I ask. "He's dangerous."

"You don't know that."

"I do. He hit you!"

Finn shrugs. "I hit him back."

"But he's dealing, too, isn't he?"

Finn doesn't deny it.

"You don't owe him anything. He's not a good person."

He scoffs. "You don't even know him. What gives you the right to judge?"

"Tell me, then. Tell me how he's not all bad."

Finn rubs his hand over the back of his neck. "One of the first things I remember growing up was Johnny talking about our mom. He had all these cassette tapes she used to love and her old Walkman. He listened to them all the time. You remember the Walkman, right?"

I nod, thinking of the careful way Finn showed it to me that first day, how he wrapped it in a sweatshirt in his backpack every day after school, tucking it carefully inside.

"Johnny loved those tapes. He listened to them for hours every day. But as I got older, I got mad because he'd never share them with me. So I stole the Walkman. I had it for a few months before he saw you that day on the playground."

Finn's face tightens. "Johnny was upset it broke. He said it was all my fault." His mouth clenches shut.

"What happened?"

"When Dad came home that night, he found Johnny whaling on me. So he started beating the crap out of Johnny."

I hold my breath, afraid to say anything, not wanting him to stop but scared to hear what will come next.

"Dad was hitting Johnny so hard, I thought he was going to kill him. So I went to the neighbors, who called 911. And when the police got there, they found Dad's meth lab in the garage. Fast-forward a few weeks later, Dad's in jail and his auto body shop is permanently closed, and we're at Carla's, in a new school district."

"That's why you were so mad at me when you came back to school," I say.

He shakes his head hard. "I was never mad at you. It was all my fault."

"Finn."

He looks at me, shoulders sharp. "Don't do that."

"What?"

"I told you already. I don't need saving, Parker."

"But . . ."

"But nothing. It's just how it was. How it is."

"None of that was your fault. You were just a kid. Your dad should have never hit Johnny. Johnny should have never hit you. That's not right."

He sucks in his breath, leans back, his eyes meeting mine evenly.

I realize then that for the first time since I met him, Finn is mad. Beyond mad—he's furious. This must be what he looks like when he fights, all his angles getting sharper, his hollows emptier, his face harder.

"You don't know me," Finn says, each word a hit. "You don't know my family."

I flinch. "I guess I don't."

I sit back, emptied out from the morning, and look out the window, realizing Finn's family isn't the only one I don't know.

I can't even make things right with my own brother.

But the longer I sit there, stewing in the silence between Finn and me, an idea starts to take root, small and careful, a seed of hope.

If I can't help Finn, maybe, just maybe, I can help Alice.

Forty-Two

I'M AT MY DESK, clicking through different travel websites, researching the costs of flights between Cincinnati and Austin, trying not to look at my phone.

But then I give in and check.

No message.

Even though it's been a little more than twenty-four hours since I last saw Finn and I doubt he'd text even if he did want to talk, I can't stop hoping he'll reach out. After our spat about his brother at Zip's, we didn't talk much, other than my insistence that I'd get the bill since he drove me (a proposition he didn't appreciate), and then his gruff "Sorry" when he dropped me off.

I hear Ruby's laugh from the backyard, and a quick glance out the window next to me confirms it: She and Charlie are approaching the giant hammock under my bedroom window.

I wonder if Charlie told her he knows my secret about the internship.

This morning, at breakfast, I was pretty sure the jig was up.

Dad was reading the paper while Charlie and I were doing our best to ignore each other's existence, when out of the blue, Mom asked me how things were going with Henry.

All the blood rushed from my face. "You know?" My spoon clattered in the bowl as I turned to Charlie. "I thought we had a deal! You weren't going to tell them!"

"Tell us what?" Mom asked.

"No, Parker," Charlie said, purposefully shooting meaningful eyes at me. "*You* told them about the new patient, remember?"

Relief made me dizzy. Of course. I had told them about the "new patient" Henry.

"Oh, Henry! That Henry. Sorry! Clearly I'm not entirely awake today yet. He's good. He's made some friends—Harriet and Peggy and Lorna—and I think it helped him feel a little less alone."

"I had a great-aunt named Lorna," Dad offered over the paper.

Mom looked confused. "But you said something about a deal with Charlie?"

"Parker made a deal to help me with my chem homework tonight, right?" Charlie asked.

"Yeah, of course, yes," I said, wondering why he was bailing me out, wondering if he was stacking up more material to use against me.

Mom didn't seem entirely satisfied with the explanation, but lucky for me, she decided to drop it.

As I watch him now, Charlie holds the hammock steady for

Ruby while she considers the best approach to hopping on. He's careful with her, making sure she has a steady net and then gingerly lifting himself on next to her.

I realize they're so much more coordinated than Em and me, who have more than once knocked each other off while trying to share the space. The last time, Em ended up with a bruised tailbone.

They both stretch out, Charlie's arms behind his head, a bare foot gently rocking them back and forth, Ruby with her curly hair hanging down from the side, her eyes studying the canopy of green above her. Lightning bugs are starting to wink around them.

I'm just about ready to lift the screen and call out hello when Ruby turns to him.

"So, did you make a decision on baseball next year?"

I freeze, waiting for Charlie's face to go sullen, his voice to go hostile, but instead, he says, "Lift your head for a second."

She does, and then he stretches his arm out, so Ruby can rest her head in the crook of his shoulder.

"Yeah. I don't think I'm going to go back on the team after all," he says once she's settled.

Surprise rushes through me—at the fact that he answered her and at his answer. I angle myself to the side, clicking off my desk lamp so they can't see my silhouette from below.

Charlie loves baseball. And he's a pretty sure shot for a baseball scholarship now that he's healthy again. He's obviously not thinking this out clearly.

"And you feel good about it?" Ruby asks him.

"Yeah, I actually do. I mean, Coach Franklin's going to be

disappointed. And I'm sure Dad'll be pissed and Mom will be quietly worried and Parker will chalk this all up to some chemo side effect where I'm not thinking clearly, but yeah, it's what I want to do."

I frown, immediately defensive that I'm so predictable. I turn my back to the wall, sliding down on the floor, and hug my knees to my chest.

I shouldn't be listening. But I don't get up.

"What are you going to do with all that free time?" Ruby asks.

"I don't know. But that's the good thing. For the past year, everything has been planned down to the second—chemo, doctor appointments, checkups. Now the whole world is open in front of me, and it's mine to fuck up however I want."

"Charlie," Ruby starts, her voice worried.

"I'm kidding. I just mean that it's all up to me for the first time in ages."

For a second I feel envious of the blank slate in front of him.

"And, of course, there's this junior I have my eye on that I'm hoping to hang out with. . . . What's her name again? Rudy?" he continues.

"Hey! You'd better know my name," Ruby says, then giggles, and then they're quiet, and it takes me a few seconds to realize they're probably making out.

My face goes red. I'm being a total creeper. I start to straighten, when I hear Ruby say, "You know, you shouldn't be so hard on your sister."

I wait for Charlie's reply, but it doesn't come, and then I hear Ruby giggle.

"Charlie, stop kissing me, just for a second, okay?"

"Okay, okay," he says in mock exasperation.

"What I was trying to tell you before I was so rudely interrupted is that I've always wanted a brother or sister. You've got a really good sister. You're lucky."

It sounds like Charlie mutters something that sounds like "Hardly," and then I hear him go, "Ow!"

"I mean it. Your sister is the first real friend I've had in ages."

"Come on," Charlie starts.

"No, it's true. People don't always like me. My mom says it's because I try too hard, that I'm too much. She says on a scale of one to ten, with ten being too much, I'm, like, a thirteen." Ruby laughs, but it's hollow. "Your sister is, like, the first person in forever who actually listens to me and wants to hang out with me."

My heart breaks for her, and I hold my breath, waiting for Charlie's response.

"Meeting you is the best thing that's happened to me in ages, Ruby Collie. If other people can't see how amazing you are, it is one hundred percent their fucking loss. And I'm sorry to say that includes your mom."

I let my breath out. Charlie might actually be worthy of my bighearted friend.

It's weird seeing—or more accurately, eavesdropping on—this side of him, a side I haven't seen since Matty's surprise pool party last summer, when I discovered the broken blood vessels on Charlie's back.

I forgot how protective he can be on behalf of the people he cares about, how when he's on your side, there's nothing he won't do for you.

"That's the problem with family," Charlie continues, and my eyelid twitches. I hug my knees harder to my chest. "They think they're doing what's best and they end up destroying everything around them in the process. Take Parker, for instance."

"Charlie," Ruby says, her voice gentle, but he keeps talking.

"Do you know how hard it is to have her for a sister? It's like watching someone willingly subject themselves to torture over and over again, like when they put slivers of wood under your finger-nails or something. . . ."

My eyes start burning, and I stand up, leaving before I hear anything more of the words my brother keeps deep in his heart.

Forty-Three

THE NEXT DAY AT pottery, I'm doing everything I can to forget what I overheard last night.

I focus instead on explaining our new project.

"I thought we could paint vases and sell them to raise money for Alice," I say.

Four blank faces greet me.

"Turns out, her niece, Lily, lives in Texas. But she's a single mom and tight on cash."

"Oh dear," Lorna says with a dismayed sigh.

"But we can help her. Carla and I thought we could paint vases and mugs to sell at the Hyde Park Art Fair to help get money for plane tickets for her and her son, Jack. It's a lot to do in the next week and a half, but I know we can do it. I talked with Carla. She's already got a booth for her own stuff, and she said she could share it and that she'd donate the materials to our cause. What do you guys think?"

"That's very noble," Miss Peggy says, and I'm relieved she's talking to us again.

"Not bad," Harriet admits, and I'm grateful she's on board too.

I look over to Lorna and Henry, sitting to my left, and I try not to gasp.

The two of them are holding hands, arms resting on the table.

"We have something to say first," Lorna says. She's decked out in blues today—an indigo shirt, sky-blue pants, a periwinkle scarf, a blue crescent moon brooch. Henry has a complementary blueberry-hued pocket square.

"Well!" Miss Peggy's thin-plucked eyebrows rise higher on her face than I thought possible.

Lorna flinches, but Henry holds her hand harder. "Lorna and I are seeing each other," he announces.

"Huh," Harriet says. "Didn't see that one coming."

"Peggy, I hope you can be happy for me, for us," Lorna says, putting her hand on Miss Peggy's shoulder.

Miss Peggy pushes Lorna's hand away, and Lorna looks crushed.

I force myself to smile. "I'm excited for you both," I say to Henry, wondering if that's appropriate, but by the way he beams at me, I don't think it really matters what I say.

"Let's get this party started already!" Harriet yells. She shoves a paintbrush in Lorna's direction.

"Are we doing round-robin painting?" Henry asks.

"If you guys want," I say.

"I'll paint my own, thank you very much," Miss Peggy says, getting up and actually moving to the next table.

Harriet rolls her eyes, and Lorna looks like she's going to cry, but Henry belts out, "Fine by me!"

I try not to smile.

Despite my best efforts, as Miss Peggy sulks and the rest of us paint, I find myself going back to what I overheard last night, Charlie's words still stinging.

I sigh and put down my paintbrush.

"You okay?" Lorna asks.

I nod. "Yeah. I just need to stretch for a little bit."

I stand, rolling my shoulders back. Harriet says something that makes Henry burst out in a loud laugh, and Lorna giggles, looking hopefully over toward Miss Peggy to see if she's joining in. But Miss Peggy just glowers, and Lorna lets out an unhappy sigh.

I fiddle with my paintbrush, and much to my surprise, I realize my heart is hurting a little on Miss Peggy's behalf.

I walk over toward her, sitting in the chair next to her.

"I don't need any help," she says, her tone clipped.

"I know. I'm not offering any."

She clicks her tongue against her teeth and shakes her head. "Impertinent."

Okay, let's try this again. "That's very beautiful," I say to her, pointing toward her vase.

It's a total lie.

She's currently painting angry-looking red, purple, and brown flowers all over the edges, with smears of orange around the bottom. In fact, I'd be hard-pressed to figure out a way to make it more visually unappealing. It looks like something Mustard threw up.

"I did take art classes in college, you know."

"It really shows," I say.

I'm lying through my teeth, but it works, because I see her shoulders soften just a half inch or so.

"Miss Peggy, I was hoping you could help me with something," I say.

She keeps painting. "I'm listening."

"I need a co-chair for the fund-raiser. I could really use someone who can make sure we have all the right supplies the weekend of the show."

"I'm very busy, as you know," she says, dipping her brush into a heinous-looking army green. As she dabs it lightly on the vase, to my surprise it somehow helps, bringing all the terrible colors together.

"Okay, maybe I can ask Harriet instead."

"No, no! I'll do it," Miss Peggy says. "I'll fit it in somehow."

"Good. I really appreciate it," I say.

She nods primly, then stands and smooths her slacks before rejoining the main table. When she gets settled, she taps Lorna on the shoulder. "Pass me that when you're done. It could use some of this green," she says, pointing to the vase Lorna is holding.

"Of course!" Lorna sends me a grateful look.

The rest of the afternoon goes by smoothly, everyone diligently painting and mostly getting along. We have a lot to finish in the next week and a half to make enough for the tickets, and I wonder if I've gotten myself in over my head. But as I watch the ladies and Henry paint, I remind myself that even if Charlie can't stand to be around me, I'm doing something good here.

I try to pretend that's enough.

Forty-Four

WALKING SLOWLY DOWN THE hallway, my Converse dangling from my hands, I hear the ten o'clock news playing in my parents' bedroom, but I make it downstairs without tipping anyone off, my whole body exhaling in relief.

Tonight, after dinner, I finally got a text from Finn:

Made it to the Fight to the Death finals—want to see me box? Around 10:45. The fair space at Huron Park.

My whole body warmed in response.

So now I'm sitting on the living room floor, lacing up my high-tops, ready to sneak out past curfew to go to an amateur boxing competition.

I don't even know who I am anymore. But I don't care.

I tell myself this is no big deal. I'm just supporting a friend. I didn't want to bother Mom and Dad, and I'll be back before they even notice. Everything's good.

"Where are you going?"

I yelp in surprise, then cover my mouth, glaring at Charlie leaning against the doorframe.

"Out."

"Where?"

"Nowhere. Please just go back upstairs."

Charlie cocks his eyebrow. "I don't think nowhere is a real place."

I shake my head. "That was a Dad joke and you know it."

"Huh. Maybe he knows where you're going." He moves toward the stairs.

"Charlie!" I hiss between clenched teeth.

He smiles, and I realize he's enjoying this.

I relent. "I'm going to see Finn box in some contest."

His face tightens at the mention of Finn's name. "Now?"

"He made it to the finals," I say.

"I'm coming with you."

"No. You aren't."

"Well, maybe I'll just stay home and talk to Mom and Dad about pottery. How about that?"

"God. Are you going to hold this over me forever?"

He shrugs, and frustration courses through me. "Why do you even want to hang out? Isn't being around me pretty much torture?"

He frowns. "What are you talking about?"

I remind myself tonight is about Finn, not Charlie, and I shake my head, relenting. "Never mind. But I'm driving."

"What time do we need to be there?"

I look at my phone. "In about forty minutes."

"And where is it again?"

"On the West Side, at Huron Park."

He gives me a skeptical look, and I sigh, tossing him Mom's keys so quickly, he almost drops them.

"If you get us stopped for a speeding ticket, I'm going to kill you," I warn as I open the door to the garage and head outside, the sound of my brother's footsteps behind me.

Forty-Five

GROWING UP, I'D SEEN posters stapled to telephone poles around town advertising "Fight to the Death" contests. They were in bright neon colors—always at intersections right when you pulled off the highway, the aggressive capital letters and exclamation points demanding your attention.

I didn't know what the contests entailed, but I couldn't understand why anyone would want to fight so much they died.

And even after I eventually read an article about the amateur boxing contests in the newspaper, if you had asked me if I'd ever be watching one unfold in front of me, I would have laughed you out of the room.

But I'm currently pushing through a crush of sweaty cheering people who are watching two large guys dance and duck and grunt as they attempt to knock each other out.

I'd never admit it out loud, but I'm secretly relieved Charlie came. There's no way I would have found this place on my own. And, of course, when we arrived, the first person I saw in the crowd was Johnny Casper. He didn't see me because I shoved Charlie so hard in the opposite direction, he actually stumbled.

He turned around and scowled at me. "Sorry," I muttered.

But right now, even if Johnny were standing two feet away from me, I don't know if I could see him. Charlie's trying to get us closer, but there are people everywhere, and I feel that familiar panic of being short in a crowd of people—stuck in a mess of torsos and shoulders. I'm just getting to the point where I think I'm going to scream when Charlie moves to the side and I realize we made it to the edge of the ring, right as one of the guys currently boxing falls to the ground, his weight slamming to the floor in front of me.

Charlie nods appreciatively. "Badass."

"I don't know why people like this."

"'Cause it's sweet," Charlie says, his eyes lighting up as the guy on the floor stumbles up and begins boxing again, only to get knocked out again—this time for good. He points to the scoreboard. "Finn's up next."

I look around at the rest of the crowd. It's mostly men, but I see an occasional woman here and there. Most everyone has plastic cups of beer, and the floor is littered with cigarette butts.

People start cheering when a super-tanned woman in a bright-orange bikini comes out and makes a slow circle around the inner ring, holding a sign that reads ROUND 1 so that everyone can see it.

The announcer calls out, "And now our level-two finalists, up first . . . Finn Casper!"

At first I'm relieved he's up, because as soon as he's done, I can leave. But then I see him—shirtless, skull tattoo dark against his pale skin, his hair knotted up in a bun—lifting the elastic ropes at the edge of the ring. Someone hands him headgear, and my stomach knots as he straps it on. Even from the other side of the ring, I can make out his lingering bruises, his sinewy abdomen, his breakable bones.

I want to jump right up there and pull him out of the ring, take him away from here, never let him come back.

My eyelid twitches.

Charlie puts his hand on my shoulder. "It'll be okay," he says. "He wouldn't have gotten this far if he didn't know what he was doing."

Finn waits in the corner, putting in a mouth guard, then sliding on his gloves. My eyes dart around the ring, and I see Johnny on the other side. He's chewing something, his focus on the guy next to him, who's stealthily counting out some money, which Johnny slips into his back pocket.

Everything around me suddenly seems louder than it was just a second ago, but I can't make out any of it—it's just a rush of noise.

I can't tell if the tenor of the crowd is changing or it's just in my head.

"And his opponent, Joe Castanelli!"

A guy with a shaved head climbs into the ring. They're the same height, but Finn's opponent looks like a bulldog, thick arms and thicker torso.

I hug myself harder.

Even Charlie looks uneasy.

The bell rings, and both boxers move forward. Finn's jogging in place, while his opponent lumbers: slow, focused, and sure.

As the guy makes his first swing, Finn's whole body arches back, graceful, and he throws a quick uppercut, hitting the guy in the ribs. The guy stumbles back a few steps, and in surprise, Charlie murmurs, "Finn's really good." The crowd cheers, and I look over at Johnny, his eyes locked on Finn, but I can't watch him for too long, my eyes going back to Finn.

Finn dances around his opponent like David and Goliath, like Jack and the Giant, before throwing a right hook. This time the guy's ready, jerking back, faster than I thought he could with all that bulk, and he quickly lands one right on Finn's jaw.

I grip Charlie's arm hard as Finn staggers backward. But even though Finn's eyes are glazed, he catches his balance, pushing his shoulders forward, and before the guy can register, Finn hits back, knocking him right in the face.

The crowd erupts in more yelling, whistling, and Johnny hollers, "Get him, Finny!"

The giant wipes his face with his arm, and Finn leaps toward his opponent, throwing a light rain of punches against the guy's gut.

The other guy is pissed now, and using all his mass, he launches himself at Finn, one huge fist meeting Finn's face again. This time, Finn tumbles to the ground in front of us. I want so badly to close my eyes, but I can't stop looking at the outline of his ribs, his chest heaving up and down, his eyes scrunched closed, the trickle of blood from his nose.

"Get up," Charlie says under his breath as the judge begins to count, the crowd starting to count along with him.

Johnny pushes close to the side, yelling, "Don't blow this, Finn!" The judge shoots him a stern look, and Johnny backs up, holding his hands in front of him.

The giant paces, restless, knocking his gloves together.

From the ground, Finn turns his head and opens his eyes. He sees me then, his eyes locking onto mine, and for the first time since I met him, the storm in them has calmed, now just the quiet still gray of a winter afternoon.

The judge finishes his count, declaring the giant the winner. I glance at Johnny and see the disgust and fury on his face as he shoves a big wad of money at a guy, then pushes away through the crowd.

I go back to Finn, holding his gaze, until hands lift him up, slinging his arm around a shoulder, Finn's eyes fluttering shut and jerking back open, his gait woozy, and then I realize it's my brother holding him up, that Charlie's the one walking him toward me, that Charlie's the one getting us home.

Forty-Six

WHEN WE STEP OUTSIDE, Finn still propped against Charlie, Johnny's waiting across the parking lot, smoking. His eyes hone in on Finn.

"Shit," Finn says under his breath, his body tensing. He turns to us. "I'll talk to you guys later?"

"Sure," Charlie says.

I give them both a hard look. "No."

"Parker," Finn starts.

Maybe it's the sleepy glaze in Finn's eyes or the way Johnny responded to Finn's loss, but I'm not leaving him right now. I shake my head. "You're coming home with us."

"Johnny's right over there. He's got my truck keys. He'll drive me home," he insists, stepping away from Charlie. He's gotten a little steadier on his feet.

"I see him over there, but um, yeah, NO."

"Parker, if he wants to—" Charlie says, but I shoot him a glare that immediately shuts him up.

By this point, Johnny has stalked over to us. He drops his cigarette, grinds it out with the heel of his boot, giving me a long look and a nod before turning his attention to Finn. "What the fuck was that, Finny?"

His voice is casual, but everything else about him is projecting barely controlled fury.

Finn shrugs, but it's not nearly as lazy as he's making it look. His whole body is alert, the animal instincts in him poised for fight or flight. "He got me. I didn't see it coming. It happens."

"'It happens'? You know how much your little fuckup just cost me?"

"Cost *you*?" I ask.

"Back off, princess," Johnny snarls.

Finn steps between us, turning his back to his brother. "Can you give us a few seconds?" he asks.

"No," I say, clenching Mom's keys in my fist.

Finn looks to Charlie—for help, I'm guessing—but Charlie's eyes go to me, and I shake my head firmly. He turns back to Finn. "Uh, no, man. Why don't you just come with us?"

Johnny laughs. "Hiding with your fancy friends?"

"What a dick," Charlie mutters under his breath.

"Come on, Finn. Please," I say. I take his hand in mine, wrap my fingers through his.

He searches my eyes, then lets out a small sigh, nodding before turning back to Johnny. "You go. I'll see you later. And be careful with the truck."

Johnny shakes his head in disgust, a two-fingered point from his eyes to Finn's. "This isn't over, Finny. You lost us a shit ton tonight."

"What's he talking about?" I ask as we watch Johnny leave.

"Nothing," Finn says.

"Finn."

"Can you just drop it?" he snaps. And then more quietly, "Please?"

The three of us walk to Mom's car.

As we're walking, the fear I felt watching Finn starts to recede. My eyelid is still occasionally twitching, but with each step away from the boxing crowd, I feel my resolve strengthen.

Finn might not want to talk about what just happened with his brother, but he needs someone to take care of him right now.

I can help him.

I open the back door of the car, pushing a stack of Mom's student papers out of the way.

"I guess this means I owe you a gift card sometime?" Finn jokes.

"Keep your nose tilted back," I say, ignoring the gift card comment as he climbs in, an involuntary groan escaping his lips as he settles against the seat.

I can't help it, letting my hand rest against his cheek for a second, wanting to take away all his hurt.

I turn to Charlie, who's just standing there looking at me like he's seeing me for the first time.

"What are you waiting for? Let's go," I say, hiking my thumb toward the driver's seat.

"Yeah, okay."

As Charlie pulls out of the lot, I dig through Mom's glove compartment until I find a packet of tissues and hand them over the seat to Finn.

"Thanks," he mumbles.

In the rearview mirror, I watch him shove one up the nostril with the dried blood.

As Charlie drives, Finn closes his eyes, but I can tell he's still awake by the way he winces every time we go over a bump.

For the next half hour, the only sound in the car is Charlie's jam-band music. When we finally reach our exit, I realize my eye hasn't twitched since we got on the highway.

Charlie looks at me expectantly. "Where to?"

Finn's breathing sounds sticky. I can't imagine leaving him with no one to watch over him but Johnny and a ghost with sharp teeth.

"Our house," I say. "I don't think he should be alone."

I expect Charlie to argue, to tell me I'm worrying too much, but to my surprise, he nods. "Yeah, you're right."

We decide to leave the car in the driveway so the sound of the garage door doesn't wake up Mom and Dad. Charlie comes to the passenger side to help me ease Finn out of the backseat, Finn suppressing a yelp when he stands.

Between the both of us, we get him into the house, me kicking the front door shut behind us.

"Family room," I say.

Mustard winds between Charlie's legs and then yelps when Charlie gets part of his tail. "Ugh, Mustard."

"Here," I say, nudging Mustard out of the way, and then scoot ahead of them so I can push aside the coffee table.

Charlie helps Finn onto the couch, and with a sigh, Finn lies down, resting his head against Mom's hand-embroidered Queen City pillow—the one that took her ten years to finish. The previously bleeding side of his nose is now precariously close to the image of the suspension bridge.

A nervous giggle escapes my lips before I clap my hand over my mouth, and Charlie shoots an exasperated look at me.

"Really?" he asks.

"I'll put a towel under there," I say. "It's just, this whole evening has been . . ." I throw up my hands.

"I know. Me too." He surveys the situation. Finn's eyes are closed, his body slumped on the couch. "Do you need any more help?"

"No. I have it," I say. "Since he's talking and can walk and his pupils aren't weird, it's okay for him to sleep."

"All right there, Dr. McCullough."

I roll my eyes at the name, but before he reaches the stairs, I look over my shoulder. "Charlie, thank you for tonight."

He pauses, then says, his voice low, "Parker, you know Johnny was betting on Finn, right? That's what he was mad about."

"But gambling on that isn't legal," I start, and Charlie gives me a look, like, *Really?*

"He can't be happy Finn lost," Charlie says.

"Well, maybe he should get in the ring himself, then. What a jerk."

"Just be careful, and stay away from him, okay?"

"Of course," I say.

He stands there for a second longer. "Finn's lucky to have you watching out for him," he says before turning to go upstairs.

I watch Charlie's back, shocked he complimented me, and wonder if I misheard him. I chalk it up to adrenaline and exhaustion and turn back to Finn.

His breathing is a little less labored than before, but the entire left side of his face looks puffy.

"I seriously don't get the allure of boxing. Why would you do this?" I say, more to myself than him.

In the kitchen, I fill a plastic bag with ice and grab a kitchen towel.

When I get back to the family room, Finn hasn't moved, so I push down on the pillow, carefully sliding the towel under there so he doesn't bleed all over Mom's ten-year project. Then I turn off the lights and squeeze onto the couch next to him, the pillow and Finn's head practically in my lap.

Mustard hops onto the back of the couch, nudging his wet nose against my neck and head, purring frantically in the hopes of a few good pets, but instead, I rest the bag of ice against the side of Finn's face. I wait for him to flinch at the cold, but he doesn't, only lifts his hand and holds the bag against his face too, his hand on top of mine.

I have no clue how I'm going to explain any of this to Mom and Dad tomorrow. But that's a problem for tomorrow. For now I let myself just listen to the sound of Finn's breathing evening out.

Mustard falls asleep behind me, his head lying flat on the back of the couch, soft cat breath against my neck.

I wonder if Finn's sleeping too, but then he whispers, "I really blew that one, didn't I?"

"Well, at least you tried," I offer, and Finn lets out a low chuckle.

I think that's it, but then he says, his voice still quiet, "When I fight, everything else goes away. Johnny and my dad and my uncle and everything else about this shitty, shitty town. That's why I do it."

I hold my breath.

"But tonight, when I was fighting, you didn't go away with the rest of it."

"Oh," I say. "I'm sorry."

"It's okay. I didn't want you to."

I blush, glad he can't see my face.

"So here we are," I say, my voice quiet.

"Here we are," Finn echoes.

I sit there for a long time, waiting for him to fall asleep, trusting his breath to stay steady with mine.

Forty-Seven

A HAND SHAKES MY shoulder, and I jerk up.

Mom's looking down at me with this super-serious expression on her face, and I realize sometime in the night I fell asleep with Finn on the couch. The bag of ice has become a sloshy bag of water, and Finn looks relaxed, all his sharp edges softened from sleep and the morning light, the bruising hidden in the sun. But when I look up at Mom, I see what she's seeing—her daughter entwined on the couch with a boy, one who has dried blood on his face to boot.

I extricate myself, careful not to wake up Finn, and follow her into the kitchen. Dad's sitting at the table, his face tightly knitted with fury, and I reflexively straighten. I can't think of the last time I've seen either of them this mad.

"Want to tell us what's going on?" Mom asks, leaning against the kitchen counter and folding her arms against her chest.

"I'm sorry—my friend Finn needed help last night."

"Your friend?" Dad asks. "How come we've never heard of this friend before?"

Mom does a double take. "Is this the same Finn . . . ?"

I nod, cringing as the eyelid twitch returns.

"The same Finn what?" Dad asks.

"Parker's friend from first grade."

"The Casper kid?" Dad's face is so red, it looks like he might keel over.

"Seriously, Dad?" I snap.

Mom's frown furrows all the way up into her brows.

"Yeah, he is a Casper, and he's my friend. He needed me," I say, my voice getting louder, daring either of them to contradict me.

"This is the type of person you want as your friend?" Dad says, but Mom shoots him a look.

"Phil," she says, and he flops back in his seat, irritated with both of us now.

I cling to the fact that Mom has a soft spot for underdogs.

"He was boxing in some amateur contest—"

"For chrissakes," Dad mutters.

"Boxing?" Mom asks.

"Yeah, and he got punched really hard"—I mentally cross my fingers against the lie I'm about to tell—"so he called me and came over here, because he was worried he had a concussion."

"He drove here while he had a concussion?" Mom says. "He should have gone to the emergency room!"

"No. Someone dropped him off. And his dad and brother?

They aren't the best. So we figured it was better he was here." I've lowered my voice, praying Finn isn't awake and listening to all of this from the other room.

Dad looks doubtful, but Mom's face is softening a bit already. Time to bring it home.

I look at my father, channeling my best valedictorian voice. "Dad, he knows I want to be a doctor, so he thought I could help. I figured it was better than nothing, you know?"

He's still grimacing, but he gives a tight nod. "You should have woken us up."

"You're right. I should have. I'm sorry."

Finn appears in the doorway then, plastic bag of water in hand, looking pretty terrible. His face is starting to bruise, and he's holding his side gently, like it hurts.

"I'll get that," I say, taking the bag from him and then turning to my parents.

"Mom and Dad, this is my friend Finn. Finn, these are my parents, Phil and Jean McCullough."

Finn stands there awkwardly in front of my parents, and I watch it happen when they don't say anything, his face starting to harden, all his defenses going up, but then Mom steps forward. Stopping just short of hugging him, she puts a hand on his shoulder.

"Finn, let me get you some more ice. Sit down, please."

Surprise crosses his face. "Um, okay, thanks."

"Coffee?" she asks.

"Water is fine, thank you, ma'am."

Mom smiles at the "ma'am." "So, Parker tells us you were

boxing last night. How are you feeling this morning?" she asks, handing him back the bag, now filled with fresh ice.

Dad's still scowling from across the table.

"Okay. A little sore, I guess," Finn replies.

"Would you like some aspirin?"

"Um, yeah, I mean yes. Thank you, ma'am."

"You can call me Jean," she says, handing him a glass of water and aspirin.

"Thank you, Jean," Finn says as Dad grunts.

Charlie comes clattering down the steps into the kitchen. He freezes when he sees us all: me and Finn sitting next to our glowering father, Mom doing her thing bustling about and trying to make everything better with small talk.

I jump in before Charlie outs us. "Charlie, this is my friend Finn. He came over here last night after his boxing match," I say significantly, as much for Finn as for him, mentally begging Charlie to roll with it.

"Nice to meet you, man," Charlie says, stepping forward and shaking Finn's hand.

"You too," Finn says, doing that guy-nod thing.

"You were lucky to have my daughter taking care of you last night," Dad finally says.

"I know, sir. You're right. She's going to be a good doctor."

Nice one, Finn.

"Humph," Dad replies, but I can tell he's thawing just a little bit.

It's quiet for a moment, but then Finn clears his throat. "Parker said you like music, sir?"

Dad gives a reluctant nod.

"I was just reading online the other day how Charlie Parker's nickname was Bird," he says.

I let out a small breath of surprise.

"Humph," Dad says again, not disagreeing.

"Phil just got a new Charlie Parker recording for Father's Day, didn't you, hon?" Mom asks. "Why don't you go put it on?"

"It's not new," Dad says. "It's just a digitally remastered recording."

"I'd like to hear it," Finn offers.

"Go on, Dad," I say.

"All right. I guess so," Dad says as he heads out to the stereo in the family room.

I turn to Finn. "Why were you looking up Charlie Parker stuff?"

He shrugs. "I wanted to learn more about your namesake. And when I read about Bird, I thought it might make for a better nickname than Parking Lot."

I blush.

"Finn, can you stay for pancakes?" Mom asks.

Finn looks at me, checking to make sure it's okay.

"Stay," I say.

He turns back to my mom. "I'd like that. Thank you, ma'am."

"Jean," Mom reminds him.

Dad comes back in, the music starting to fill the room, and Finn nods appreciatively.

"It's pretty good, right?" Dad asks.

"It is, sir," Finn replies as Dad nods and grabs his paper, settling down across from Finn.

And just like that, I know it's okay, that Mom and Dad are going to let this go.

I realize then what all my years of being the good daughter have earned me: my family's willingness to trust me, to let Finn in despite all their better instincts.

I shift uncomfortably in the seat, making myself smile, trying not to think too hard what this moment would be like if they knew how much their good daughter was keeping from them.

Forty-Eight

"DO YOU SEE THEM?" Ruby asks, balancing four hot dogs in her hands as she stands on her toes.

I stop and stand on mine, too, trying to find Charlie and Finn in the crowd of parade-goers. "Charlie's text said they were right around here. Let's check the other side of the street."

Ruby nods and I follow her to the crosswalk, weaving between the families with screaming kids in strollers, tattooed hipsters, and swarthy old men who populate Northside, trying not to drop our tray of drinks.

I've never gone to the Northside Fourth of July parade, but Ruby insisted we should all go. Her exact words: "It's my only day off from the Float for the whole week. I guess I'd understand if you hated awesome things, but since you all seem to like awesome things, you have no reason not to come."

We split up after Finn squeezed his truck into a spot that defied normal people's parallel-parking skills. Ruby and I went to get food, while Charlie and Finn went to stake out space along the parade route.

"Do you have everything ready for the art fair on Sunday?" she asks.

"Yeah, we do. There was a lot of painting there at the end, but we did it. The rest home is letting us borrow a folding table, and Carla's helping me get the crew down to Hyde Park Square to work the booth. We ended up with about fifty vases to sell and a few dozen mugs."

I hear the rumblings of a band down the street, and Ruby and I both rush to cross before they close the street to the parade.

"That's awesome," Ruby says over her shoulder.

I feel a little burst of pride. "It turns out Henry's daughter is a florist. She was able to get her store to donate daisies and sunflowers the day of, so anyone who goes home with a vase will go home with flowers, too."

"Do you think you're going to have enough for Alice's niece's and grandnephew's tickets?"

I nod happily. "Yeah, and the rest home activities director is so excited about the way the summer sessions have been going, she's booked Carla for two new groups of seniors during the fall. That made Carla so happy, she offered me a bonus, but I told her to put it toward the tickets. We're going to be in good shape."

"That's so badass." Ruby stops for a second, debating. "Have you told your parents about the internship yet? Everything that you're doing with Carla is so cool. I bet they'd be really proud of you."

"Ha, as if."

"I'm serious, Parker."

"You've met our parents, right? Mom would be epically disappointed, and Dad might literally keel over from a rage heart attack." I shudder. "No way. Maybe when I'm fifty. Maybe."

"But don't you think they'd come around? People are good at surprising us. I mean look at me—when you first met me, you thought I was the most irritating person on the planet."

"No I didn't!"

"Oh, please. You totally did. I come on pretty strong. I know that."

I stop and gently pull at her shoulder. "Ruby. I don't think you should say that anymore."

"But it's true."

"So? There's nothing wrong with being enthusiastic. And I'm sorry I ever made you feel like there was. It's really amazing how you immediately let everyone in, how open you are. I'm so happy you're my friend."

Ruby shakes her head. "You don't have to say that."

"I know. But I want to. You're fearless and bright, and you should own it. And anyone who doesn't like it is a . . . a . . ." I struggle to find a good description. "A jerk."

Ruby tries not to smile. "You can do better than that."

"A . . ." I cringe. "A jerkface?"

"Better," she says, chewing on her lip for a second. "How about this: I'll try to own it if you think about telling your parents."

"Ruby—"

"I'm serious. Just think about it."

"Okay, okay," I say.

"Good." She chucks me on the arm. "Let's go find your brother."

When we finally locate Finn and Charlie—a good three and a half blocks from where they said they'd be—the parade's already started.

"Hey," Finn says, his face brightening as he sees me. His bruises from the boxing contest have hit the deep red and purple stage, but he seems to be moving a bit easier in his body today.

I hand him the hot dog. "Relish and sauerkraut. Disgusting."

"Only way to eat it," he replies.

From the corner of my eye, I see Charlie pull Ruby close, and she nestles against his chest, giggling. Embarrassed, Finn and I immediately turn our heads to the street.

"Want to sit on the curb?" I ask.

He takes his red sweatshirt from his bag and spreads it out so we can both sit on it. It's close, but I don't mind. We pull our knees up and eat the grilled hot dogs, watching the people start to stream by.

There's a marching band of teenagers playing a somewhat recognizable version of Led Zeppelin's "Immigrant Song," followed by a group of scantily clad women wearing red, white, and blue, gyrating enthusiastically.

"Sexy," Charlie says, dropping next to Finn.

Ruby leans into his arm, sending him a gentle elbow in the ribs. "Watch it."

Finn raises an eyebrow at me, and I laugh, shaking my head.

"Oooh, good job!" Ruby calls out as a bunch of ladies and a

few guys Hula-Hoop their way past us. "I love Hula-Hooping," she says to us.

We watch the vice mayor go by, his aides throwing out hard candy and Dum Dum lollipops. Finn raises his hand and snaps one of the lollipops midthrow, then hands it to me.

"Yes! Cream soda!" I unwrap it and pop it in my mouth. "My hero," I say.

Finn snorts and turns his attention to a bunch of kids in front of us, each one balancing precariously on a unicycle.

My favorite is the group of ladies holding a banner that says LAWN CHAIR LADIES BRIGADE. The dozen or so middle-aged women that follow are all holding up foldable lawn chairs, clicking them open and clacking them shut, whirling them in elaborate synchronized patterns.

"Sweet!" Charlie yells.

"Seconded," Finn says.

The parade continues, but I keep sneaking glances at Charlie and Ruby and Finn.

Ruby is clapping in time to the music of another plucky high school band. Of course they're playing a Taylor Swift song, and of course Finn is humming along, I'm sure without realizing what the song is.

I meet Charlie's eyes. He's got his arm slung around Ruby's shoulders, and for the first time I can remember, his skin doesn't look translucent anymore. I can't see the shadowy river of blue veins up his arm where they poked IVs. I can't see the soft skin of his scalp under his hair. I just see my brother, whole.

As if he can feel the weight of my stare, Charlie turns my way. "What?" he asks.

"Nothing," I say.

But that's not exactly true.

I can't stop looking at him.

He's not making terrible choices. He's not hiding cancer bruises or holding back a bloody nose. He's not faking a good mood with Erin or lashing out at Matty or me.

Instead, he's taking care of himself. He's taking care of Ruby.

He's healthy. He's happy.

His future could be anything.

It could be everything.

Right then I realize something, and I have to look away, the weight of it making me suddenly dizzy.

Charlie isn't *going* to be okay.

Charlie already is.

Forty-Nine

"DO YOU REMEMBER THE year we went to Lake Michigan and watched the Fourth of July fireworks from the lake?" Charlie asks as we follow Ruby and Finn. The two of them are in a heated discussion about something Float-related, and after trying to make sense of it, Charlie and I fell back, letting them lead the way.

"Yeah. You kept insisting each one was the best," I say, remembering the look of sheer glee on my brother's face as his neck craned up, watching the lights.

"Yeah, and you kept saying, 'This one must be the finale,'" Charlie says.

I realize I don't even remember the finale now, only the feeling of dread each time, not wanting it to be over.

"That was the last summer before I got sick," he continues. "Though I guess I was probably already sick—I just didn't know it."

Ahead of us, Ruby punches Finn in the arm. "You are being the Emperor of Assholes right now."

Finn stops and looks over his shoulder at us, rubbing his arm. "Did you see that? She's a menace."

"Watch it, Casper," Charlie says. "You're talking about my girl there."

Ruby grins happily at "my girl" and marches forward.

Charlie catches me watching him and immediately stiffens.

"What?" he asks.

"Nothing. It's just that Ruby seems happy," I offer.

"Oh," he says, clearly surprised. Then his shoulders soften. "Thanks."

We walk awkwardly next to each other, but it's not angry. It's just been a long time since we've talked without hurting each other.

"You know what else I remember about that year at Michigan?" I ask.

"Let me guess: your refusal to hike the trail to the lighthouse?"

"No! And besides, that trail was too long for nine-year-old kids; sand dunes are hard to walk on!"

"I did just fine," Charlie brags.

"What I wanted to say was that I loved that house we stayed at on Hamlin Lake," I say. "Do you remember it?"

"Yeah, I do."

He and I slept on twin beds on the screened-in porch. "Twins on the twin beds," Dad kept joking, and every night we'd whisper to each other until there were longer and longer pauses between our conversation, and we'd fall asleep with the sound of the lake lapping at the shore below us, the crickets and tree frogs going mad with summer in the trees around us.

One night it stormed, and the entire room lit up with lightning, my heart clamoring with each thunderclap. I sat up, clutching my sheet around me, looking over. Charlie was awake too, but his eyes were wide with wonder, like they had been during the fireworks. Seeing him like that quieted my pulse, let me sink back to the bed, to fall asleep amid the noise.

We stopped going to Michigan after he got sick. I think my parents were worried about Charlie's immune system, and soon enough, there were the mounds of hospital bills they had to catch up on.

And then we just never went again.

"When I got chemo for the first time, they told me to think of the last time I was happy, and so I closed my eyes and pretended we were back on that porch," Charlie says.

I stop for a second, surprised our memories of it are the same. "You did?"

But before he can answer, Ruby's voice jolts us back into the present.

"Parker! Charlie! You gotta see this!"

She and Finn are stopped in front of us, at the side of a building on Hamilton.

Charlie starts walking forward, turning to see if I'm following him, almost like he's making sure he hasn't left me behind.

When we reach them, Finn points to the brightly colored image painted on the wall: a yellow figure riding a horse, holding up what looks like a puppet, small white birds patterned all around and behind them. The horse has small flutters near its feet, like it's flying, lifting off from the street into a luminous blue-purple space.

It's gorgeous, a fairy tale come to life in the middle of Cincinnati.

"This is by Brazilian street artists. Os Gemeos," Finn says.

"They're twins, like you two," Ruby adds. Charlie looks at her, impressed. "Finn just told me," she admits.

"It's really cool," I say, getting up close to lightly trace one of the small birds. "Maybe we should become a street-art duo, Charlie." I turn to him to gauge his reaction, but the expression on his face is frozen.

Erin's standing there next to us, her brown hair pulled back in a pert ponytail with a red-white-and-blue ribbon, her skin tanned and even, her Xavier University tee bright blue and white. The only thing not perfect on her is the uncomfortable expression on her face, the one currently mirroring Charlie's.

She steps forward, reaching an arm out to Charlie and then stopping herself. "It's really good to see you."

Charlie lets out an exhale. "You too," he says.

Next to me, Ruby stiffens.

No one says anything then until Erin breaks the awkward silence. "How are you feeling?"

Charlie shoves his hands in his pockets. "Good. Really good, actually. My blood cell count is looking normal again."

Her face lights up, her shoulders falling in relief. "Oh my God, I'm so happy to hear that! You must be really happy to hear that too. Your whole family must be, right?"

Erin looks hopefully at me, and I offer her a small smile. "Yeah, it's good."

Ruby rubs the bridge of her nose under her glasses.

Charlie's still got this stricken look on his face, like a deer in headlights, so I clear my throat. "Hey, Erin. These are our friends Finn and Ruby. Guys, this is . . ." I don't know how to describe her.

"Erin," she says, smiling and shaking Finn's hand before turning to Ruby, taking in her proximity to Charlie.

"Hi. I'm Ruby Collie," Ruby offers, extending her hand. "Charlie's told me a lot about you. I heard you're going to Xavier next year to major in communication? That's awesome. I thought about double minoring in that, because I think it's good when doctors have good bedside manners, and I figure it can't hurt to have a lot of skills at my fingertips, you know? Oh, yeah, I'm going to be a doctor, too, maybe cardiology or neurology, but definitely some time with Doctors Without Borders. . . ." She stops, catching herself midstream, and I can see her mom's words echoing through her head.

"Um, so that's cool. Nice to meet you," Erin says, returning the handshake, clearly unsure how to respond.

I shoot Ruby a reassuring smile, but she looks vaguely sick to her stomach.

Erin turns back to Charlie. "So, I've been wanting to call you. It would be really good to hang out before I start freshman orientation at Xavier. Maybe we can catch up this week?"

"Maybe," Charlie echoes.

Ruby's shoulders fall and she lets out an audible sigh.

"Come on, Roo." Finn guides her away from us. "We're going to get some ice cream at the truck over there," he says to me.

I nod.

"So, do you think you'll do baseball again when you're back at school?" Erin asks Charlie. "You know, Xavier's got a team, if you ever want to come check it out."

"I don't know. I don't know what's happening a month from now, let alone next year."

"Oh, okay," Erin says, surprised and clearly a little hurt by Charlie's tone.

I see myself in her now, in how she wants to make sure he's okay. After worrying about him for so long, it's hard to stop.

"I just have to figure some stuff out still," he explains.

"Sure, I get that."

Charlie starts rubbing his hand over his scalp, like he's trying to figure out what to talk about, and Erin folds her arms, chewing on her lip.

The awkwardness is making my eyelid twitch just by proximity. "Sooo, I guess I'll get some ice cream too," I say. "It was good seeing you, Erin."

But she's scanning Charlie's face. "Babe, your cheeks are getting pretty red. Do you need some sunscreen? I know I have some in my bag. You know, skin cancer and all."

He jerks back. "No."

"You don't need sunscreen?" Erin asks.

"No, that's not what I meant. I have it on already. I meant no, I can't meet up with you later this week."

She falters. "What?"

Charlie hikes a thumb over his shoulder in the direction of the ice cream truck. "Her. I'm seeing Ruby." His response is lacking eloquence, for sure, but his tone is gentle.

"Oh," Erin replies, her voice small, and even though Erin and I have never been super close, my heart hurts for her.

"I should probably get back to Ruby." Charlie leans down, gives Erin a hug. "Good luck at Xavier next year, Erin. I mean it. I wish you nothing but good things. You ready, Parker?"

He doesn't wait for me as he breaks into a jog, then an all-out run toward Ruby and Finn, calling out, "Wait up, guys. Roo!"

From where I'm standing, I can see the way Ruby's face breaks into a smile when Charlie reaches her, one that gives the July sun a run for its money, and I wish not for the first time I were as brave as my brother.

I turn back to Erin.

She's got a lost look on her face, and as soon as she sees me notice, she begins digging through her bag. "I know my phone's in here somewhere," she mutters, and I realize she's trying not to cry in front of me.

"Thanks for watching out for my brother for all those years," I say to her.

Erin looks up, surprised, but then she gives me a small smile. "You're welcome, Parker."

I'm sure it won't be easy for her to figure out who she is without Charlie, the same way it's been tough for Charlie to figure out who he is without cancer, for me to figure out who I am period. But Erin is unstoppable and devoted—a fierce star for the people she loves. I know she'll be okay.

As I walk to join Finn and Charlie and Ruby, for the first time in a long time, I feel strangely hopeful (a sky of fluttering birds, a horse that can fly). Charlie really is okay.

And with that, I start to wonder if I can be too, if maybe my future is coming into shape with my own two hands, crooked and new, something that's unexpected and all my own.

Fifty

"WE SHOULD BE ABLE to see some fireworks from here,"
Finn says, pulling his truck to the side of the back road, right next
to a field of sunflowers. All of them are closed up for the night, the
blooms nodding heavily, barely able to support the weight of themselves after the sun goes down.

"Are we that close to Kings Island?" I ask, checking my watch.
We have only a few more minutes until they start.

"Yeah, we should be good," Finn says. "Come on." He hops
out of the truck, goes to the back, and climbs up. He offers me
a hand, and I scoot next to him, both of us leaning against the
truck cab right as the first firework explodes above us, so loud it
makes me start.

"Wow," I say, my neck angled back, watching red and blue
blooms burst into existence above us.

"Just a second," he says, opening the window to the cabin and grabbing a grass-covered old red plaid blanket from the backseat. He spreads it out.

"Lie down. It's easier to see them this way," he says.

With any other guy, it would be a come-on line, but with Finn, it's what he means. So I do.

"You know, for a while after I met you, every time I looked at the sky, I wondered if I'd see Major Tom up there," I say, watching the sky explode with silver and gold light. It reminds me of the patterns in Finn's tunnel. "My dad finally told me the song wasn't real, but I guess I was still hoping."

"Sorry about that," Finn says.

"You really loved that song, didn't you?"

A new round of fireworks come to life, silver shimmers like stars.

"I think I just thought if I could find Major Tom, I'd be a hero, you know?" he finally says.

"Finn," I say.

"Everyone knows my brother's an asshole and my dad's an asshole and his brother is too. But when I was little, I thought if I could bring Major Tom back, people would know I was different." He looks briefly at me, then turns back to the fireworks. "It's ridiculous, I know."

But I get it.

Little parts of my heart break off then, for Finn, for Ruby, for Charlie, for me, for all the ways we've let ourselves become who people think we should be instead of who we really are.

"That's not ridiculous," I say, looking over at him. He won't look at me, so I take his chin gently and turn it toward me. "That's not ridiculous, Finn."

His eyes hold mine, and I trace my thumb along the line of his jawbone. "You are the best person I've ever met," I say, my voice soft as the night around us.

He smiles. "You're here, Bird McCullough."

"You're here, Finn Casper."

I wonder if this is what it feels like to be a helium person, your heart on the outside, vulnerable and open in the sky.

And then I forget to watch for any fireworks finale, because Finn pushes himself up and leans in to me, his lips meeting mine, tentative at first, and then, when I don't pull away, harder, more insistent, like we're crashing into each other, my fingers in his hair, his hands on my back, and he smells like the field, like summer and goldenrod and sweat and evening. Around us, I swear the sunflowers are opening to the fireworks, to the explosions of light above us and between us.

Fifty-One

MISS PEGGY SMILES AT an elderly man browsing through the selection of vases. He grins back.

"Only fifteen dollars. Such a bargain, no?"

"But we'll take more," Harriet barks from behind her. "Fifteen is just the *suggested* price."

"Have you seen this one?" Ruby asks him, holding up a vase painted in brilliant shades of blues with Harriet's black slash marks around the edges.

The fund-raiser is going better than I could have dreamed. Ruby came to help us set up and ended up enjoying the ladies and Henry so much, she offered to stay for the afternoon. We still have another two hours of the art fair to go, and there are only a few vases stamped LAPPHH left on the table (LAPPHH being the extremely eloquent name Harriet came up with for our enterprise, signifying each of our first names—Lorna, Alice, Parker, Peggy, Harriet, Henry—after having shot down Miss Peggy's suggested name of "Flowers for Alice" on the grounds that Alice wasn't dead and it was too corny). In fact, we've sold so many of our creations, Carla had to go back to the studio to get some of her vases so we didn't completely run out of merchandise. Not to mention the fact that Carla's e-mail sign-up list is well onto the fourth page.

Henry chuckles as Lorna pulls out a bunch of sunflowers from a box. They match her outfit today: golden yellows and warm oranges.

"They're too big for the vases," she says in dismay.

"Give 'em to me," Harriet says, and when Lorna hands them over, Harriet begins hacking at the stems with a pair of blunt scissors.

"Atta girl," Henry says as she hands him shortened sunflower stems. He stuffs them in the vases so sunflowers are bursting out the top.

Seeing the flowers makes me blush, and I busy myself with counting the money before anyone notices.

Finn and I stayed in the sunflower field well after the fireworks ended. I have mosquito bites up and down my legs, and even though it's five days later, my lips just stopped feeling puffy from making out.

"This is going so well, Parker. And Harriet and Miss Peggy are actually getting along," Carla says to me under her breath.

"Don't jinx it," I say as I finish counting the change, then look up, smiling. "Sweet. We've already raised more than enough for the tickets!"

"Bravo!" Carla says, and Harriet lets out a loud whoop from across our booth. Ruby claps.

"Maybe you can use the extra money to get some new glazes for the studio?" I say as I'm putting the cash in the lockbox.

"I had another idea," Carla says.

"Yeah?"

"I was thinking we could start some art classes at Wild Meadows, for the residents who aren't mobile enough to get to the studio, like Alice."

"That's awesome," I say.

"And I know I'm losing you to Harvard this fall, but maybe you can help me get it set up before you go?" she asks.

"Really?"

"Of course! You have a gift working with these people—you're way better with them than I am."

I snort. "Well, it's clear my gifts aren't in the throwing-pottery realm."

"Patience, Parker. You can't be good at everything right away."

I scoff, but inside, the idea of setting up classes with the people at Wild Meadows makes me wish I could stick around to run the program full-time.

And then a revolutionary thought sneaks into my consciousness: *Maybe I can.*

I stop in place, the world of the art fair buzzing around me.

The realization is like sun bursting through the clouds—all the nagging dread and heart-racing anxiety I've been feeling since I got the acceptance letter pushed aside by one single clear thought: *I don't have to go to Harvard.*

I feel giddy, clear, and light.

I have no clue how I'd tell my parents or how I'd make it working at Carla's, but while normally those things would paralyze me in place, the rightness of the notion—of not doing something that I don't really want to do—is so obvious, I don't know why it's taken me so long to get here.

"You look pretty pleased with yourself," Harriet says to me, nudging me in the stomach with her elbow.

"Ow," I say.

"Oh, you're fine. You're stronger than you think, girl."

"I am, aren't I?" I ask.

"You remind me of Alice that way, before her Alzheimer's kicked in," Harriet says.

I look over at her, surprised.

"I've known her for the past six years, and it's only been the last two that she started withdrawing more and more, you know."

"I didn't."

"Did you know she used to be a writer? Wrote a bunch of spy thrillers. Kind of violent stuff. Tiny little lady with a core of iron on the inside. Oh, don't look so shocked. We all had glamorous lives back in the day. I used to be a burlesque dancer in Coney Island."

"I know," I say.

Harriet winks at me and goes to help a girl who's trying to decide between one of Carla's vases—a sedate, graceful light-green glazed piece—and one of ours—raucous and clashy and mismatched.

"You definitely want this one," Harriet says, pushing ours forward and setting Carla's vase to the side. The girl holds it up, taking in the glaze, examining the vase at different angles.

I slide my phone out of my pocket to check the time, and that's when I see three missed phone calls from Charlie and one from Finn, all from the past forty-five minutes. He and Charlie promised to stop by and help us clean up after the fair, but there are at least another two hours to go, not to mention the thirty minutes of last-minute stragglers I'm sure we'll get.

I wonder what's going on.

I look up to ask Ruby if she's heard from either of them, but she's talking to a customer. I move to the back of our booth where it's a little quieter and dial Charlie.

He picks up right away. "Parker?" he asks. But the connection cuts out with a beep.

"Ugh." I dial right back and am relieved when he picks up. "I just lost you. What's going on?"

"Um, I was with Finn . . ." His voice cuts out for a good ten seconds. ". . . to the ER at Bethesda North."

ER?

"What?" My vision narrows in on the overflowing trash can in front of me. "You're cutting out. Did you say ER?"

". . . in the ambulance . . ."

"*What?* Charlie, I can't hear you!" I say louder this time, clenching the phone.

Ruby shoots a worried glance over her shoulder.

" . . . wouldn't stop bleeding . . . going to be okay . . ."

The phone beeps as the call drops.

"No. No. *No.*"

I hit redial, and the call goes straight to Charlie's voice mail.

I hit redial again.

Ruby's at my side.

"Can you try Charlie?" I ask, voice shaking.

As she dials, I try Finn, but he doesn't pick up.

Ruby shakes her head. "Voice mail. What's going on, Parker?"

My heart is racing, and I dial Charlie again, then again, sucking in air, but it's not enough.

All my breath swoops out of me, and I'm sweating everywhere, my eyes watering, but I can't talk. I lean against the building, my hands on my knees. My heart is coming straight up my throat, out of my body.

He was fine at the Fourth of July.

He was finally okay again.

I start gasping for breath.

But he's not okay.

Nothing's okay.

No matter what I do to save Charlie, it's not enough.

"Parker?" Ruby asks, but she's eight million miles away. I hear her bark out a sharp "Help!" and then Henry's got my arm and is leading me to a shady spot against a store, making me sit down and rest my head between my knees.

"In and out, in and out," he says, rubbing my back, and the small part of me that's watching from a distance recognizes how calm he is, how he knows what he's doing, how he was probably a very good doctor.

Ruby has my hand.

From the tent of my head against my knees, I see Carla come over. She squats down. "Parker, can I help?"

I hear Lorna ask Henry what's going on and Harriet snapping at a passerby to mind his own business.

When my heart finally finds its way back to me, I feel mortified at the scene I've caused, and it takes me a second to work up the courage to look up.

"I need to get to Charlie. He's at Bethesda Hospital," I say.

"Is he okay?" Ruby asks, her hand squeezing mine harder.

"I don't know."

"Parker, you should rest a little longer," Henry says.

"I can't. I need to go." I try to stand, my legs shaky.

"I'll go with you," Ruby says.

"Of course. I'll take you both," Carla says immediately. "Harriet and Lorna, can you help Miss Peggy at the booth while I drive Parker to the hospital? Ruby, can you get Parker some water?" She hands her a five.

Ruby nods, running to the refreshment booth.

"I'll bring the car around," Carla says.

Before they leave for the booth, Lorna smiles at me, and Harriet gives me a gentle pat on the back.

After they all leave, I can't bear to look at Henry. "I'm so sorry."

"Why are you sorry?"

I shake my head.

"Look at me. Look at me," he says.

When I do, his eyes are bright, his face furrowed in concern. "I think you had a panic attack. It's not your fault. Has this happened before?"

I nod slowly, thinking of the day I got my Harvard acceptance letter, my valedictorian speech, my first day at the internship, the night at the bridge with Finn. "But not this bad. I thought I was dying."

"You're not, but you should talk to someone. Are you seeing a doctor?"

I shake my head.

"I can give you some names. It can really help to talk this stuff out, Parker."

"I don't know."

I hear a short honk and then see Carla waving from a car at the curb, Ruby jumping into the backseat.

"I need to go see my brother. But thanks, Henry."

"Promise me you'll think about it at least?"

But I can't promise Henry that right now. I just need to get to Charlie, to make sure he's okay.

I'm pretty sure I'm going to be sick, but right then a nurse comes by, touches Charlie on the arm. "You can see your friend. One at a time."

"I'll go," I say.

"Of course," Charlie says.

Ruby lets go of him and comes over and gives me a hug.

"I'm really scared," I whisper against her ear.

She steps back, eyes glistening. "I know. I'm here for you, okay?"

I nod, then follow the nurse down the hall into the room.

Finn's stretched out on the bed. He looks awful. Most of his face is swollen into reds and purples, and his bottom lip is huge. There's a cut on his cheekbone, another on his chin.

I cover my mouth with my hand, my eyes welling up.

"Bird," he whispers with a drowsy smile. "Hey."

"Only a few minutes," the nurse says. "He's on some pain medication and needs to rest."

I pull over the chair, leaning forward, my hands in a knot.

"Who did this?" Even though I'm crying, my voice is steady. "Tell me."

"I don't know."

"Did anyone call the police?"

He shakes his head.

"We should call them. Does the gym have security cameras?"

"I'm okay," Finn whispers.

"Finn, you have broken ribs. It's not okay." I wipe my eyes with my arm. "I'll go to the gym and ask them to call the police. We'll find out who did this."

"Parker. Please. You have to let this go," he says, and I'm surprised at the hint of desperation I hear in his voice.

I straighten, my voice cautious. "Why should I let it go?"

He shakes his head slowly.

"Finn, tell me now, why?"

He sighs, turning his head away from me. "Maybe you should leave."

"What are you talking about?"

"I don't need this right now. I don't need you. I want you to go." His voice is distant, like he's in space, like he's Major Tom leaving the rest of us behind.

I sit back in the chair, stunned and hurt.

I don't know why he wouldn't want the police to go after the person who did this.

I don't know why he's pushing me away.

And then a dark wave of understanding sweeps over me, stealing my breath, the realization leaving me reeling.

Finn in first grade, his quiet days, the anger inside him.

When he pummeled Johnny on the playground, his words. *You can't hurt her, too.*

His bruises back then.

His bruises at the airfield.

Johnny's threat after the boxing match.

The fights he and Johnny get in aren't just everyday brother fights.

I hold my hands tight, so Finn can't see the way they're shaking, and I lean forward. "Did your brother do this?"

He doesn't say anything.

"Finn, please, look at me. Did Johnny do this?"

He still won't meet my eyes, but at his brother's name, his whole body shudders, and I know I'm right.

"Him and another guy," he mutters. "If it was just one of them, I could have held my own."

"Oh my God," I say, shaking my head, tears streaming down my face. I'm sick to my stomach at how I've failed Finn for all these years, how everyone has. "I'm so sorry. I'm so sorry. I'm so sorry."

I can't stop saying it.

Finn reaches out, grabbing my hand. I can barely see his eyes with all the swelling.

"Stop. It's not your fault, okay?"

"You should tell your dad at least."

Finn exhales, letting go. "Where do you think Johnny picked up the habit, Parker?"

I feel sick all over again. "My parents can help. Or Carla."

"Parker, I messed up things all those years ago when I went to the neighbors. It's my fault the police arrested my dad. Johnny's got two strikes and I'm not sending someone else in my family to jail, okay? Let it go. I'm asking you to do this for me."

"Why do you want to protect him?" I finally ask.

"He's blood. Promise me you'll let this go."

I look at him, the boy who told me he could fly, who made me swear not to tell his secret all those years ago, who's asking me again.

"I don't know if I can," I say right as the nurse comes back in the room.

"He should probably get some rest soon," she says, picking up the chart at the end of Finn's bed.

"Okay, yeah, I'm heading out." I'm relieved at her arrival. I don't want to make a promise I'm not sure I can keep. "When will he be discharged?"

"Tomorrow," she said. "The doctor wants to make sure there's no internal bleeding."

I lean over to kiss Finn's forehead. "I'll be back tomorrow, okay? Call if you need anything."

But he grabs my hand firmly, not letting go. His eyes search mine, panicked, his voice a hoarse whisper. "Don't tell anyone about my brother. Promise, Parker. You have to promise me."

"I promise," I finally say, trying to hide the reluctance in my voice.

His whole body relaxes at my words, his shoulders releasing into the sheets, his face losing its hardness, his eyes drifting shut.

"Thank you," he says, the relief in his voice breaking my heart all over again.

Fifty-Three

"HOW'S FINN?" RUBY ASKS, searching my face when I meet her in the lobby.

"A mess," I say. "But the nurse is watching him, and it's good he came to the hospital. They want to make sure he doesn't have internal bleeding."

"Crap," Charlie mutters. "That's serious."

"Yeah, it is," I say, turning more carefully toward my brother. I can feel it starting as soon as I look at him: a restless anger, my hands twitchy, my thoughts sharp.

For the first time in my life, I'm pretty sure I could actually hurt someone.

I want to plow a car into Johnny, want to hear the thud of his body as it breaks against the fender.

I want to curl my fingers into a fist and hit Finn's dad right in the face for letting it happen, for hitting Johnny first.

I want to hear cartilage snap. I want to see blood coming from a nose.

Focusing on the anger is the only way to avoid looking at the black hole of guilt behind me, for not realizing what was happening earlier, for not helping my friend.

I should have known.

It's not enough.

"So," I say to Charlie, trying to keep the volume of my voice at an acceptable level for a hospital waiting room. "Why were you at the boxing gym with Finn? Were you picking him up for the art fair?"

He takes a careful breath. "No, not exactly."

"Charlie, why were you at the boxing gym." It's not a question this time.

"Um, I think I'm going to go check on Finn? Or go to the cafeteria?" Ruby says, nervousness making her fidgety.

Charlie watches her leave before stretching his neck, rubbing his head, bracing himself. "I was there for beginner boxing lessons," he finally says.

"Boxing lessons," I repeat.

"Yeah."

"With Finn?"

"He doesn't know I was taking them. But trust me, it's not a big deal," he says. "You don't need to worry."

It's not enough.

"I'm fine," he continues, motioning to his body. "Totally one hundred percent healthy, boxing and all."

It's not enough.

I can't save him.

At that point I don't know if the "him" is Finn or Charlie, but I've had it. The last nine years, the last two months, the last two hours—all of it rushes inside me like a tornado whirling into existence.

And the eye of the storm? Pure, quiet anger, a "no" startling in its clarity.

"I'm not worried," I say, my voice steely. "Livid? Irritated? Infuriated? Yes. But worried? No."

"Parker," Charlie starts, his voice mildly exasperated. "Come on."

"Boxing? Why in the world would you do that?" I shoot back.

I watch my brother transform: his expression tightening, his shoulders jutting back, every muscle in him rigid and defensive, ready for this fight.

"Because I'm not a dying boy anymore."

It's his mean voice. But I don't back down.

Instead I drive my finger at his chest with each word. "Then stop acting like one!"

"I *have!*" he yells.

Charlie's angrier than I've ever seen him, his whole body stiff with it. But then, like he's reminding himself, he sucks in his breath and breathes it out slowly, flexes his fingers and stretches, before he continues, forcing calm into his voice until it comes on its own. "Listen, I know I wasn't great at the beginning of the summer."

"That's an understatement."

"Can you just listen?" he snaps.

I nod warily.

"People expect that when you hit remission, everything will just go back to normal. I expected it the first time. But I'm not normal. Instead I've got this tangled mess of dark, angry stuff inside me . . . here." He touches his chest. "And there are times I hate everything. You, Mom, Dad, Matty, school, baseball, everything. It doesn't make sense, I know. And at the beginning of the summer, I wasn't dealing with it in the right ways. I fully acknowledge that."

I snort, but he ignores me.

"But, Parker, I'm changing now, I really am. Being with Ruby helps. Doing things on my own terms helps. Talking with my therapist and the support group helps. I know my body is still healing, that I have to be careful. I really do. But watching Finn box that night at the Fight to the Death?" Charlie whistles. "I got why he does it—he just loses himself in that ring. He takes all the tangled stuff inside him and makes it work for him. I wanted that. So, I signed up for lessons."

"But—"

He holds up his hand. "Before you freak out, yes, the coach knows I had cancer. We're only using the bag. I'm not in the ring with people. But when I put on those gloves and swing? It's like when I used to pitch. I know I'm in control, that what happens next all comes down to me. It's good because things are good, Parker. They're finally good, okay? Do you get that? I'm sorry you found out this way, but I need you to trust me on this, please."

I think of how when I'm trying to throw a pot, I'm so focused on making, I forget the anxious voices in my head.

I think of Finn describing boxing, how during the contest I saw the storm in his eyes finally clear.

But then I think of Finn in that hospital bed, of the bruises on his ribs, of how he's broken.

I think of Charlie sailing across the river, of Charlie letting go, of Charlie leaving us all behind.

I want to trust him, but I'm so scared if I do, if I let go of my grip, something bad will happen to him.

"It's not that easy," I start.

"Ugh!" he yells. "Parker, for fuck's sake, will you give me a break? I'm not like you, doing everything perfectly the first time around."

I ignore the dig, how wrong he is about me, and shake my head, folding my arms across my chest, holding myself tight. "You can't box. You have to stop. No more."

"You've got to be fucking kidding me."

"No. You stop now, or I tell Mom and Dad. And I don't care if you tell them about the internship, Charlie. Do it. I don't care. If that's what it takes to keep you safe—"

Charlie cuts me off again. "God, enough already! I was never going to tell them, all right? I'm not going to do that to you!"

I freeze.

"What are you talking about?"

A tall orderly comes over to the two of us, his voice polite. "Um, could you two please keep it down?"

"Not now," Charlie barks, and the orderly steps back, shaking his head.

I grab Charlie's arm to get his attention back. "What do you mean you weren't going to tell?"

"I mean that it's your decision to share that stuff, not mine."

I exhale in disgust. "You are unbelievable. This is all a passive-aggressive dig on the fact that you think I tell Mom and Dad too much, isn't it? You're not going to tell on me to make a point?"

"I wasn't going to tell on you because it's your own fucking business!" he yells, and I flinch, surprise coursing through my veins.

Charlie meets my gaze square on.

"Listen, I get it, okay? I was not happy you got me grounded and into therapy this summer. And the baseball camp stuff last year? I was fucking furious with you. But . . ." He looks away, at the floor, at the ceiling, at the people around us, then back to me, his voice softening. "I get it, Parker. I get that you have to make hard decisions for people when they can't do it themselves. I get it, okay? But there are also times you need to step back and let people figure it out for themselves, to listen to them instead of ratting them out. That's how I feel with your internship. The decision to tell is up to you, not me."

My heart skips at his words, and hot tears well in my eyes. I shake my head. "But you're blackmailing me because you hate me."

"I don't hate you, Parker."

"But I heard you. With Ruby. You hate me. You said it's not easy having me as a sister. You said it's like torture." My words end in a choked sob.

He rolls his eyes, the height of exasperation. "That's not at all what I said. What I said was that it was torture watching you do all this shit you hate out of some sense of obligation to me. Because of *me*, you're going to be a doctor. Because of *me*, you spent most of high school studying and taking SAT prep tests and doing all the right extracurriculars. Because of *me*, you're going to Harvard. But you hate it. I didn't deserve cancer, okay? But that doesn't mean you're responsible for making that right. And until you get that, we're both going to be stuck in the shitty in-between place—remember that?"

I nod, caught in the middle of a storm of tears.

"It's time to stop worrying about my future, Parker, and to start making your fucking own."

When I meet his gaze, even though he still looks angry enough to burn down the whole city, he's also crying.

They're angry tears, the kind of tears that can only come when there's nothing left holding you back.

In the hallway behind him, I see our parents and Ruby heading our way. They don't look terrified, so Ruby must have filled them in on what is going on.

"It's Mom and Dad," I say to Charlie.

He wipes his wet face with his arm and then turns in their direction, trying to smile.

Ruby grabs his arm, her face worried. "Is Finn okay?"

"Yeah." He pulls her close, kissing the top of her head.

I look to our parents, trying to get ahold of myself. "I'm so sorry I didn't call you guys to tell you Charlie was okay."

"It's okay, hon. I'm sorry we missed your calls. Your dad and I were at the park and I left my phone at home and his reception was bad." Mom shakes her head. "I'm just happy to hear Finn's all right."

"What happened to him?" Dad asks. "Ruby was saying something about a fight."

In the split second I'm debating how much to tell Mom and Dad, a girl with white-blond hair walking behind them pauses and does a double take when she sees me.

My heart stops.

It's Laurel from the internship.

Move along. Move along. Please move along.

But she leans closer. "Um, hi?"

She never remembered my name at the internship. Surely she doesn't remember me now?

"Um, Parker, right? I've been wondering how you were doing. Mono, right?"

No no no no no.

Like it's been biding its time, waiting for the perfect moment to return, my eyelid twitches.

Mom and Dad have confused looks on their faces, but Ruby's expression is growing increasingly alarmed, and Charlie's clearly trying to piece together who Laurel is.

"Not exactly," I say quickly, "but now's not really a good time."

She ignores my attempt at dismissing her. "I was soooo surprised when I heard about you leaving. Getting in was such a competitive process. I can't imagine how awful it would be to have mono and to miss out on the intern—" she starts right as Charlie moves, blocking Laurel from our parents.

"Guys, I have to tell you something, since I figure you'll find out soon enough. Parker caught me drinking on Friday."

Mom turns to him, startled.

My mouth opens, then shuts again, everything around me happening too fast.

"What did you just say, Charlie?" Dad asks.

He shrugs. "I had a bad day at tutoring, so I used my fake ID and bought some Jack Daniel's on the way home from therapy. Parker found the bottle in the car."

I try to focus on keeping my balance, the waiting room dizzyingly bright.

"You were drinking and *driving*?" Dad yells, and Mom's shoulders fall as she shakes her head, the heartbreak evident on her face.

At that, Laurel cringes, beating a steady retreat. I see Charlie register her departure, and he nods at me, but I'm unable to move, watching the scene in front of me play out like I'm not part of it.

"But, Charlie, we were hanging out on Friday," Ruby says, and he shakes his head firmly at her.

"That was Thursday night, Roo."

"I can't believe you, Charlie," Dad says, his face as red as Charlie's was a few minutes ago. "Throwing away your health? It's selfish and asinine. What is wrong with you?"

Mom clears her throat. "This isn't the time or place to talk about this, but we're having a serious conversation when we get home, Charlie," she says, her voice scarily calm, before turning to Ruby. "We can drop you off on our way, okay?"

Ruby nods helplessly.

"You might as well enjoy the ride now," Dad says to Charlie, the anger in his voice just barely controlled. "As it's the last time you'll be seeing Ruby or anyone other than your therapist and tutor for a long time."

Mom and Dad start toward the exit, Dad shaking his head in disgust, Mom clutching her purse against her side. Ruby watches them go before turning back to Charlie, pure anguish on her face.

"But you lied," she says.

Charlie pulls her into a hug. "I'll explain later," he says, resting his chin on her head. "It'll be okay."

He meets my eyes then, and I shake my head at him, holding myself tight.

"Why?" I ask.

He mouths the words, and they are clear as a cloudless blue sky.

I got you.

Fifty-Four

AFTER AN AWKWARD RIDE back from the hospital, in which the only people talking were Mom and Ruby, home feels like relief. As soon as we get in the house, I motion for Charlie to follow me upstairs.

I need to ask him why he did this for me.

But before we get far, Dad stops him at the bottom of the steps. "We need to talk."

"Can't it wait until dinner?" Charlie asks.

"*Now.*"

Charlie lets out a heavy sigh and turns, reluctantly, to follow Dad.

I freeze on the steps, unsure of what to do.

This is on me.

Charlie is in trouble for something he didn't even do because of me, *for* me.

But as if he can sense my hesitation, he looks over his shoulder, gives me a brief shake of the head.

As soon as they're out of eyesight, I sit on the top step, where they can't see me, pulling my knees close. It reminds me of the year Charlie and I tried to stay up to see Santa, hanging out at the top of the steps until our parents caught us there, half asleep and confused, and made us go to bed.

I hear Mom say, "Have a seat, Charlie."

He clears his throat. "Listen, I'm sorry. It was a one-time thing. I won't do it again—"

Dad interrupts him. "You sure won't do it again. Because you're grounded. No cell phone. No car. No computer."

"Come on," Charlie says. "That seems kind of extreme. I'm eighteen."

"And still living in our house!" Dad snaps.

"Listen," Charlie starts.

"No, *you* listen. If you can't take care of your new health, the health we have all worked so hard for—"

Mom cuts them both off. "Charlie, we just don't understand why you'd be so irresponsible. I really thought that with remission and the strides you were making with therapy, things were better. But I'm with Dad on this. If you can't act like an adult, we can't treat you like one."

"But how will I see Ruby?" he asks, desperation making his voice break.

I can't listen to this anymore.

Guilt moves over me in a cold sweat, and I stand, hugging myself hard, and go to my room, carefully shutting the door.

Oblivious to the family drama, Mustard hops down from the window, letting out a sassy chirp, and jumps up on my lap. I grab my laptop and reread the e-mail sitting in my in-box, the one I've left unanswered for the past five days.

Park, where are you? I miss you and I'm so
sorry again.

oxo, em

I wonder how this summer would have unfolded if Em were in town, if I hadn't quit the internship, if I'd never discovered Carla's, if I hadn't become friends with Ruby, if I hadn't let myself trust Finn, if Charlie hadn't just sacrificed his new happiness to keep my secret for me.

I wonder what would happen if I let the secret free.

I don't know what to do.

I miss Em so much right now, it's a physical ache. I wish she were sitting next to me on the bed, a bag of M&M's between us, and I could tell her everything. She'd know what to do.

But then I hear a voice: *You have to tell them.*

I swallow hard, digging my nails into my palms.

It's not Em's voice. It's mine.

Yeah, Em and Ruby have been telling me it the whole summer. But I realize, sitting there, that in light of Charlie's sacrifice, of Finn's secrets, I'm finally discovering a voice of my own, the words I want to say.

I need to tell my parents.

And I'm going to have to tell them everything.

The realization makes me feel a little nauseated, and I don't know if I'm brave enough to do it just yet, so instead I pick up my phone and text my best friend.

Remember when you told me to call if I needed you? I need you. Can I call you? I'll get the charges.

Immediately, the three dots appear.

Yes, sitting by the Seine, so timing is perfect. But even if the timing wasn't perfect, you can call me anytime, Park.

"Em?" I ask tentatively as she picks up.

"Park." I can hear the sound of laughter behind her, the gentle lilt of French accents. "Oh, I have missed you so much. You have no idea," she says.

Relief floods through me at hearing her voice, and I stretch back on my bed, letting my feet dangle over the edge. If I close my eyes, I can almost pretend she's right there next to me, her curls spread wild on the bedspread, both of us talking so much we forget to stop.

"Me too. How's Paris?"

"I could talk about the cheese sandwich I had this morning for about five hours. It's beautiful here, and I'm probably going to gain at least ten pounds before I leave. But that's not why you called. Park, what's going on?"

I close my eyes. "You were right."

"Right about what?"

"About being a doctor. I don't want to be a doctor. I don't want to go to Harvard."

She lets out a low whistle. "Wow, that's no joke, Park."

"And, Em, I was mad at you. But only because you were right. I just wasn't ready to hear it. I'm really sorry."

"You were going through a lot. I get it," she says.

"You always get it before I do," I say. "How do you do that?"

She laughs.

"I'm serious. For all these years, you've gotten me better than I've gotten myself. It's like you translate me to the world, you know?"

"It sounds like you have a pretty good sense of yourself right now all on your own, Park."

"I need to thank you," I say. "You did a hard, hard thing by calling me on the internship and the doctor stuff. You said something I didn't want to hear because you love me, and then you gave me the space to listen, to finally get it on my own. Thank you."

I'm pretty sure I hear Em sniff on the other end.

"Also, I have to apologize. I was being a total . . ." I scramble for the right Ruby-esque phrase. "I was being a total, full-fledged, one hundred percent certified asshat."

She sniffs and giggles again. "Wow. That's one way to put it."

"Are we okay?"

"We're always okay, no matter how much of a certified asshat you're being."

I want to hug her so badly right then.

"Just a second. Matty is hollering at me that we're going to miss our nighttime Paris canal tour. Let me tell him I'll skip it."

"No, it's okay. We can catch up on e-mail."

"You promise to tell me everything?"

"I do."

"I mean it. *Everything.*"

"I promise. Love you, Em. Tell Matty I say hi."

"Love you too, Park."

I hang up but keep the phone in my hands.

I realize what a gift Em's given me, telling me I shouldn't keep my internship decision a secret, but also letting me make my own way through it, nudging me to the edge but never pushing me over, letting me figure out myself when I was ready to test my wings.

And weirdly enough, even though it seemed like blackmail at the time, Charlie did too: He never told.

I don't know how I can ever pay them back, but with Charlie, at least, I have an idea.

There's still time to make things right.

For a second I wonder if I should do that with Finn, too, if I should keep his secrets about his brother like he asked.

But for the first time in my life, I can see the difference. I should have tried to have an honest conversation with Charlie after the party this summer instead of just going straight to our parents. I shouldn't have taken that choice away from him so quickly, not when he's already had so many choices taken from him. But now I know that there are times to nudge and trust and hope, and then there are times when someone's holding so many heavy things inside them—bruised skin and splintered ribs and broken wings— they can't fly on their own yet.

They need someone else to be brave for them.

I swallow hard, scrolling through my contacts, then hit dial.

Carla picks up right away, the sound of the art fair still buzzing in the background.

"Parker, what's going on? How's Charlie?" she asks.

"He's good. He's safe. But, Carla, it wasn't Charlie who was hurt."

I pause, knowing not only that what I say next will scare Carla, but that it will make Finn furious, that even though I kept his superhero secret, this secret is one I can't keep.

I'm pretty sure I will lose him for good after this.

But if losing him means saving him, I'll do it. I'll do it a thousand times over.

I take a deep breath. "Finn's in trouble. He needs help, Carla. More than I can give him. I should have known. I should have figured it out."

I hear her suck in her breath, then a worried exhale.

"Tell me everything."

Fifty-Five

AFTER THE CALL WITH Carla, I find my family in the kitchen.

Dad's got his arms folded across his chest, looking like he's doing everything he can not to combust.

Mom's got streaks on her face, like she's been crying.

Charlie's getting up from the table. He looks sadder than I've seen him in ages. But he also looks resigned. And it's the resignation that breaks my heart, that lets me know I'm doing the right thing.

I don't want him giving up his new life, the one he's working so hard to earn, not when it's time to start finally owning my own.

"I have to talk to you guys," I say.

All three of them look at me.

For a second I falter, and the bad feelings start: my heart speeding up, heavy and intense, the sound around me becoming extra keen, my palms sweating, my head dizzy.

This is the last second my parents will look at me with absolute trust, the last second I can be the daughter who's going to be a doctor, the girl who makes everything right.

But then, just like the roller coaster, the moment before the drop, Charlie's hand on mine, I hear the words again.

I got you.

They make me brave.

He looks at me, understanding dawning on his face. "Parker, you don't have to do this."

I give him a small smile, shaking my head slowly. "I got you, Charlie." And then I turn toward our parents. "Charlie wasn't drinking and driving or any of that."

"What?" Mom says, looking quickly between the two of us. Dad frowns.

"He just said that to cover for me."

"Why would he need to cover for you?" Dad asks.

"Because that girl at the hospital, that girl who stopped by? She was close to telling you guys my secret. Which is . . ." I take a deep breath. "I quit my internship."

Mom looks confused. "What did you say?"

"I quit the internship. At the hospital. I'm not doing it."

"That can't be right. I'm sure you can go back. You can call them on Monday."

"I quit at the beginning of the summer," I say. "I didn't like it."

"Jesus Christ, are you kidding me?" Dad asks.

"No," I say.

"What are you going to tell Harvard?" he demands. "Are you

going to tell them you 'didn't like it'? This isn't how the adult world works, Parker."

"I know."

Charlie moves closer to me, standing next to me, and just having him there makes me stronger.

"This is because of that Casper boy, right?"

"Phil," Mom says, trying to cut him off.

"No. It's not because of Finn," I insist.

"Well, then why are you throwing this away? Do you know how many people would kill to be given the opportunities in life that you've been given? Your brother's one of them."

I suck in my breath. "I'm not throwing it away."

Dad turns to Mom like he can't even bear to look at me one second longer. "It was nice for a while, not having to worry about the future of one kid, you know? But I guess that's too much to ask for."

"Now, Phil," Mom starts. "Maybe we can fix this. I can call Dr. Travis's office and see if they know of any internships or office jobs for Parker."

I tune her words out, thinking about the last time Dad was this mad at me, that day all those years ago when I told him I wished Charlie was dead.

He had just given up the writing career he loved to better take care of his family.

He was exhausted from the traffic.

He was probably really, really worried about Charlie.

Meanwhile, I was only a kid.

A selfish, bratty kid.

A hungry and tired and confused kid.

A kid whose heart was breaking for her brother.

Charlie didn't ask for cancer, but neither did I.

I shake my head. "No," I say.

"What'd you say, Parker?" Dad asks, turning to me, furious.

When I said *sorry* all those years ago, Dad said: *That's not enough!*

He was blinking back tears. I remember that, too.

"No," I say more loudly.

I can't save Charlie. I never could. None of us can. All we can do is try to be there for one another, loving each other the best we can in the process.

"I don't want to be a doctor."

"Jesus," Dad mutters, and Mom blanches. She leans forward, touching his arm. "There are a lot of other majors at Harvard—maybe Parker could try a few other things out."

"I don't want to go to Harvard. I don't want to be a doctor, and I don't want to go to Harvard," I say.

Dad's face falls, and I see the disappointment. It's palpable, what I'm taking from him right now. But I can't. I shake my head. "I need to figure out who I'm going to be. And I can't do that at Harvard."

Charlie squeezes my shoulder then, quickly.

"Parker," Dad says, trying to regain control. "Let's talk about this. You've always wanted to be a doctor."

I muster up all the bravery and honesty inside me, and I feel it then, helium moving through my veins, as light as eyelashes you wish on, as light as relief, even as my feet are on the ground, gravity steadying me, balancing me. "No. I just didn't want you guys to worry when Charlie was sick. My body's been telling me this for the past three months, and I need to listen. I can't do it. I won't. And I'm sorry if you won't support me in that, but it doesn't change anything."

"Oh, Parker. I wish you could have told us all this before now." Mom sounds so disappointed in me; my eyes start to water. But then she stands, pulling me into a hug, and my arms go slack with the relief of it. "But I'm glad you finally did. We'll get through this."

When she lets go, I look over at Dad, but he won't meet my eyes. Mom sees, and loops her arm around Charlie's waist. "Let's go outside, you and me, and talk some more, okay?"

"You going to be okay?" Charlie asks me.

"Yeah, as much as I can be," I say.

He nods, following Mom, leaving Dad and me alone.

I pull up the chair next to him, sit down. "I'm sorry," I whisper.

"I just don't understand why you're insisting on throwing away everything," he says, shaking his head.

I bite my lip, trying to figure out how to say what I want to say next. "Dad, a few weeks ago, Ruby asked me what I wanted to be when I grew up, before I wanted to be a doctor."

"What does this have to do with anything?"

"I told her I wanted to be you when I grew up."

He stills.

"I remember you coming home with new music, I guess from bands you were writing about? You'd get out your old record player and put on the vinyl album and turn up the volume so loud, the entire living room would vibrate. And Charlie and I would dance, and Mom would tell you to turn it down, but she never really meant it."

Dad's whole body sighs.

"I didn't know exactly what you did back then. I think I was too little to totally get it. But I could tell you were happy. And I just figured that's who I wanted to be when I grew up—someone who was happy. But, Dad, being a doctor? That's not it."

He closes his eyes for a second, then rests his head in his hands. I angle myself closer, put my arm around his shoulder.

"I know you gave up your writing to take care of Charlie and me and Mom. I can't imagine how hard that was. That was such a brave thing to do. But, Dad, Charlie doesn't need me to take care of him anymore. He doesn't need saving. Right now it's time for me to save myself."

I realize that I'm crying, but then Dad looks over at me and hugs me hard.

I let myself rest in his arms, not knowing if I've finally said the right words, but realizing it doesn't matter, because I've finally said the true ones.

Fifty-Six

"THE HOWRYS ARE HOSTING the euchre tournament tonight," Dad says. "But we should be home by ten."

"What are you guys up to tonight?" Mom asks.

"*Game of Thrones* marathon with Ruby," I say.

"Tell her we say hi," Dad adds.

"Will do," Charlie replies, grabbing another slice of pizza.

"Have fun," I call out as they leave.

As soon as the garage door shuts, Charlie turns to me, chewing while he talks. "It's still weird, right?"

I nod.

It's been three and a half weeks since all hell broke loose.

In an effort to move forward, we're all trying out what our family therapist calls "radical transparency" and what Charlie calls "telling everyone everything all the time." This translates into a lot of detailed updates from all of us on what we're doing and thinking at pretty much every hour of the day.

But even though we complain about it, the results haven't been terrible.

For the first time ever, Mom's talking about teaching. Right now her current batch of students is making her wish she'd "never gone into education." I don't think she's quite used to unloading about her day on us, but the second time she did, Charlie offered for him and me to make dinner so she could relax for a little bit, and Mom was so happy, she teared up.

Dad's still disappointed about Harvard, but he's stopped calling me Dr. McCullough, and he made a point of getting down some of his old clips the other day, showing me his first published music review from his high school newspaper. And earlier this week, he mentioned how he's been waiting for a new album by the National to come out, which resulted in the two of us taking a trip together to Shake It Records to meet the band at the release party last night. I can't think of the last time just Dad and I hung out together in the world. It felt good.

As for me, I'm working on not lying. It seems strange to tell my parents that I'm spending the afternoon with Carla composing a grant application, even stranger to tell them that sometimes I worry too much about snakes and cult compounds, that after talking with my own new therapist, I'm trying to stop making so many bargains with fate, that what happened to me over the past year wasn't just nerves, but panic attacks, like Henry said.

But even though it feels uncomfortable to talk—like breaking in a new pair of shoes—it's not impossible.

And every time I do it, I'm convinced it will just keep getting easier, until it's as second nature as breathing.

Charlie, of course, is taking the transparency business to the extreme, his answers to what he's doing later ranging from "making out with my girl" or "wondering about the jerk who invented the SATs" to "taking out the garbage because Mustard's cat barf is stinking up the kitchen."

But underneath that all, he's there, with us, with me.

I've been helping him with his chemistry homework.

He's been teaching me how to play poker.

Every night, we binge-watch *Game of Thrones*.

We aren't finding our way back to who we were before he got sick—those people are gone. Instead, we're getting to know who we are now.

But when I try to tell Charlie that, he rolls his eyes and tells me I sound like a Hallmark card.

"You better save some of that pizza for Ruby," I say as Charlie grabs yet another piece.

Right then, the doorbell rings.

"I'll get it!" Charlie says, dropping the slice back in the box, his whole body lighting up, and I smile to myself at how wrong I was to worry about him and Ruby. He, quite rightfully, worships the ground she walks on.

"You ready for the Red Wedding?" Ruby asks me as she enters the kitchen. She takes off her Float visor and grabs the seat next to me. In a matter of seconds, Charlie appears at her side with a piece of pizza, a napkin, a glass of Diet Coke, and a jar of maraschino cherries, like he's a waiter in a four-star restaurant.

"I could get used to this," Ruby says, laughing. "Will you be this way in the school cafeteria next year?"

"Anything for you, Roo," Charlie says.

"How about you carry my purse for me?"

Charlie frowns, and I laugh.

"Oh man, the thought of that almost makes me wish I could go back to high school," I say.

"But you'll still be around next year?" Ruby asks.

I nod. "Yep. I officially withdrew from Harvard yesterday. Dad wanted me to defer for a year, but I don't want to have it hanging over my head. I talked with Carla and she's going to hire me on full-time. For however long I need. I'm going to help her set up an art outreach program at the Wild Meadows Retirement Community."

Charlie leans forward. "Parker's underplaying it. She's actually going to run the whole thing—set it up, design the programming, maybe even roll it out to other retirement homes."

"So no college at all?" Ruby asks.

"Not for now. But Carla's going to help me research art therapy programs. She said she could help with recommendations, too, when I'm ready."

"Well, if you're happy, then I'm happy," Ruby declares.

"I'm getting there," I say.

She puts her slice down and wipes her mouth. "Um, Parker, there's something I have to tell you. You know Finn's leaving for New York tonight, right?"

My heart skips. "I do," I say, though the news didn't come from Finn.

Unlike Charlie and Ruby, who see each other every day, Finn hasn't talked to me since that day at the hospital. He hasn't responded to any of the texts I've sent or the messages I've left, and he refused to see me when I stopped by Carla's house after work last week.

Carla tells me to give him space, that he'll come around. But I'm not so sure.

Carla's been my Finn lifeline ever since the afternoon at the hospital. She and her husband were the ones who checked him out that day, refusing to let him go back to his family's house. He's been at their home ever since, recovering slowly, quietly.

He had a broken nose, three broken ribs, numerous cuts and bruises.

He refuses to press charges.

He won't talk about what happened.

Carla told me Johnny came by once, early on, but Carla wouldn't let him see Finn, threatening to call the police and to report him for assault if he didn't leave. He hasn't been around since.

"I failed Finn," she said to me last week, her face grim. "When they were with me, Johnny and Finn fought, but it was never more than brothers picking on each other. And after he moved back home, Finn was always so quick to reassure me the bruises I saw were from boxing. But I should have pushed him harder. I should have known. I didn't do enough." She shook her head, looked outside.

It was hard to hear her say those words, my words.

I know how much she loves Finn. I know what she's given him. And I know how guilt can creep inside of you, spreading like a stain. Even now, I can feel it pushing at my edges, that I didn't see what was happening with Finn earlier, that I didn't help him earlier.

But just like I couldn't make everything right for Charlie, I can't make everything right for Finn. The only person I can do that for is myself.

All I can do is love them both the best way I know how, to be brave, so that they know when they need me, I got them.

I'm here.

When Carla told me last week that Finn was leaving, that she'd found a place for him to stay in New York with a former art professor and his wife so he could get a fresh start, I knew how important it was to tell her she was doing the right thing.

Even though inside I wanted to keep him here.

Even though I missed him so much already, it was like missing a part of myself.

"I just wish he'd talk to you before he leaves," Ruby says unhappily, rubbing the bridge of her nose under her glasses, her silver bracelets jangling. I see the new one Charlie got her, with a small silver charm in the shape of a cherry, in homage to her love of Cherry Coke.

"It's okay," I say.

"But you didn't do anything wrong."

Ruby doesn't know everything that happened with Finn, that Johnny was the one who hurt him, who'd been hurting him. It's not my story to tell, but I hope it will be Finn's someday.

"It's all right," I say.

"No, it isn't! He never listens to me. It's like that time I told him that he had the flu and he kept insisting it was just allergies, and then he barfed all over the kitchen at the Float."

Charlie smiles at her. "You're so cute when you're feeling self-righteous."

"'Cute'? 'Self-righteous'?" She bristles. "How about 'I admire how badass you are when you're clearly right'?"

Charlie drops his head to his hands, and I high-five Ruby.

"Have I ever told you how amazing you are?" Charlie says, looking back up at her with a big smile.

Ruby rolls her eyes at him before turning back to me. "I just wanted to make sure you were okay with him leaving."

"I'm fine," I say. "This is good for Finn. He needs a fresh start. It's the best thing for him. I'm fine," I repeat, more firmly this time.

Ruby looks doubtful.

Charlie takes a deep breath. "It can still be the best thing for him and not fine for you, Parker. You don't have to be okay right now."

I turn away, looking out the window.

Mustard is leaping around in the backyard, intent on killing some small animal. He pounces, then proudly lifts his head, a small, dead brown something clenched in his teeth.

I yelp in dismay, making Charlie and Ruby both start.

I point outside. "It's Mustard," I mumble. "He just killed something. It's really sad. . . ." I trail off because Charlie and Ruby are both staring at me with these terrible looks of pity and understanding.

And then the tears come.

Not in a big heaving release or sputtering sobbing.

Instead they're quiet tears: the simple devastation of not being okay.

Ruby rubs my back.

Charlie starts drumming his fingers on the table.

"What are you thinking?" Ruby asks.

"What time does Finn's bus leave?"

"Eight," she replies, understanding dawning on her face. "We can do it, I think."

Charlie nods immediately. "I'll get the keys."

I look at them, confused. Ruby stands, like she's waiting for me to do something, then leans down, pinching me lightly on the arm, her bracelets jangling.

"Ow," I say.

"His bus doesn't leave until eight," she repeats.

Finn. She's talking about Finn.

Charlie holds up the extra set of keys Mom leaves in the odds-and-ends drawer. "Come on, little sister. You're saying good-bye to Finn."

And then I look at Charlie, the way he's bouncing on his heels, impatient to leave, how he's trying to save me.

"Get that chicken ass of yours moving," Ruby cries impatiently. Charlie snorts, and I realize yet again how lucky the McCullough twins are to know her.

I try not to smile. "Chicken ass?"

"Not my best effort, I know," she says, giving me a gentle push on the back toward Charlie, toward the car, toward Finn.

Fifty-Seven

CHARLIE PULLS IN FRONT of the entrance of the Cincinnati Greyhound Station and jerks to a stop. My stomach drops, and I wipe my palms across my forehead, queasy.

Ruby groans. "Can Parker drive on the way back?"

"I was trying to get us here in time," Charlie says.

"I would have stayed under the speed limit," I say, unclicking my seat belt.

"Yeah, and you would have missed the bus. Thanks to me, though, you have seven minutes," Charlie retorts.

I lean between the two front seats. "Do you guys want to come in too?" I ask, suddenly anxious about seeing Finn by myself.

"I said good-bye already," Ruby says.

"What about you?" I ask Charlie.

"Parker, get off your ass and get in there," he says. "Now."

"Okay. Okay." I scramble out of the backseat, then lean down to Ruby's open window.

"Thanks, you guys."

Ruby smiles while Charlie waves his hand. "Six minutes now. Go!"

I jog into the bus terminal.

It's a grim place—the industrial lighting a sickly yellow-green color, bright-blue plastic benches inhabited by a ragged assortment of tired-looking people, the air-conditioning on so high I get instant goose bumps. I look for Finn, my eyes darting to the announcement board, trying to find the bus to New York City. No luck.

But then I see the line of people in the far corner. They're moving forward slowly, bags slung over shoulders, pillows stuffed under arms, as a woman in a navy-blue shirt takes their tickets.

At the end, I see a guy with a red hooded sweatshirt, hood up, those beat-up cargo shorts, paint-spattered old shoes, a heavy backpack at his feet. A woman with brown hair has her arm wrapped gently around his shoulder.

"Carla!" I call out, my yell sharp against the murmur of white noise in the station. "Finn!"

I move toward them, around a small child holding a ragged Elmo doll, a woman with numerous bags of newspapers, a guy in a trucker hat scowling.

"Finn!" He turns around then, sliding his hood down, and finds me in the crowd. He doesn't smile, doesn't send radiant beams of forgiveness across the room.

I slow down, scared to reach him.

But I don't stop.

Carla pulls me into a hug when I get to them, whispering, "Be patient with him." She steps back. "I'll give you guys a few minutes. But, Finnegan, promise me you won't get on that bus without saying good-bye."

"I promise," he mutters.

I watch Carla leave before turning to Finn. He's watching me with his storm-wary eyes. His face is mostly healed, just a few lingering yellow spots, but his nose is newly crooked at the bridge.

"Hey," I say, shifting nervously in place. "I'm glad I caught you. Charlie was driving like he was possessed so we could get here in time. Ruby's out there too. And since you didn't return any of my messages, I really wanted to see you before you leave."

I stop, waiting for Finn to say something, for his face to soften, for his shoulders to ease.

But his mouth is clenched shut, jaw jutted out. Even though he's standing right in front of me, he's so far away, he could be lost in space.

"So, New York, huh?" I ask.

Nothing.

I remind myself of hidden street-art cathedrals, of fields of sleeping sunflowers, of what it's like to let your heart live on the outside.

I look at the boy who pushed me away in first grade, the boy who's pushing me away now.

I swallow hard.

No more small talk.

"So, I came here thinking I'd tell you I was sorry for telling Carla. I was practicing my apology the whole way down I-71. But, Finn, I'm not sorry."

He sucks in his breath—sharp and surprised. Angry.

I see lightning in his eyes.

"You promised me," he says, his voice low.

I nod slowly. "I did. But, Finn . . ." I struggle to find the right words. "It's like you're Major Tom. I know I can't save you. But I still had to try. 'Cause how else would you know I love you?"

I hold my breath.

Finn shakes his head and rubs his hand over the back of his neck, tries to hold it back, to keep it in, but I see it: the second when the storm breaks and all the hardness falls away, the boy underneath beginning to cry.

I step forward, put my arms gently around him, not wanting to hurt any of his broken parts.

"I have to leave," he whispers against my hair, his voice broken.

"I know," I say.

"You did the right thing. I don't like it, but I love you for it. Thank you."

My shoulders release as he kisses my forehead hard, and I wonder if I could just hold on forever. Maybe if I don't let go, he won't leave.

But Finn deserves better than the in-between. We both do.

He whispers against my skin, "I'm so sorry I'm leaving you, Bird. I'm sorry for everything."

I pull back, turn his chin gently toward me so he can see

my eyes, so I can see his. "I'm not sorry for anything. You know why?"

He shakes his head.

"Without you I never would have quit the internship. I never would have found Carla's. Without you, I never would have learned to fly." I take in his crooked nose, the ragged and worn edges of his sweatshirt sleeves, that small space between his two front teeth, the storm in his eyes, trying to memorize as much of it as I can. "I'm going to miss you."

He doesn't say anything, but our lips meet.

In the kiss, there's the bittersweet taste of what might have been, the quiet acceptance of something like forgiveness for each of us.

But behind all that, there's more: the promise of flight, of gravity-bound objects moving faster and faster, the world passing by in a blur, until the moment of lift, that glorious beautiful second of finally letting go.

Fifty-Eight

"HOW WAS THE VISIT with Alice's niece?" Ruby asks from the front seat.

"Here," I say, pointing to the side of the road. Charlie frowns and gives me an accusing look as the car sinks to a stop in the muddy ditch.

I shrug and turn back to Ruby. "It was amazing. The whole visit was great. Lily, Alice's niece, was so appreciative, and her son, Jack, was really sweet with Alice. He kept making her pictures for her room."

"Awww," Ruby says.

"Oh, and I almost forgot. Lorna and Henry are moving in together."

Ruby cheers and claps.

"Are they allowed to do that?" Charlie asks.

"Why wouldn't they be?" I say.

"Because they're old people?"

"You're kidding, right?" I turn back to Ruby. "I didn't even tell you the best part. Harriet's going to be Miss Peggy's new roommate."

"What?" Ruby practically yells.

"I know. It's literally the worst decision in the history of bad decisions. But Carla says it was their idea." I shrug. "Come on, this way."

We start walking through the field and then into the woods, hitting the top of the hill.

I realize it then, as I make my way down the slope: Charlie's following me. For once, I'm leading the way.

"Here, Roo," Charlie says behind me, taking Ruby's hand, the two of them moving down the hill together.

I remember Finn holding my hand the first time he brought me here and feel the familiar shiver of missing him.

The moods pass over me a lot these days, like clouds over the sun.

We've talked almost every night since he left. He tells me about the brownstone he's living in, how he thinks it might be haunted, but with a sad ghost, not a vengeful one. He describes the old man up the street, who every afternoon takes a shirtless nap stretched out on his stoop. He shares stories about his neighbors, a six-year-old boy named Archer who loves web-footed tenrecs and his three-year-old sister, Ramona, who's going to be a superprincess when she grows up.

415

In exchange, I fill him in on the dinner party Harriet and Miss Peggy hosted for all of us in their new apartment at Wild Meadows, how I stopped by to see Alice afterward, how Alice is still silent but likes looking at the brand-new picture of her, Lily, and Jack next to her bed. I tell him how Ruby and Charlie and I go swimming at Caesar Creek every Saturday afternoon, how when they're in the water, I browse the classes for the pre–art therapy certification at University of Cincinnati.

I talk with him about therapy, too, sharing some of what I'm discovering with my family and on my own. Finn tells me he's talking to someone too, but that's as far as he'll go.

After every call, he texts me pictures of New York City—of green leaves in Central Park, old guys playing chess in Washington Square, an explosion of street art in Brooklyn. That's when I hear his voice the most, when I see the world finally opening itself up for him, the way it always should have, the way he deserves.

But it was the message he sent me last night that's prompted our visit today.

"Where in the world are we going?" Ruby asks as all three of us come to a stop at the bottom of the hill.

"This better not be some cult compound, Parker," Charlie says, and I smile to myself.

I walk toward the tunnel, and just like Finn did with me, I pull out a flashlight from the bag on my shoulder. "This way."

I click it on, step forward, letting the light shine.

I look over my shoulder. Ruby and Charlie are at the front of the tunnel, frozen. His arm is wrapped around her shoulder, hers around his waist, and I'd almost think they were statues except for their faces, heads tilted back, eyes taking in the wonder.

"I can't believe that crap bird didn't tell me about this," Ruby whispers, her voice filled with awe.

Charlie looks down long enough to give Ruby a kiss on the top of her head.

I move farther into the tunnel. It's the first time I've been since Finn brought me.

When I reach the back wall, I freeze.

Finn was clearly busy before he left.

In front of me is a mural featuring dozens of sunflowers, some closed tight, others only starting to bloom. Only one is fully open, a small flower standing bravely by the side, and from its petals, dozens of birds are emerging. They're flying upward, a rush of them, small and large, fantastical and real, a stream of feathered creatures pouring out from the bloom, all rising up into a night sky, a black canvas filled with stars and explosions, space debris and rings.

They soar there, like they've found their home, and my breath rushes out in an exhale, lightness moving through me like feathers, like flying.

Above it all, the words YOU ARE HERE.

I give myself a few minutes, taking it all in, the way the sunflower roots meet the real dirt of the tunnel, the way some of the birds look like they're half creature, half constellation, how the whole thing is more beautiful than anything I could have ever dreamed, how at the same time, it's as familiar as the lines on my hand.

I catch my breath, wipe my eyes on my sleeve, then squat down at the side of the tunnel, digging out the can of sky-blue spray paint I bought yesterday. I had to ask the guy at Vinchesi's to get it out of a locked case, probably to make sure people weren't buying it for exactly the use I'm anticipating.

And then I slide out my phone, clicking on Finn's latest text.

It's a photo of a wall somewhere in New York City. It's night, a streetlight casting a glow on the image, a Dumpster protruding from the left corner. But I don't spend much time studying that. Instead, I read the message on the brick, all in capital letters and bright-red paint: MAJOR TOM TO CHARLIE BIRD PARKER: COMMENCING COUNTDOWN.

My eyes scan the tunnel in front of me for the perfect spot around the rim. I like how the opening frames the world of color outside.

"I'm ready," I call out to Charlie. I start shaking the can, the rattle loud.

"Crap, that's noisy. Why don't you just call the police already and let them know what we're doing?" Charlie asks, coming up behind me.

"We are literally in the middle of nowhere." I stop, raising my eyebrow. "Oh my gosh, are you nervous?"

He frowns. "No."

"You are!"

"No, I'm not. I just don't really want to get arrested."

"You won't," I say, savoring the new sensation of helium rushing through me—my heart racing, my palms sweating, the world around me vibrant—and marveling at the gravity I'm seeing in my brother for the first time: the way he keeps looking over his shoulder, checking to make sure Ruby's okay, the cautious jut of his shoulders.

"Boost me up," I say.

He cups his hands together, and I use the momentum to leap up, my free hand scrambling for purchase in the stone wall, the spray paint can in the other.

"I don't know why I let you talk me into this," Charlie says from below as I scale higher, finally finding a small ridge on the side, one I can stand upon.

I'm not as nimble as Finn. My message isn't going to span the width of the entrance, and as soon as I start spraying the paint, I remember there's an art to it, one that, like throwing pottery on the wheel, I haven't mastered.

Yet.

But my arm still moves with something like grace, the spray paint taking on a life of its own, as I make the small loops.

I'm breathless and alive, my heart pounding against my ribs, outside of them, completely vulnerable and gloriously open to the world around me.

"Looking good, Parker!" Ruby calls out from below.

When I'm done, I hold the can out to Charlie.

"Heads up," I say.

He scrambles to catch it, giving me the finger once he does.

I start to scale back down.

Halfway there, my left foot slips, my fingers going white-knuckled against the stones in order to hold my weight, but I can hear Charlie below, murmuring, "Easy, easy," and, "I've got you," and I know he does.

When I get to the bottom, I turn to Charlie and Ruby.

"How does it look?"

"Come see," Ruby says, beckoning me toward them.

I look up at the tunnel's exit, and there around the circular rim, in all lowercase cursive letters, is *my* message to the world—not Finn's, not Charlie's, not my parents', but *mine*.

I grab my phone and snap a picture to send to Finn.

And then I stand next to my brother and my friend, all of us looking at the words I've written, the ones I never thought I could, my heart beating as steady as the flap of wings:

fly fly fly

Acknowledgments

A MILLION THANKS TO ...

Steven Leder, for offering feedback on an early version of this manuscript and also just for being my brother.

The rest of the Leders—Jack (you're first in this list!), Clara, Pat, Jim, and Tina—for having my back no matter what.

My agent, Michael Bourret, for his unflappable calm and constant support.

Lauren Abramo, for helping share my words in different parts of the world.

Liesa Abrams, for her clear and steady wisdom every step of the way.

Sarah McCabe, the Em to this book's Parker, who knew what I wanted to do with it before I did.

Jessi Smith, for her invaluable insights into what made Parker and Charlie tick.

The rest of the Simon Pulse and Riveted Lit team: Mara Anastas, Elizabeth Mims, Russell Gordon, Katherine Devendorf, Lauren Hoffman, Catherine Hayden, Amy Hendricks, Anna Jarzab, Janine Perez, Penina Lopez, Erica Stahler, Rebecca Vitkus, and Jodie Hockensmith.

Cam Montgomery and Meghan Hopkins, for their willingness to teach and guide.

Kathleen Glasgow, for her generosity and her always-luminous words.

Jen of *Pop! Goes the Reader*, Patty of *Bookish Wanderlove*, Emma of *Miss Print*, Nicole of *Nicole's Novel Reads*, Tiff of *Mostly YA Lit*, and all the other amazing and dedicated bloggers out there whose love for books encourages anxious writers like me to keep creating.

Jenny Clark, Meredith Dros, Chris Dufault, Tara Felleman, Lance Fitzgerald, Shannon Kelly, Nancy Lambert, P. J. Mark, Holly McGhee, Dolores McMullan, Jake Morrissey, Patrick Nolan, Caitlin O'Shaughnessy, Micol Ostrow, Vim Pasupathi, Steven Reese, Rebecca Reiss, Pippa Wright, my colleagues at Penguin Books, the Sweet 16s, and all my other friends, for their words and acts of encouragement, from leaving flowers on my desk from an anonymous "well-respected reviewer" to being first in line at my event with a stack of books for me to sign.

Kelly Bean, Kim Brock, Brittney Gabbard, Olivia Horrox, Alexa Marciano, Michael Link, and Cristin Stickles, for making the world a better place for book lovers.

The baristas at Kos Kaffe, for the endless supply of hot chocolate and buttered toast.

Lastly, I want to thank artists Darius Jones (Leon Reid IV) and Buddy Lembeck. Back in late 2000, I was driving on I-71 in Cincinnati, Ohio. At the time, I hadn't quite recovered from a particularly bad breakup, and the world around me seemed very gray. I was listening to sad music and crying (a not unusual occurrence during that year) when I looked up to see a spray-painted message across an overpass: TONY DANZA IS MY DAD. It was weird and cryptic, and I immediately loved it. Over the next month, messages continued to mysteriously appear on highway overpasses, and each time, they jolted me out of my gray world into a place unexpectedly stranger and noticeably brighter. Thank you for inspiring Finn's work and for surprising me out of my sadness.

About the Author

A former bookseller and teacher, Meg Leder currently works as a book editor in New York City. She is the author of *Letting Go of Gravity* and *The Museum of Heartbreak* and is the coauthor of *The Happy Book*. She lives in Brooklyn, New York. You can visit her online on Facebook or Twitter: @megleder.